# Ida

PHOTOGRAPH
CARL VAN VECHT

# Ida

*A Novel*

Gertrude Stein

*Edited by* Logan Esdale



Yale UNIVERSITY PRESS

NEW HAVEN & LONDON

*In association with the* Beinecke Rare Book and Manuscript Library

*Ida A Novel is a co-publication of Yale University Press and the Beinecke Rare Book and Manuscript Library.*



*Yale University Press books may be purchased in quantity for educational, business, or promotional use. For information, please e-mail sales.press@yale.edu (U.S. office) or sales@yaleup.co.uk (U.K. office).*

*Designed by Mary Valencia.*
*Set in Adobe Caslon type by Newgen North America.*
*Printed in the United States of America.*

*Library of Congress Cataloging-in-Publication Data*
*Stein, Gertrude, 1874–1946.*
*Ida : a novel / Gertrude Stein ; edited by Logan Esdale.*
*p. cm.*
*Originally published: New York : Random House, c1941. A reissue of the novel with critical matter added.*
*Includes bibliographical references.*
*ISBN 978-0-300-16976-8 (pbk. : alk. paper) 1. Women—Psychology—Fiction. 2. Sex role—Fiction. 3. Self-actualization (Psychology)—Fiction. 4. Stein, Gertrude, 1874–1946 Ida. 5. Stein, Gertrude, 1874–1946—Criticism and interpretation. I. Esdale, Logan. II. Title.*
*PS3537.T323I33 2012*
*813'.52—dc23* 2011028906

*A catalogue record for this book is available from the British Library.*
*This paper meets the requirements of ANSI/NISO Z39.48–1992 (Permanence of Paper).*

10 9 8 7 6 5 4 3 2 1

*Frontispiece: Gertrude Stein in February 1935, in Richmond, Virginia, by Carl Van Vechten. Used by permission of Bruce Kellner, Successor Trustee, Estate of Carl Van Vechten.*

# *Contents*

# *Abbreviations*

*AB* Gertrude Stein. *Alphabets and Birthdays*. New Haven: Yale University Press, 1957.

*BC* *The Boudoir Companion: Frivolous, Sometimes Venomous Thoughts on Men, Morals and Other Women*. Ed. Page Cooper. New York: Farrar & Rinehart, 1938. 31–38.

*CLM* Gertrude Stein. "How Writing Is Written." *Choate Literary Magazine* 21.2 (Feb. 1935): 5–14.

*CVV* *The Letters of Gertrude Stein and Carl Van Vechten, 1913–1946*. 2 vols. Ed. Edward Burns. New York: Columbia University Press, 1986.

*EA* Gertrude Stein. *Everybody's Autobiography*. Cambridge: Exact Change, 1993.

*FF* *The Flowers of Friendship: Letters Written to Gertrude Stein*. Ed. Donald Gallup. New York: Alfred A. Knopf, 1953.

*GSW* *Gertrude Stein: Writings, 1932–1946*. Vol. 2. Ed. Catharine R. Stimpson and Harriet Chessman. New York: Library of America, 1998.

*HHR* Duchess of Windsor. *The Heart Has Its Reasons*. New York: David McKay, 1956.

*HWW* *How Writing Is Written*. Ed. Robert Bartlett Haas. Los Angeles: Black Sparrow Press, 1974.

*LIA* Gertrude Stein. *Lectures In America*. Boston: Beacon Press, 1957.

*LOP* Gertrude Stein. *Last Operas and Plays*. Ed. Carl Van Vechten. New York: Rinehart, 1949.

*LR* Ulla E. Dydo, with William Rice. *Gertrude Stein: The Language That Rises, 1923–1934*. Evanston: Northwestern University Press, 2003.

*MR* Gertrude Stein. *Mrs. Reynolds and Five Earlier Novelettes*. New Haven: Yale University Press, 1952.

*NA* Gertrude Stein. *Narration*. Chicago: University of Chicago Press, 1935.

*PGU* *A Primer for the Gradual Understanding of Gertrude Stein*. Ed. Robert Bartlett Haas. Los Angeles: Black Sparrow Press, 1971.

*RAB* *Reflection on the Atom Bomb*. Ed. Robert Bartlett Haas. Los Angeles: Black Sparrow Press, 1973.

RHC Gertrude Stein Correspondence. Random House Collection. Rare Book and Manuscript Library. Columbia University.

*RM* W. G. Rogers. *When This You See Remember Me: Gertrude Stein in Person*. New York: Rinehart, 1948.

*SR* *A Stein Reader*. Ed. Ulla E. Dydo. Evanston: Northwestern University Press, 1993.

*TW* *The Letters of Gertrude Stein and Thornton Wilder*. Ed. Edward Burns and Ulla E. Dydo. New Haven: Yale University Press, 1996.

*WAM* *What Are Masterpieces*. Ed. Robert Bartlett Haas. Los Angeles: Conference Press, 1940.

WY "Woman of the Year." *Time* 29.1 (Jan. 4, 1937): 13–17.

YCAL Gertrude Stein and Alice B. Toklas Papers. Yale Collection of American Literature. Beinecke Rare Book and Manuscript Library. Yale University.

# *Introduction: Ida Made a Name for Herself*

This workshop edition presents *Ida A Novel* in its historical context, as it moved from composition to publication and reception.[1] The supplementary materials have been chosen to illuminate Gertrude Stein's experience of authorship from the novel's beginning in early summer 1937, through the various drafts and negotiations with her publisher, to the periodical reviews that began appearing in February 1941.

We can re-create Stein's workshop experience because concurrent with the start of *Ida* she began constructing her archive at the Yale University Library. Having a public archive motivated her to systematically keep the novel's draft materials, something she had never done before. The decision to save the drafts, as well her correspondence and related, unpublished texts, was Stein's invitation to us to study her creative process. This edition of *Ida* has therefore been designed according to how Stein herself presented the novel, not only in print, through her publisher Random House, but also in her archive.[2]

Such an approach contradicts the myth of Stein's genius that she had created with *The Autobiography Of Alice B. Toklas* (1933). In fact, we can read her enthusiasm for an archive a few years later as her effort to counterbalance both that myth and its opposite, her expressions of self-doubt. When she gave the lecture "How Writing

Is Written" (1935), for instance, she told an audience of students, "I didn't know what I was doing any more than you know." Neither the doubt nor the myth captures Stein in her complex reality. She was disappointed when readers accepted her status as a famous artist without also enjoying her writing, and expressions of doubt were invitations to join her thinking, not admissions that her writing was a haphazard game.

The archive offers a complexity that debunks caricature. The *Ida* record shows that Stein followed a conscious, step-by-step process. Seeing the extant manuscripts and her commitment to revision makes her look ironically ordinary—ironic because the more ordinary she appears, the more singular she becomes, free of the reductive "genius or charlatan" binary. This is Stein the serious writer working through a problem of narration: how to tell an unpredictable story about someone who becomes well known simply for being herself.

So whereas a critical edition typically includes documents that reveal the era's attitude on gender, for example, or some intellectual touchstones, as well as critical essays from the novel's publication to the present, this workshop edition contextualizes primarily through Stein's writing. The supplementary materials reveal the novel's composite nature and Stein's particular brand of intertextuality: not only did she rewrite *Ida* multiple times, but she borrowed from many other of her texts. This edition enables us to track that process.

In the mid-1930s Stein worried that her famous personality had overtaken her life as a writer and made her too self-conscious. With *Ida* she moved on and wrote with a palpable sense of fun, in her language and in the strange, oddly charmed life she gave her title character. Stein also made the novel, as a composite text, a personal reflection on her career. Working in the archive space she created in the late 1930s, she could separate herself from identity and focus on the act of writing.

One of the novel's key lines is "If nobody knows you that does not argue you to be unknown," in part for its reassuring aspect—one need not be famous to matter—and in part because it has a sly self-referentiality, alluding to Stein's aim as a writer to be in a state of mind where "nobody knows you," free of identity, and to the difficulty of achieving that aim (you can never be "unknown"?). Moreover, it addresses the novel's central theme, the significance of being known to others and how that affects who we are, where we live, and who we love.

## THE COMEDY OF IDENTITY

The novel begins with Ida's birth and follows her to middle adulthood. In practically every scene we see Ida having to respond to the desires and behavior of others. Rarely does she have a moment alone with herself, and, in the novel's First Half especially, new relations and locations are her only constants. Her parents quickly abandon her, and although orphan Ida has other family members to raise her, the routine of moving from one companion to another continues in the years to come. Having few obligations, either regional or familial, Ida often allows her unfixed identity to function as a blank screen for the projections of others. They see what they want to see. At other times, instead of adapting to the occasion she forces it to end with silence or an about-face: she will leave or wait until the other person does. This suggests both a need for continuity, a stable identity, and also, when someone wants her to be "Ida," a refusal to perform according to expectation.

Our attention in the opening three chapters is drawn to Ida's relationship with a twin. She is born with one, the narrator says, though that twin subsequently goes unmentioned. The narrator is joking with us that even at the moment of creation, in the womb, Ida could not be alone. Then in her late teens, Ida decides that she needs a twin who can function as her double or decoy.[3] Ida names her self-made twin Winnie, in honor of her pageant-winning beauty. As Ida-Winnie transitions into adulthood, she meets a number of men who have propositions for her, including marriage, and shortly before she meets her first of five husbands, Frank Arthur, she leaves the Winnie persona behind. Now a husband becomes her twin.[4] Also at this time Ida "began to be known." Her emerging public status appears based not on what she does, but on who she is. With a circular logic at play, Ida becomes famous for being Ida. Her mere existence excites people; they are excited that she exists. Everyone wants to know—where is she now?

Although Stein de-emphasizes plot, focusing instead on Ida's constantly adjusting relation to stillness and movement, there are two main discernible narrative lines, one about becoming a celebrity and the other involving romance. More subtle is a narrative strand on the identity of someone who is born a celebrity, Andrew, a prince. While Ida was well known before she married Andrew, the addition of his daily script further compromises her independence. All four identities for Ida—the twin, the wife, the celebrity, and the quasi-royal—have something in common: wherever she is she has accompaniment. Having made a name for herself, she is recognized at every turn; "Ida" becomes public property.[5] Written in dark times, with disturbing echoes from the world of economic depression and war, *Ida* describes a woman's life that from its inception is singularly not her own.[6] When Ida is Winnie, men follow her; when Ida is a wife, she moves as her husband moves; and when Ida is famous, anyone might visit her.

To the extent that people feel they do not exist unless others recognize them, they depend on the moment of encounter that says, "I know you." Ida certainly does, and beyond all the people she meets, dogs help with the process of coming into and maintaining existence. She always has a dog, one of whom was "almost blind not from age but from having been born so and Ida called him Love, she liked to call him naturally she did and he liked to come even without her calling him." Without sight and even when no words reach his ear, Love still recognizes Ida. That is devotion and love, the dog's name matching the essence of their relationship. Having a dog or husband not only creates evidence that she exists but also eventually leads to, as Harriet Chessman has argued, the "achievement of identity through difference," where measuring our distance from others, from who they are and what they want from us, generates self-understanding (169).

The phrase "achievement of identity through difference" describes the self-other dynamic as it generally occurs, but *Ida* requires significant interpretive open-mindedness. For one thing, while Ida depends on the look of recognition, very often she seems to be escaping identity rather than "achieving" one. Nor does "achievement" acknowledge the plurality of Ida's identity (public and private), or her effort to convince people, through silence or walking away, that they have misidentified her. And what of the

power of romance to overcome difference, when two lovers (such as Ida and Andrew) become as one?

Rae Armantrout puts the issue this way in her poem "Back":

> We were taught
>
> to have faces
> by a face
>
> looking back[7]

These lines capture Ida's almost constant predicament: all too often her face reflects those who have come to look at her. In Ida's world are many who would do anything to have a celebrity recognize them. Aiming to copy her, they demand that she look back—and this uncalled-for devotion unsettles her. Ida is like the "tourist attraction known as the most photographed barn in America" in Don DeLillo's *White Noise*, which everyone photographs but no one sees—or they see "only what others see."[8] The more well known Ida becomes, the more her existence feels evanescent. She might be here or there, with them or them; it is all the same. The odds of her "achieving" self-possession appear slim.

While there are foreboding aspects to *Ida*, I read the novel as lighthearted overall. The comical side to Ida's experience of fame and romance eventually outweighs the oppressive side. *Ida* marks a shift in Stein's career, away from the anxiety about public identity that she had expressed from 1933 to 1937, in books such as *Four In America*, *The Geographical History Of America*, and *Everybody's Autobiography*. In those years, she worried that fame from *The Autobiography Of Alice B. Toklas* had put her creative and private life at risk. But in *Ida*, what seems a threat often turns into a phantasm. In one episode, for instance, Ida is walking home with her aunts when "all of a sudden some one a man of course jumped out from behind the trees and there was another with him. Ida said to the aunts go on go on [ . . . and] she turned toward the men but they were gone." Readers of *Ida* have called it a dream or fairy tale; this and other scenes in which a danger abruptly disappears give evidence for those suggestions. Ultimately, one of the great pleasures of *Ida* lies in this tension between real threats—fame against self-possession, men against women—and their comic undoing.

In Stein's analysis, a type of modern celebrity is like the modern prince, known for who they are—their identity—rather than what they do or make. For both, their public life is their private life. What they eat for lunch can be newsworthy. Stein thus has Ida, known for being Ida, perfectly matched with Andrew, whose royal status is a key point of reference. Although she is an orphan, a divorcée, and an American, she can be the wife of a monarch because her experience with fame is similar to his. Stein reveals the American celebrity class, created by the media, to be a version of the aristocracy in England, created through tradition. The old and new worlds are not so different. A 1938 press release on *Ida* talked about the reverence the media creates for certain people and how that reality informs the novel:

> [It is] a novel about publicity saints.
>
> The idea of the book is that religion has been replaced by publicity.
>
> A "publicity saint" is a new entity in history and requires a little explaining. Never in the whole world before has anybody occupied the peculiar status that [Charles] Lindbergh occupies, Miss Stein believes. He is publicity saint No. 1. He is a saint with a certain mystical something about him which keeps him a saint; he does

> nothing and says nothing, and nobody is affected by him in any way whatsoever.
>
> The Duchess of Windsor, the former Mrs. Simpson, is another case in point. [. . .] Miss Stein admitted that she, herself, is a publicity saint, but of a minor order. (YCAL 16.337)[9]

Befitting her status as a "publicity saint," then, as well as Stein's aim to write a narrative relatively free of cause-and-effect logic, Ida's rise to fame is never explained—it just happens.

As a young girl, Ida watches people visit her great-aunt, but as she grows older and adds her Winnie persona, she no longer has an observer's distance: she becomes a favorite consumer object for those who like to see what others see. At one point, two people, not knowing what else to do, "went to look at Winnie." After that, Ida's social importance goes through an incipient period: "there was nothing written about her [. . . ] [s]o they just waited"; if they came to see her "she would not be there, not just yet." And then in the city of power politics, Ida "saw a great many who lived in Washington and they looked at her when they saw her. Everybody knew it was Ida." She soon marries her fourth husband, Gerald Seaton, and one day "they went to another country." This is apparently England, given that her friend there is Lady Helen Button and Ida learns a new intonation for the expression "How are you?" There she falls in love with a prince, who brings to their relationship his own notoriety. By the end, "everybody talked all day and every day about Ida and Andrew."

Being the object of scrutiny is thus a given for the adult Ida and then for the couple, a background noise that threatens private talk. The narrator has sardonic moments as she considers the amazing volume of that noise: "It is wonderful how things pile up even if nothing is added." But Ida also uses that background chatter, leveraging her power as someone important to enter marriages as an equal and leave them too, if that is her choice. Indeed, as Chessman has said, *Ida* is "one of Stein's most openly feminist works" (167). The narrator brings equality and balance to the act of marrying in statements such as "He married her and she married him." So while a public identity leads to undesirable encounters and pressures for Ida, it also loosens up marriage, making it less about bondage and more about open friendship. In a letter to Stein from her friend William G. Rogers in April 1941, he praised the feminist aspect of *Ida*:

> I think it's probably your best piece of fiction. [. . .] [T]he story is really interesting, I mean, I don't read it because it's you and because it's got an experimental value but because it makes me read it. From the very start, the very first sentence, it has something that holds my attention, and held [his wife] Mildred's too. In the first place, it is a love story, it's a man-and-woman yarn—and Mildred thought (rightly) that you showed more admiration for women than for men in it. But there is a definite one-sex-against-the-other conflict in it, that hasn't been in your books ever before. (YCAL 121.2617)

When Ida arrives in England, marriage with Gerald involves neither friendship nor spirited conflict. "They talked together at least some time every day," the narrator dryly notes, "and occasionally in the evening." Their emotional distance grows to appear even more absolute in contrast with Ida's intimacy with Andrew. The narrator offers a number of eloquent descriptions of Ida's new love; for example,

> Andrew, she called him, Andrew, not loudly, just Andrew and she did not call him she just said Andrew. Nobody had just said Andrew to Andrew.
>
> [. . .] Ida liked it to be dark because if it was dark she could light a light. And if she lighted a light then she could see and if she saw she saw Andrew and she said to him. Here you are.

Later, playing on Andrew's new status as a king, the narrator jokes that "he was Andrew the first. All the others had been others." After Andrew leaves the throne, he still remains "first" in Ida's affections.

At the end of the novel Ida goes away to begin again.[10] The narrator voices our question, "where was Andrew," answering that "he was not there yet" and then "little by little Andrew came." Ida's relationship with Andrew has the convergence of a "love story," as Rogers said, but there are times when Ida takes the lead.[11] Where she goes he will follow. This is not the stalking that Winnie experienced, this is devotion. Andrew is therefore like Ida's dog Love, who "liked to come even without her calling him." And so the novel concludes with a paradox on the comedy of identity: although life with Andrew brings more publicity than ever to Ida, she experiences more intimacy with him than with her earlier husbands. And we ask ourselves: if a woman is not known for what she does, but only for an identity that others have constructed for her, then how can we know her? In the margin this question affords, there exists an untold story. As the novel closes, we consider the possibility that Ida not only has her life with Andrew but also a life of her own.

*Ida* depicts a world in which the threshold for celebrity status is fairly low. In the 1930s, decades before the social networking technologies of today, being well known had become a common experience. Indeed, the narrator largely assumes that Ida is well known and never really explains why this happened to her in particular. As we see that Ida's life is more typical than exceptional, we note that Ida being a celebrity is partly a figurative condition: in male-dominated societies, women function as celebrities. Men feel entitled to approach women as if they were movie stars. Stein's novel critiques this sense of entitlement. Eventually, and happily, Ida finds a man who was likewise born into this condition and can appreciate both the almost inescapable nature of this problem and the necessity to try. The hopeful ending reinforces the feminist spirit that Stein gave to *Ida*.

Readers will find the novel's Second Half quite different from the First, which has a hectic mode appropriate to the life of an orphan and a young adult who wants to travel "all around the world." Ida's geographic restlessness mirrors her developing erotic consciousness. In the Second Half, however, Ida settles down with one man, and whereas in the First Half we are given the names of Ida's various American locations, her home address with Andrew remains unspoken. Despite their many visitors, they live quietly. The two halves are practically opposite in this regard: whereas in the First Half Ida tries to rest as she moves from place to place, in the Second she experiences movement internally.[12] Memories surface. As well, the Second Half presents a number of narrative interruptions. (There are some in the First, but they are more seamlessly integrated.) Along with two terse chapters (Part Two and Part Three) that delve into Ida's nervousness at the prospect of marrying Andrew, Stein inserts two texts first written separately from *Ida* that have been known by the titles "My Life With Dogs" (Part One) and "Superstitions" (Part Five).[13]

I will say more on the formal significance of these insertions in a moment. For now, I want to assure readers that they belong in the novel. Stein wrote them while she worked on *Ida*, and both pieces add to the novel's meditation on identity. The various dogs that Ida has known have also known her: "A dog has to have a name and he has to look at you." Every dog that Ida has called also calls her—recognition goes both ways—and as the narrator describes the dogs one by one, we consider yet again how tied Ida's identity is to those who accompany her, whether people or dogs. The "Superstitions" episode addresses the belief systems we construct that are riddled with arbitrariness. If something bad happens, it's because we own goldfish. (Think of everything we own—what luck will they bring us?) We try to control events by predicting them. If only I had not looked at that spider! (Think of all we see and do not see.) Earlier in the novel we are told that Ida has a superstitious side: "Ida was funny that way, it was so important that all these things happened to her just when and how they did." This "Superstitions" episode perhaps leads Ida to question her funny habit. When the idea that one might "believe in everything" is proposed, Ida remains silent. The conclusion seems to mock those who are superstitious.

Yet Ida's silence may mean something else, for she frequently uses silence in the face of provocation. Her inscrutability offers resistance to those who want to possess her. And as Susan Sontag argues in an essay titled "Performance Art," Ida's silence also makes her funny. Sontag compares Ida to three heroes of the silent-film era, Buster Keaton, Harry Langdon, and Charlie Chaplin.[14] All of them refused the tragic plot wherein "choices have to be made and things which are opposite truly oppose." Instead, their performances suggest "the equivalence of contraries," which drains affect and "the possibility of tragic reaction" (94). Because Stein texts such as *Ida* have the "encyclopedic idea of happiness," which is "the essence of the comic vision," and because Stein drew from the world of theater and film, she is "not only one of the greatest comic writers of literature written in English," asserts Sontag, "but probably the most original" (93). So when Ida "believes in everything" or stymies her visitors with a blank "yes" to everything, refusing to uphold the necessity of choice, we should laugh.

While Sontag was the first to put *Ida* in a silent-film context, readers have long pointed to its comedy, starting with Stein herself in a letter to Carl Van Vechten shortly after the novel was published: "I am so pleased and happy about it and it is funny, funnier than I remembered it" (see "Selected Letters"). Then in a book review, Dorothy Chamberlain concluded that "*Ida* is entertaining, stimulating, often funny" (see "Reviews"). Later in the 1940s Rosalind S. Miller said that Stein's "exquisite sense of humor" was openly accessible in *Ida* (93). Miller compared Stein's humor with Lewis Carroll's, as did Neil Schmitz in the 1980s: "It is the humor that governs any reading of *Ida*" (231). Two of Stein's foremost critics have also insisted on her comic brilliance more generally: in his introduction to *The Geographical History Of America*, Thornton Wilder defined Stein as "an artist in a mood of gaiety," and Ulla E. Dydo has written that Stein's work, "though it is not religious," recalls the saints who "speak as an act of devotion in the tradition of the comic spirit, free of the regimentation of the world" (*LR* 22).

Gathered together, these comments point us to *Ida*'s comedy of incident and comedy of language. When readers refer to Stein's humor they are usually thinking about the latter type, her use of repetition, disjunction, and play on words to create surprise.[15] During Wilder's visit with Stein in 1939, he said that her writing was "really funny because it makes you suddenly laugh" (YCAL

74.1356). The delight of *Ida* is in the rhythm of its words and in Ida's actions too, her inscrutable assent and rejection of stasis.

Ida "did not really run away, she did not go away. It was something in between. She took her umbrella and parasol. Everybody knew she was going, that is not really true they did not know she was going but she went they knew she was going. Everybody knew." Describing how Ida moved away (go or run), how she prepared (with umbrella and parasol: her future, whether rain or sun, was unpredictable), and who knew about her plans, Stein created a language that echoes Ida's rhythms, her "something in between" manner, both forward and elusive. Stein combined a discernible plot with her signature style so that her comic spirit would be manifest in all aspects of the novel.

## REWRITING *IDA*

In the 1938 press release cited above, we learn that Stein included herself among the publicity saints, although one of "a minor order," and that a publicity saint did nothing and affected no one. Stein included herself because of a lingering anxiety that she had become famous for her personality alone. It is evident, however, that as she worked on *Ida* she affirmed her identity as a writer. She regained her confidence that she would be known for what she did and not for who she was. She did this in part by making *Ida* a composite text, a decision motivated by the concurrent project of building an archive of her life's work. The two together, *Ida*'s composite identity and the archive, proved that she was no publicity saint. Her confidence also shows itself in the novel's lighthearted conclusion, where the publicity Ida and Andrew receive does not compromise their intimacy.

Stein's use of a composite style makes *Ida* remarkable in a number of ways. First, her writing is not known for its citations. As she liked to say, hers was "writing as it is written," made with immediacy. While that approach does not preclude spontaneous recall or echo, she consciously avoided literary allusion so that her readers would not be distracted by things remembered, external to the page. In addition, not only are such references unusual in a novel (composite gleanings more often occur in poetry), but the references are to her own work: Stein's intertextuality was internal to her career. "My Life With Dogs" and "Superstitions" have already been mentioned; Stein also borrowed from some fiction she wrote as an undergraduate student (see "Hortense Sänger") and from a movie scenario (see "Film Deux Soeurs Qui Ne Sont Pas Soeurs"). Whether Stein's action was incorporation or begetting, as when *Ida* led to another text ("Ida has become an opera [*Doctor Faustus Lights The Lights*]"; see "Selected Letters"), she demonstrates a family relation among them all. The paradox in the scenario's title, which translates to "Two Sisters Who Are Not Sisters," nicely sums this up.[16] *Ida* has many "relatives" who can also be read on their own.

Besides *Doctor Faustus Lights The Lights*, Stein wrote *Ida* alongside many shorter pieces and three other books: *The World Is Round*, *Paris France*, and *To Do: A Book Of Alphabets And Birthdays*. The borders between these texts were porous. Sometimes they shared a notebook, and phrases and methods could transfer from one to another. This textual networking was an act of repetition at a metalevel[17] and a dramatic rendering of her personal theory of authorship: "You can have historical time, but for you the time does not exist, and if you are writing about the present, the time element must cease to exist. [. . .] There should not be a sense of time, but an existence suspended in time" (*PGU* 20). To the extent that Stein took her theory literally, she could be "writing about the present" and incorporate not only a concurrent text into *Ida* but also one from 1895 or 1929, because everything she had written was "suspended in time." At a more material level, in the archive at Yale, where decades of Stein's writings are in boxes and the manuscripts are organized alphabetically by title, a text from 1910 might be adjacent to one from 1932—the archive's organization agrees with Stein's nonlinear imagination.

The composite identity of *Ida* was not recognized until Richard Bridgman's *Gertrude Stein in Pieces* (1970): "[M]ore than any single composition," he wrote, "*Ida* incorporates a variety of material from Gertrude Stein's other pieces" (306). Stein would have been disappointed at the lag in recognition. After she finished the novel in May 1940, she sent its draft materials (eleven manuscript notebooks and more than 370 manuscript and typescript sheets) to the Yale Library in time for an exhibition to celebrate her already voluminous archive.[18] By coincidence, *Ida* was published in February 1941, one week before the exhibition opened.[19] Stein's friend Rogers wrote to her after visiting it: "Among other items we saw was the Ida done first, which Mildred [his wife] read, or started to read in mss in 1937 [when they visited her in France], and also of course the new Ida [the book]" (YCAL 121.2617). Rogers did not take this observation further, but it was the sort of beginning that Stein wanted. The story being told in February 1941 was about more than just a woman marrying a number of times; it was also about the archive and Stein's intertextual practices. She arranged for both the product and the process to be on display, and for us to read the manuscripts alongside the book.

Just as Stein began *Ida*, in early summer 1937, she received a letter from Charles Abbott at the University of Buffalo requesting draft material for the library. Abbott believed that modernist writers would be better understood if readers had access to their creative process, and to that end he was building an archive with draft work by English and American writers. In August 1937, Stein rejected the Buffalo offer in favor of a competing one: Thornton Wilder convinced Stein to join him in preserving their life's work at Yale. In June 1937, just before he left for Europe, Wilder had deposited at Yale some of his own manuscripts, and three Stein typescripts: *Four In America*, "An American And France," and "What Are Master-pieces." He brought with him "Yale's ecstatically eager attitude in the matter" (*TW* 165n). Stein became increasingly excited about this development, and when Wilder returned to the States in December, he brought with him two "large valises full of her MSS [including] several 'layers' of parts of The Making of Americans; there is A Long Gay Book; Tender Buttons, etc. There are also her daily themes at Radclyffe" (*TW* 184n).[20] Stein immediately designed her archive to be comprehensive, adding to the three texts from the mid-1930s her early writing from 1894 into the 1910s. So while she rejected the Buffalo offer, she kept to the spirit of Abbott's request, his rationale for the modernist archive.

More shipments followed until war suspended the project in 1940. (It resumed in 1946.) By 1938 Stein's sorting through her manuscripts was having its effect as *Ida* began to take on a composite identity. More intertexts would be added in 1939 and 1940. In addition, one of the passages she added to *Ida* in the final months of composition speaks to her construction of the novel as an analogue to her archive, with intertexts from the start of her writing life ("Hortense Sänger") to its most recent moments ("My Life With Dogs"): "Sometimes in a public park [Ida] saw an old woman making over an old brown dress that is pieces of it to make herself another dress. She had it all on all she owned in the way of clothes and she was very busy." We can read the old woman as Stein and the public park as the Yale Library. The old dress represents the early *Ida* manuscripts and even her career's work as a whole (she "had it all on"); the new dress is what she will send to her publisher. With this sewing metaphor in mind, this edition of *Ida* not only draws attention to the seams in the dress-novel but gives a selection of those other "pieces," so that we can follow the cut of her scissors and path of her needle.

Stein designed *Ida* to be composite to draw attention to the continuity of her writing career and the contingent relation of one text with others. Dydo has said about Stein's writing in general that one "piece engenders the next, so that each becomes a context for the next. Her life's work is not only a series of discrete pieces but also a single continuous work" (*LR* 78). This is manifestly true for *Ida*, and in that way the novel was designed as an advertisement to readers, exhorting them to read more of what Stein had written in the mid- to late 1930s and earlier too. Even though *Doctor Faustus Lights The Lights* and *To Do: A Book Of Alphabets And Birthdays* were not published in Stein's lifetime, she could reassure herself that eventually we would read *Ida* in its historical context, and the "continuous work" quality would be recognized. Again, from 1937 until she died, she knew that any writing she saved (drafts included) would have a public home at Yale. The archive came as a tremendous relief because for many years she had been anxious about her unpublished writing, and now all of it would survive and be seen.

To this point I have connected how Stein wrote *Ida* with her archive and the need to affirm her identity as a writer (not just a personality).[21] This need arose three years before the archive's inception, however, when *The Autobiography Of Alice B. Toklas* brought her the fame she had long hoped would be hers. Two texts written in the wake of that event, early in 1934, anticipate the textual identity and composition of *Ida*: "And Now," which Stein published in the September 1934 issue of *Vanity Fair*, and "George Washington," the final text in *Four In America* (1933–1934).

As Stein reflected on her new celebrity in "And Now," she thought of Paul Cézanne's belated success: "I remember when [Cézanne received] his really first serious public recognition, they told the story that he was so moved he said he would now have to paint more carefully than ever. And then he painted those last pictures of his that were more than ever covered over painted and painted over" (*HWW* 64). Then she offers a comparison that again reaches back to the early twentieth century: "I write the way I used to write in *The Making Of Americans* [1903–1911], I wander around. I come home and I write, I write in one copy-book and I copy what I write into another copy-book and I write and I write" (*HWW* 66). So as both a younger and older writer, Stein had to write and reread and unwrite her way into a state of unself-consciousness, where she felt relatively free of audience expectation. This comment on recursive method is from 1934, but it exactly describes the *Ida* manuscripts: for three years (1937–1940) Stein moved from one copybook or draft sequence to another.

Alongside "And Now" and "The Superstitions Of Fred Anneday, Annday, Anday A Novel Of Real Life" (included here), Stein was finishing *Four In America*, with its chapters on four quintessential American men: Ulysses Grant, Wilbur Wright, Henry James, and George Washington. When *Four In America* was published in 1947, it contained a note alerting readers that the first part of "George Washington" had previously been published, in a 1932 issue of *Hound and Horn*. It was not recognized until Dydo's 2003 book *Gertrude Stein: The Language That Rises, 1923–1934*, however, that other preexisting texts had been used, which makes *Four In America* a precedent for *Ida*. "The amazing number of piecemeal inclusions from many sources," Dydo writes, "along with hesitations about uncertain progress, suggest how Stein cut and pasted the Washington section together" (*LR* 593). Further critical discoveries of this kind may come to light. All of the moving among notebooks, as well as working concurrently on different pieces, blurred the line between texts and encouraged cross-fertilization.

After the American lecture tour (1934–1935), Stein wrote *The Geographical History Of America*, which introduced an important binary in her aesthetic lexicon: human nature (or identity) and human mind (or entity). "Events are connected with human nature," she says, "but they are not connected with the human mind and therefore all the writing that has to do with events has to be written over, but the writing that has to do with writing does not have to be written again, again is in this sense the same as over."[22] The term "human mind" is in part a spiritual directive, a challenge to imagine existing without identity. As Wilder understood human mind, it happened when one could "realize a non-self situation," when the creative self was experienced without external recognition. Just as a true believer does not remember God as if God had an identity but instead experiences God, Stein's human mind was experienced in the mystery of living and writing. Events, like linear time and relational identity, usually prohibit "non-self situations," and events are the meat of narrative—conflict, character development, closure. Stein limits those typical events in *Ida*, but marriages and moves do happen, and in consequence, "writing that has to do with events has to be written over," into abstraction.

As Stein went from draft to draft of *Ida*, she thus generated a textual world to work within. She used her writing to make more writing. She sewed a "dress" and then cut it apart and sewed again. Besides copying from one notebook to another, she also used preexisting texts unmotivated by the current occasion, texts written prior to her fame. To reach human mind for *Ida*, she put into action both the writing-over method described in "And Now" and the cut-and-paste method used in *Four In America*. Stein would refer to the former in a 1941 letter to Carl Van Vechten: "Ida you know was done over and over again, before it finally became what it is" (see "Selected Letters"). These methods have only slowly been recognized in Stein scholarship, and this edition of *Ida* puts both on display.

I conclude with three examples that show incorporation and radical rearrangement. (See the genealogy of the novel for a complete description of the writing process.) The first two are from typescript copies of the second version of *Ida*, which Stein wrote by hand on loose sheets in 1938–1939 and titled "Arthur And Jenny." (The Jenny character was named Ida in the 1937–1938 version of the novel, and later in 1939 Stein changed Jenny back to Ida.) In 1938 Stein wrote an episode for Jenny that vaguely alluded to "Hortense Sänger":

> [Jenny] did want to go to a meeting whenever there was one.
>
> One day she went to one, a great many were crowded together and she was crowded with them and then well she was more crowded than any of them. Did she stop it. She did not. Her name

> was Jenny and she did not stop it stop being more crowded than any of them there inside that building. Later she wondered about it. Could she have stopped being more crowded than any of them there in that building and did she like it. (YCAL 26.534)

Then in 1939, after writing another 250 sheets of "Arthur And Jenny," Stein had Toklas produce the typescript we see here, on which she added a handwritten note: "The story of the church and her relatives" (Figure 1). The note indicates her decision to expand the episode and reposition it. Indeed, the version we see in *Ida* is over four times longer and offers more detail on Ida's erotic indiscretion in a church in front of some relatives. The second example is another handwritten note on a 1939 typescript, an addition that Stein copied from a text she had recently written, *Lucretia Borgia A Play* (Figure 2).

The third example involves a sequence of fourteen paragraphs in *Ida* (see 28) that Stein cut and pasted from five locations in "Arthur And Jenny," covering eighty pages and two separate draft sequences (YCAL 26.534, pp. 78–85, 101–106, 143–146, 158; YCAL 26.536, pp. 22–23). Using "Arthur And Jenny" as raw material, Stein

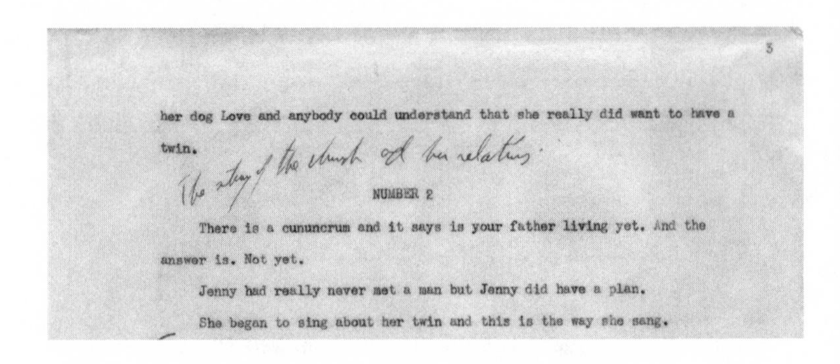

5

her dog Love and anybody could understand that she really did want to have a twin.

The story of the church and her relatives

NUMBER 2

There is a cununcrum and it says is your father living yet. And the answer is. Not yet.

Jenny had really never met a man but Jenny did have a plan.

She began to sing about her twin and this is the way she sang.

*Figure 1:* "The story of the church and her relatives" (YCAL 27.541).

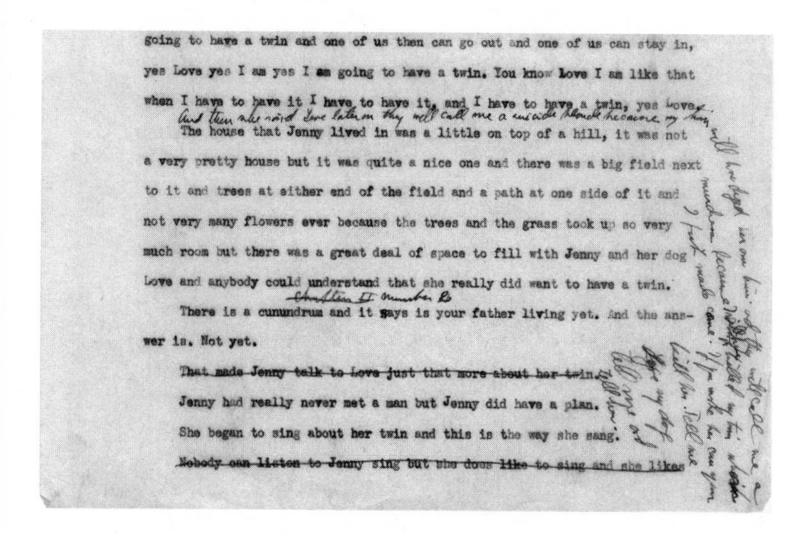

going to have a twin and one of us then can go out and one of us can stay in, yes Love yes I am yes I am going to have a twin. You know Love I am like that when I have to have it I have to have it, and I have to have a twin, yes Love.

The house that Jenny lived in was a little on top of a hill, it was not a very pretty house but it was quite a nice one and there was a big field next to it and trees at either end of the field and a path at one side of it and not very many flowers ever because the trees and the grass took up so very much room but there was a great deal of space to fill with Jenny and her dog Love and anybody could understand that she really did want to have a twin.

There is a cunundrum and it says is your father living yet. And the answer is. Not yet.

~~That made Jenny talk to Love just that more about her twin.~~

Jenny had really never met a man but Jenny did have a plan.

She began to sing about her twin and this is the way she sang.

~~Nobody can listen to Jenny sing but she does like to sing and she likes~~

*Figure 2:* "And then she said Love later on they will call me a suicide blonde because my twin will have dyed her hair and they will call me a murderess because I will have killed my twin which I first made come. If you make her can you kill her. Tell me Love my dog tell me and tell her" (YCAL 27.540).

wrote these paragraphs for the final *Ida* version in winter 1939–1940, at which time she added two completely new paragraphs.[23] She started the rewriting process by copying from pages 78–85, which begin, "He [Arthur] tried several ways of going and finally he went away on a boat and was shipwrecked and had his ear frozen." Page 83 in that section illustrates the remarkable complexity of this cut-and-paste process (Figure 3).

Stein retained, in modified form (see the paragraph that begins "It was a nice time then"), only the first sentence and a half from this page ("As he woke he was not all awake and he talked about sugar and cooking. He also talked about medicine glasses"). She dropped some altogether ("and meaning and all of this meant that

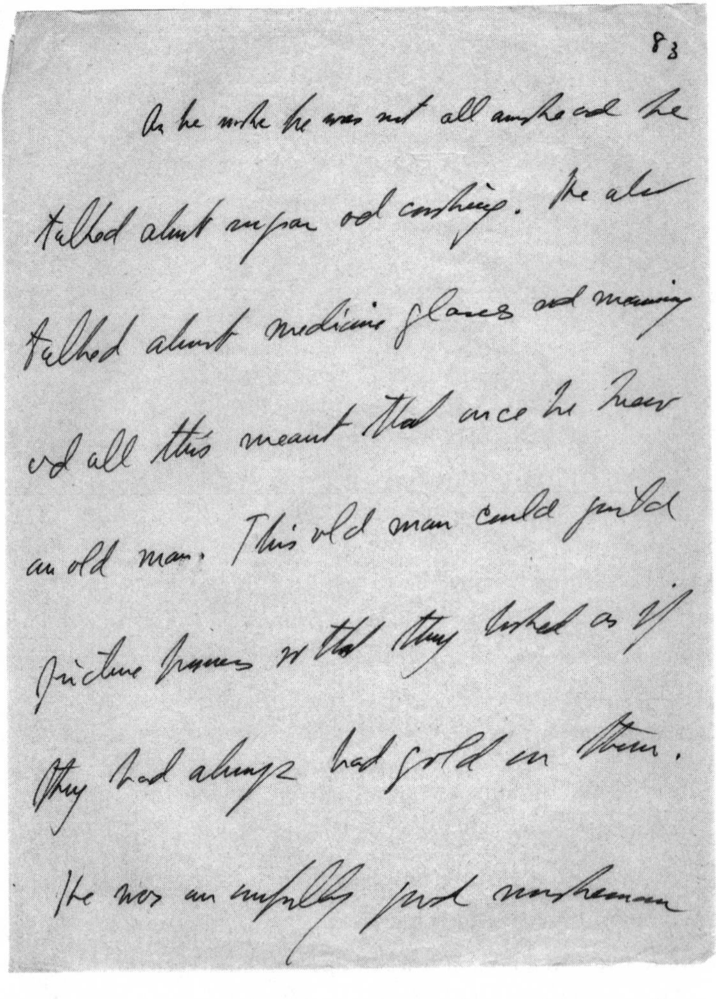

83

As he woke he was not all awake and he
talked about sugar and cooking. He also
talked about medicine glasses and meaning
and all this meant that once he knew
an old man. This old man could gild
picture frames so that they looked as if
they had always had gold on them.
He was an awfully good workman

*Figure 3:* "As he woke he was not all awake and he talked about sugar and cooking. He also talked about medicine glasses and meaning and all of this meant that once he knew an old man. This old man could gild picture frames so that they looked as if they had always had gold on them. He was an awfully good workman" (YCAL 26.534).

once he knew an old man") and used the rest many paragraphs further on ("This old man could gild picture frames so that they looked as if they had always had gold on them. He was an awfully good workman"). After "medicine glasses" in *Ida* is a paragraph that begins "Arthur never fished in a river," which came from pages 101–106. "Arthur often wished on a star" and the following three paragraphs came from pages 143–146, and the paragraph with "they managed to make their feet keep step" came from page 158. The paragraph in *Ida* that begins "Well anyway he went back" came from pages 22–23 in another manuscript sequence:

> Philip was his name Philip Arthur but until then he had only been known as Arthur.
>
> He was in the middle of his country which was a big one, and he commenced to cry. He sat down and wept. He was so nervous when he found himself weeping that he lay down full length on the ground turned on his stomach and dug his palms into the ground.
>
> He had come back and he was there.
>
> Five years he had been going all around and had looked at everybody and listened to everybody and slept everywhere. (YCAL 26.536)

Stein's three-year journey with *Ida* ends much more happily than Philip Arthur's five-year one. Her going all around and looking and listening occurred within both the country of the draft material and the world of her career, among the texts from years earlier and those written concurrently. While these methods were not absolutely new—she had used them early in her career and again following *The Autobiography Of Alice B. Toklas*—they had a new significance because she had planned for the evidence of her writing process to be made available. Through her archive and through *Ida*, through incorporation and rearrangement, Stein delineated her identity as an intertextual writer so that we would consider how closely networked her writing was across her career, and she gave indisputable evidence of her commitment to the creative act.

# Ida

*A Novel*

# First Half

## Part One

There was a baby born named Ida. Its mother held it with her hands to keep Ida from being born but when the time came Ida came. And as Ida came, with her came her twin, so there she was Ida-Ida.

The mother was sweet and gentle and so was the father. The whole family was sweet and gentle except the great-aunt. She was the only exception.

An old woman who was no relation and who had known the great-aunt when she was young was always telling that the great-aunt had had something happen to her oh many years ago, it was a soldier, and then the great-aunt had had little twins born to her and then she had quietly, the twins were dead then, born so, she had buried them under a pear tree and nobody knew.

Nobody believed the old woman perhaps it was true but nobody believed it, but all the family always looked at every pear tree and had a funny feeling.

The grandfather was sweet and gentle too. He liked to say that in a little while a cherry tree does not look like a pear tree.

It was a nice family but they did easily lose each other.

So Ida was born and a very little while after her parents went off on a trip and never came back. That was the first funny thing that happened to Ida.

The days were long and there was nothing to do.

She saw the moon and she saw the sun and she saw the grass and she saw the streets.

The first time she saw anything it frightened her. She saw a little boy and when he waved to her she would not look his way.

She liked to talk and to sing songs and she liked to change places. Wherever she was she always liked to change places. Otherwise there was nothing to do all day. Of course she went to bed early but even so she always could say, what shall I do now, now what shall I do.

Some one told her to say no matter what the day is it always ends the same day, no matter what happens in the year the year always ends one day.

Ida was not idle but the days were always long even in winter and there was nothing to do.

Ida lived with her great-aunt not in the city but just outside.

She was very young and as she had nothing to do she walked as if she was tall as tall as anyone. Once she was lost that is to say a man followed her and that frightened her so that she was crying just as if she had been lost. In a little while that is some time after it was a comfort to her that this had happened to her.

She did not have anything to do and so she had time to think about each day as it came. She was very careful about Tuesday. She always just had to have Tuesday. Tuesday was Tuesday to her.

They always had plenty to eat. Ida always hesitated before eating. That was Ida.

One day it was not Tuesday, two people came to see her great-aunt. They came in very carefully. They did not come in together. First one came and then the other one. One of them had some orange blossoms in her hand. That made Ida feel funny. Who were they. She did not know and she did not like to follow them in. A third one came along, this one was a man and he had orange blossoms in his hat brim. He took off his hat and he said to himself here I am, I wish to speak to myself. Here I am. Then he went on into the house.

Ida remembered that an old woman had once told her that she Ida would come to be so much older that not anybody could be older, although, said the old woman, there was one who was older.

Ida began to wonder if that was what was now happening to her. She wondered if she ought to go into the house to see whether there was really anyone with her great-aunt, and then she thought she would act as if she was not living there but was somebody just coming to visit and so she went up to the door and she asked herself is any one at home and when they that is she herself said to herself no there is nobody at home she decided not to go in.

That was just as well because orange blossoms were funny things to her great-aunt just as pear trees were funny things to Ida.

And so Ida went on growing older and then she was almost sixteen and a great many funny things happened to her. Her great-aunt went away so she lost her great-aunt who never really felt content since the orange blossoms had come to visit her. And now Ida lived with her grandfather. She had a dog, he was almost blind not from age but from having been born so and Ida called him Love, she liked to call him naturally she did and he liked to come even without her calling him.[1]

It was dark in the morning any morning but since her dog Love was blind it did not make any difference to him.

It is true he was born blind nice dogs often are. Though he was blind naturally she could always talk to him.

One day she said. Listen Love, but listen to everything and listen while I tell you something.

Yes Love she said to him, you have always had me and now you are going to have two, I am going to have a twin yes I am Love, I am tired of being just one and when I am a twin one of us can go out and one of us can stay in, yes Love yes I am yes I am going to have a twin. You know Love I am like that when I have to have it I have to have it. And I have to have a twin, yes Love.

The house that Ida lived in was a little on top of a hill, it was not a very pretty house but it was quite a nice one and there was a big field next to it and trees at either end of the field and a path at one side of it and not very many flowers ever because the trees and the grass took up so very much room but there was a good deal of space to fill with Ida and her dog Love and anybody could understand that she really did have to have a twin.

She began to sing about her twin and this is the way she sang.

Oh dear oh dear Love, that was her dog, if I had a twin well nobody would know which one I was and which one she was and so if anything happened nobody could tell anything and lots of things are going to happen and oh Love I felt it yes I know it I have a twin.

It was winter and Ida never wondered because thunder rumbled in winter, that lightning struck and thunder rumbled in winter. It just did.

Ida paid no attention to that but she did one day see a man carrying an advertisement on his back, a sandwich man, that was all right but what was funny was that he stopped and he was talking as if he knew him to a big well dressed rich man.

Ida very quickly went off home.

Then she went to live with another great-aunt outside of the city and there she decided and she told her dog Love about it, she decided that she would be a twin.

She had not yet decided to be a twin when another funny thing happened to her.

She was walking with her dog Love, they were walking and suddenly he left her to bark at something, that something was a man stretched out by the side of the road, not sleeping, because his legs were kicking, not dead, because he was rolling, not happy, because he just was not, and he was dressed in soldier's clothing. Love the dog went up to him, not to sniff, not to bark, he just went up to him and when Ida came near she saw he was not a white man, he was an Arab, and of course the dog Love did not bark at him. How could he when an Arab smells of herbs and fields and not of anything human. Ida was not frightened, he got up the Arab and he began to make motions of drinking. Ida might have been frightened if it had been toward evening, which it was, and she had been all alone, which she was, but she motioned back that she had nothing, and the Arab got up, and stood, and then suddenly, he went away. Ida instead of going on the way she was going went back the way she had come.

She heard about religion but she never really did happen to have any. One day, it was summer, she was in another place and she saw a lot of people under the trees and she went too. They were there and some one was moving around among them, they were all sitting and kneeling, not all of them but most of them and in the middle there was one slowly walking and her arms were slowly moving and everybody was following and some when their arms were started moving could not stop their arms from going on moving. Ida stayed as long as she could and then she went away. She always stayed as long as she could.

One day, it was before or after she made up her mind to be a twin, she joined a walking marathon. She kept on moving, sleeping or walking, she kept on slowly moving.[4] This was one of the funny things that happened to her. Then she lived outside of a city, she was eighteen then, she decided that she had had enough of only being one and she told her dog Love that she was going to be two she was going to be a twin. And this did then happen.

Ida often wrote letters to herself that is to say she wrote to her twin.

Dear Ida my twin,

Here I am sitting not alone because I have dear Love with me, and I speak to him and he speaks to me, but here I am all alone and I am thinking of you Ida my dear twin. Are you beautiful as beautiful as I am dear twin Ida, are you, and if you are perhaps I am not. I can not go away Ida, I am here always, if not here then somewhere, but just now I am here, I am like that, but you dear Ida you are not, you are not here, if you were I could not write to you. Do you know what I think Ida, I think that you could be a queen of beauty, one of the ones they elect when everybody has a vote. They are elected and they go everywhere and everybody looks at them and everybody sees them. Dear Ida oh dear Ida do do be one. Do not let them know you have any name but Ida and I know Ida will win, Ida Ida Ida,

from your twin

Ida

Ida sat silently looking at her dog Love and playing the piano softly until the light was dim. Ida went out first locking the door she went out and as she went out she knew she was a beauty and that they would all vote for her. First she had to find the place where they were going to vote, but that did not make any difference anywhere would do they would vote for her just anywhere, she was such a beauty.

As she went she saw a nicely dressed little girl with a broken arm who threw a stone at a window. It was the little girl's right arm that was broken. This was a sign.[5]

So when Ida arrived they voted that she was a great beauty and the most beautiful and the completest beauty and she was for that year the winner of the beauty prize for all the world. Just like that. It did happen. Ida was her name and she had won.

Nobody knew anything about her except that she was Ida but that was enough because she was Ida the beauty Ida.

# Part Two

There was an older man who happened to go in where they were voting. He did not know they were voting for the prize beauty but once there he voted too. And naturally he voted for her. Anybody would. And so she won. The only thing for her to do then was to go home which she did. She had to go a long way round otherwise they would have known where she lived of course she had to give an address and she did, and she went there and then she went back outside of the city where she was living.

On the way, just at the end of the city she saw a woman carrying a large bundle of wash. This woman stopped and she was looking at a photograph, Ida stopped too and it was astonishing, the woman was looking at the photograph, she had it in her hand, of Ida's dog Love. This was astonishing.[6]

Ida was so surprised she tried to snatch the photograph and just then an automobile came along, there were two women in it, and the automobile stopped and they stepped out to see what was happening. Ida snatched the photograph from the woman who was busy looking at the automobile and Ida jumped into the automobile and tried to start it, the two women jumped into the automobile threw Ida out and went on in the automobile with the photograph. Ida and the woman with the big bundle of wash were left there. The two of them stood and did not say a word.

Ida went away, she was a beauty, she had won the prize she was judged to be the most beautiful but she was bewildered and then she saw a package on the ground. One of the women in the automobile must have dropped it. Ida picked it up and then she went away.

So then Ida did everything an elected beauty does but every now and then she was lost.

One day she saw a man he looked as if he had just come off a farm and with him was a very little woman and behind him was an ordinary-sized woman. Ida wondered about them. One day she saw again the woman with a big bundle of wash. She was talking to a man, he was a young man. Ida came up near them. Just then an automobile with two women came past and in the automobile was Ida's dog Love, Ida was sure it was Love, of course it was Love and in its mouth it had a package, the same package Ida had picked up. There it all was and the woman with the bundle of wash and the young man and Ida, they all stood and looked and they did not any one of them say anything.

Ida went on living with her great-aunt, there where they lived just outside of the city, she and her dog Love and her piano. She did write letters very often to her twin Ida.

Dear Ida, she said.

Dear Ida,

So pleased so very pleased that you are winning, I might even call you Winnie because you are winning. You have won being a beautiful one the most beautiful one. One day I was walking with my dog Love and a man came up to him, held out his hand to him and said how do you do you the most beautiful one. I thought he was a very funny man and now they have decided that you are the one the most beautiful one. And one day the day you won, I saw a funny thing, I saw my dog Love belonging to some one. He did not belong to me he did belong to them. That made me feel very funny, but really it is not true he is here he belongs to me and you and now I will call you Winnie because you are winning everything and I am so happy that you are my twin.

Your twin, Ida-Ida

And so Winnie was coming to be known to be Winnie.

Winnie Winnie is what they said when they saw her and they were beginning to see her.

They said it different ways. They said Winnie. And then they said Winnie.

She knew.

It is easy to make everybody say Winnie, yes Winnie. Sure I know Winnie. Everybody knows who Winnie is. It is not so easy, but there it is, everybody did begin to notice that Winnie is Winnie.

This quite excited Ida and she wrote more letters to Winnie.

Dear Winnie,

Everybody knows who you are, and I know who you are. Dear Winnie we are twins and your name is Winnie. Never again will I not be a twin,

Your twin

Ida

So many things happened to Winnie. Why not when everybody knew her name.

Once there were two people who met together. They said. What shall we do. So what did they do. They went to see Winnie. That is they went to look at Winnie.

When they looked at her they almost began to cry. One said. What if I did not look at her did not look at Winnie. And the other said. Well that is just the way I feel about it.

After a while they began to think that they had done it, that they had seen Winnie, that they had looked at her. It made them nervous because perhaps really had they.

One said to the other. Say have we and the other answered back, say have we.

Did you see her said one of them. Sure I saw her did you. Sure he said sure I saw her.

They went back to where they came from.

One day Ida went to buy some shoes. She liked to look at yellow shoes when she was going to buy red ones. She liked to look at black shoes when she was not going to buy any shoes at all.

It was crowded in the shoe store. It was the day before Easter.

There were a great many places but each one had some one, it is hard to try on shoes standing, hard, almost impossible and so she waited for her turn, a man was sitting next to his wife who was trying on shoes, he was not, and so not Ida but the saleswoman told him to get up, he did, and he did not look at Ida. Ida was used to that.

The place was full, nobody looked at Ida. Some of them were talking about Winnie. They said. But really, is Winnie so interesting. They just talked and talked about that.

So that is the way life went on.

There was Winnie.

Once in a while a man is a man and he comes from Omaha, where they catch all they can. He almost caught Ida. It happened like this.

He went out one night and he saw Winnie. Winnie was always there. She went everywhere.

He followed Winnie.

He did it very well.

The next day he went and rang the bell.

He asked for Winnie.

Of course there was no Winnie.

That was not surprising and did not surprise him.

He could not ask for Ida because he did not know Ida. He almost asked for Ida. Well in a way he did ask for Ida.

Ida came.

Ida was not the same as Winnie. Not at all.

Ida and he, the man from Omaha said. How do you do. And then they said. Good-bye.

The Omaha man went away. He did follow Winnie again but he never rang the bell again. He knew better.

Ida lived alone. She tried to make her dog Iris notice birds but he never did. If he had she would have had more to do because she would have had to notice them too.

It is funny the kind of life Ida led but all the same it kept her going day after day.

But all the same something did happen.

One day she was there doing nothing and suddenly she felt very funny. She knew she had lost something. She looked everywhere and she could not find out what it was that she had lost but she knew she had lost something. All of a sudden she felt or rather she heard somebody call to her. She stopped, she really had not been walking but anyway she stopped and she turned and she heard them say, Ida is that you Ida. She saw somebody coming toward her. She had never seen them before. There were three of them, three women. But soon there was only one. That one came right along. It is funny isn't it. She said. Yes said Ida. There, said the woman, I told them I knew it was.

That was all that happened.

They all three went away.

Ida did not go on looking for what she had lost, she was too excited.

She remembered that one day in front of the house a man with a hat a cane and a bottle stopped. He put down the cane but then he did not know what to do with his hat, so he began again. He put his cane into a window so that stuck out, and he hung his hat on the cane and then with the bottle he stood up. This, he said, is a bottle and in it there is wine, and I who am drunk am going to drink this wine. He did.

And then he said.

It might be like having a handkerchief in a drawer and never taking it out but always knowing it was there. It would always be new and nobody ever would be through with having it there.

What is peace what is war said the man, what is beauty what is ice, said the man. Where is my hat said the man, where is my wine said the man, I have a cane, he said, I have a hat, he said, I have a bottle full of wine. Goodbye, he said, but Ida had gone away.

She had certain habits. When she counted ten she always counted them on her fingers to make ten times ten. It was very hard to remember how many times she had counted ten when once she had counted them because she had to remember twice and then when she had counted a hundred then what happened. Really nothing. Ida just sat down. Living alone as she did counting was an occupation.

She was walking and she saw a woman and three children, two little girls and a littler boy. The boy was carrying a black coat on his arms, a large one.

A woman said to Ida, I only like a white skin. If when I die I come back again and I find I have any other kind of skin then I will be sure that I was very wicked before.

This made Ida think about talking.

She commenced to talk. She liked to see people eat, in restaurants and wherever they eat, and she liked to talk. You can always talk with army officers. She did.

Army officers do not wear their uniforms in the cities, soldiers do but officers do not. This makes conversation with them easier and more difficult.

If an officer met Ida he said, how do you do and she answered very well I thank you. They were as polite as that.

He said to her. Thank you for answering me so pleasingly, and she said. You are very welcome.

The officer would then go on conversing.

What is it that you like better than anything else, he asked and she said. I like being where I am. Oh said he excitedly, and where are you. I am not here, she said, I am very careful about that. No I am not here, she said, it is very pleasant, she added and she turned slightly away, very pleasant indeed not to be here.

The officer smiled. I know he said I know what you mean. Winnie is your name and that is what you mean by your not being here.

She suddenly felt very faint. Her name was not Winnie it was Ida, there was no Winnie. She turned toward the officer and she said to him. I am afraid very much afraid that you are mistaken. And she went away very slowly. The officer looked after her but he did not follow her. Nobody could know in looking at him that he was an officer because he did not wear a uniform and he did not know whether she knew it or not.

Perhaps she did and perhaps she did not.

Every day after that Ida talked to some officer.

If I am an officer, said an officer to Ida, and I am an officer. I am an officer and I give orders. Would you, he said looking at Ida. Would you like to see me giving orders. Ida looked at him and did not answer. If I were to give orders and everybody obeyed me and they do, said the officer, would that impress you. Ida looked at him, she looked at him and the officer felt that she must like him, otherwise she would not look at him and so he said to her, you do like me or else you would not look at me. But Ida sighed. She said, yes and no. You see, said Ida, I do look at you but that is not enough. I look at you and you look at me but we neither of us say more than how do you do and very well I thank you, if we do then there is always the question. What is your name. And really, said Ida, if I knew your name I would not be interested in you, no, I would not, and if I do not know your name I could not be interested, certainly I could not. Good-bye, said Ida, and she went away.

Ida not only said good-bye but she went away to live somewhere else.

Once upon a time way back there were always gates, gates that opened so that you could go in and then little by little there were no fences no walls anywhere. For a little time they had a gate even when there was no fence. It was there just to look elegant and it was nice to have a gate that would click even if there was no fence. By and by there was no gate.

Ida when she had a dog had often stood by a gate and she would hold the dog by the hand and in this way they would stand.

But that was long ago and Ida did not think of anything except now. Why indeed was she always alone if there could be anything to remember. Why indeed.

And so nothing happened to her yet. Not yet.

One day Ida saw a moth that was flying and it worried her. It was one of the very few things that ever worried Ida. She said to an officer. This was another officer. There is an army and there is a navy and there are always lots of officers. Ida said to this one. When you put your uniform away for the summer you are afraid of moths. Yes said the officer. I understand that, said Ida, and she slowly drifted away, very thoughtfully, because she knew of this. Alone and she was alone and she was afraid of moths and of mothballs. The two go together.

Ida rarely coughed. She had that kind of health.

In New England there are six states, Maine, Massachusetts, Vermont, New Hampshire, Connecticut and Rhode Island.

Ida turned up in Connecticut. She was living there quite naturally, quietly living there. She had a friend who was tall and thin and her eyes were gray and her hair was messed and she dressed in black and she was thin and her legs were long and she wore a large hat. She did not mind the sun but she did wear a wide-brimmed hat. Yes she did. She was like that. Yes she was.

This friend did not interest Ida. She saw her, yes, but she did not interest her.

Except this one woman nobody knew Ida in Connecticut. For a while she did not talk to anybody there. She spent the day sitting and then that was a day. On that day she heard somebody say something. They said who is Winnie. The next day Ida left Connecticut.

She began to think about what would happen if she were married.

As she was leaving Connecticut she began to listen to a man. He was an officer in the army. His name was Sam Hamlin. He was a lively Sam Hamlin. He said if he had a wife he could divorce her. He came originally from Connecticut and he was still in Connecticut. He said the only way to leave Connecticut was to go out of it. But he never would. If he had left Connecticut he might have gotten to Washington, perhaps to Utah and Idaho, and if he had he might have gotten lost. That is the way he felt about Connecticut.

Little by little very little by little he said it all to Ida. He said I know, and he said when I say I know I mean it is just like that. I like, he said to Ida, I like everything I say to be said out loud.

He said I know. He said I know you, and he not only said it to Ida but he said it to everybody, he knew Ida he said hell yes he knew Ida. He said one day to Ida it is so sweet to have soft music it is so sweet.

He told her how once upon a time he had been married and he said to her. Now listen. Once upon a time I was married, by the time you came to Connecticut I wasn't. Now you say you are leaving Connecticut. The only way to leave Connecticut is to go out, and I am not going out of Connecticut. Listen to me, he said, I am not going out of Connecticut. I am an officer in the army and of course perhaps they will send me out of Connecticut there is Massachusetts and Rhode Island and New Hampshire and Vermont and Maine but I am going to stay in Connecticut, believe it or not I am.

Ida left Connecticut and that was the first time Ida thought about getting married and it was the last time anybody said Winnie anywhere near her.

There was a woman in California her name was Eleanor Angel and she had a property and on that property she found gold and silver and she found platinum and radium. She did not find oil. She wrote to everybody about it and they were all excited, anybody would be, and they did believe it, and they said it was interesting if it was true and they were sure it was true.

Ida went out to stay with her.

Ida was never discouraged and she was always going out walking.

As she walked along, she thought about men and she thought about presidents. She thought about how some men are more presidents than other men when they happen to be born that way and she said to herself. Which one is mine. She knew that there must be one that could be hers one who would be a president. And so she sat down and was very satisfied to do nothing.

Sit down, somebody said to her, and she sat.

Well it was not that one. He sat too and then that was that.

Ida always looked again to see if it was that one or another one, the one she had seen or not, and sometimes it was not.

Then she would sit down not exactly to cry and not exactly to sit down but she did sit down and she felt very funny, she felt as if it was all being something and that was what always led her on.

Ida saw herself come, then she saw a man come, then she saw a man go away, then she saw herself go away.

And all the time well all the time she said something, she said nice little things, she said all right, she said I do.

Was she on a train or an automobile, an airplane or just walking.

Which was it.

Well she was on any of them and everywhere she was just talking. She was saying, yes yes I like to be sitting. Yes I like to be moving. Yes I have been here before. Yes it is very pleasant here. Yes I will come here again. Yes I do wish to have them meet, I meet them and they meet me and it is very nice.

Ida never sighed, she just rested. When she rested she turned a little and she said, yes dear. She said that very pleasantly.

This was all of Ida's life just then.

She said. I do not like birds.

She liked mechanical birds but not natural birds. Natural birds always sang.

She sat with her friend and they talked together. Ida said, I am never tired and I am never very fresh. I change all the time. I say to myself, Ida, and that startles me and then I sit still.

Her friend said, I will come again.

Do said Ida.

It was very quiet all day long but Ida was ready for that.

Ida married Frank Arthur.

Arthur had been born right in the middle of a big country.

He knew when he was a tiny boy that the earth was round so it was never a surprise to him. He knew that trees had green leaves and that there was snow when time for snow came and rain when time for rain came. He knew a lot.

When Arthur was little he knew a handsome boy who had a club-foot and was tall and thin and worked for a farmer.

The boy with the club-foot rode a bicycle and he would stand and lean on his bicycle and tell Arthur everything.

He told him all about dogs.

He told him how a little dog, once he had found out about it, would just go on making love to anything, the hind leg of a big dog, a leg of a table, anything, he told him how a young hunting dog's voice changed, it cracked just like boys' voices did and then it went up and down and then finally it settled down. He told him about shepherds' dogs, how shepherds only could work their dogs eight years that when the dog was nine years old the shepherd had to hang him, that often the shepherd was awfully sad and cried like anything when he had to hang his dog to kill him but he could not keep him after the dog was eight years old, they did not really care anything for sheep after that and how could you feed a dog if he did not care about sheep any more and so the shepherds sometimes cried a lot but when the dog was eight years old they did hang him. Then he told Arthur about another dog and a girl. She always used to give that dog a lump of sugar whenever she saw him. She was a girl in a store where they sold sugar, and then one day she saw the man come in who had the dog, and when he came she said where is the dog and he said the dog is dead. She had the piece of sugar in her hand and when he said that she put the piece of sugar in her mouth and ate it and then she burst out crying.[7]

He told Arthur about sheep, he told him that sheep were curious about everything but mostly about dogs, they always were looking for a dog who looked like a sheep and sometimes they found one and when they did they the young ones the baby sheep were pleased, but the older ones were frightened, as soon as they saw a dog who really looked like a sheep, and they ran at him and tried to butt him.

He also told Arthur about cows, he said cows were not always willing, he said some cows hated everything. He also told him about bulls. He said bulls were not very interesting.

He used to stand, the boy with a club-foot, leaning on his bicycle and telling Arthur everything.

When Arthur was a little bigger he came to know a man, not a tall man. He was a fairly little man and he was a good climber. He could climb not only in and out of a window but out of the top of a door if the door was closed. He was very remarkable. Arthur asked him and he then heard him say that he never thought about anything else than climbing. Why should he when he could climb anything.

Arthur was not very good at climbing. All he could do was to listen to the little man. He told about how he climbed to the top of a gate, to the top of a door, to the top of a pole. The little man's name was Bernard. He said it was the same name as that of a saint. Then well naturally then he went away. He finally did go away alone.

Arthur was almost old enough to go away. Pretty soon he did go away.

He tried several ways of going away and finally he went away on a boat and got shipwrecked and had his ear frozen.

He liked that so much that he tried to get shipwrecked again but he never did. He tried it again and again, he tried it on every kind of boat but they never were wrecked again. Finally he said, Once and not again.

He did lots of things before he went back to the middle of the big country where he had been born.

Finally he became an officer in the army and he married Ida but before that he lived around.

One of the things he did was to sleep in a bed under a bridge. The bed was made of cardboard. He was not the first to make it. Somebody else made it but when Arthur had no place to go because he had used up all his money he used to go to sleep there. Some one always was asleep there. Day and night there was always somebody sleeping there. Arthur was one who when he woke up shaved and washed himself in the river, he always carried the things with him.

It was a nice time then. Instead of working or having his money Arthur just listened to anybody. It made him sleepy and he was never more than half awake and in his sleep he had a way of talking about sugar and cooking. He also used to talk about medicine glasses.

Arthur never fished in a river. He had slept too often under a bridge to care anything about going fishing. One evening he met a man who had been fishing. They talked a little and the man said that he was not much good at fishing, he saw the fish but he never could catch them. Finally he said to Arthur, do you know who I am. No said Arthur. Well said the man taking off his hat, I am chief of police. Well why can't you catch fish, said Arthur. Well I caught a trout the other day and he got away from me. Why didn't you take his number said Arthur. Because fish can't talk was the answer.

Arthur often wished on a star, he said star bright, star light, I wish I may I wish I might have the wish I wish tonight.

The wish was that he would be a king or rich.

There is no reason why a king should be rich or a rich man should be a king, no reason at all.

Arthur had not yet come to decide which one was the one for him. It was easy enough to be either the one or the other one. He just had to make up his mind, be rich or be a king and then it would just happen. Arthur knew that much.

Well anyway he went back to where he came from, he was in the middle of his country which was a big one and he commenced to cry. He was so nervous when he found himself crying that he lay full length on the ground turned on his stomach and dug his palms into the ground.

He decided to enter the army and he became an officer and some few years after he met Ida.

He met her on the road one day and he began to walk next to her and they managed to make their feet keep step. It was just like a walking marathon.

He began to talk. He said. All the world is crying crying about it all. They all want a king.

She looked at him and then she did not. Everybody might want a king but anybody did not want a queen.

It looks, said Arthur, as if it was sudden but really it took me some time, some months even a couple of years, to understand how everybody wants a king.

He said. Do you know the last time I was anywhere I was with my mother and everybody was good enough to tell me to come again. That was all long ago. Everybody was crying because I went away, but I was not crying. That is what makes anybody a king that everybody cries but he does not.

Philip was the kind that said everything out loud.[8]

I knew her, he said and he said he knew Ida, hell he said, yes I know Ida. He said it to every one, he said it to her. He said he knew her.

Ida never saw Arthur again.

She just did not.

She went somewhere and there she just sat, she did not even have a dog, she did not have a town, she lived alone and just sat.

She went out once in a while, she listened to anybody talking about how they were waiting for a fall in prices.

She saw a sign up that said please pay the unemployed and a lot of people were gathered around and were looking.

It did not interest her. She was not unemployed. She just sat and she always had enough. Anybody could.

Somebody came and asked her where Arthur was. She said, Arthur was gone.

Pretty soon she was gone and when she was gone nobody knew what to say.

They did not know she was gone but she was.

They wanted to read about her but as there was nothing written about her they could not read about her. So they just waited.

Ida went to live with a cousin of her uncle.

He was an old man and he could gild picture frames so that they looked as if they had always had gold on them. He was a good man that old man and he had a son, he sometimes thought that he had two sons but anyway he had one and that one had a garage and he made a lot of money. He had a partner and they stole from one another. One day the son of the old man was so angry because the partner was most successful in getting the most that he up and shot him. They arrested him. They put him in jail. They condemned him to twenty years hard labor because the partner whom he had killed had a wife and three children. The man who killed the other one had no children that is to say his wife had one but it was not his. Anyway there it was. His mother spent all her time in church praying that her son's soul should be saved. The wife of their doctor said it was all the father and mother's fault, they had brought up their son always to think of money, always of money, had not they the old man and his wife got the cousin of the doctor's wife always to give them presents of course they had.

Ida did not stay there very long. She went to live with the cousin of the doctor's wife and there she walked every day and had her dog. The name of this dog was Claudine. Ida did not keep her. She gave her away.

She began to say to herself Ida dear Ida do you want to have two sisters or do you want to be one.

There were five sisters once and Ida might have been one.

Anybody likes to know about then and now, Ida was one and it is easy to have one sister and be a twin too and be a triplet three and be a quartet and four and be a quintuplet it is easy to have four but that just about does shut the door.

Ida began to be known.

As she walked along people began to be bewildered as they saw her and they did not call out to her but some did begin to notice her. Was she a twin well was she.

She went away again. Going away again was not monotonous although it seemed so. Ida ate no fruit. It was the end of the week and she had gone away and she did not come back there.

Pretty soon she said to herself Now listen to me, I am here and I know it, if I go away I will not like it because I am so used to my being here. I would not know what has happened, now just listen to me, she said to herself, listen to me, I am going to stop talking and I will.

Of course she had gone away and she was living with a friend.

How many of those who are yoked together have ever seen oxen.

This is what Ida said and she cried. Her eyes were full of tears and she waited and then she went over everything that had ever happened and in the middle of it she went to sleep.

When she awoke she was talking.

How do you do she said.

First she was alone and then soon everybody was standing listening. She did not talk to them.

Of course she did think about marrying. She had not married yet but she was going to marry.

She said if I was married I'd have children and if I had children then I'd be a mother and if I was a mother I'd tell them what to do.

She decided that she was not going to marry and was not going to have children and was not going to be a mother.

Ida decided that she was just going to talk to herself. Anybody could stand around and listen but as for her she was just going to talk to herself.

She no longer even needed a twin.

Somebody tried to interrupt her, he was an officer of course but how could he interrupt her if she was not talking to him but just talking to herself.

She said how do you do and people around answered her and said how do you do. The officer said how do you do, here I am, do you like peaches and grapes in winter, do you like chickens and bread and asparagus in summer. Ida did not answer, of course not.

It was funny the way Ida could go to sleep and the way she could cry and the way she could be alone and the way she could lie down and the way anybody knew what she did and what she did not do.

Ida thought she would go somewhere else but then she knew that she would look at everybody and everything and she knew it would not be interesting.

She was interesting.

She remembered everything and she remembered everybody but she never talked to any of them, she was always talking to herself.

She said to herself. How old are you, and that made her cry. Then she went to sleep and oh it was so hard not to cry. So hard.

So Ida decided to earn a living. She did not have to, she never had to but she decided to do it.

There are so many ways of earning a living and most of them are failures. She thought it was best to begin with one way which would be most easy to leave. So she tried photography and then she tried just talking.

It is wonderful how easy it is to earn a living that way. To be sure sometimes everybody thinks you are starving but you never are. Ida never starved.

Once she stayed a week in a hotel by herself. She said when she saw the man who ran it, how often do you have your hotel full.

Quite often he answered. Well, said Ida, wait awhile and I will leave and then everybody will come, but while I am here nobody will come. Why not said the hotel keeper. Because said Ida, I want to be in the hotel all alone. I only want you and your wife and your three boys and your girl and your father and your mother and your sister in it while I am here. Nobody else. But do not worry, you will not have to keep the others out, they will not come while I am here.

Ida was right. The week she was there nobody came to eat or sleep in the hotel. It just did happen that way.

Ida was very much interested in the wife of the hotel keeper who was sweet-voiced and managed everything because Ida said that sooner or later she would kill herself, she would go out of a window, and the hotel would go to pieces.[9]

Ida knew just what was going to happen. This did not bother her at all. Mostly before it happened she had gone away.

Once she was caught.

It was in a hilly country.

She knew two young men there, one painted in water colors and the other was an engineer. They were brothers. They did not look alike.

Ida sat down on a hillside. A brother was on each side of her.

The three sat together and nothing was said.

Then one brother said. I like to sit here where nothing is ever said. The other brother said. I I like bread, I like to sit here and eat bread. I like to sit here and look about me. I like to sit here and watch the trees grow. I like to sit here.

Ida said nothing. She did not hear what they said. Ida liked sitting. They all three did.

One brother said. It pleases me very much that I have discovered how prettily green looks next to blue and how water looks so

It is not easy to count, said he to himself because when I count, I lose count.

Oh dear he said, it is lovely in Montana, there are mountains in Montana and the mountains are very high and just then he looked up and he saw them and he decided, it was not very sudden, he decided he would never see Montana again and he never did.

He went away from Montana and he went to Virginia. There he saw trees and he was so pleased. He said I wonder if Ida has ever seen these trees. Of course she had. It was not she who was blind, it was her dog Iris.

Funnily enough even if Ida did see trees she always looked on the ground to see what had fallen from the trees. Leaves might and nuts and even feathers and flowers. Even water could fall from a tree. When it did well there was her umbrella. She had a very pretty short umbrella. She had lost two and now she had the third. Her husband said, Oh Ida.

Ida's husband did not love his father more than he did his mother or his mother more than he did his father.

Ida and he settled down together and one night she dreamed of a field of orchids, white orchids each on their stalk in a field. Such a pretty girl to have dreamed of white orchids each on its stalk in a field. That is what she dreamed.

And she dreamed that now she was married, she was not Ida she was Virginia. She dreamed that Virginia was her name and that she had been born in Wyoming not in Montana. She dreamed that she often longed for water. She dreamed that she said. When I close my eyes I see water and when I close my eyes I do see water.

What is water, said Virginia.

And then suddenly she said. Ida.

Ida was married and they went to live in Ohio. She did not love anybody in Ohio.

She liked apples. She was disappointed but she did not sigh. She got sunburned and she had a smile on her face. They asked her did she like it. She smiled gently and left it alone. When they asked her again she said not at all. Later on when they asked her did she like it she said. Perhaps only not yet.

Ida left Ohio.

As she left they asked her can you come again. Of course that is what she said, she said she could come again. Somebody called out, who is Ida, but she did not hear him, she did not know that they were asking about her, she really did not.

Ida did not go directly anywhere. She went all around the world. It did not take her long and everything she saw interested her.

She remembered all the countries there were but she did not count them.

First they asked her, how long before you have to go back to Washington.

Second they said, how soon after you get back to Washington will you go back to Ohio.

Thirdly they asked her. How do you go back to Washington from Ohio.

She always answered them.

She did not pay much attention to weather. She had that kind of money to spend that made it not make any difference about weather.

Ida had not been in love very much and if she were there she was.

Some said, Please like her.

They said regularly. Of course we like her.

Ida began to travel again.

She went from Washington to Wyoming, from Wyoming to Virginia and then she had a kind of feeling that she had never been in Washington although of course she had and she went there again.

She said she was going there just to see why they cry.

That is what they do do there.

She knew just how far away one state is from another. She said to herself. Yes it is all whole.

And so there she was in Washington and her life was going to begin. She was not a twin.

Once upon a time a man had happened to begin walking. He lived in Alabama and walking made it seem awfully far away. While he was walking all of a sudden he saw a tree and on that tree was a bird and the bird had its mouth open. The bird said Ida, anyway it sounded like Ida, and the man, his name was Frederick, Frederick saw the bird and he heard him and he said, that kind of a bird is a mocking bird. Frederick went on walking and once every once in a while he saw another tree and he remembered that a bird had said Ida or something like Ida. That was happening in Alabama.

Frederick went into the army became an officer and came to Washington. There he fell in love with a woman, was she older was she younger or was she the same age. She was not older perhaps she was younger, very likely she was not the same age as his age.

Her name was not Ida.

Ida was in Washington.

If there are two little dogs little black dogs and one of them is a female and the other a male, the female does not look as foolish as the male, no not.

So Ida did not look foolish and neither she was.

She might have been foolish.

Saddest of all words are these, she might have been.

Ida felt very well.

# Part Four

So Ida settled down in Washington. This is what happened every day.

Ida woke up. After a while she got up. Then she stood up. Then she ate something. After that she sat down.

That was Ida.

And Ida began her life in Washington. In a little while there were more of them there who sat down and stood up and leaned. Then they came in and went out. This made it useful to them and to Ida.

Ida said. I am not careful. I do not win him to come away. If he goes away I will not have him. Ida said I can count any one up to ten. When I count up to ten I stop counting. When she said that they listened to her. They were taken with her beginning counting and she counted from one to ten. Of course they listened to her.

Ida knew that. She knew that it is not easy to count while anybody listens to them, but it is easy to listen to them while they are counting.

More and more came to see Ida. Frederick came to see Ida.

Little by little Frederick fell in love with Ida. Ida did not stop him. He did not say that he was in love with her. He did not say that, not that.

And then he was and then they were all there together.

He married her and she married him.

Then suddenly not at all suddenly, they were sent there, he was in the army, they got up and had decided to leave for Ohio. Yesterday or today they would leave for Ohio.

When they got to Ohio, Ohio is a state, it is only spelled with four letters. All of a sudden there they were in Ohio.

Ohio very likely was as large as that.

Everybody said to Ida and they said it to Frederick too. Smile at me please smile at me.

Ida smiled.

They settled down in Ohio.

What did they do in Ohio.

Well they did not stay there long.

They went to Texas.

There they really settled down.

It is easier for an officer in the army to settle down in Texas than in Ohio.

Ida said one day.

Is there anything strange in just walking along.

One day in Texas it was not an accident, believe it or not, a lizard did sit there. It was almost black all over and curled, with yellow under and over, hard to tell, it was so curled, but probably under.

Ida was not frightened, she thought she was thinking. She thought she heard everybody burst out crying and then heard everybody calling out, it is not Ohio, it is Texas, it is not Ohio.

Ida was funny that way, it was so important that all these things happened to her just when and how they did.

She settled down and she and Frederick stayed there until they were not there together or anywhere.

All this time Ida was very careful.

Everything that happened to her was not strange. All along it was not strange Ida was not strange.

It is so easy not to be a mother.

This too happened to Ida.

She never was a mother.

Not ever.

Her life in Ohio which turned out to be her life in Texas went on just like that. She was not a mother. She was not strange. She just knew that once upon a time there was a necessity to know that they would all leave Texas. They did not leave Texas all together but they all left Texas. She left Texas and he left Texas, he was Frederick, and they left Texas. They were all the people they knew when they were in Texas.

As they one and all left Texas, they all fastened their doors and as they fastened their doors nobody saw them leave. That is a way to leave.

Ida always left everywhere in some way. She left Texas in this way. So did they.

She left Texas never to return.

She never went back anywhere so why would she go back to Ohio and to Texas. She never did. Ida never did.

She did not go back to Frederick either.

Ida never did.

She did not remember just how many years she had been with Frederick and in Ohio and in Texas.

She did not remember even when she was with him and there because when she was there she did not count, that is she could count up to ten but it did not give her any pleasure to count then.

How pleasant it is to count one two three four five six seven, and then stop and then go on counting eight nine and then ten or eleven.

Ida just loved to do that but as she certainly was not in Ohio or in Texas that long and certainly not with Frederick that long counting was not anything to do.

Ida liked to be spoken to.

It happened quite often.

How do you do they said and she said it to them and they said it to her. How do you do.

Would you never rather be Ida, they said, never rather be Ida, she laughed, never, they said never rather be Ida.

Of course not, of course she would always rather be Ida and she was.

They all said everybody said, Never rather be Ida, it got to be a kind of a song.

Never, never rather be Ida, never rather be Ida.

Ida never heard anybody sing it. When she heard her name she never heard it. That was Ida.

And so it was all over that is Frederick was all over, Ida left Texas just as it was.

Before she left Texas she talked to Duncan. Old man Duncan they called him but he was quite young. He was forty-five and he had been a policeman and now he was a head of police and not in uniform, of course not, otherwise she would not have been talking to him.

He said to her, where were you before you came to Texas. He asked her that after they had shaken hands several times together and it was evening. It often was evening in Texas.

It is very easy to leave Texas, Ida said, not to Duncan, she just said it.

There is no harm in leaving Texas, no harm at all.

Ida said, I have not left Texas yet, but tell them, you and he, what are you, tell them that he has left Texas and tell them that you and he, well tell them about Texas, you and he.

So then suddenly, she was called away, they thought in Ohio, but she was called away to wherever she was. Just like that Ida was called away.

She was not there any more, because she was called away.

Duncan told her, that is he did not tell her because she was called away, but anyway he told her that he had not left Texas.

Duncan never did leave Texas except once when he went to Tennessee. But by that time he never wanted to leave Texas. No use saying that he only remembered Ida because he didn't.

Once upon a time there was a meadow and in this meadow was a tree and on this tree there were nuts. The nuts fell and then they plowed the ground and the nuts were plowed into the ground but they never grew out.

After Ida left Texas she did not live in the country, she lived in a city. She lived in Washington.

That is the way it went on. Washington is a city and a city well a city is well it is a city. Ida lived there.

Once upon a time every time Ida lived in a city she was careful, she really was. She might lose it lose being careful but really every time she lived in a city she was careful. She was careful in Washington. All who came in would say to her, well Ida how about it.

That is what did happen.

By the time it was all comfortable for Ida and everybody knew better, she knew just what would not be there for her. And it was not. It just was not there for her.

Just then somebody came in and he said here I am. He said to Ida if you were with me I would just say, say she is with me. By golly that is what we are like in Minnesota, Minnesota is just like that.

Hello Ida, said some one. And they said, no Ida we are not. Ida said, no I am not.

Ida felt that way about it. She said well sit down and cry, but nobody did, not just then.

So life began for Ida in Washington.

There were there Ida and two more, Ida kept saying to herself.

There whether there whether whether who is not.

That might have been the motto for Minnesota.

She did have to see those who came from Minnesota and hear them say, Minnesota is not old, believe it or not Minnesota is not old.

Ida began a daily life in Washington.

Once upon a time there was a shotgun and there were wooden guinea hens and they moved around electrically, electricity made them move around and as they moved around if you shot them their heads fell off them.

I thought I coughed said Ida and when I coughed I thought I coughed.

Ida said this and he listened to her he was not from Minnesota.

Once upon a time Ida stood all alone in the twilight. She was down in a field and leaning against a wall, her arms were folded and she looked very tall. Later she was walking up the road and she walked slowly.

She was not so young any more. It almost happened that she would be not sad not tired not depressed but just not so young any more.

She looked around her, she was not all alone because somebody passed by her and they said, it is a nicer evening than yesterday evening and she said, it was.

Ida married again. He was Andrew Hamilton and he came from Boston.

It is very usual of them when they come from Boston to be selfish, very usual, indeed. He and Ida sat together before they sat down.

But not, said some one seeing him, and who had heard of Ida, not, he said.

In Boston the earth is round. Believe it or not, in Boston the earth is round. But they were not in Boston, they were in Washington.

In Boston they hear the ocean as well. Not in Washington. There they have the river, the Potomac.

They were being married, it was not exciting, it was what they did. They did get married.

Once upon a time all who had anywhere to go did not go. This is what they did.

Ida was married again this time he came from Boston, she remembered his name. She was good friends with all her husbands.

This one came from Boston. They said Massachusetts, and when they said Massachusetts they remembered how fresh and green they were there, all of it, yes that is what they said.

In Washington it was different.

There it was in Washington it was come carefully and believe what they said.

Who is careful.

Well in a way Ida is.

She lives where she is not.

Not what.

Not careful.

Oh yes that is what they say.

Not careful.

Of course not.

Who is careful.

That is what they said.

And the answer was.

Ida said.

Oh yes, careful.

Oh yes, I can almost cry.

Ida never did.

Oh yes.

They all said oh yes.

And for three days I have not seen her.

That is what somebody did say somebody really somebody has said. For three days I have not seen her.

Nobody said Ida went away.

She was there Ida was.

So was her husband. So was everybody.

# Part Five

## *Politics*

They said, they do not want to buy from Ida. Why should they want to buy.

Ida and he.

He did not come from Louisiana, no. He was that kind. He did not only not come from Louisiana but he had had a carriage hound, a white and black spotted one and he the black and white spotted one was killed not killed but eaten by other dogs, they were all looking at a female dog and no one told him that the dog was nearly dead.

No one told him.

A young woman had silently had a way of giving the dog sugar and when she heard the dog was dead she ate the sugar.

And the man who was not from Louisiana added that, Oh yes he added that.

He and Ida.

He would have bought from Ida bought and well not well yes well no well why why not bought from Ida.

Ida was a friend.

She stayed in Washington.

She came to do what she knew each one of them wanted.

Easy enough in Washington.

She did not sell anything although they all wanted to buy.

Not at Bay Shore.

No not in Louisiana.

But in Carolina.

Not in North Carolina.

But in South Carolina.

Yes he would have bought from Ida in South Carolina but Ida was not there never there. She never was in either North or South Carolina. She was in Washington.

And so well yes so he did he did not buy from Ida.

Only Ida.

Well what did Ida do.

Ida knew just who was who.

She did. She did know.

They did not not an awful lot of them know Ida, just enough knew Ida to make Ida be just the one enough of them knew.

There are so many men.

What do you call them there.

There are so many men.

They did not all know Ida.

Now then.

In Washington, some one can do anything. Little by little it was Ida. She knew Charles and she smiled when she saw him. He wanted her to give him the rest of the morning. The rest of the morning. She was too busy too. She said, she never had anything to do but she did not give him the rest of the morning.

Woodward would not die of chagrin when he did not get what he had bought from Ida.

They all buy twice a day but the morning is the best time to buy. Woodward was a great buyer and he never did die of chagrin.

If he was no longer in Washington would Woodward die of chagrin.

Ida smiled every morning. She rested a good deal, she rested even in the evening.

Would Woodward come in and go out just as he liked.

Now that is a question a great question and Ida might answer, she might answer any question, but she did not find it as interesting as anything.

Would Woodward die of chagrin if he left Washington. Somebody stopped Ida and asked her this thing and she said nothing.

Then she said yes, Yes she said and she said nothing.

Yes they said yes would Woodward die of chagrin if he left Washington.

Almost at a loss Ida said yes, she did stand still and then she went on again.

Nobody ever followed Ida. What was the use of following Ida.

Ida had a dream. She dreamed that they were there and there was a little boy with them. Somebody had given the little boy a large package that had something in it and he went off to thank them. He never came back. They went to see why not. He was not there but there was a lady there and she was lying down and a large lion was there moving around. Where said they is the little boy, the lion ate him the lady said, and the package yes he ate it all, but the little boy came to thank you for it, yes I know but it did happen, I did not want it to happen but it did happen. I am very fond of the lion. They went away wondering and then Ida woke up.

Ida often met men and some of them hoped she would get something for them. She always did, not because she wanted them to have it but because she always did it when it was wanted.

Just when it was not at all likely Ida was lost, lost they said, oh yes lost, how lost, why just lost. Of course if she is lost. Yes of course she is lost.

Ida led a very easy life, that is she got up and sat up and went in and came out and rested and went to bed.

But some days she did rest a little more than on other days.

She did what she could for everybody.

Once in a while a father when he was young did not do it himself but a friend of his did. He took something.

When the policeman came nobody knew him. Most certainly he who later was a father refused to know him. They did not come from Africa, they came from North Carolina and Colorado. Later on the father had a son a young son and the young son began to go with men who stole. They were all then in Michigan so when they did steal they stole it again. The father was so worried, worried lest the police come and say to him your son is stealing, had he not refused when he was young and in North Carolina to recognize a friend who had stolen. He did say to the policeman then that he had never known that man although of course he had. And now, here in Michigan perhaps his own son was stealing. The policeman might come and how could he say he did not know his son. He might say it of course he might, he almost probably would.

Ida said to him I'll ask him. She meant that it was all right, it would be just like that, no trouble to anybody. Ida always did that.

She saw the one who was all right and who would say yes yes it is all right and of course it was all right.

Ida did not need to be troubled, all she need do was to rest and she did rest. Just like that.

Once very often every day Ida went away. She could not go away really not, because she had no mother and she had no grandmother no sister and no aunt.

She dreamed that clothes were like Spanish ice-cream. She did not know why she dreamed of Spain. She was married in Washington, there was ice-cream there were clothes, but there was no Spain. Spain never came, but ice-cream and clothes clothes and ice-cream, food and clothes, politics, generals and admirals, clothes and food, she was married and she was in Washington.

She was not away from Washington.

No no more was there any day. She dreamed, if you are old you have nothing to eat, is that, she dreamed in her dream, is that money.

Ida had a companion named Christine. Christine had a little Chinese dog called William. Soon Christine went away taking William. She thought of leaving him behind but she changed her mind.

When Christine went away she accomplished a great deal.

Oh Ida.

Ida was not married any more. She was very nice about it.

All around were what they found. At once they seemed all to like coming.

Ida did not leave Washington.

She rested.

Somebody said. Where is Ida.

Should she go away, somebody said. Go away like what.

Like what, they said.

Like Ida.

No said Christine and for this they thanked her.

All alone in Montana was a little man fragile but he smoked a pipe. Not then but later.

All alone there he was pale. Not tall. Not tall at all. All alone there he went about. He knew nobody was stout in Montana.

For this every little while he tried not to be thinner.

Dear Montana and how he went away.

It does not take long to leave Montana but it takes a long time to get stout, to put flesh on, get rosy and robust, get vaccinated, get everything.

In Montana he was never at a loss. Very likely not because he was careful of Montana.

He knew how to be careful and he was careful of Montana.

And so he plans everything.

He was a great success in Washington. Of course he was.

Politically speaking.

All of a sudden the snow had fallen the mountains were cold and he had left Montana.

That was when he began to smoke his pipe.

That was when he was a success in Washington.

That was when Christine had left him, naturally she had gone again. Now he knew Ida. Not to marry her. It was going to be quite a little while before Ida married again.

Ida moved around, to dance is to move around to move around is to dance, and when Ida moved around she let her arms hang out easily in front of her just like that.

She kept on being in Washington.

Once upon a time, once very often a man was in Washington who was cautious. He came from Wisconsin although he had been born in Washington, Washington city not Washington state.

All right he liked it.

After a little while he was nervous again and then for them it was just as if he was cautious. How do you like it, they said. Then he said no. For that they were very willing that they could just as much as ever they could be used to it.

Oh believe me, he said, and then mountains, he said.

Of course there are no mountains in the city of Washington but there are monuments. Oh believe me, he said, there are mountains in Wisconsin. And everybody believed him.

Once when it happened to snow he stayed at home. I will, he said, I will stay at home and as I am at home I will think and as I am thinking I will say I am thinking. He did, he did stay at home, he did think and as he thought he did think that he would think. He did.

Gradually he wondered what it was he was thinking. He thought how very nice it is and then he said I can not help it.

Of course not of course he could not help it, dear Madison, dear Wisconsin.

He was born in the city of Washington but that just happened.

Ida was in Washington she was not thinking, all the time she was suffering because of his thinking and then he was not thinking about his thinking.

Dear Ida.

Ida very likely Ida was not only in Washington but most likely he would not forget to cry when he heard that Ida was never to leave Washington.

Never to leave Washington.

Of course she finally did.

But in the meantime Ida could not believe that it was best.

To be in Washington.

She knew only knew that she did not rest.

She did it all.

Ida did.

But enough, said some one.

And then Ida came in and sat down and she did rest.

When anybody needed Ida Ida was resting. That was all right that is the way Ida was needed.

Once upon a time there was a city, it was built of blocks and every block had a square in it and every square had a statue and every statue had a hat and every hat was off.

Where was Ida where where was Ida.

She was there. She was in Washington and she said thank you very much, thank you very much indeed. Ida was in Washington.

Thank you very much.

While she was in Washington it was a long time.

There it was.

She was kind to politics while she was in Washington very kind. She told politics that it was very nice of them to have her be kind to them. And she was she was very kind.

She really did not get up in the morning. She wished that she could and they wished that she could but it was not at all necessary.

When she was up and she did see them she was kind.

She saw seven, or eight of them and she saw them one or perhaps two and each time it was a very long time. She never went away she always did stay.

This was what they did say.

How do you do, said Ida, how do you feel when I see you, said Ida, and she did say that and they liked it.

Of course they liked it. And then she was not tired but she did lie down in an easy-chair.

It was not really politics really that Ida knew. It was not politics it was favors, that is what Ida liked to do.

She knew she liked to do them.

Everybody knew she liked to do favors for them and wanting to do favors for everybody who wanted to have favors done for them it was quite natural that those who could do the favors did them when she asked them to do them.

It does go like that.

Once upon a time there was a man his name was Henry, Henry Henry was his name. He had told everybody that whatever name they called him by they just had to call him Henry. He came to Washington, he was born in San Francisco and he liked languages, he was not lazy but he did not like to earn a living. He knew that if anybody would come to know about him they would of course call him Henry. Ida did.

She was resting one day and somebody called, it was somebody who liked to call on Ida when she was resting. He might have wanted to marry her but he never did. He knew that everybody sooner or later would know who Ida was and so he brought Henry with him. Henry immediately asked her to do a favor for him, he wanted to go somewhere where he could talk languages and where he would have to do nothing else. Ida was resting. She smiled.

Pretty soon Henry had what he wanted, he never knew whether it was Ida, but he went to see Ida and he did not thank her but he smiled and she smiled and she was resting and he went away.

That was the way Ida was.

In Washington.

When it was a year Ida did not know how much time had passed. A year had passed. She was not married when a year had passed.

She was in Washington when a year had passed.

They asked her to stay with them and she did.

Once upon a time a man was named Eugene Thomas. He was a nice man and not older than Ida. He was waiting after he had been careful about coming in and going out and everybody invited him. They said Eugene are you married and he said perhaps he had been. He never had been. That was the funny part of it he never had been married. He liked to think that Ida had been married and she had, of course she had been.

So that went on.

Ida was not tired, she went on staying in Washington.

Eugene Thomas pretty well stayed there too.

If a house has windows and any house has them anybody can stand at the window and look out.

He was funny Eugene Thomas, he used to say, There is a treasure, That is a pleasure, It is a pleasure to her and to him.

All these things did not really make Ida anxious to see him. Ida was never anxious. Ida was tired. Once in a while she knew all about something and when this happened everybody stood still and Ida looked out of the window and she was not so tired.

It is hard for Ida to remember what Ida said.

She said, I could remember anything I ever said. She did say that.

Eugene Thomas was caught in a flood. And so he did not marry Ida. The flood caught him and carried him away. The flood was in

Connecticut and he was so nearly being drowned that he never came back to Washington.

But in the meanwhile Ida had begun to wonder, to wonder whether she had perhaps better begin to leave Washington and go elsewhere.

Not that she really went then, she was still resting. She saw a great many who lived in Washington and they looked at her when they saw her. Everybody knew it was Ida, not when they saw her, seeing her did not bring it home to them but hearing about her, hearing that she was Ida, it was that that made them know everything that Ida was to do. It was a pleasant Ida. Even when she was just tired with having besides everything had to come in after she had been out, it was a very pleasant Ida.

And so Ida was in Washington.

One day, it had happened again and again some one said something to her, they said Oh Ida, did you see me. Oh yes she said. Ida never did not see anybody, she always saw everybody and said she saw them. She made no changes about seeing then.

So he said to her Ida, your name is Ida isn't it, yes she said, and he said I thought your name was Ida, I thought you were Ida and I thought your name is Ida.

It is, she said.

They sat down.

She did not ask his name but of course he told her. He said his name was Gerald Seaton, and that he did not often care to walk about. He said that he was not too tall nor was he too stout, that he was not too fair and that he often had thought that it was very pleasant to live in Washington. He had lived there but he thought of leaving. What did Ida think. She said she thought that very often it was very well to rest in the afternoon. He said of course, and then they did not leave, they sat there a little longer and they drank something and they thought they would eat something and pretty soon they thought that the afternoon was over which it was not.

How are you Ida said Gerald Seaton and she said, very well I thank you, and she said that they knew that.

Ida was not sure that she did want to marry not that Gerald Seaton had asked her, but then if Ida did want to marry well Gerald Seaton might go away and he might come back again and if while he was away she would want to marry and then when he was back again she still wanted to marry would she marry him.

They neither of them really said anything about any such thing. Gerald Seaton had not yet gone away and Ida had not yet wanted to marry, but but. Ida had friends, she stayed with them and they thought perhaps they thought that Ida would marry again perhaps marry Gerald Seaton.

Who is Gerald Seaton said the husband to his wife, who is any one said the wife to the husband and they liked to sit with Ida while Ida was resting.

Ida could always stay with a married couple, neither the husband nor the wife did not like to have her, they always wanted to make her life easy for her, it always was easy for her and they always wanted her to keep right on going to marry Gerald Seaton or whoever it was, now it was Gerald Seaton and he was going away. Nobody could say that he was not going away.

You see Edith and William are still talking about Ida as everybody is. Does it make any difference to Edith and William. Just enough so that like everybody they go on talking and they talk about Ida.

Edith and William were the married couple with whom Ida was staying.

They were not the ones who were anxious and ambitious, nor were they the ones who collected anything they were a quiet couple even though they were rich and they talked together.

Positively, said Edith, can you go on doing what you do do. Can you go on doing what you did do. This is what Edith told William she had said to Ida.

And William, laughed and then he broke into poetry.

At a glance

What a chance.

He looked at Edith and laughed and they laughed.

Edith went on being worried and William began again.

That she needs

What she has.

Edith said that William was foolish and Gerald Seaton was going away.

And they have what they are, said William.

Looking at William you never would have thought that he would talk poetry.

He liked to be in a garden.

Edith was worried not really worried but she liked to feel worried and she liked to look as if she felt worried, of course only about Ida.

Oh dear she said, and they have what they are said William chucking her under the chin.

Cheer up Edith he said let us talk about Ida.

And they like where they go

He murmured,

And Edith said Shut up.

Which is all after a while said William and then he and Edith said all right they would talk about Ida and Ida came in, not to rest, but to come in. They stopped it, stopped talking about her.

So Edith and William did not look at Ida, they started talking. What do you think said William what do you think if and when we decide anything what do you think it will be like. This is what William said and Edith looked out of the window. They were not in the same room with Ida but they might have been. Edith liked an opportunity to stand and so she looked out of the window. She half turned, she said to William, Did you say you said Ida. William then took to standing. This was it so they were standing. It is not natural that if anybody should be coming in that they would be standing. Ida did not come in, Edith went away from the window and William stood by the window and saw some one come in, it was not Gerald Seaton because he had gone away.

Let it be a lesson to her said Edith to William, but naturally William had said it first. Life went on very peacefully with Edith and William, it went on so that they were equally capable of seeing Ida all day every day, for which they might not feel it necessary to be careful that they shall after all realize what it is.

It is not early morning nor late in the evening it is just in between.

Edith and William had a mother but not living with them. She was waiting to come to see them but she was not coming any particular day. William had been married before and had a boy, Edith had been married before and had a girl, so naturally they did not have another one. It was very comfortable with them but Ida might go away.

It was a pleasant home, if a home has windows and any house has them anybody can stand at the window and look out.

Ida never did. She rested.

It was summer, it is pretty hot in Washington and Edith and William were going away to the country. Ida did not mind the heat and neither did Gerald Seaton. He was back in Washington.

How hot Washington is in summer and how much everybody in Washington feels the heat to be hot.

It was easy, Ida was Mrs. Gerald Seaton and they went away to stay.

It was a long time before they said all they had to say, that is all Washington had to say about Ida and Gerald Seaton. But they were there naturally not since they were man and wife and had gone away.

This was not the only thing to do but they did it. They lived together as man and wife in other places. Which they were they were married, Ida was Mrs. Gerald Seaton and Seaton was Gerald Seaton and they both wore their wedding rings.

# Part Six

They lived in a flat not too big not too small. And they lived there almost every day. They were not in Washington, they were far away from Washington, they were in Boston. There they lived almost as if Ida had not been Ida and Gerald Seaton had married any woman. They lived like this for quite a while. Some things did happen one of them was that they left Boston. Ida rested a good deal she liked to live in a smallish flat, she had never lived in a big one because she and Gerald could hear each other from one end of the place to the other and this was a pleasure because Ida liked to hear some one she liked to rest and Gerald Seaton did content her. Almost anything did content Ida although everybody was always talking about her.

Gerald Seaton did not look as if he had any ideas he was just a nice man but he did have some. He was always saying Ida knows a lot of people and if I have known them I have admired the ones I have known and if I have admired the ones I have known I have looked like them that is to say I do not look like them but they are like the ones I have known.

Ida did like to know that Gerald was in the house and she liked to hear him.

Gerald often said, I do not mean, I myself when I say I mean I mean, I do know how much I feel when once in a while I come in and I do. I am very busy, said Gerald and thinking does not take very much of my time, I do not think that is I do not feel that I do not like thinking.

All this would interest Ida also the way he would say I never think about Ida, everybody talks about Ida but I do not talk about Ida nor do I listen when they are all talking about Ida. I am thinking, Gerald would say, I am thinking of another person not any one whom I could possibly think would be at all like Ida not at all. This is what Gerald said and he did say that and that was the way it was.

Ida was not idle but she did not go in and out very much and she did not do anything and she rested and she liked Gerald to be there and to know he was talking.

So they went on living in their apartment but they did not live in Washington and later on they did not live in Boston.

If nobody knows you that does not argue you to be unknown, nobody knew Ida when they no longer lived in Boston but that did not mean that she was unknown.

She went away and she came again and nobody ever said they had enough of that.

What happened. She felt very well, she was not always well but she felt very well.

One day she saw him come, she knew he was there but besides that she saw him come. He came. He said, oh yes I do and she said thank you, they never met again.

Woodward George always worked, and he was always welcome. Ida said do come again. He came very often. When he came he came alone and when he came there were always at least a half dozen there and they all said, oh dear, I wish it was evening.

It almost looked as if Ida and Woodward would always meet, but Woodward went away and as they were not on the same continent, Ida was on one and Woodward was on another it looked as if they would not meet. But a continent can always be changed and so that is not why Ida and Woodward did not always meet.

Very likely Ida is not anxious nor is Woodward. Well said Ida, I have to have my life and Ida had her life and she has her life and she is having her life.

Oh dear said Ida and she was resting, she liked to get up when she was resting, and then rest again.

Woodward started in being a writer and then he became a dressmaker but not in Washington and not in Boston. Ida almost cried when she met his brother. She said what is your name and he answered Abraham George. Oh dear said Ida and she looked at him. Abraham George was a writer and he did not become a dressmaker like his brother and he and Ida talked together all the time. Abraham George even asked her questions, he said, you know I really think you are a very pleasant person to know, and Ida said of course, and she said I do like to do favors for anybody and he said do one for me, and she said what is it, and he said I want to change to being a widower and she said yes of course, and she did not really laugh but she did look very pleasant resting and waiting. Yes she did. After all it was Woodward George who was important to her but he was far far away.

She was still married to Gerald Seaton and houses came and houses went away, but you can never say that they were not together.

One day they went away again, this time quite far away, they went to another country and there they sat down. It was a small house, the place was called Bay Shore, it was a comfortable house to live in, they had friends among others she had a friend whose name was Lady Helen Button.[10] How are you they said to each other. Ida learned to say it like that. How are you.

Ida liked it at Bay Shore. It did not belong to her but she well she did belong to it. How are you, she said when they came to see her.

A good many people did come to see her. Well of course she was married there was Gerald Seaton. How are you, was what they said to her, and they did sometimes forget to say it to Gerald but Gerald was nice and always said, oh yes, do, oh yes do.

She lived there and Gerald Seaton lived there, they lived in the same apartment and they talked to each other when they were dining but not much when they were resting and each in their way was resting.

Ida knew a vacant house when she saw it but she did not look at it, would she be introduced to some one who did look at a vacant house. Never at any time did tears come to Ida's eyes.

Never.

Everybody knew that Andrew was one of two. He was so completely one of two that he was two. Andrew was his name and he was not tall, not tall at all.

And yet it did mean it when he came in or when he went out.

Ida had not known that she would be there when he came in and when he went out but she was.

Ida was.

Andrew, there were never tears in Andrew's voice or tears in his eyes, he might cry but that was an entirely different matter.

Ida knew that.

Slowly Ida knew everything about that. It was the first thing Ida had ever known really the first thing.

Ida somehow knew who Andrew was and leave it alone or not Ida saw him.

If he saw her or not it was not interesting. Andrew was not a man who ever noticed anything. Naturally not. They noticed him.

Feel like that do you said Ida.

Ida was busy resting.

Ida when she went out did not carry an umbrella. It had not rained enough not nearly enough and once a week Ida went walking and today was the once a week when she went walking.

Once a week is two days one following another and this was the second one and Ida was dreaming.

So much for Andrew.

There was hardly any beginning.

There never could be with Andrew when he was there there he was. Anybody could know that and Ida well she just did not know that and Andrew looked about him when she was there and he saw her.

She was married to Gerald and she and Gerald were just as old as ever but that did not bother them. They talked together at least some time every day and occasionally in the evening but that was all and when they talked she called out to him and he did not answer and he called out to her and mostly she did not answer but they were sometimes in their home together. Anyway they were married and had been for quite some time.

Andrew did not notice Ida but he saw her and he went away to meet some one who had been named after a saint, this one was named after a saint called Thomas and so his name was Thomas and so Andrew met Thomas that is to say Andrew went out to meet that is to say he would meet Thomas who was out walking not walking but reading as he was walking which was his habit.

Andrew was there and then Thomas came to him.

Everybody was silent and so were they and then everybody went away. Andrew went away first.

Ida went out walking later on and the rain came down but by that time Ida was at home reading, she was not walking any more. Each one reads in their way and Ida read in her way.

Andrew never read.

Of course not.

Ida was careless but not that way. She did read, and she never forgot to look up when she saw Andrew.

Ida went out walking instead of sitting in a garden which was just as well because in this way she often met everybody and stopped and talked with them, this might lead her to meet them again and if it did she sometimes met some one who cried for one reason or another. Ida did not mind anybody crying, why should she when she had a garden a house and a dog and when she was so often visiting. Very often they made four and no more.

This had nothing to do with Andrew who in a way was never out walking and if he was then of course nobody did meet him.

Andrew never disappeared, how could he when he was always there and Ida gradually was always there too. How do you do. That is what she said when she met him.

She did not really meet him, nobody did because he was there and they were there and nobody met him or he them, but Ida did, she met him.

Andrew, she called him, Andrew, not loudly, just Andrew and she did not call him she just said Andrew. Nobody had just said Andrew to Andrew.

Andrew never looked around when Ida called him but she really never called him. She did not see him but she was with him and she called Andrew just like that. That was what did impress him.

Ida liked it to be dark because if it was dark she could light a light. And if she lighted a light then she could see and if she saw she saw Andrew and she said to him. Here you are.

Andrew was there, and it was not very long, it was long but not very long before Ida often saw Andrew and Andrew saw her. He even came to see her. He came to see her whether she was there or whether she was not there.

Ida gradually was always there when he came and Andrew always came.

He came all the same.

Kindly consider that I am capable of deciding when and why I am coming. This is what Andrew said to Ida with some hesitation.

And now Ida was not only Ida she was Andrew's Ida and being Andrew's Ida Ida was more than Ida she was Ida itself.

For this there was a change, everybody changed, Ida even changed and even changed Andrew. Andrew had changed Ida to be more Ida and Ida changed Andrew to be less Andrew and they were both always together.

# Second Half

## Part One

The road is awfully wide
With the snow on either side.

She was walking along the road made wide with snow. The moonlight was bright. She had a white dog and the dog looked gray in the moonlight and on the snow. Oh she said to herself that is what they mean when they say in the night all cats are gray.

When there was no snow and no moonlight her dog had always looked white at night.

When she turned her back on the moon the light suddenly was so bright it looked like another kind of light, and if she could have been easily frightened it would have frightened her but you get used to anything but really she never did get used to this thing.

She said to herself what am I doing, I have my genius and I am looking for my Andrew and she went on looking.

It was cold and when she went home the fire was out and there was no more wood. There was a little girl servant, she knew that the servant had made a fire for herself with all that wood and that her fire was going. She knew it. She knocked at her door and walked in. The servant was not there but the fire was. She was furious. She took every bit of lighted wood and carried it into her room. She sat down and looked at the fire and she knew she had her genius and she might just as well go and look for her Andrew. She went to bed then but she did not sleep very well. She found out next day that Andrew came to town every Sunday. She never saw him. Andrew was very good looking like his name. Ida often said to herself she never had met an Andrew and so she did not want to see him. She liked to hear about him.

She would if it had not been so early in the morning gone to be a nurse. As a nurse she might seek an Andrew but to be a nurse you have to get up early in the morning. You have to get up early in the morning to be a nun and so although if she had been a nun she could have thought every day about Andrew she never became a nun nor did she become a nurse. She just stayed at home.

It is easy to stay at home not at night-time but in the morning and even at noon and in the afternoon. At night-time it is not so easy to stay at home.

For which reason, Andrew's name changed to Ida and eight changed to four and sixteen changed to twenty-five and they all sat down.

For which all day she sat down. As I said she had that habit the habit of sitting down and only once every day she went out walking and she always talked about that. That made Ida listen. She knew how to listen.

This is what she said.

She did not say Ida knew how to listen but she talked as if she knew that Ida knew how to listen.

Every day she talked the same way and every day she took a walk and every day Ida was there and every day she talked about his walk, and every day Ida did listen while she talked about his walk. It can be very pleasant to walk every day and to talk about the walk and every day and it can be very pleasant to listen every day to him talk about his every day walk.

You see there was he it came to be Andrew again and it was Ida.

If there was a war or anything Andrew could still take a walk every day and talk about the walk he had taken that day.

For which it made gradually that it was not so important that Ida was Ida.

It could and did happen that it was not so important.

Would Ida fly, well not alone and certainly it was better not to fly than fly alone. Ida came to walking, she had never thought she would just walk but she did and this time she did not walk alone she walked with Susan Little.

For this they did not sing.

Such things can happen, Ida did not have to be told about it nor did she have to tell about it.

There was no Andrew.

Andrew stayed at home and waited for her, and Ida came. This can happen, Andrew could walk and come to see Ida and tell her what he did while he was walking and later Ida could walk and come back and not tell Andrew that she had been walking. Andrew could not have listened to Ida walking. Andrew walked not Ida. It is perhaps best so.

Anybody can go away, anybody can take walks and anybody can meet somebody new. Anybody can like to say how do you do to somebody they never saw before and yet it did not matter. Ida never did, she always walked with some one as if they had walked together every day. That really made Ida so pleasant that nobody ever did stay away.

And then they all disappeared, not really disappeared but nobody talked about them any more.

So it was all to do over again, Ida had Andrew that is she had that he walked every day, nobody talked about him any more but he had not disappeared, and he talked about his walk and he walked every day.

So Ida was left alone, and she began to sit again.

And sitting she thought about her life with dogs and this was it.[11]

The first dog I ever remember seeing, I had seen cats before and I must have seen dogs but the first dog I ever remember seeing was a large puppy in the garden. Nobody knew where he came from so we called him Prince.

It was a very nice garden but he was a dog and he grew very big. I do not remember what he ate but he must have eaten a lot because he grew so big. I do not remember playing with him very much. He was very nice but that was all, like tables and chairs are nice. That was all. Then there were a lot of dogs but none of them interesting. Then there was a little dog, a black and tan and he hung himself on a string when somebody left him. He had not been so interesting but the way he died made him very interesting. I do not know what he had as a name.

Then for a long time there were no dogs none that I ever noticed. I heard people say they had dogs but if I saw them I did not notice them and I heard people say their dog had died but I did not notice anything about it and then there was a dog, I do not know where he came from or where he went but he was a dog.

It was not yet summer but there was sun and there were wooden steps and I was sitting on them, and I was just doing nothing and a brown dog came and sat down too. I petted him, he liked petting and he put his head on my lap and we both went on sitting. This happened every afternoon for a week and then he never came. I do not know where he came from or where he went or if he had a name but I knew he was brown, he was a water dog a fairly big one and I never did forget him.

And then for some time there was no dog and then there were lots of them but other people had them.

A dog has to have a name and he has to look at you. Sometimes it is kind of bothering to have them look at you.

Any dog is new.

The dogs I knew then which were not mine were mostly very fine. There was a Pekinese named Sandy, he was a very large one, Pekineses should be tiny but he was a big one like a small lion but he was all Pekinese, I suppose anywhere there can be giants, and he was a giant Pekinese.

Sandy was his name because he was that color, the color of sand. He should have been carried around, Pekinese mostly are but he was almost too heavy to carry. I liked Sandy. When he stood up on a table all ruffled up and his tail all ruffled up he did look like a lion, a very little lion, but a fierce one.

He did not like climbing the mountains, they were not real mountains, they were made of a man on two chairs and Sandy was supposed to climb him as if he were climbing a mountain. Sandy thought this was disgusting and he was right. No use calling a thing like that climbing the mountains, and if it has been really mountains of course Sandy would not have been there. Sandy liked things flat, tables, floors, and paths. He liked waddling along as he pleased. No mountains, no climbing, no automobiles, he was killed by one. Sandy knew what he liked, flat things and sugar, sugar was flat too, and Sandy never was interested in anything else and then one day an automobile went over him, poor Sandy and that was the end of Sandy.

So one changed to two and two changed to five and the next dog was also not a big one, his name was Lillieman and he was black and a French bull and not welcome. He was that kind of a dog he just was not welcome.

When he came he was not welcome and he came very often. He was good-looking, he was not old, he did finally die and was buried under a white lilac tree in a garden but he just was not welcome.

He had his little ways, he always wanted to see something that was just too high or too low for him to reach and so everything was sure to get broken. He did not break it but it did just get broken. Nobody could blame him but of course he was not welcome.

Before he died and was buried under the white lilac tree, he met another black dog called Dick. Dick was a French poodle and Lillieman was a French bull and they were both black but they did not interest each other. As much as possible they never knew the other one was there. Sometimes when they bumped each other no one heard the other one bark it was hard to not notice the other one. But they did. Days at a time sometimes they did.

Dick was the first poodle I ever knew and he was always welcome, round roly-poly and old and gray and lively and pleasant, he was always welcome.

He had only one fault. He stole eggs, he could indeed steal a whole basket of them and then break them and eat them, the cook would hit him with a broom when she caught him but nothing could stop him, when he saw a basket of eggs he had to steal them and break them and eat them. He only liked eggs raw, he never stole cooked eggs, whether he liked breaking them, or the looks of them or just, well anyway it was the only fault he had. Perhaps because he was a black dog and eggs are white and then yellow, well anyway he could steal a whole basket of them and break them and eat them, not the shells of course just the egg.

So this was Dick the poodle very playful very lively old but full of energy and he and Lillieman the French bull could be on the same lawn together and not notice each other, there was no connection between them, they just ignored each other. The bull Lillieman died first and was buried under the white lilac, Dick the poodle went on running around making love to distant dogs, sometimes a half day's run away and running after sticks and stones, he was fourteen years old and very lively and then one day he heard of a dog far away and he felt he could love her, off he went to see her and he never came back again, he was run over, on the way there, he never got there he never came back and alas poor Dick he was never buried anywhere.

Dogs are dogs, you sometimes think that they are not but they are. And they always are here there and everywhere.

There were so many dogs and I knew some of them I knew some better than others, and sometimes I did not know whether I wanted to meet another one or not.

There was one who was named Mary Rose, and she had two children, the first one was an awful one. This was the way it happened.

They say dogs are brave but really they are frightened of a great many things about as many things as frighten children.

Mary Rose had no reason to be frightened because she was always well and she never thought about being lost, most dogs do and it frightens them awfully but Mary Rose did get lost all the same not really lost but for a day and a night too. Nobody really knew what happened.

She came home and she was dirty, she who was always so clean and she had lost her collar and she always loved her collar and she dragged herself along she who always walked along so tidily. She was a fox-terrier with smooth white hair, and pretty black marks. A little boy brought back her collar and then pretty soon Chocolate came, it was her only puppy and he was a monster, they called him Chocolate because he looked like a chocolate cake or a bar of chocolate or chocolate candy, and he was awful. Nobody meant it but he was run over, it was sad and Mary Rose had been fond of him. Later she had a real daughter Blanchette who looked just like her, but Mary Rose never cared about her. Blanchette was too like her, she was not at all interesting and besides Mary Rose knew that Blanchette would live longer and never have a daughter and she was right. Mary Rose died in the country, Blanchette lived in the city and never had a daughter and was never lost and never had any worries and gradually grew very ugly but she never suspected it and nobody told her so and it was no trouble to her.

Mary Rose loved only once, lots of dogs do they love only once or twice. Mary Rose was not a loving dog, but she was a tempting dog, she loved to tempt other dogs to do what they should not. She never did what she should not but they did when she showed them where it was.

Little things happen like that, but she had to do something then when she had lost the only dog she loved who was her own son and who was called Chocolate. After that she just was like that.

I can just see her tempting Polybe in the soft moonlight to do what was not right.

Dogs should smell but not eat, if they eat dirt that means they are naughty or they have worms, Mary Rose was never naughty and she never had worms but Polybe, well Polybe was not neglected but he was not understood. He never was understood. I suppose he died but I never knew. Anyway he had his duty to do and he never did it, not because he did not want to do his duty but because he never knew what his duty was.

That was what Polybe was.

He liked moonlight because it was warmer than darkness but he never noticed the moon. His father and his sister danced on the hillside in the moonlight but Polybe had left home so young that he never knew how to dance in it but he did like the moonlight because it was warmer than the dark.

Polybe was not a small dog he was a hound and he had stripes red and black like a zebra only a zebra's stripes are white and black but Polybe's stripes were as regular as that and his front legs were long, all his family could kill a rabbit with a blow of their front paw, that is really why they danced in the moonlight, they thought they were chasing rabbits, any shadow was a rabbit to them and there are lots of shadows on a hillside in the summer under a bright moon.

Poor Polybe he never really knew anything, the shepherds said that he chased sheep, perhaps he did thinking they were rabbits, he might have made a mistake like that, he easily might. Another little little dog was so foolish once he always thought that any table leg was his mother, and would suck away at it as if it was his mother. Polybe was not as foolish as that but he almost was, anyway Mary Rose could always lead him astray, perhaps she whispered to him that sheep were rabbits. She might have.

And then Mary Rose went far away. Polybe stayed where he was and did not remember any one. He never did. That was Polybe.

And he went away tied to a string and he never did try to come back. Back meant nothing to him. A day was never a day to Polybe. He never barked, he had nothing to say.

Polybe is still some place today, nothing could ever happen to him to kill him or to change anything in any way.

The next dog was bigger than any other dog had been.

When a dog is really big he is very naturally thin, and when he is big and thin when he moves he does not seem to be moving. There were two of them one was probably dead before I saw the second one. I did not know the first one but I heard what he could do I saw him of course but when I saw him he came along but he was hardly moving.

It did not take much moving to come along as fast as we were going. There was no other dog there which was lucky because they said that when he saw another dog well he did not move much but he killed him, he always killed any dog he saw although he hardly moved at all to kill him. I saw this dog quite a few times but there was never any other dog anywhere near. I was glad.

The other one well he looked gentle enough and he hardly moved at all and he was very big and he looked thin although he really was not.

He used to walk about very gently almost not at all he was so tall and he moved his legs as if he meant them not to leave the ground but they did, just enough, just a little sideways just enough, and that was all. He lived a long time doing nothing but that and he is still living just living enough.

The next dog and this is important because it is the next dog. His name is Never Sleeps although he sleeps enough.[12]

He was brown not a dark brown but a light brown and he had a lot of friends who always went about together and they all had to be brown, otherwise Never Sleeps would not let them come along. But all that was later, first he had to be born.

It was not so easy to be born.

There was a dog who was an Alsatian wolf-hound a very nice one, and they knew that in the zoo there was a real wolf quite a nice one. So one night they took the dog to see the wolf and they left her there all night. She liked the wolf and the wolf was lonesome and they stayed together and then later she had a little dog and he was a very nice one, and her name was Never Sleeps. She was a gentle dog and liked to lie in the water in the winter and to be quiet in the summer. She never was a bother.

She could be a mother. She met a white poodle he was still young and he had never had a puppy life because he had not been well. His name was Basket and he looked like one. He was taken to visit Never Sleeps and they were told to be happy together. Never Sleeps was told to play with Basket and teach him how to play. Never Sleeps began, she had to teach catch if you can or tag, and she had to teach him pussy wants a corner and she taught him each one of them.

She taught him tag and even after he played it and much later on when he was dead another Basket he looked just like him went on playing tag. To play tag you have to be able to run forward and back to run around things and to start one way and to go the other way and another dog who is smaller and not so quick has to know how to wait at a corner and go around the other way to make the distance shorter. And sometimes just to see how well tag can be played the bigger quicker dog can even stop to play with a stick or a bone and still get away and not be tagged. That is what it means to play tag and Never Sleeps taught Basket how to play. Then he taught him how to play pussy wants a corner, to play this there have to be trees. Dogs cannot play this in the house they are not allowed to and so they have to have at least four trees if there are three dogs and three trees if there are two dogs to play pussy wants a corner. Never Sleeps preferred tag to pussy wants a corner but Basket rather liked best pussy wants a corner.[13]

Ida never knew who knew what she said, she never knew what she said because she listened and as she listened well the moon scarcely the moon but still there is a moon.

Very likely hers was the moon.

Ida knew she never had been a little sister or even a little brother. Ida knew.

So scarcely was there an absence when some one died.

Believe it or not some one died.

And he was somebody's son and Ida began to cry and he was twenty-six and Ida began to cry and Ida was not alone and she began to cry.

Ida had never cried before, but now she began to cry.

Even when Andrew came back from his walk and talked about his walk, Ida began to cry.

It's funny about crying. Ida knew it was funny about crying, she listened at the radio and they played the national anthem and Ida began to cry. It is funny about crying.

But anyway Ida was sitting and she was there and one by one somebody said Thank you, have you heard of me. And she always had. That was Ida.

Even Andrew had he had heard of them, that was the way he had been led to be ready to take his walk every day because he had heard of every one who came in one after the other one.

And Ida did not cry again.

One day, she saw a star it was an uncommonly large one and when it set it made a cross, she looked and looked and she did not hear Andrew take a walk and that was natural enough she was not there. They had lost her. Ida was gone.

So she sat up and went to bed carefully and she easily told every one that there was more wind in Texas than in San Francisco and nobody believed her. So she said wait and see and they waited.

She came back to life exactly day before yesterday.[14] And now listen.

Ida loved three men. One was an officer who was not killed but he might have been, one was a painter who was not in hospital but he might have been one and one was a lawyer who had gone away to Montana and she had never heard from him.

Ida loved each one of them and went to say good-bye to them.

Good-bye, good-bye she said, and she did say good-bye to them.

She wondered if they were there, of course she did not go away. What she really wanted was Andrew, where oh where was Andrew.

Andrew was difficult to suit and so Ida did not suit him. But Ida did sit down beside him.

Ida fell in love with a young man who had an adventure. He came from Kansas City and he knew that he was through. He was twenty years old. His uncle had died of meningitis, so had his father and so had his cousin, his name was Mark and he had a mother but no sisters and he had a wife and sisters-in-law.

Ida looked the other way when they met, she knew Mark would die when he was twenty-six and he did but before that he had said, For them, they like me for them and Ida had answered Just as you say Mark. Ida always bent her head when she saw Mark she was tall and she bent her head when she saw Mark, he was tall and broad and Ida bent her head when she saw him. She knew he would die of meningitis and he did. That was why Ida always bent her head when she saw him.

Why should everybody talk about Ida.

Why not.

Dear Ida.

# Part Two

Ida was almost married to Andrew and not anybody could cloud it. It was very important that she was almost married to Andrew. Besides he was Andrew the first. All the others had been others.

Nobody talked about the color of Ida's hair and they talked about her a lot, nor the color of her eyes.

She was sitting and she dreamed that Andrew was a soldier. She dreamed well not dreamed but just dreamed. The day had been set for their marriage and everything had been ordered. Ida was always careful about ordering, food clothes cars, clothes food cars everything was well chosen and the day was set and then the telephone rang and it said that Andrew was dying, he had not been killed he was only dying, and Ida knew that the food would do for the people who came to the funeral and the car would do to go to the funeral and the clothes would not do dear me no they would not do and all of this was just dreaming. Ida was alive yet and so was Andrew, she had been sitting, he had been walking and he came home and told about his walk and Ida was awake and she was listening and Andrew was Andrew the first, and Ida was Ida and they were almost married and not anybody could cloud anything.

# Part Three

Any ball has to look like the moon. Ida just had to know what was going to be happening soon.

They can be young so young they can go in swimming. Ida had been. Not really swimming one was learning and the other was teaching.

This was being young in San Francisco and the baths were called Lurline Baths.[15] Ida was young and so was he they were both good both she and he and he was teaching her how to swim, he leaned over and he said kick he was holding her under the chin and he was standing beside her, it was not deep water, and he said kick and she did and he walked along beside her holding her chin, and he said kick and she kicked again and he was standing very close to her and she kicked hard and she kicked him. He let go her he called out Jesus Christ my balls and he went under and she went under, they were neither of them drowned but they might have been.

Strangely enough she never thought about Frank, that was his name, Frank, she could not remember his other name, but once when she smelled wild onion she remembered going under and that neither were drowned.

It is difficult never to have been younger but Ida almost was she almost never had been younger.

# Part Four

And now it was suddenly happening, well not suddenly but it was happening, Andrew was almost Andrew the first. It was not sudden.

They always knew what he could do, that is not what he would do but what they had to do to him. Ida knew.

Andrew the first, walked every day and came back to say where he had walked that day. Every day he walked the same day and every day he told Ida where he had walked that day. Yes Ida.

Ida was just as much older as she had been.

Yes Ida.

One day Ida was alone. When she was alone she was lying down and when she was not alone she was lying down. Everybody knew everything about Ida, everybody did. They knew that when she was alone she was lying down and when she was not alone she was lying down.

Everybody knew everything about Ida and by everybody, everybody means everybody.

It might have been exciting that everybody knew everything about Ida and it did not excite Ida it soothed Ida. She was soothed.

For a four.

She shut the door.

They dropped in.

And drank gin.

I'd like a conversation said Ida.

So one of them told that when his brother was a soldier, it was in summer and he ate an apple off an apple tree a better apple than he had ever eaten before, so he took a slip of the tree and he brought it home and after he put it into the ground where he was and when he took it home he planted it and now every year they had apples off this apple tree.

Another one told how when his cousin was a soldier, he saw a shepherd dog, different from any shepherd dog he had ever seen and as he knew a man who kept sheep, he took the shepherd dog home with him and gave it to the man and now all the shepherd dogs came from the dog his cousin had brought home with him from the war.

Another one was telling that a friend of his had a sister-in-law and the sister-in-law had the smallest and the finest little brown dog he had ever seen, and he asked the sister-in-law what race it was and where she had gotten it. Oh she said a soldier gave it to me for my little girl, he had brought it home with him and he gave it to my little girl and she and he play together, they always play together.

Ida listened to them and she sighed, she was resting, and she said, I like lilies-of-the-valley too do you, and they all said they did, and one of them said, when his sister had been a nurse in a war she always gathered lilies-of-the-valley before they were in flower. Oh yes said Ida.

And so there was a little conversation and they all said they would stay all evening. They said it was never dark when they stayed all evening and Ida sighed and said yes she was resting.

Once upon a time Ida took a train, she did not like trains, and she never took them but once upon a time she took a train. They were fortunate, the train went on running and Andrew was not there. Then it stopped and Ida got out and Andrew still was not there. He was not expected but still he was not there. So Ida went to eat something.

This did happen to Ida.

They asked what she would have to eat and she said she would eat the first and the last that they had and not anything in between. Andrew always ate everything but Ida when she was alone she ate the first and the last of everything, she was not often alone so it was not often that she could eat the first and the last of everything but she did that time and then everybody helped her to leave but not to get on a train again.

She never did get on any train again. Naturally not, she was always there or she was resting. Her life had every minute when it was either this or that and sometimes both, either she was there or she was resting and sometimes it was both.

Her life never began again because it was always there.

And now it was astonishing that it was always there. Yes it was.

Ida

Yes it was.

# Part Five

Any friend of Ida's could be run over by any little thing.

Not Andrew, Andrew was Andrew the first and regular.

Why are sailors, farmers and actors more given to reading and believing signs than other people. It is natural enough for farmers and sailors who are always there where signs are, alone with them but why actors.

Well anyway Ida was not an actress nor a sailor nor a farmer.

Cuckoos magpies crows and swallows are signs.

Nightingales larks robins and orioles are not.

Ida saw her first glow worm. The first of anything is a sign.

Then she saw three of them that was a sign.

Then she saw ten.

Ten are never a sign.

And yet what had she caught.

She had caught and she had taught.

That ten was not a sign.

Andrew was Andrew the first.

He was a sign.

Ida had not known he was a sign, not known he was a sign.

Ida was resting.

Worse than any signs is a family who brings bad luck. Ida had known one, naturally it was a family of women, a family which brings bad luck must be all women.

Ida had known one the kind that if you take a dog with you when you go to see them, the dog goes funny and when it has its puppies its puppies are peculiar.

This family was a mother a daughter and a granddaughter, well they all had the airs and graces of beauties and with reason, well they were. The grandmother had been married to an admiral and then he died and to a general and then he died. Her daughter was married to a doctor but the doctor could not die, he just left, the granddaughter was very young, just as young as sixteen, she married a writer, nobody knows just how not but before very long she cried, every day she cried, and her mother cried and even her grandmother and then she was not married any longer to the writer. Then well she was still young not yet twenty-one and a banker saw her and he said he must marry her, well she couldn't yet naturally not the writer was still her husband but very soon he would not be, so the banker was all but married to her, well anyway they went out together, the car turned over the banker was dead and she had broken her collar-bone.

Now everybody wanted to know would the men want her more because of all this or would they be scared of her.

Well as it happened it was neither the one nor the other. It often is not.

The men after that just did not pay any attention to her. You might say they did not any of them pay any attention to her even when she was twenty-three or twenty-four. They did not even ask not any of them. What for.

And so anybody could see that they could not bring good luck to any one not even a dog, no not even.

No really bad luck came to Ida from knowing them but after that anyway, it did happen that she never went out to see any one.

She said it was better.

She did not say it was better but it was better. Ida never said anything about anything.

Anyway after that she rested and let them come in, anybody come in. That way no family would come that just would not happen.

So Ida was resting and they came in. Not one by one, they just came in.

That is the way Andrew came he just came in.

He took a walk every afternoon and he always told about what happened on his walk.

He just walked every afternoon.

He liked to hear people tell about good luck and bad luck.

Somebody one afternoon told a whole lot.

Andrew was like that, he was born with his life, why not. And he had it, he walked every afternoon, and he said something every minute of every day, but he did not talk while he was listening. He listened while he was listening but he did not hear unless he asked to have told what they were telling. He liked to hear about good luck and bad luck because it was not real to him, nothing was real to him except a walk every afternoon and to say something every minute of every day.

So he said and what were you saying about good luck and bad luck.

Well it was this.[16]

The things anybody has to worry about are spiders, cuckoos goldfish and dwarfs.

Yes said Andrew. And he was listening.

Spider at night makes delight.

Spider in the morning makes mourning.

Yes said Andrew.

Well, said the man who was talking, think of a spider talking.

Yes said Andrew.

The spider says

Listen to me I, I am a spider, you must not mistake me for the sky, the sky red at night is a sailor's delight, the sky red in the morning is a sailor's warning, you must not mistake me for the sky, I am I, I am a spider and in the morning any morning I bring sadness and mourning and at night if they see me at night I bring them delight, do not mistake me for the sky, not I, do not mistake me for a dog who howls at night and causes no delight, a dog says the bright moonlight makes him go mad with desire to bring sorrow to any one sorrow and sadness, the dog says the night the bright moonlight brings madness and grief, but says the spider I, I am a spider, a big spider or a little spider, it is all alike, a spider green or gray, there is nothing else to say, I am a spider and I know and I always tell everybody so, to see me at night brings them delight, to see me in the morning, brings mourning, and if you see me at night, and I am a sight, because I am dead having dried up by night, even so dead at night I still cause delight, I dead bring delight to any one who sees me at night, and so every one can sleep tight who has seen me at night.

Andrew was listening and he said it was interesting and said did they know any other superstition.

Yes said the man there is the cuckoo.

Oh yes the cuckoo.

Supposing they could listen to a cuckoo.

I, I am a cuckoo, I am not a clock, because a clock makes time pass and I stop the time by giving mine, and mine is money, and money is honey, and I I bring money, I, I, I. I bring misery and money but never honey, listen to me.

Once I was there, you know everybody, that I I sing in the spring, sweetly, sing, evening and morning and everything.

Listen to me.

If you listen to me, if when you hear me, the first time in the spring time, hear me sing, and you have money a lot of money for you in your pocket when you hear me in the spring, you will be rich all year any year, but if you hear me and you have gone out with no money jingling in your pocket when you hear me singing then you will be poor poor all year, poor.

But sometimes I can do even more.

I knew a case like that, said the man.

Did you said Andrew.

She, well she, she had written a lovely book but nobody took the lovely book nobody paid her money for the lovely book they never gave her money, never never never and she was poor and they needed money oh yes they did she and her lover.

And she sat and she wrote and she longed for money for she had a lover and all she needed was money to live and love, money money money.

So she wrote and she hoped and she wrote and she sighed and she wanted money, money money, for herself and for love for love and for herself, money money money.

And one day somebody was sorry for her and they gave her not much but a little money, he was a nice millionaire the one who gave her a little money, but it was very little money and it was spring and she wanted love and money and she had love and now she wanted money.

She went out it was the spring and she sat upon the grass with a little money in her pocket and the cuckoo saw her sitting and knew she had a little money and it went up to her close up to her and sat on a tree and said cuckoo at her, cuckoo cuckoo, cuckoo, and she said, Oh, a cuckoo bird is singing on a cuckoo tree singing to me oh singing to me. And the cuckoo sang cuckoo cuckoo and she sang cuckoo cuckoo to it, and there they were singing cuckoo she to it and it to her.

Then she knew that it was true and that she would be rich and love would not leave her and she would have all three money and love and a cuckoo in a tree, all three.

Andrew did listen and the man went on.

And the goldfish.

Yes said a goldfish I listen I listen but listen to me I am stronger than a cuckoo stronger and meaner because I never do bring good luck I bring nothing but misery and trouble and all no not at all I bring no good luck only bad and that does not make me sad it makes me glad that I never bring good luck only bad.

They buy me because I look so pretty and red and gold in my bowl but I never bring good luck I only bring bad, bad bad bad.

Listen to me.

There was a painter once who thought he was so big he could do anything and he did. So he bought goldfish and any day he made a painting of us in the way that made him famous and made him say, goldfish bring me good luck not bad, and they better had.

Everything went wonderfully for him, he turned goldfish into gold because everything he did was bold and it sold, and he had money and fame but all the same we the goldfish just sat and waited while he painted.

One day, crack, the bowl where we were fell apart and we were all cracked the bowl the water and the fish, and the painter too crack went the painter and his painting too and he woke up and he knew that he was dead too, the goldfish and he, they were all dead, but we there are always goldfish in plenty to bring bad luck to anybody too but he the painter and his painting was dead dead dead.

We knew what to do.

Andrew was more interested, and the dwarfs he said.

Well this is the way they are they say we are two male and female, if you see us both at once it means nothing, but if you see either of us alone it means bad luck or good. And which is which. Misfortune is female good luck luck is male, it is all very simple.

Oh yes anybody can know that and if they see one of us and it is the female he or she has to go and go all day long until they see a dwarf man, otherwise anything awful could happen to them. A great many make fun of those who believe in this thing but those who believe they know, female dwarf bad luck male dwarf good luck, all that is eternal.

Silence.

Suddenly the goldfish suddenly began to swish and to bubble and squeak and to shriek, I I do not believe in dwarfs neither female nor male, he cried, no not in a cuckoo, no not in spiders, no, the only thing I believe in besides myself is a shoe on a table, oh that, that makes me shiver and shake, I have no shoes no feet no shoes but a shoe on a table, that is terrible, oh oh yes oh ah.

And the cuckoo said,

Oh you poor fish, you do not believe in me, you poor fish, and I do not believe in you fish nothing but fish a goldfish only fish, no I do not believe in you no fish no, I believe in me, I am a cuckoo and I know and I tell you so, no the only thing I believe in which is not me is when I see the new moon through a glass window, I never do because there is no glass to see through, but I believe in that too, I believe in that and I believe in me ah yes I do I see what I see through, and I do I do I do.

No I do not believe in a fish, nor in a dwarf nor in a spider not I, because I am I a cuckoo and I, I, I.

The spider screamed. You do not believe in me, everybody believes in me, you do not believe in spiders you do not believe in me bah. I believe in me I am all there is to see except well if you put your clothes on wrong side to well that is an awful thing to do, and if you change well that is worse than any way and what do I say, if you put your clothes on wrong everything will go well that day but if you change from wrong to right then nothing will go right, but what can I do I am a green spider or a gray and I have the same clothes every day and I can make no mistake any day but I believe oh I believe if you put your clothes on wrong side to everything will be lovely that you do, but anyway everybody has to believe in me, a spider, of course they do, a spider in the morning is an awful warning a spider at night brings delight, it is so lovely to know this is true and not to believe in a fish or in dwarfs or in a cuckoo, ooh ooh, it is I, no matter what they try it is I I. I.

The dwarfs said, And of whom are you talking all of you, we dwarfs, we are in the beginning we have commenced everything and we believe in everything yes we do, we believe in the language of flowers and we believe in lucky stones, we believe in peacocks' feathers and we believe in stars too, we believe in leaves of tea, we believe in a white horse and a red-headed girl, we believe in the moon, we believe in red in the sky, we believe in the barking of a dog, we believe in everything that is mortal and immortal, we even believe in spiders, in goldfish and in the cuckoo, we the dwarfs we believe in it all, all and all, and all and every one are alike, we are, all the world is like us the dwarfs, all the world believes in everything and we do too and all the world believes in us and in you.

Everybody in the room was quiet and Andrew was really excited and he looked at Ida and that was that.

# Part Six

Good luck and bad luck

No luck and then luck.

Ida was resting.

She was nearly Ida was nearly well.

She could tell when she had been settled when she had been settled very well.

Once she had been and she liked it, she liked to be in one room and to have him in another room and to talk across to him while she was resting. Then she had been settled very well. It did not settle everything, nothing was unsettling, but she had been settled very well.

Andrew had a mother.

Some still have one and some do not still have one but Andrew did still have a mother.

He had other things beside
But he had never had a bride.

Flowers in the spring succeed each other with extraordinary rapidity and the ones that last the longest if you do not pick them are the violets.

Andrew had his life, he was never alone and he was never left and he was never active and he was never quiet and he was never sad.

He was Andrew.

It came about that he had never gone anywhere unless he had known beforehand he was going to go there, but and he had, he had gone to see Ida and once he was there it was as if he had been going to see Ida. So naturally he was always there.

Andrew knew that he was the first Andrew.

He had a nervous cough but he was not nervous.

He had a quiet voice but he talked loudly.

He had a regular life but he did what he did as if he would do it and he always did. Obstinate you call him. Well if you like. He said obstinate was not a word.

Ida never spoke, she just said what she pleased. Dear Ida.

It began not little by little, but it did begin.

Who has houses said a friend of Ida's.

Everybody laughed.

But said Andrew I understand when you speak.

Nobody laughed.

It was not customary to laugh.

Three makes more exchange than two.

There were always at least three.

This was a habit with Andrew.

Ida had no habit, she was resting.

And so little by little somebody knew.

How kindly if they do not bow.

Ida had a funny habit. She had once heard that albatrosses which birds she liked the name of always bowed before they did anything. Ida bowed like this to anything she liked. If she had a hat she liked, she had many hats but sometimes she had a hat she liked and if she liked it she put it on a table and bowed to it. She had many dresses and sometimes she really liked one of them. She would put it somewhere then and then she would bow to it. Of course jewels but really dresses and hats particularly hats, sometimes particularly dresses. Nobody knew anything about this certainly not anybody and certainly not Andrew, if anybody knew it would be an accident because when Ida bowed like that to a hat or a dress she never said it. A maid might come to know but naturally never having heard about albatrosses, the maid would not understand.

Oh yes said Ida while she was resting. Naturally she never bowed while she was resting and she was always resting when they were there.

Dear Ida.

It came to be that any day was like Saturday to Ida.

And slowly it came to be that even to Andrew any day came to be Saturday. Saturday had never been especially a day to Andrew but slowly it came to be Saturday and then every day began to be Saturday as it had come to be to Ida.

Of course there was once a song, every day will be Sunday by and by.

Ida knew this about Saturday, she always had, and now Andrew slowly came to know it too. Of course he did walk every day walk even if every day was Saturday. You can't change everything even if everything is changed.

Anybody could begin to realize what life was to Andrew what life had been to Andrew what life was going to be to Andrew.

Andrew was remarkable insofar as it was all true. Yes indeed it was.

Saturday, Ida.

Ida never said once upon a time. These words did not mean anything to Ida. This is what Ida said. Ida said yes, and then Ida said oh yes, and then Ida said, I said yes, and then Ida said, yes.

Once when Ida was excited she said I know what it is I do, I do know that it is, yes.

That is what she said when she was excited.

# Part Seven

Andrew knew that nobody would be so rude as not to remember Andrew. And this was true. They did remember him. Until now. Now they do not remember Andrew. But Andrew knew that nobody would be so rude as not to. And pretty well it was true.

But again.

Andrew never had to think. He never had to say that it was a pleasant day. But it was always either wet or dry or cold or warm or showery or just going to be. All that was enough for Andrew and Ida never knew whether there was any weather. That is the reason they got on so well together.

There was never any beginning or end, but every day came before or after another day. Every day did.

Little by little circles were open and when they were open they were always closed.

This was just the way it was.

Supposing Ida was at home, she was almost at home and when she was at home she was resting.

Andrew had many things to do but then it was always true that he was with Ida almost all day although he never came to stay and besides she was resting.

One of the things Ida never liked was a door.

People should be there and not come through a door.

As much as possible Ida did not let herself know that they did come through a door.

She did not like to go out to dinner at a house because you had to come in through a door. A restaurant was different there is really no door. She liked a room well enough but she did not like a door.

Andrew was different, he did just naturally come through a door, he came through a door, he was the first to come through a doorway and the last to come through a doorway. Doorways and doors were natural to him. He and Ida never talked about this, you might say they never talked about anything certainly they never talked about doors.

The French say a door has to be open or shut but open or shut did not interest Ida what she really minded was that there was a door at all. She did not really mind standing in a portiere or in a hall, but she did not like doors. Of course it was natural enough feeling as she did about doors that she never went out to see anybody. She went out she liked to go out but not through a doorway. There it was that was the way she was.

One day she was telling about this, she said, if you stand in an open place in a house and talk to somebody who can hear that is very nice, if you are out or in it is very nice but doors doors are never nice.

She did not remember always being that way about doors, she kind of did not remember doors at all, it was not often she mentioned doors, but she just did not care about doors.

One day did not come after another day to Ida. Ida never took on yesterday or tomorrow, she did not take on months either nor did she take on years. Why should she when she had always been the same, what ever happened there she was, no doors and resting and everything happening. Sometimes something did happen, she knew to whom she had been married but that was not anything happening, she knew about clothes and resting but that was not anything happening. Really there really was never anything happening although everybody knew everything was happening.

It was dark in winter and light in summer but that did not make any difference to Ida. If somebody said to her you know they are most awfully kind, Ida could always say I know I do not like that kind. She liked to be pleasant and she was but kind, well yes she knew that kind.

They asked her to a dinner party but she did not go, her husband went, she had a husband then and he wore a wedding ring. Husbands do not often wear wedding rings but he did. Ida knew when he came home that he had worn his wedding ring, she said, not very well and he said oh yes very well.

Three things had happened to Ida and they were far away but not really because she liked to rest and be there. She always was.

Andrew next to that was nothing and everything.

Andrew knew a great many people who were very kind. Kind people always like doors and doorways, Andrew did. Andrew thought about Ida and doors, why should he when doors were there. But for Ida doors were not there if they had been she would not have been. How can you rest if there are doors. And resting is a pleasant thing.

So life went on little by little for Ida and Andrew.

It all did seem just the same but all the same it was not just the same. How could anybody know, nobody could know but there it was. Well no there it wasn't.

Ida began talking.

She never began but sometimes she was talking, she did not understand so she said, she did not sit down so she said, she did not stand up so she said, she did not go out or come in, so she said. And it was all true enough.

This was Ida

Dear Ida.

Ida was good friends with all her husbands, she was always good friends with all her husbands.

She always remembered that the first real hat she ever had was a turban made of pansies. The second real hat she ever had was a turban made of poppies.

For which she was interested in pansies and gradually she was not. She had liked pansies and heliotrope, then she liked wild flowers, then she liked tube-roses, then she liked orchids and then she was not interested in flowers.

Of course she was not interested. Flowers should stay where they grow, there was no door for flowers to come through, they should stay where they grew. She was more interested in birds than in flowers but she was not really interested in birds.

Anything that was given to her she thanked for she liked to thank, some people do not but she did and she liked to be thanked. Yes she said.

She was careful to sit still when she thanked or was thanked, it is better so.

Some people like to stand or to move when they thank or are thanked but not Ida, she was not really resting when she thanked or was thanked but she was sitting.

Nobody knew what Ida was going to do although she always did the same thing in the same way, but still nobody knew what Ida was going to do or what she was going to say. She said yes. That is what Ida did say.

Everybody knew that they would not forget Andrew but was it true.

Not so sure.

You did not have to be sure about any such thing as long as it was happening, which it was not.

Andrew come in said Ida.

Andrew was in.

Andrew do not come in said Ida. Ida said Andrew is not coming in. Andrew came in.

Andrew had not been brought up to come in but little by little he did come in he came in and when Ida said he is not to come in he came in. This was natural as he came to know Ida. Anybody came in who came to know Ida but Ida did not say come in. To Andrew she had said yes come in and Andrew had come in.

It was not a natural life for Andrew this life of coming in and this was what had been happening to Andrew, he had commenced to come in and then he never did anything else, he always came in. He should have been doing something else but he did not he just came in.

Little by little it happened that except that he took his walk in the afternoon he never did anything but come in. This little by little was everything Andrew did.

Ida tried to stop, not anything but she tried to stop but how could she stop if she was resting how could she stop Andrew from coming in.

And in this way it might happen to come to be true that anybody would forget Andrew.

That would not happen little by little but it could come to be true.

Even in a book they could be rude and forget Andrew but not now. Andrew said not now, and Ida said Andrew said not now and Ida said she said not now but really Ida did not say not now she just said no.

Ida often sighed not very often but she did sigh and when somebody came in she said yes I always say yes, if you say no then you say no but if you say yes then you just say yes.

This was very natural and Ida was very natural.

So much happened but nothing happened to Ida.

To have anything happen you have to choose and Ida never chose, how could she choose, you can choose hats and you can choose other things but that is not choosing. To choose, well to choose, Ida never chose.

And then it looked as if it happened, and it did happen and it was happening and it went on happening. How excited, and Ida was excited and so was Andrew and his name might have been William.

He had a great many names Andrew did and one of them was William but when he became Andrew the first he could not be William.

Ida often wished gently that he had been William, it is easier to say William than Andrew and Ida had naturally to say a name. Every time Andrew came in or was there or was anywhere she had to say his name and if his name had been William she could have said it easier. But all the same it was easy enough to say Andrew and she said Andrew.

Sometimes she called him Andy and sometimes she would say Handy Andy it is handy to have Andy, and her saying that did please Andrew. Naturally enough it pleased him.

It is not easy to lead a different life, much of it never happens but when it does it is different.

So Ida and Andrew never knew but it was true they were to lead a different life and yet again they were not.

If one did the other did not, and if the other did then the other did not.

And this is what happened.

If they had any friends they had so many friends.

They were always accompanied, Andrew when he came and went and wherever he was, Ida was not accompanied but she was never alone and when they were together they were always accompanied.

This was natural enough because Andrew always had been and it was natural enough because Ida always had been.

Men were with them and women were with them and men and women were with them.

It was this that made Ida say let's talk.

It was this that made Ida say, I like to know that all I love to do is to say something and he hears me.

It was this that made Ida say I never could though they were not glad to come.

It was this that made Ida say how do you do do come. It was this that made Ida say yes anything I can do I can always ask Andrew and Andrew will always do anything I ask him to do and that is the reason I call him Handy Andy.

Ida never laughed she smiled and sometimes she yawned and sometimes she closed her eyes and sometimes she opened them and she rested. That is what Ida did.

It did look as if nothing could change, nothing could change Ida that was true, and if that was true could anything change Andrew.

In a way nothing could but he could come not to be Andrew and if he were not Andrew Ida would not call him Handy Andy and as a matter of fact when he was not any longer Andrew she never did call him Handy Andy. She called him Andy, and she called him Andrew then but that was not the same thing.

But it was natural enough. Nature is not natural and that is natural enough.

Ida knew that is she did not exactly know them but all the same she did know them some people who always were ready to be there.

The larger the house these people had the more ready they were to be there.

Ida might have to come to that but if she did she could not rest.

Oh dear she often said oh dear isn't it queer.

More than that she needed no help, but she might come to need help, and if she would come to need help she would help herself and if she helped herself then she certainly would be needing help.

I let it alone, she told everybody, and she did. She certainly did. But most gradually Andrew it was true was a way to do, not for Ida, but for Andrew, and that made a lot of trouble, not for Ida, but for Andrew.

What was because was just what was a bother to Ida because she saw that Andrew was across from where he was.

Nobody knew whether it was happening slowly or not. It might be slowly and it might not.

Once in a great while Ida got up suddenly.

When she did well it was sudden, and she went away not far away but she left. That happened once in a way.

She was sitting just sitting, they said if you look out of the window you see the sun. Oh yes said Ida, and they said, do you like sunshine or rain and Ida said she liked it best. She was sitting of course and she was resting and she did like it best.

They said, well anybody said, More than enough. Oh yes said Ida, I like it, yes I do, I like it.

Somebody said, well let us go on. No said Ida I always say no, no said Ida. And why not they asked her, well said Ida if you go away. We did not say we were going away, they said. Believe it or not we did not say we were going away, they said. Well said Ida I feel that way too. Do you they said. Yes said Ida I feel that way too.

It was not then that she got up suddenly. It was considerably after. She was not startled, a dog might bark suddenly but she was not startled. She was never startled at once. If she was, well she never was.

But after all, if she got up suddenly, and she did not very often. And once she got up suddenly she left.

That did not as a matter of fact make very much difference.

More than enough she never really said, but once well really once she did get up suddenly and if she did get up suddenly she went away.

Nobody ever heard Andrew ever mention what he did because he never did it.

Everybody always said something, they said let's have it again, and they always had it again.

For this much they did come in, of course there never really was a beginning, for which it was fortunate.

Ida was mostly fortunate even if it did not matter. It really did not matter, not much.

So whether it was slowly or not was not enough because nobody was scared. They might be careful Ida was careful.

For which reason she was never worried not very likely to be.

She once said when this you see remember me, she liked being like that. Nicely.

For this reason she was rested. She will get up suddenly once and leave but not just now. Not now.

They could exchange well she knew more about hats than cows.

Andrew was interested in cows and horses. But after all there was much more in the way they sat down. Believe it or not they did sit down.

# Part Eight

Well he said Andrew said that he could not do without Ida. Ida said yes, and indeed when she said yes she meant yes. Yes Andrew could not do without Ida and Ida said yes. She knew she might go away suddenly, but she said yes.

And so it came to be not more exciting but more yes than it had been.

Ida did say yes.

And Andrew was not nervous that is to say Andrew trembled easily but he was not nervous. Ida was nervous and so she said yes. If you are resting and you say yes you can be nervous, and Ida was nervous. There was no mistake about Ida's being nervous. She was not nervous again, she was just nervous. When she said yes she was not nervous. When she was resting she was nervous. Nearly as well as ever she said she was, she said she was nearly as well as ever, but nobody ever asked her if she is well, they always knew she was nearly as well as ever.

It happened that when she went out she came in. Well she did go out and when she went out she came in.

Andrew went in and went out, but Ida did not.

When she went out she came in.

This was not just in the beginning it came to be more so, the only time that it ever was otherwise was when she got up suddenly and this did happen soon.

And so Andrew well Andrew was not careless nothing ever made Andrew careless.

He was much prepared.

Neither Andrew nor Ida was astonished but they were surprised. They had that in common that they were surprised not suddenly surprised but just surprised.

They were not astonished to learn but they were surprised.

This is what happened.

Ida had an aunt, she remembered she had an aunt but that had nothing to do with Ida nothing at all. Next to nothing to do with Ida.

Her aunt well her aunt sometimes did not feel that way about it but not very often and really it had nothing to do with Ida or with what happened.

What happened was this.

Ida returned more and more to be Ida. She even said she was Ida.

What they said. Yes she said. And they said why do you say yes. Well she said I say yes because I am Ida.

It got quite exciting. It was not just exciting it was quite exciting. Every time she said yes, and she said yes any time she said anything, well any time she said yes it was quite exciting.

Ida even was excited, well not altogether but she really was excited. Even Andrew was excited and as for the rest of all of them, all of them were excited.

And in between, well Ida always did have a tendency to say yes and now she did say, she even sometimes said oh yes.

Everybody was excited, it was extraordinary the way everybody was excited, they were so excited that everybody stopped everything to be excited.

Ida was excited but not very excited. At times she was not excited but she did always say yes.

Andrew was excited, he was not excited when he took his walk but he was quite often excited. Ida did say yes.

They went out together of course but it was difficult as the more excited he was the faster he went and the more excited she was the slower she went and as she could not go faster and he could not go slower. Well it was all right.

They lived from day to day. Ida did. So did they all. Some of their friends used to look at clouds, they would come in and say this evening I saw a cloud and it looked like a hunting dog and others would say he saw a cloud that looked like a dragon, and another one would say he saw a cloud that looked like a dream, and another he saw a cloud that looked like a queen. Ida said yes and Andrew said very nicely. They liked people to come in and tell what kind of clouds they had seen. Some had seen a cloud that looked like a fish and some had seen a cloud that looked like a rhinoceros, almost any of them had seen a cloud.

It was very pleasant for Ida that they came and told what the clouds they had seen looked like.

Ida lived from day to day so did they all but all the same a day well a day was not really all day to Ida, she needed only a part of the day and only a part of the night, the rest of the day and night she did not need. They might but she did not.

Andrew did not need day nor night but he used it all he did not use it up but he used it, he used it all of it it was necessary to use all of it and it was always arranged that he did everything that was necessary to do and he did. It was necessary that he used all of the night and all of the day every day and every night. This was right.

Ida chose just that piece of the day and just that piece of the night that she would use.

All right.

They did not say it but she said it and that was why she said yes.

And then something did happen.

What happened was this.

Everybody began to miss something and it was not a kiss, you bet your life it was not a kiss that anybody began to miss. And yet perhaps it was.

Well anyway something did happen and it excited every one that it was something and that it did happen.

It happened slowly and then it was happening and then it happened a little quicker and then it was happening and then it happened it really happened and then it had happened and then it was happening and then well then there it was and if it was there then it is there only now nobody can care.

And all this sounds kind of funny but it is all true.

And it all began with everybody knowing that they were missing something and perhaps a kiss but not really nobody really did miss a kiss. Certainly not Ida.

Ida was not interested, she was resting and then it began oh so slowly to happen and then there it was all right there it was everybody knew it all right there it was.

Dear Ida.

What happened.

Well what happened was this. Everybody thought everybody knew what happened. And everybody did know and so it was that that happened. Nothing was neglected that is Ida did nothing Andrew did nothing but nothing was neglected.

When something happens nothing begins. When anything begins then nothing happens and you could always say with Ida that nothing began.

Nothing ever did begin.

Partly that and partly nothing more. And there was never any need of excuses. You only excuse yourself if you begin or if somebody else begins but with Ida well she never began and nobody else began. Andrew although he was different was the same, he was restless all day and Ida was resting all day but neither one nor the other had to begin. So in a way nothing did happen.

That was the way it was nothing did happen. Everybody talked all day and every day about Ida and Andrew but nothing could happen as neither the one of them or the other one ever did begin anything.

It is wonderful how things pile up even if nothing is added. Very wonderful.

Suppose somebody comes in, suppose they say, well how are we today. Well supposing they do say that. It does not make any difference but supposing they do say that. Somebody else comes in and says that too well how are we today. Well if Ida has not answered the first one she could not answer the second one because you always have to answer the first one before you answer the second one.

And if there was still a third one and mostly there was and a fourth one and a fifth one and even a sixth one and each one said well and how are we today, it is natural enough that Ida would have nothing to say. She had not answered the first one and if you are resting you cannot hurry enough to catch up and so she had nothing to say. Yes she said. It is natural enough that she said yes, because she did not catch up with anything and did not interrupt anything and did not begin anything and did not stop anything.

Yes said Ida.

It looks the same but well of course one can run away, even if you are resting you can run away. Not necessarily but you can. You can run away even if you say yes. And if you run away well you never come back even if you are completely followed.

This could be a thing that Ida would do. She would say yes and she was resting and nothing happened and nothing began but she could run away. Not everybody can but she could and she did.

What happened.

Before she ran away.

She did not really run away, she did not go away. It was something in between. She took her umbrella and parasol. Everybody knew she was going, that is not really true they did not know she was going but she went they knew she was going. Everybody knew.

She went away that is she did get away and when she was away everybody was excited naturally enough. It was better so. Dear Ida.

Little by little she was not there she was elsewhere. Little by little.

It was little by little and it was all of a sudden. It was not entirely sudden because she was not entirely there before she was elsewhere.

That is the way it happened.

Before it happened well quite a while before it happened she did meet women. When they came she was resting, when they went she was resting, she liked it and they did not mind it. They came again and when they came again, she was obliging, she did say yes. She was sorry she was resting, so sorry and she did say yes. She thought they liked it and they did but it was not the same as if she had ever said no or if she had not always been resting.

If she had not always been resting they would not have come nor would they have come again. They said thank you my dear when they went. She had said yes Ida had and she said yes again.

That is the way it was before going away, they had not really come nor had they said Thank you my dear.

That is really the reason that Ida ran away not ran away or went away but something in between. She was ready to be resting and she was ready to say yes and she was ready to hear them say thank you my dear but they had almost not come again.

So Ida was not there. Dear Ida.

She knew she would be away but not really away but before she knew she was there where she had gone to she was really away.

That was almost an astonishment, quite to her, but to all the others, not so much so once she was not there.

Of course she had luncheon and dinners to eat on the way.

One of the menus she ate was this.

She ate soft-shell crabs, she had two servings of soft-shell crabs and she ate lobster à la Newburg she only had one helping of that and then she left.

She often left after she ate. That is when she was not resting but she mostly was resting.

And so there she was and where was Andrew, well Andrew moved quickly while Ida moved slowly that is when they were both nervous, when each one of them was nervous. But he was not there yet. Not really.

Ida was resting. Dear Ida. She said yes.

Slowly little by little Andrew came, Andrew was still his name.

He was just as nervous as he was and he walked every afternoon and then he told about his walk that afternoon. Ida was as nervous as she was and she was resting.

For a little time she did not say yes and then she said yes again.

Gradually it was, well not as it had been but it was, it was quite as it was Ida was resting and she was saying yes but not as much as she had said yes. There were times when she did not say yes times when she was not resting not time enough but times.

It is all very confused but more confused than confusing, and later it was not interesting. It was not confused at all, resting was not confused and yes was not confused but it was interesting.

When any one came well they did Ida could even say how do you do and where did you come from.

Dear Ida.

And if they did not come from anywhere they did not come.

So much for resting.

Little by little there it was. It was Ida and Andrew.

Not too much not too much Ida and not too much Andrew.

And not enough Ida and not enough Andrew.

If Ida goes on, does she go on even when she does not go on any more.

No and yes.

Ida is resting but not resting enough. She is resting but she is not saying yes. Why should she say yes. There is no reason why she should so there is nothing to say.

She sat and when she sat she did not always rest, not enough.

She did rest.

If she said anything she said yes. More than once nothing was said. She said something. If nothing is said then Ida does not say yes. If she goes out she comes in. If she does not go away she is there and she does not go away. She dresses, well perhaps in black why not, and a hat, why not, and another hat, why not, and another dress, why not, so much why not.

She dresses in another hat and she dresses in another dress and Andrew is in, and they go in and that is where they are. They are there. Thank them.

Yes.

# Contexts I

# Stein's Life and Publications

1864 Daniel Stein (b. 1832) and Amelia ("Milly") Keyser (b. 1842) are married

1865 The Steins' first child, Michael ("Mike"), is born (d. 1938), followed by Simon in 1867 (d. 1906), Bertha in 1870 (d. 1924), and Leo in 1872 (d. 1947)

1874 February 3: Gertrude Stein is born in Allegheny, Pennsylvania; late in the year, or early in 1875, the Stein family moves to Vienna, Austria

1877 April 30: Alice Toklas is born

1878 The Stein family (minus Daniel, who is back in America) moves to Paris

1879 After a few weeks in London, the family moves to Baltimore

1880 The family moves to Oakland, California

1888 Milly dies (cancer)

1891 Daniel dies (in his sleep); with Mike as guardian, the five children move to San Francisco

1892 Gertrude and Bertha move to Baltimore to live with a Keyser aunt; Leo begins studies at Harvard University

1893 Stein enrolls at Radcliffe College (then Harvard Annex, renamed Radcliffe in 1894), where her studies include literature, philosophy, psychology, and biology

1896 Summer: In Europe with Leo

September: Stein's article "Normal Motor Automatism," co-written with Leon Solomons, is published in the *Psychological Review*

1897 Stein leaves Radcliffe, but because of an unfulfilled Latin requirement does not receive her bachelor of arts degree until 1898

Summer: In San Francisco with Mike and his wife, Sarah ("Sally") Samuels (again in summer 1898 and summer 1899 as well)

Fall: Stein enrolls at Johns Hopkins School of Medicine, where her studies include anatomy, pathology and bacteriology, surgery, pharmacology and toxicology, and gynecology

1898 May: Stein's article "Cultivated Motor Automatism" is published in the *Psychological Review*

1900 Summer: In Italy and France with Leo

1901 Stein leaves Johns Hopkins School of Medicine without degree

Summer: In Morocco, Spain, and France with Leo

Fall: In Baltimore doing biological studies

1902 Spring: In Italy with Leo

Summer–Fall: In London with Leo

1903 Winter–Spring: In New York; begins *The Making Of Americans*

Summer: In Italy with Leo

Fall: Stein moves to 27 rue de Fleurus, Paris, with Leo and they begin collecting Paul Cézanne paintings; Stein writes *Q.E.D.* (not published until 1950)

1904 Winter–Spring: In New York

Summer: In Italy and then back to Paris (Stein does not return to the United States for thirty years)

1905 Spring: Stein begins *Three Lives* (finished by February 1906)

Fall: Stein and Leo begin collecting Pablo Picasso and Henri Matisse paintings

Winter: Stein meets Picasso, who begins a portrait of her (finished by fall 1906)

1906 Stein continues writing *The Making Of Americans*

Summer: In Italy with Leo (these annual Italian holidays continue until 1912)

1907 Fall: Alice Toklas arrives in Paris and meets Stein

1908 Toklas begins secretarial work for Stein, typing *The Making Of Americans*

1909 July: Stein's first book, *Three Lives* (New York: Grafton Press), is published

1910 December: Toklas moves in with Stein and Leo

1911 Fall: Stein finishes *The Making Of Americans* (not published until 1925)

1912 Spring–Summer: Stein and Toklas in Spain and Morocco

August: Stein's first portraits, "Matisse" and "Picasso," are published in the magazine *Camera Work*

September: In Italy (final Italian holiday)

1913 January: In England

August–September: In Spain

Fall: Leo moves to Italy (Stein and Leo never speak to one another again)

1914 June: *Tender Buttons* (New York: Claire Marie)

July–October: In England

August: War begins

October: Stein and Toklas return to Paris

1915 March: Stein and Toklas go to Barcelona, then Palma, Majorca

1916 June: They return to Paris from Majorca

1917 March: Stein and Toklas drive a supply truck for American Fund for French Wounded

1919 June: They return to Paris after more than two years of relief work

1922 Fall–Winter: In Saint-Rémy

December: *Geography And Plays* (Boston: Four Seas)

1923 March: Stein and Toklas return to Paris

Fall: In Nice (visits Belley, France)

Winter: In Paris

1924 Summer: In Belley (summer living at a Belley hotel continues until 1929)

1925 September: *The Making Of Americans* (Paris: Contact Editions)

1926 June: Stein reads "Composition As Explanation" at Cambridge and Oxford universities

Fall: Stein finishes *A Novel Of Thank You* (not published until 1958)

December: *A Book Concluding With As A Wife Has A Cow A Love Story* (Paris: Galerie Simon)

1928 September: *Useful Knowledge* (New York: Payson and Clarke)

1929 April: *An Acquaintance With Description* (London: Seizin Press)

Summer: Stein leases a home in Bilignin, France, a mile from Belley, and for the next decade has a city-and-country lifestyle, living in Paris for the winter and spring, and in Bilignin for the summer and fall; Stein and Toklas get Basket, a standard poodle

1930 January: *Lucy Church Amiably* (Paris: Plain Edition); this marks the first of five books to be published under the Stein and Toklas imprint Plain Edition

May: *Dix Portraits* (Paris: Editions de la Montagne)

1931 May: *Before the Flowers of Friendship Faded Friendship Faded* (Paris: Plain Edition)

November: *How To Write* (Paris: Plain Edition)

1932 August: *Operas And Plays* (Paris: Plain Edition)

Summer: Stein and Toklas get Byron, a Chihuahua; he dies in early spring 1933 and in May 1933 is replaced by another Chihuahua, Pépé (d. 1943)

1933 February: *Matisse Picasso And Gertrude Stein* (Paris: Plain Edition)

August: *The Autobiography Of Alice B. Toklas* (New York: Harcourt, Brace) quickly becomes a best seller

September: Stein finishes *Blood On The Dining Room Floor* (not published until 1948)

1934 February: *Four Saints In Three Acts* (New York: Random House)

April: Stein finishes *Four In America* (not published until 1947)

October 24: Stein and Toklas arrive in New York City; over the next six months, Stein gives more than seventy lectures in cities across the country, including New York, Chicago, St. Paul, Madison, Columbus, Cleveland, Detroit, Ann Arbor, Amherst, Cambridge, Philadelphia,

Baltimore, Washington, Charlottesville, New Orleans, Austin, Oklahoma City, Pasadena, San Francisco, and Oakland

November: *Portraits And Prayers* (New York: Random House)

1935 March: *Lectures In America* (New York: Random House); Stein teaches for two weeks at the University of Chicago

May 4: Stein departs for France

December: *Narration* (Chicago: University of Chicago Press)

1936 February: Stein lectures again at Oxford and Cambridge ("What Are Master-pieces")

October: *The Geographical History Of America Or The Relation Of Human Nature To The Human Mind* (New York: Random House)

1937 April: In London for opening of ballet *A Wedding Bouquet*

Summer–Fall: Stein begins constructing archive of her writing at Yale University Library

December: *Everybody's Autobiography* (New York: Random House); after thirty-four years, Stein's lease terminated at 27 rue de Fleurus by landlord

1938 January: Stein and Toklas move to 5 rue Christine, Paris

October: *Picasso* (London: B. T. Batsford)

November: Basket dies, and early in 1939, they get another standard poodle, Basket II (d. 1952)

1939 August: *The World Is Round* (New York: William R. Scott)

September: War having begun, Stein and Toklas quickly visit the Paris apartment and then return to Bilignin

1940 April: *Paris France* (London: B. T. Batsford)

1941 February 15: *Ida A Novel* (New York: Random House)

February 22–March 29: First exhibition of Stein archive (notebooks, typescripts, first editions, letters, photographs) at Yale University Library

1942 Summer: Stein finishes *Mrs. Reynolds* (not published until 1952)

1943 February: Stein moves from Bilignin to nearby Culoz

1944 August: Stein sees American soldiers, marking end of the war

December: Stein returns to Paris for the first time in more than five years

1945 March: *Wars I Have Seen* (New York: Random House)

June: Stein tours U.S. Army bases in occupied Germany

1946 March: Stein finishes libretto *The Mother Of Us All* (published in 1947)

July: Stein sends Yale University Library most of her remaining papers; *Brewsie And Willie* (New York: Random House)

July 27: Stein dies following operation for cancer

October: *Selected Writings of Gertrude Stein* (New York: Random House)

1947 March 22–June 1: Second exhibition of Stein archive at Yale University Library

1951–1958 Yale University Press publishes eight volumes of Stein's previously unpublished writing

1967 March 7: Toklas dies

# Compositions, 1935–1940

Although Stein did not begin *Ida A Novel* until 1937, this chronology of composition begins two years earlier, in 1935, when Stein was in the middle of her American lecture tour, seeing again the geography of her homeland and experiencing the life of a marked woman, a celebrity. In text after text that year, she meditated on the effects. What was the relationship between a successful writer and her audience? Could Stein the *writer* still exist in a creative space free of her public identity? This experience and her response to it, including her second life narrative, *Everybody's Autobiography*, are behind *Ida*. While not all-inclusive, this chronology lists most of her writing in these years, and with it we can read laterally and test the idea that any act of writing for Stein was embedded within her career: as she worked on a new text, she was thinking about—and sometimes even using words from—earlier ones.

Following the date of composition is information on first publication and selected later publications (for abbreviations, see p. vii). An asterisk indicates that information on first publication is in "Stein's Life and Publications." To supplement this chronology, see Richard Bridgman's *Gertrude Stein in Pieces* (365–385), which covers her entire career, and Ulla Dydo's *The Language That Rises* (*LR* 633–643) for a more accurate record of the years 1923–1934.

1935 January: "How Writing Is Written" (*CLM*; *Oxford Anthology of American Literature*, vol. 2, ed. William Rose Benét and Norman Holmes Pearson [New York: Oxford University Press, 1938], 1446–1451; *HWW* 151–160)

Winter–Spring: Six articles on America for the *New York Herald Tribune* (*HWW* 73–105)

February–March: *Narration**

June–September: *The Geographical History Of America** (*GSW* 365–488)

August: "Identity A Poem" (*WAM* 71–79; *PGU* 117–123; *SR* 588–594)

(Fall?): "A Political Series" (*Painted Lace And Other Pieces* [New Haven: Yale University Press, 1955], 71–77)

Fall: "What Are Master-pieces And Why Are There So Few Of Them" (*WAM* 83–95; *GSW* 353–363)

Winter: "An American And France" (*WAM* 61–70)

1936 March: *Listen To Me A Play* (*LOP* 387–421)

March: *A Play Called Not And Now* (*LOP* 422–439)

Summer: Begins *Everybody's Autobiography*

Summer–Fall: Five articles on money for the *Saturday Evening Post* (*HWW* 106–112)

(Summer?): "A Waterfall And A Piano" (*New Directions in Prose and Poetry, 1936* [Norfolk, CT: New Directions, 1936], 16–18; *HWW* 31–32)

(Summer?): "Is Dead" (*Occident* 30.3 [Apr. 1937]: 6–8; *HWW* 33–36)

(September?): "Butter Will Melt" (*Atlantic Monthly* 159.2 [Feb. 1937]: 156–157; *HWW* 37–38)

October: "The Autobiography Of Rose" (*Partisan Review* 6.2 [Winter 1939]: 61–63; *HWW* 39–42)

Fall: "What Does She See When She Shuts Her Eyes A Novel" (*MR* 375–378; *GSW* 491–493)

1937 Winter–Summer: *Daniel Webster Eighteen In America A Play* (*New Directions in Prose and Poetry, 1937* [Norfolk, CT: New Directions, 1937], 162–188; *RAB* 95–117)

May: Finishes *Everybody's Autobiography**

May: Begins *Ida A Novel*

(Summer?): "Why I Like Detective Stories" (*Harper's Bazaar* 17.2 [Nov. 1937]: 70, 104, 106; *HWW* 146–150)

November–December: *Picasso** (*GSW* 497–533)

1938 February–June: *Doctor Faustus Lights The Lights* (*LOP* 89–118; *SR* 595–624; *GSW* 575–607)

May: "Ida" (*BC*; *HWW* 43–47)

Summer: Continues *Ida A Novel* as "Arthur And Jenny"

September–October: *The World Is Round** (*GSW* 537–574)

1939 (Winter?): *Lucretia Borgia A Play* (*Creative Writing* 1.8 [Oct. 1939]: 15; *RAB* 118–119)

(April?): "A Portrait Of Daisy To Daisy On Her Birthday" (YCAL 67.1200)

June: "Les Superstitions" (translated and incorporated into *Ida A Novel*)

Summer–Winter: *Paris France**

Fall: "Helen Button A Story Of War-Time" (incorporated into *Paris France*)

1940 Winter: "My Life With Dogs" (incorporated into *Ida A Novel*)

May: Finishes *Ida A Novel** (*GSW* 611–704)

May: *To Do: A Book Of Alphabets And Birthdays* (*AB* 3–86)

July–August: "The Winner Loses, A Picture Of Occupied France" (*Atlantic Monthly* 166.5 [Nov. 1940]: 571–583; *HWW* 113–132)

July: Begins *Mrs. Reynolds* (finishes it by the summer of 1942; *MR* 1–267)

# Genealogy of *Ida A Novel*

Gertrude Stein wrote *Ida A Novel* over the course of three years, from May 1937 to May 1940, and the manuscripts reveal four stages of composition. While the last two stages present Stein knowing the narrative, in the first two she is finding her way—copying and copying again, expanding, excising, and rearranging. To illuminate the novel's evolution, a number of excerpts are offered here, in particular from the first two stages. This narrative of genealogy, while not a complete variorum, allows readers the opportunity to compare draft versions of the novel with the published text. Readers will also want to acquaint themselves with the chronology of composition in this period (see "Compositions, 1935–1940")—*Ida* rested a number of times as Stein wrote other, often closely related texts. The four stages occurred as follows.

*1. May 1937 to early 1938*: In four notebooks and on ten-plus manuscript sheets, Stein worked on a first draft of what she was calling "Ida A Novel." She recycled some of this material for the second stage, and again for the third stage, primarily for Parts Three through Six in the novel's First Half. In August 1937, Stein showed the second notebook to Thornton Wilder, who wrote some notes that have since been published (see *TW* 366–368).

*2. Summer 1938 to fall 1939*: On three hundred manuscript sheets and thirty-two-plus typescript sheets—the latter being copies of the former, but with handwritten additions—Stein began the novel again, changing the Ida character to Jenny and the title to "Arthur And Jenny A Novel." In the third stage Stein transformed this material into Parts One and Two in the novel's First Half. Appearing in this second stage are versions of two preexisting texts—an early fiction work, "Hortense Sänger" (1895), and a movie scenario, "Film Deux Soeurs Qui Ne Sont Pas Soeurs" (1929)—that would be further modified in the third stage.

*3. Winter 1939–1940*: In two notebooks, Stein used the materials from the preceding two and a half years to write the novel's First Half, with the title reverting back to "Ida A Novel." This stage involved a radical rearrangement of the already existing text (see the end of the Introduction for an example), some new text, and a reconceptualization of the narrative structure. From these two notebooks Alice Toklas produced a typescript (not extant) that Stein sent to Bennett Cerf early in 1940.

*4. April–May 1940*: In five notebooks and on thirty manuscript sheets, Stein wrote the Second Half of *Ida*. Into the novel she incorporated two recent texts, "My Life With Dogs" and "Les Superstitions." Toklas's typescript was 102 sheets—she noted her page count on the manuscript—and Stein sent copies to Cerf and Carl Van Vechten in June (neither is extant).

**1937–1938**

Stein appears to have begun *Ida* in two slim notebooks (thirty and forty-eight sheets). In the first she used only a couple of pages, and in the second she used a little less than half of them. (*Ida* shares these notebooks with two versions of "Why I Like Detective Stories.") Here, then, is Stein making a start:

> Good-by now.
>
> In the beginning when forty-eight made them ask how old they were a little noise was heard. If they heard a little noise everybody asked them not to make it.
>
> Ida was fifteen she looked older, she had a tall way of holding herself. Ida.
>
> Ida was lost that is to say a man followed her and that frightened her so that she was crying when she got back. In a little while it was a comfort to her. Ida.
>
> In a little while a cherry tree does not look like a pear tree. She said and she was so much older so old that not anybody could be older although one was she said, her grandfather had said that a cherry tree never did have to have pears on it or a pear tree cherries. There was no use in not saying this.
>
> Welcome Nelly and welcome Ida Ida's sister was much smaller. She had a suit-case. Think of this thing.
>
> And so everything introduces it or finishes it.
>
> And not yet.
>
> Ida. (YCAL 27.552)

The second notebook—the one Wilder read—has nine vignette chapters, five of which are transcribed here (Chapters I, IV–VII). Chapters VIII and IX are not transcribed here, but they contain two exemplary sentences that play with dislocations in time to give Ida an evanescence. The sentence was Stein's primary unit of style in *Ida*, and throughout the writing process she would play with the possibilities: length, level of abstraction, and number in a paragraph.[1]

From Chapter VIII: "Ida went on walking later on the rain came down more but that was much later and Ida was not walking any more." The phrase "went on walking" pushes Ida into her future, and at first Ida walking appears linked with the rain coming down, as if the two were happening together. Moreover, the material language of this sentence relates them: it moves from "went on" to "later on" to "much later," and from "came down more" to "walking any more." But Ida's future ultimately appears separate from the rain, and we ask: where was she when the rain came down, and where was she when it came down *more*? Ida has an umbrella in this chapter, but did she need it? In the context of this draft, we cannot be sure. Ida disappears.[2]

From Chapter IX: "Ida was careless she sent her dog Iris to look for her what she had forgotten but she had not forgotten it, he did not find it the dog did not but he found a hat, oh yes a hat and he brought that." Poor Iris (who is blind) could not find what was not there, and when Ida recovers the memory on her own she does not need Iris to know herself; she has self-possession. But a new hat could unsettle Ida's identity by canceling the old memory and moving her into an alternative future. So with careless Ida and Iris the blind hunter, predicting what happens next in the narrative is no simple matter.

# Ida
# A Novel

## Chapter one.
## Good-by now.

It was just here that Ida was. Ida walked as if she was tall young very young not sixteen yet and tall very tall as tall as any one.

Ida was very careful about Tuesday. She always had to have Tuesday just had to have Tuesday.

Ida knew another Ida who was thirty and had a blind dog who was born blind and his name was Iris.

It is true Ida is a woman you can generally tell by their name. Ida is and was a woman. Once in a while she knew all about something and when this happened everybody stood still and they did look they looked out of the window.

She that is Ida hesitated before eating. It was dark in the morning.

Ida always talked not very much but she did always talk unless she was alone and she was never alone not even when she was waiting. Ida can wait long enough. Which Ida had done she had waited long enough and what she had to have had begun. Ida did not know just what she had to have until she had it but when she had it she had to have it.

## IV
## A plan.

Woodward was the man he was soliloquizing. He was saying I have known and if I know I have admired the ones I have known and if I have admired the ones I have known I have looked like them. Woodward never sighed. He had not known Ida and he had never sighed. He soliloquized. This is what he said. I do not mean said Woodward as he soliloquized, I do not mean I when I say I I mean I do not know how much I feel when once in a while I have never come to know Ida. I can know about Ida analyzed Woodward, I do not think about Ida because as I am very busy and thinking does not take very much of my time I do not think about Ida. I do not think said Woodward that is I do not feel that I do not like thinking. All this interested Woodward in Ida. He had not met Ida very likely he would never meet Ida. He might have tears in his eyes not Woodward not Ida at not meeting Ida. He said to himself Everybody talks about Ida but I do not talk about Ida nor do I listen when they are all talking about Ida, I am thinking of another person said Woodward to himself not any one I could possibly think would be at all like Ida not at all like Ida.

And that was the way it was.

## Chapter V
## It was.

If Ida was on the front page of the newspaper Ida was Idle.

Ida and idle both begin with I but Ida was not idle nobody ever is, if they all talk about what everybody does nobody is idle.

~~Woodward and work both begin with w and that does make them welcome.~~

Work and we both begin with w and that does make them welcome.

It almost does seem that Ida and Woodward would meet but they will not. Woodward will not meet Ida and Ida would not meet any one who came to where she then was. Very likely Ida is not anxious. Woodward is.

## Chapter VI
## Is.

There is a place called Bayshore and at Bayshore there is a house and this house is a comfortable house to live in. Ida was living there.

Like everybody Ida has lived not everywhere but she had lived in quite a number of houses and in a good many hotels. Believe her. She liked it at Bayshore. Bayshore did not belong to her but she belonged to Bayshore.

## Chapter VII
## Bayshore.

Ida had a little white dog his name was Iris. Iris is the name of a flower it might be the name of a girl it was the name of a little white dog he jumped up and down. Bayshore was not near the water that is unless you call a little stream water or quite a way off a little lake water, and rocks beyond it water. If you do not call all these things water then Bayshore was not at all near any water but its name was Bayshore and it was in the country where there are vipers only most of the time nobody sees them. Ida almost did not nor the little white dog Iris but on the path there must have been a yellow viper and as Ida watched the little dog Iris jump up and down bouncing like a ball she must have stood on the tail of the viper because she felt a sharp thing that was not like a sting on the side of her foot and as she stooped to look she saw something disappearing, she did not think it could be a viper but she looked down and took down her stocking she was wearing stockings while she was walking and there were two sharp little marks and she remembered that she had read that that was what a serpent's bite looked like.

> Therefore she went on meditating and then as she went on she met some woman who belonged there, Ida of course did not, and Ida said to her could I have been bitten by a viper, yes said the woman not often but it does happen, well said Ida what shall I do, better go and see a doctor, so Ida went back to where she had come from and pretty soon she found a doctor and he said oh yes and injected a serum into her, it did not hurt her but it made a big red patch where the sting had been, it will make another one where the poison has been stopped higher up said the doctor and it did. Some one said sometimes the big red patch comes back every spring said some one they knew some one to whom this did happen but this did not do this to Ida. Then there was the dog Iris he had not been stung by the viper. (YCAL 27.552)

Certain of these passages are in the novel's final version, such as "Ida hesitated before eating" and "Very likely Ida is not anxious," but Woodward loses his status as potential companion to Ida, and the viper episode morphs into *Doctor Faustus Lights The Lights*.[3] Around the time that Stein was working in these first two notebooks, she also drafted some episodes on loose sheets of paper. Here are excerpts from four of them:

> Ida Isabel lived with her aunt. It was her aunt's house. Ida had a poodle whose name was Love. She often talked to him she also often went out with him and when they did once when they went out they saw a man holding a cat which had gotten caught and hurt badly by a hay mower and the man did not want to kill it but he felt he had to. And once they saw a big bird flying high and being attacked by little birds. [. . . They brought the big bird to the ground and] began pecking at his head one after the other of them until the big bird fell down dead. (YCAL 27.539)

> I am going to have a sister a sister who looks as like me as two peas (not that peas do) and no one will know which is she and which is me. I tell you my Love I am going to have a sister. / This idea kept running around in the head of this young girl until she really thought she was two and that the other sister did not want to stay at home all the time and so she went out. (YCAL 27.539)

> Woodward was away, away from Belvedere. His wife and daughter and his son they were old enough to be called. [. . . He] called them upon the long distance telephone, he said I am away from home. He was. He never went home again. [. . . ] His wife divorced him, but and this was natural enough he was good friends with them with his wife and his daughter and his son. / And so he went out into the world. / Ida. (YCAL 27.539)

> [Woodward] was born in Kansas [. . . and] a good many knew his name [. . . but he] was never more there. [. . . Gradually everybody knew that Ida was there and] it relieved everybody of their gloom. [. . .] Woodward looked at anybody who knew him but Ida did not. (YCAL 26.535)

Stein then turned to a third notebook and started with the by now well-used chapter title:

> Good-by now.
>
> Positively, can you go on doing what you did do. This is what Edith said to William. Naturally they were talking about something. So then they broke into poetry.
>
> At a glance  
> What a chance  
> ___________

> That they need
> What they have
>
> ---
>
> And they have
> What they are
>
> ---
>
> And they like
> Where they go
> Which is all.
> After a while
> They stopped it.
>
> ---
>
> So then poetry having been spoken Edith and William went on talking. (YCAL 27.545)

This chapter, with changes, makes it to the final version (see 64). Then, after three more paragraphs with Edith and William and a few more lines of poetry, the narrative starts over: Stein copies and expands on the nine-chapter narrative of the second notebook, and then adds nine new chapters (more on these in a moment). So after the Edith-and-William episode, the third notebook begins again:

> Chapter one.
> The story of Ida.
>
> Ida it is true Ida is a woman you can generally tell by their name. Ida is and was a woman. Once in a while she knew all about something and when this happened everybody stood still and as they were standing they did look and as they did look they looked out of the window. (YCAL 27.545)

This chapter begins as the second notebook did, except the first five sentences are missing ("It was just here that Ida was. Ida walked [. . .]"). Stein uses sixty sheets (both sides) of this third notebook and leaves the last half blank, until the very end, where—voilà—we find the five sentences. At some point she changed her mind about their value and made sure they remained in view for later drafts. Indeed, opening the fourth notebook we see those sentences again, and while episodes in the third notebook often expand on those in the second,[4] the fourth presents the familiar opening chapters in truncated form. As Stein moved from one notebook to another, the act of copying drew her into the landscape of the text as it had been and she was readied for a new surge of attention:

Ida A novel.

Chapter one.
Good-by now.

It was just here that Ida was. Ida walked as if she was tall young very young not sixteen yet and tall very tall as tall as any one.

Ida was very careful about Tuesday. She always had to have Tuesday just had to have Tuesday. That was so Ida.

Chapter II
Sight Unseen.

Another Ida who was thirty and had a blind dog who was born blind and his name was Iris.

She that is Ida hesitated before eating. It was dark in the morning.

Ida said I am like a dog I am affected by the tones of their voices and not by what they say.

> Ida always talked not very much but she did always talk unless she was alone and she was never alone. Ida did not know just what she had to have until she had it but when she had it she had to have it.
>
> Now you know all about Ida.
>
> Chapter III
>
> Now and then.
>
> There is a place called Bayshore and at Bayshore there is a house and this house is a comfortable house to live in. Ida was living there. Believe her. She liked it at Bayshore. (YCAL 27.547)

To understand the evolution of *Ida*, we need to know the order in which these drafts were written. At the same time, a later draft for Stein did not necessarily supersede an earlier one—there was a nonlinear aspect to her rewriting process. For instance, if we jump ahead for a moment to the third stage (winter 1939–1940), we see the reappearance of a passage which had been dropped (Figure 4). Stein may have simply recalled the passage and inserted it. However, given her habit of review as she worked on this novel, it seems more likely that she double-checked what she had written against the fourth notebook in this first stage (late 1937 or early 1938), which reads, "Well what did he know. He knew Ida. Hell yes he knew Ida. He never went to Bay Shore but then why did he know Ida. Well and listen. Of course he knew Ida" (YCAL 27.547), and made the change. As we saw above, fidelity to an earlier draft was evident in the case of the "missing" five sentences, and here it is again.

Back in the third notebook, following the expanded version of material from the second, Stein wrote a lengthy narrative involving Ida and a Spanish refugee, Harold: "[H]e was the only man among all those Spaniards the rest were women and children they

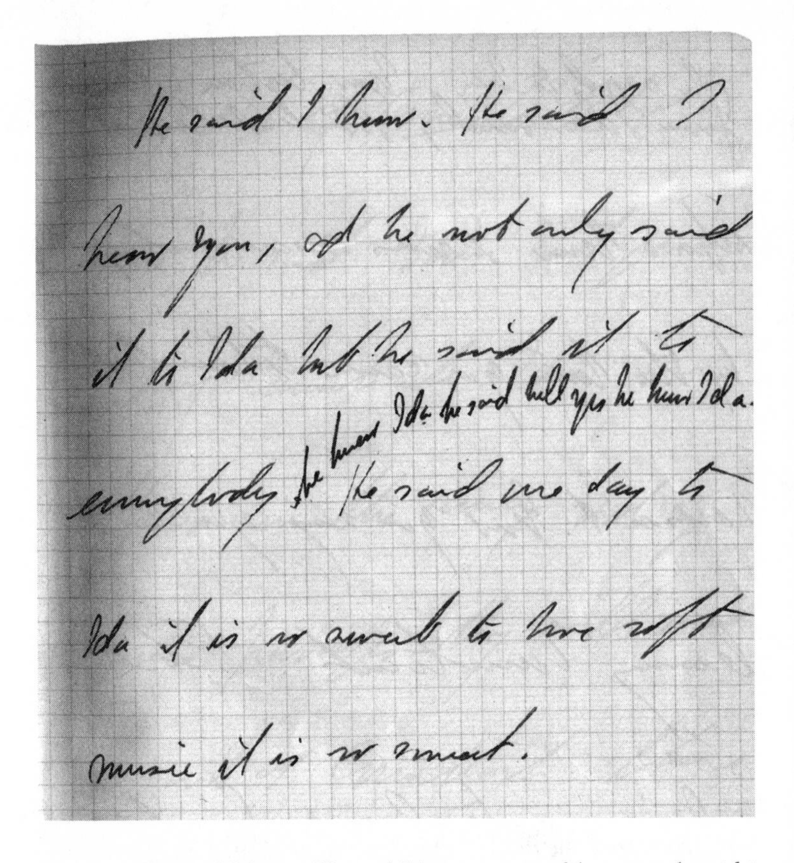
He said I know. He said I
know you, and he not only said
it to Ida but he said it to
he knew Ida he said hell yes he knew Ida.
everybody he He said one day to
Ida it is so sweet to have soft
music it is so sweet.

*Figure 4:* "He said I know. He said I know you, and he not only said it to Ida but he said it to everybody <he knew Ida he said hell yes he knew Ida>. He said one day to Ida it is so sweet to have soft music it is so sweet" (YCAL 27.543).

had come out of the city that was bombarded and they had a long trip and nothing to eat [. . .] he had come dressed as a woman" (YCAL 27.545). By implication, we understand that Ida was then living in England and Harold had escaped his country's civil war (1936–1939), assimilating with a new, English name. This topical reference, as well as the commentary on political turmoil and its identity effects ("every day Harold and Ida met and when they met Harold said I am a Spaniard and she said you have no country now and he said Harold said I have no country now because nobody has a country now"), appears in this notebook alone—none of the Harold narrative appears in *Ida*.

The text in the fourth notebook is the longest by far, with Stein using more than 140 sheets (both sides) in the 164-sheet notebook. It opens in the fictional city of Bayshore, as the others did, but soon Ida and the narrative begin to move. In October 1937 Stein asked Wilder to send a map of the United States: "I kind of need it to make Ida go on" (see "Selected Letters"). Indeed, references to a multitude of American states—California, Kentucky, Alabama, and so on—appear almost systematic. Brazil, Africa, and France also become part of Ida's consciousness, and her social geography expands too. In earlier drafts, the narrative had aligned her with one man, Woodward or Harold; now there are many, including Sam Hamlin, Benjamin William, William Benjamin, Joseph, and Frederick.[5] In this notebook, Woodward becomes a powerful man in Washington, a public figure, maybe even the president. People turn to him when they need something done. For instance, in a bizarre episode with Arthur Alexander, who finds "the original dahlia" in Mexico and wants to bring it to America but is denied entrance, Woodward writes to help "but Alexander never had the letter because he had gone off in a boat [. . .]. This is what happens in America and they all laugh" (YCAL 27.547). These Harold-the-Spaniard and dahlia stories refer to the growing nationalism of the late 1930s and the thickening borders between countries. Within the United States, though, Ida moves easily in a light echo of Depression-era drifting.

As in the first two notebooks, the narrative in the latter two is structured in brief vignette chapters, with those in the fourth (almost forty of them) being especially short. Apparently Stein did not give these first-stage manuscripts to Toklas for typing, which means that the narrative she had written over and again did not yet fully satisfy her. Early in 1938, after moving from 27 rue de Fleurus to 5 rue Christine, she set the novel aside to write the play *Doctor Faustus Lights The Lights* and the "Ida" story.

### 1938–1939

When Stein returned to *Ida* in the summer of 1938, she started by copying from the notebooks in the first stage. Now, however, Ida had become Jenny, and she was sharing the narrative with Arthur; the novel's new title gives equal billing to both. On two and then five loose sheets, Stein reacquaints herself with the narrative:

~~Ida~~
Arthur and Jenny
A Novel
Chapter one.
Good by now.

> Jenny was very careful about Tuesday. She always had to have Tuesday just had to have Tuesday. ~~She had to have Arthur too and that is why the title of this is Arthur and Jenny~~. Jenny always hesitated before eating. That was Jenny. Jenny She was very young not sixteen yet. She walked as if she was tall, very tall, as tall as any one.
>
> Jenny lived with her great aunt, ~~Where did she live. She lived just on the Well she lived just outside of the a city. outside a city any city, Paris or Chicago or London. She just lived there with~~ not in the city but just outside. (YCAL 26.535)

A Novel
Arthur and Jenny
Chapter I
Good-by now.

Jenny was very careful about Tuesday. She always had to have Tuesday just had to have Tuesday.

Jenny always hesitated before eating. That was Jenny.

Jenny was very young not sixteen yet. She walked as if she was tall, very tall, as tall as any one.

Jenny lived with her great aunt, not in the city but just outside.

Once she was lost that is to say a man followed her and that frightened her so that she was crying when she got back. In a little while it was a comfort to her.

In a little while as her grandfather told her a cherry tree does not look like a pear tree. An old woman told her that she would come to be so much older that not anybody could be older, although said the old woman, there was one who was older. Then her grandfather had told her that a cherry tree never did have to have pears on it nor a pear tree cherries. Her grandfather said there was no use in not saying this. He also said and so everything introduces it or finishes it, and then he said. And not yet.

The old woman told her that her great aunt had had something happen to her oh many years ago, it was a soldier, and then her great aunt had had little twins born to her, and she quietly buried them under a pear tree and nobody knew.

Jenny did not believe her, perhaps it was true perhaps the old woman had told it as it was but Jenny did not believe her. (YCAL 26.535)

On one of the loose sheets from the first stage of composition cited above (see 152), Stein had tested the idea of Ida having a twin: "I am going to have a sister a sister who looks as like me as two peas (not that peas do) and so no one will know which is she and which is me" (YCAL 27.539). This idea returns here with the great aunt and her twins. It is also in Tuesday (Two-s-day); in Jenny being followed; in the old woman's story being a true copy of the real event (or not); and in the cherry and pear (pair) trees, which in winter, without their leaves, appear similar, though "in a little while" when their fruit comes in they will "not look like" each other.[6] This last example suggests that two entities in a condition of infancy or stasis can appear identical, and that they become distinct by growing or moving.

Ida's wish for a twin sister returns in the next sequence of "Arthur And Jenny," 178 sheets arranged in ten chapters. ("Arthur And Jenny" has three primary sequences, the other two being fifty-seven sheets in four chapters and forty-five sheets in six chapters.) Here are the first twelve sheets:

~~A Novel.~~

Arthur and Jenny.

A Novel

Chapter I

Good-by now.

I

Jenny lived with her great aunt, not in the city but just outside.

She was very young not sixteen yet. She walked as if she was tall, very tall, as tall as any one.

Once she was lost that is to say a man followed her and that frightened her so that she was crying when she was lost. In a little while it was a comfort to her.

Jenny was very careful about Tuesday. She always had to have Tuesday just had to have Tuesday. Tuesday was Tuesday to her.

Jenny always hesitated before eating. That was Jenny.

Her grandfather once told her, and that she could remember, that in a little while a cherry tree does not look like a pear tree. He also always told her that a cherry tree did not have to have pears on it and a pear tree did not have to have cherries on it. Her grandfather often then said. And not yet.

Then there was an old woman who was no relation and she told her that she Jenny would come to be so much older that not anybody could be older, although, said the old woman, there was one who was older.

This old woman once told her that Jenny's great aunt had had something happen to her oh many years ago, it was a soldier, and then her great aunt had had little twins born to her, and she had quietly, they were dead then, buried them under a pear tree, and nobody knew.

Jenny did not believe the old woman, perhaps it was true perhaps the old woman had told it as it was but Jenny did not believe it, she looked at every pear tree, Jenny did, but she did not believe it.

And now Jenny was eighteen and she lived with her great aunt outside of a city, she had a dog, he was almost blind not from age but from having been born so, and Jenny called him Love, she liked to call him, naturally she did and he liked to come even without her calling him.

It was dark in the morning any morning but since her dog Love was blind it did not make any difference to him.

It is true he was born blind nice dogs often are.

And so Jenny lived with her great aunt. Jenny always talked not very much but she did always talk unless she was alone and she was never alone not even when she was waiting. She always had her dog and though he was blind naturally she could always talk to him.

One day she said listen Love,[7] but listen to everything and listen while I tell you something.

Yes Love, she said to him, you have always had me and I am your little mother yes I am Love, and now you are going to have an aunt, yes you are Love, I am going to have a twin yes I am Love, I am tired of being just one I am going to have a twin and one of us then can go out and one of us can stay in, yes Love yes I am yes I am going to have a twin. You know Love I am like that when I have to have it I have to have it, and I have to have a twin, yes Love.

The house that Jenny lived in was a little on top of a hill, it was not a very pretty house but it was quite a nice one and there was a big field next to it and trees at either end of the field and a path at one side of it and not very many flowers ever because the trees and the grass took up so very much room but there was a good deal of space to fill with Jenny and her dog Love and anybody could understand that she really did want to have a twin. (YCAL 26.534)

Note Stein's revision of the paragraph about the great aunt's twins: it now includes a clarifying aside, "they were dead then." This aside lessens some of the ambiguity surrounding the great aunt's past that was in the earlier draft. The twins were stillborn and there was no infanticide. Stein's revisions did not always clarify what she had written in an earlier draft, but here is one example.

The multitude of references and allusions to twins in this opening chapter is suggestive of the larger narrative trajectory. In this stage, Stein is working even more overtly on a romance novel, wherein Jenny will find Arthur and ostensibly become one with him. Stein gives to the romance of lovers as twins a dark frame, however. She is thinking about older (grandfathers and great aunts) and younger (teenage girls) generations and the absence of a middle adult generation. The references to birth are antisentimental, with stillborn twins and Love the dog being blind from birth, not from age as would be more natural. Indeed, as we read above, "[i]t was dark in the morning."

Readers of *Ida* will recognize this opening chapter as similar to the finished text, albeit with further additions and rearrangement. For one thing, while *Ida* opens with Ida's birth, and a few paragraphs later we learn that her parents "went off on a trip and never came back," in "Arthur And Jenny" we wait until the second section of Chapter I (on page 19) for Jenny's birth and orphanhood (Figure 5).

Here is one more substantial transcription from "Arthur And Jenny" (numbered 100–134 in the 178-sheet sequence) for readers to compare with *Ida*:

Chapter III
Sight Unseen.

> Arthur knew that Jenny was a name of a woman. He knew that and it made him nervous. She knew it was a name of a twin. What was the other twin's name. She thought and she thought and she

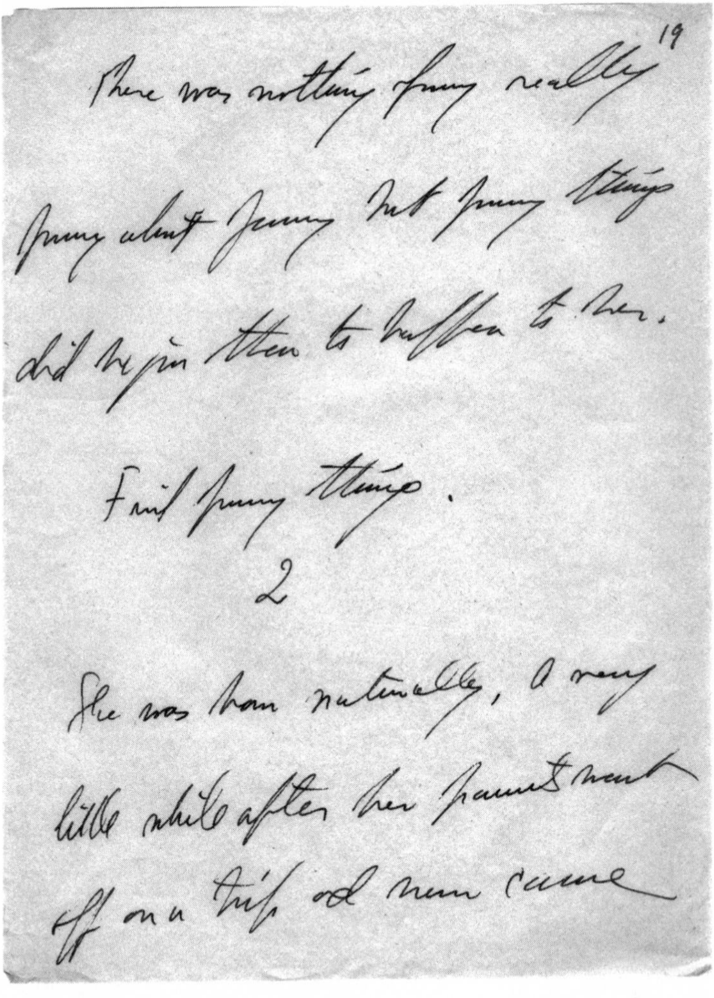

19

There was nothing funny really
funny about Jenny but funny things
did begin then to happen to her.

First funny thing.

2

She was born naturally, a very
little while after her parents went
off on a trip and never came

*Figure 5:* "There was nothing funny really funny about Jenny but funny things did begin then to happen to her. / First funny thing. / 2 / She was born naturally, a very little while after her parents went off on a trip and never came [back. That was the first funny thing that happened to her]" (YCAL 26.534).

finally decided it would be Winnie which is short for Winnifred, Jenny and Winnie would go very well together.

## Chapter IV

Arthur never did fish in the river he slept too often under a bridge to care anything about going fishing but he did one evening meet a man who had been fishing, they talked a little and the man said that he was not much good at it, he was a[w]kward at fishing, he saw the fish but he never could catch them. Finally he said to Arthur do you know who I am. No said Arthur, well said the man ~~I am~~ taking off his hat, I am chief of police, well why can't you catch fish, said Arthur. Well I caught a trout the other day and he got away from me. Why didn't you take his number said Arthur, because fish can't talk was the answer.

Well anyway Arthur went on and it made him be what he was and then one day little by little he went back to the country he had come from, right in the middle of it, and things began to happen. Everybody began to know who he was, he did not have to take his hat off and tell them like the chief of police when he was fishing, everybody knew who Arthur was without even looking. That is what happened to him. And this is the way it was.

## Chapter [V].

Jenny often wrote letters to herself that is to say she did not write to herself she wrote to her twin she wrote to Winnie, here is one of them.

Dear dear Winnie

Here I am sitting alone not alone because I have dear Love with me and I speak to him and he speaks to me but here I am all alone and I am thinking of you Winnie dear twin. Are you beautiful as beautiful as I am dear twin Winnie are you and if you are perhaps I am not perhaps you are but do you know what I think Winnie, I cannot go away I am here always here I am always somewhere and just now I am always here, I am like that, I am always here, but you dear Winnie, you are not, if you were I could not write to you not if you were here but you are not and do you know Winnie what I think, I think you could be queen of beauty one of those they elect everybody votes for them and they are elected and they go everywhere and everybody looks and everybody sees them, dear Winnie do dear Winnie do do be one, be an elected queen of beauty and everybody will know you are one, do not let them know you have any name but Winnie and I know Winnie will win, Winnie Winnie Winnie,

from your twin
Jenny.

If you know that nobody knows then you know that she knows, sang Jenny and it was a pretty tune, and she sang it again. And then she suddenly said I am a twin and I begin.

She sat silently looking at her dog Love and playing the piano softly until the light was dim and then she was Winnie. Winnie was there and Winnie was the kind that never did care where she was so Winnie went out, first locking the door she went out and as she went out she knew she was a beauty and that they would all vote for her. First she had to find the place where they were going to vote, but that did not make any difference, anywhere would do they would vote for her just anywhere, she was such a beauty they just had to and so they would too and really and truly they did. They voted that she was a great beauty and the most beautiful and the completest beauty and she was for that year the winner of the beauty prize for all the world. Just like that it did happen, Winnie was her name and she had won.

Nobody [knew] anything about her except that she was Winnie but that was enough because she was Winnie the beauty.

As she came out from winning she saw a woman [carrying] a large bundle of linen and this woman stopped and she was looking at a photograph, Winnie stopped too and it was astonishing, the woman was looking at the photograph she had it in her hand of Jenny's dog Love. That was astonishing.

Winnie was so surprised she tried to snatch the photograph and just then an automobile came along there were two women in it and the automobile stopped and they stept out to see what was happening, Winnie snatched the photograph from the woman, she was busy looking at the automobile and Winnie jumped into the automobile and tried to start it, the two women jumped into the automobile threw Winnie out and went off with the photograph and left Winnie there with the woman and the big bundle of linen, and the two of them just stood and said never a word.

Winnie went away, she was a beauty and she had the prize but she was bewildered and then she saw a package one of the women in the automobile must have dropped it and Winnie picked it up and went away. Why not.

Winnie was a beauty and she had been elected as the most beautiful woman and what if Jenny did sing, if you know that nobody knows then you know that she knows. It is a pretty song.

So then Winnie did everything an elected beauty does, but every now [and] then she was lost, and once when she was lost she saw again the woman with a big package of linen and she was talking to a man and Winnie came up to them and there they stood and just then an automobile with two women came past, and in the automobile was Jenny's dog Love, Winnie was sure it was Love, of course it was Love, and in its mouth it had the package that Winnie had picked up when the others had dropped it. There it all was and the woman with the package of linen and the man and Winnie they all just stood and looked and their mouths were open and they did not say anything and the man's name was Arthur, but Winnie did not know that then.

Winnie went on living her quiet life with her great aunt, there where they lived just outside of a city, she and her dog Love and her piano, she did write letters very often to her twin Winnie.

Winnie was coming to be known to be Winnie.

Winnie Winnie is what they said when they saw her and they were coming to see her.

They said it different ways they said Winnie, and then they said Winnie. She knew.

It is easy to make everybody say, Winnie, there goes Winnie, of course Winnie, yes Winnie. Sure I know Winnie, everybody knows Winnie, it is not so easy but there it is everybody did begin to notice that Winnie was Winnie.

This quite excited Jenny who was at home and she wrote these letters to Winnie.

Dear Winnie,

When everybody knows who you are then I know who you are, that is it I am a twin and her name is Winnie, never again will I not be a twin and her name not be Winny,

always

Jenny.

Winnie never said she was a twin she just said she was Winnie, naturally not, if she did they would know about Jenny and Jenny

> was living so quietly staying at home so quietly with her great aunt, of course Winnie never said she was a twin, of course not.
>
> So many things happened to Winnie. Why not when everybody knew her name. They were coming from everywhere to see that she was Winnie.
>
> Once there were two people who met together. They said what shall we do. Oh yes they said it is not easy but what they said what shall we do.
>
> So what did they do.
>
> They went to see Winnie that is to look at Winnie.
>
> When they looked at her they almost began to cry, and they talked together and they could not decide what to do.
>
> One said
>
> What if I did not do it and the other said well that is just the way I feel about it.
>
> After a while they began to think that it was done that they had seen Winnie, that they had looked at her but really had they.
>
> Perhaps Winnie was Jenny, they never had heard of Jenny of course not. All who came to see Winnie went away.
>
> But Winnie was never alone because there were always others coming and it was a surprise to them to have come. Like it or not they go on.
>
> But really was Winnie so interesting. They just all talked about that. (YCAL 26.534)

The most obvious difference from the first stage is, of course, as the title states, the second's shared focus on two characters. Of the opening ten chapters, three are on Jenny, three are on the two together, and four are on Arthur. However, emphasis on this obvious change would be misleading. As we saw in the first-stage manuscripts,

Stein had connected Ida with certain men before—behind Arthur are Woodward and Harold—and moreover, Arthur has much in common with Jenny. For one thing, he too desires a twin: "He had a funny idea that the only way that he could get away from where he was was if he were two, it was a time when naturally anybody thought of themselves as two. Jenny did and he did" (YCAL 26.535). Above all, while Arthur anxiously awaits a fame he believes will one day be his, a fame that comes easily to Jenny, they are both reluctant and uncertain participants in their world. In other words, Stein transformed the Ida character from the first stage by splitting her into Jenny and Arthur. Here are three Arthur passages (not used again) that echo the charming awkwardness of Jenny:

> [Arthur is in a pasture where he meets some people who ask his name. Arthur, he answers.]
>
> Oh yes said the man I know that name first name or last name.
>
> Either or both says Arthur, and then he turns his back to them and stands still.
>
> They all know what he wanted, he wanted to sit down. So they all sat down. (YCAL 26.536)

> Arthur really had adventures. He was in a saloon and there there were two men sitting one playing the mandolin and one a guitar. Arthur thought he would sing with them. No said the saloon keeper, they are playing there quite quietly. Don't sing.
>
> Arthur hesitated a moment and then he did not sing.
>
> Arthur always had adventures. (YCAL 26.536)

> Arthur when he is all alone hears the rain fall.
>
> He never talks to himself.
>
> He looks as if he was silent.

> As you look at him you wonder is he sad.
>
> Pretty soon he face lights up and he lies down.
>
> Just then the earth has a little tremor in it, not an earthquake but a kind of meeting of sun and the sun setting. (YCAL 26.536)[8]

For the finished version of *Ida*, Stein cuts Arthur's role considerably: no longer a romantic soul mate for Ida, he is just one husband among many. In *Ida* we are told that before Arthur met Ida, he grew up in the middle of a big country, learned about shepherds' dogs and climbing, went away and was shipwrecked, was homeless and listened to anybody, wished on a star, wondered if he was to be rich or a king, and became an army officer (see 26). As unusual as Arthur's life episodes might be in their telling, they depict someone inhabiting the world with a masculine sense of entitlement. The one shard of Arthur's former, uncertain self appears in a scene of emotional breakdown, where he digs "his palms into the ground." Stein ultimately uses other aspects of that former self for the Ida character: when Ida "sat down on a hillside" with two brothers, for example, an action that had first been Arthur's (see YCAL 27.537).[9] So as much as Jenny is behind the Ida we see in the finished novel, Arthur is too.

Unlike the first stage, this second one includes typescript—Stein felt satisfied with the progress she had made with "Arthur And Jenny." Toklas first typed 165 sheets of the 178-sheet sequence and some of the fifty-seven-sheet sequence, which we can call Typescript A (twenty-five sheets altogether). Working with Toklas and seeing the narrative come into "print" nurtured the writing process as Stein then used the back of this typescript as draft paper for the forty-five-sheet sequence. The final part of the second stage involves more typescript and Stein's handwritten additions. Toklas made another copy of the first 165 sheets, on which Stein made changes (Typescript B). Stein then drafted ten more sheets. Next, Toklas made two copies (C1 and C2) of B that incorporated Stein's changes and the ten new sheets, and included all of the fifty-seven-sheet sequence (to make thirty-two typescript sheets altogether). On C1 and C2 Stein then made minor but different (on each copy) changes.[10] The forty-five-sheet manuscript sequence does not appear in typescript form.

We see in this final, typescript part of the second stage the beginnings of the third stage, which involved a return to the first stage. Stein plays with Helen as an alternative to Jenny (Figure 6),

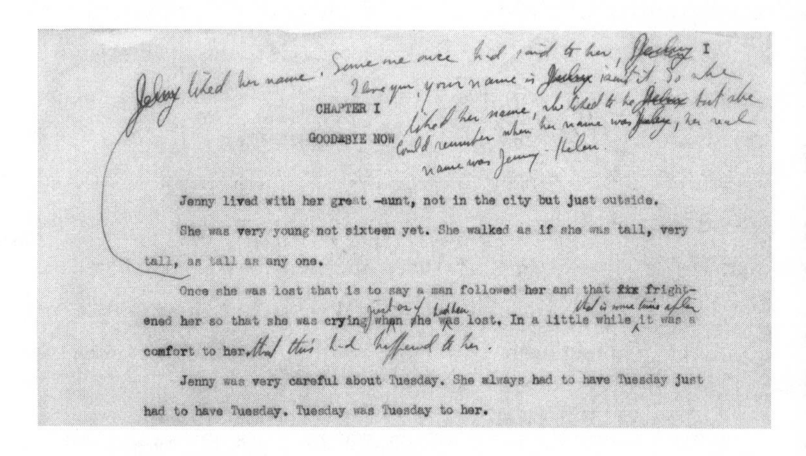

CHAPTER I

GOODBYE NOW

Jenny lived with her great -aunt, not in the city but just outside.

She was very young not sixteen yet. She walked as if she was tall, very tall, as tall as any one.

Once she was lost that is to say a man followed her and that ~~fix~~ frightened her so that she was crying when she was lost. In a little while it was a comfort to her.

Jenny was very careful about Tuesday. She always had to have Tuesday just had to have Tuesday. Tuesday was Tuesday to her.

*Figure 6:* "<Jenny ~~Helen~~ liked her name. Some one once had said to her, Jenny Helen I love you, your name is Jenny ~~Helen~~ isn't it. So she liked her name, she liked to be Jenny ~~Helen~~ but she could remember when her name was Jenny ~~Helen~~, her real name was Jenny-Helen.> / Once she was lost that is to say a man followed her and that frightened her so that she was crying ~~when~~ <just as if> she ~~was~~ <had been> lost. In a little while <that is some time after> it was a comfort to her <that this had happened to her>" (YCAL 27.540[b]). Stein copied this passage from three loose sheets that have been filed in the "Helen Button" material (YCAL 25.493), turning "Helen" into "Jenny."

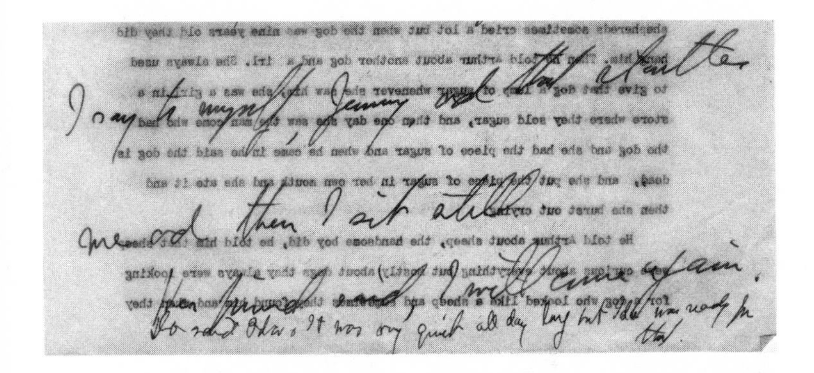

*Figure 7:* Stein shifts from Jenny to Ida: "I say to myself, Jenny, and that startles me and then I sit still. / Her friend said, I will come again. / Do said Ida. It was very quiet all day long but Ida was ready for that" (YCAL 27.537).

and then starts to bring back Ida (Figure 7). Helen and Jenny (or Guinevere) were legendary adulterers, Helen with Paris (cuckolding Menelaus) and Guinevere with Lancelot (cuckolding Arthur), and thus comparable to the already legendary Wallis Simpson, whom the Ida character was based on and who was married when she began her affair with the prince who would become King Edward VIII. However, Stein eventually rejected being obvious with historical comparisons.

This juxtaposition of Jenny and Ida appears in the forty-five-sheet sequence, and such confusion may have rendered it ineligible for typing. The first stage—the Ida stage—was reasserting its presence. Before Stein could give more manuscript to Toklas, the narrative would have to be completely rewritten.

**1939–1940**

After the palimpsestic nature of the first two stages, the last two are relatively straightforward to describe. Stein sat down with the

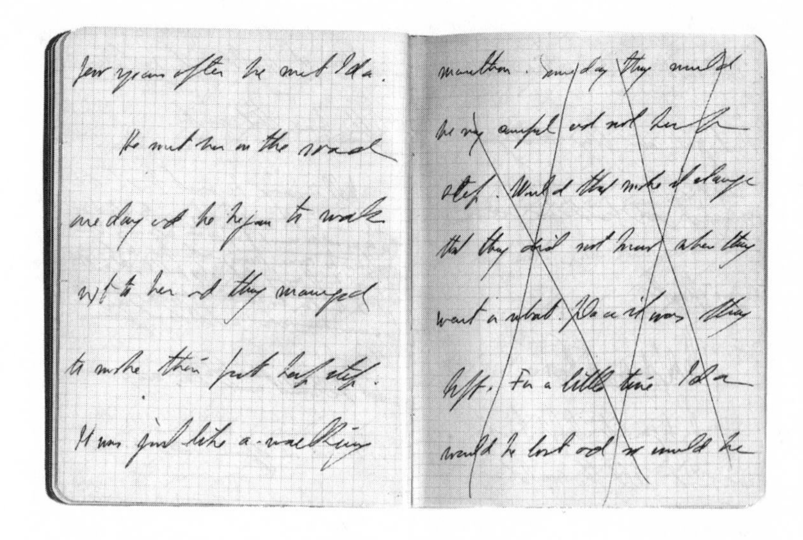

*Figure 8:* "[He became an officer and some] few years after he met Ida. / He met her on the road one day and he began to walk next to her and they managed to make their feet keep step. It was just like a walking marathon. ~~Someday they would be very careful and not keep step. Would that make it strange that they did not know when they went or what place it was they left. For a little time Ida would be lost and so would he~~" (YCAL 27.543).

manuscripts and typescripts of the previous two and a half years and set to work on a new version. She used two notebooks for this third stage.[11] After reading through the various texts that Stein left for us of the first two stages, opening these notebooks gives a shock: they offer a viable copy-text for the published novel.[12] The first one opens, "There was a baby named Ida," and goes on as *Ida* does. Stein was still testing ideas—writing, for instance, "[Ida] went to stay by the sea" and then crossing the line out. An entire page might be drafted and then canceled (Figure 8). This new version of the narrative would therefore not reach its final form until Toklas typed a copy.

At this point, early in 1940, Stein sent a typescript of the narrative to her publisher, Bennett Cerf, telling him that the novel was "about half or three quarters done." In his reply he praised the novel ("I have fallen in love with Ida and can't wait to hear the end of her adventures") and recommended that she "write just about as much more to finish the book" (see "Selected Letters"). So by April 1940 an agreement between Stein and her publisher had been reached: *Ida* was half done. Although what she wrote next was not, in the end, as long as what she produced in this third stage, Stein honored the agreement with Cerf by structuring the novel in two parts, First Half and Second Half.

And overall, Stein kept the commercially oriented expectations of Cerf in mind as she wrote this third-stage version. While she made the narrative less referential by cutting episodes involving 1930s nationalism, the Spanish Civil War, and the unemployed, itinerant men of the Depression, references that in Cerf's eyes might have given the book a greater marketability, Stein also made the narrative more linear—opening the novel with Ida's birth and following her into middle adulthood—and clarified some ambiguous phrasing.[13] As well, she normalized some of the punctuation. For example, a second-stage manuscript reads,

> If I am an officer said the officer to Jenny I give orders, would you he said looking at Jenny would you like to see me giving orders. Jenny looked at him and did not answer. If I were to give orders

> and everybody obeyed me and they do said the officer would that impress you. Jenny looked at him she looked at him and the officer felt that she must like him otherwise she would not look at him and so he said to her you do like me or else you would not look at me. But Jenny sighed she said yes and no, you see said Jenny I do look at you, but that is not enough. (YCAL 26.536)

The same passage in the third stage reads,

> If I am an officer, said an officer to Ida, and I am an officer. I am an officer and I give orders. Would you, he said looking at Ida. Would you like to see me giving orders. Ida looked at him and did not answer. If I were to give orders and everybody obeyed me and they do, said the officer, would that impress you. Ida looked at him, she looked at him and the officer felt that she must like him, otherwise she would not look at him and so he said to her, you do like me or else you would not look at me. But Ida sighed. She said, yes and no. You see, said Ida, I do look at you but that is not enough. (YCAL 27.543)

Most dramatically, Stein developed a chapter structure to reflect the changes in Ida's intimate life. In the first stage of composition Stein had broken the narrative into dozens of brief chapters, with titles that, for an air of continuity, repeated the previous chapter's final words—"A plan," "Sight unseen," "Now and then." The second-stage draft was in twenty chapters, but there was still some staccato rhythm.[14] The six-part structure that Stein devised in this third stage brings significant continuity to the narrative, as it basically corresponds to Ida's six primary relationships, starting with her dog Love and her twin Winnie and then moving through her five marriages.

## 1940

In April 1940 Stein wrote to Thornton Wilder and Carl Van Vechten about *Ida*. To Wilder she said, "I sent Bennett Cerf the first half of Ida and he liked it, so I am finishing it for him." To Van Vechten she noted what we have seen here, that "I have written it over almost three times completely" (see "Selected Letters").[15] In the fourth stage of composition, Stein wrote the Second Half (in eight parts) using thirty sheets and five slim (thirty- and fifty-sheet) notebooks, the last two being clean copies of Parts Six

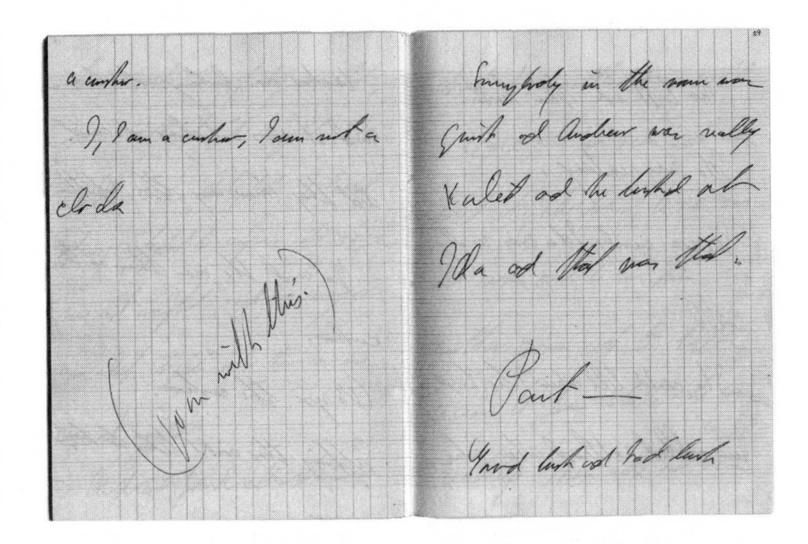
a cuckoo.
I, I am a cuckoo, I am not a
clock
(go on with this.)
Everybody in the room was
quiet and Andrew was really
excited and he looked at
Ida and that was that.
Part—
Good luck and bad luck

*Figure 9:* Stein's note to Toklas, "go on with this," refers to the rest of the superstitions episode on separate sheets: "[Supposing they could listen to] a cuckoo. / I, I am a cuckoo, I am not a clock / (go on with this.) / Everybody in the room was quiet and Andrew was really excited and he looked at Ida and that was that. / Part— / Good luck and bad luck" (YCAL 27.548).

through Eight.[16] The narrative in the first three notebooks follows a devious route, moving from one to another as she incorporated two previously written texts ("My Life With Dogs" and "Les Superstitions"). Stein was working intensively: she had Cerf's interest in publishing *Ida* by the fall, and with the German attack on France, which was frightening to her, people were fleeing and she could not know with certainty how much writing time she would

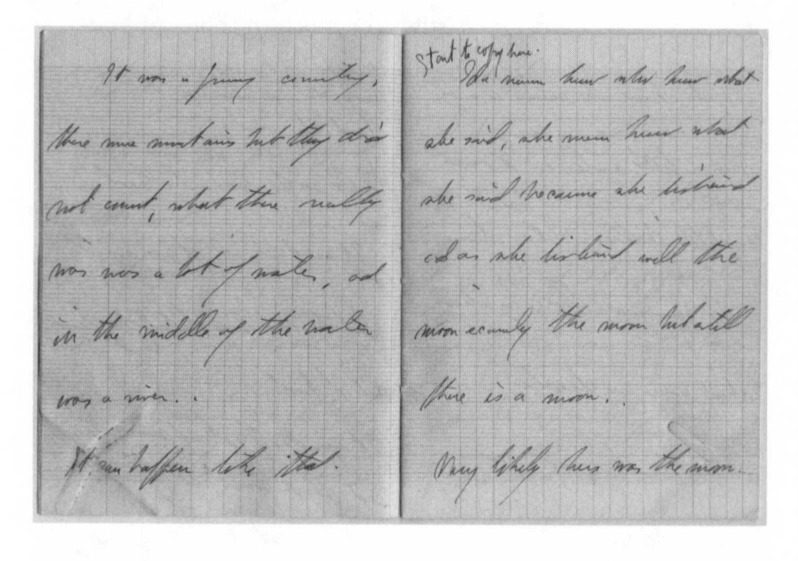
It was a funny country, there were mountains but they did not mount, what there really was was a lot of water, and in the middle of the water was a river.

It can happen like that.

Start to copy here.
Ida never knew who knew what she said, she never knew what she said because she listened and as she listened well the moon scarcely the moon but still there is a moon.

Very likely hers was the moon.

*Figure 10:* This notebook contains some passages for *To Do: A Book Of Alphabets And Birthdays*, and Stein directs Toklas where to begin copying for the *Ida* typescript: "[from *To Do*] It was a funny country, there were mountains but they did not mount, what there really was was a lot of water, and in the middle of the water was a river. / It can happen like that. [end of *To Do*] / Start to copy here. / Ida never knew who knew what she said, she never knew what she said because she listened and as she listened well the moon scarcely the moon but still there is a moon. / Very likely hers was the moon" (YCAL 27.549).

have. In the third stage, Stein had added this sentence: "(Think of all the refugees there are in the world just think)."[17]

The Second Half opens with Ida in winter, walking with her dog in the moonlight.[18] After a few pages in this first notebook, the narrative breaks away to a history of Ida's "life with dogs" in the second notebook.[19] The first notebook remains a home base for Parts One through Five, and in any case, because these notebooks provide clean copies for *Ida*, the only complication is knowing which notebook contains what part of the narrative. For Toklas, accustomed to Stein's manuscript habits, sorting heads from tails would not have been too difficult, although Stein added a couple of messages—"go on with this" (Figure 9) and "Start to copy here" (Figure 10)—to help Toklas as she finished typing the novel.

Likewise, the *Ida* manuscripts as a whole are Stein's handwritten message to us about her intertextual practices in the years after *The Autobiography Of Alice B. Toklas*, when she worked to regain her identity as someone who published "writing that has to do with writing." For two and half years (from May 1937 to winter 1939–1940) we see her telling herself to "go on with this," and in the fourth stage especially she is highlighting her composite, "copy here" method. While Stein worked to produce what the general reader (represented by Cerf) would recognize as a novel, she was also focused on the creative process and keeping a comprehensive record of that process. Showing us (and showing herself) how she worked—writing, copying, revising, rearranging, and incorporating—was as important as what she brought into print.

# Mrs. Simpson

> Gertrude Stein has completed the first forty pages of a new novel to be called "Ida" and has forwarded the manuscript to her publisher, Random House. The book is written in Miss Stein's usual cryptic style. The editors of Random House wrote to the author and asked her: "Do you think that a novel called 'Ida' by Gertrude Stein is just what the world needs right now?" Miss Stein, who is able to write good English when she really wishes to be understood, replied: "My novel, 'Ida,' could not be more timely. It is all about the Duchess of Windsor."
>
> —Source unknown, early 1940? (YCAL 28.553)

Despite newspaper articles such as the one above and Stein's comments in letters—made as she began the novel and again as she finished it—that *Ida* was based on the Duchess of Windsor, as well as the fact that Stein had a copy of *Ida* sent to the duchess, critics have made no more than passing reference to Ida's real-life twin. Knowing this context for the Ida character should not necessarily lead to the referential fallacy, in which knowing the referent definitively explains the text. Even reviewers of the novel in 1941—on the spot, historically speaking—did not see much evidence to support a one-to-one correspondence, and while this section presents the missing evidence, as it were, the aim is to promote informed readings of the novel, not definitive ones.

An informed reading, to give one example, avoids the kind of speculation that Carolyn Copeland offered in her gloss on the novel's opening: "There was a baby born named Ida. Its mother held it with her hands to keep Ida from being born but when the time came Ida came." Copeland argues, "This must be a dream [. . .] because most women in labor—far from trying to prevent the birth—would do anything to get it over with" (150). This is logical enough, but as Stein apparently knew, the duchess had been born prematurely, and a woman experiencing a premature birth may well wish to stall it. In her autobiography, *The Heart Has Its Reasons* (1956), the duchess described her beginning this way: "I started to struggle toward light and life somewhat in advance of calculations" (*HHR* 3).[1] Even if, as some biographers have argued, this tale of premature birth was a cover for sex before marriage, it still makes sense of Ida's mother's behavior. This moment of shared experience between Ida and the duchess is the first of many, which confirms that Stein was being fairly serious when she claimed that *Ida* was "all about the Duchess of Windsor."

The duchess was born Bessie Wallis Warfield on June 19, 1896, and grew up in Baltimore. *Time* magazine offered this summary when it made her "Woman of the Year" for 1936: "Her life up to

[. . .] meeting with Edward VIII was inconsequential to a degree [. . .]. She was born to one of those typical Southern families who all more or less descend from William the Conqueror, but Wallis Warfield was not going to spend her life talking about her family. She resolved early to make men her career, and in 40 years reached the top—or almost" (WY 16). The reason for "almost" was very familiar to readers by then. On December 10, 1936, the King of England, who had inherited the throne on January 20, 1936, when his father died, abdicated to be with the woman he loved, Mrs. Wallis Simpson, who had filed for divorce from her second husband on October 27. Even the king's proposal that their marriage be morganatic (she would be a wife but not queen) was considered politically unacceptable. Forced by the prime minister, Stanley Baldwin, to choose either the throne or Wallis, either his public or private life, on December 12 the king stepped down and became the Duke of Windsor.[2] Wallis's divorce entailed a six-month interregnum between marriages, and she lived out that time near Cannes, while the duke retired to Austria. The couple had just been reunited when Stein began *Ida* in May 1937, and they married on June 3.

*Time* hailed Mrs. Simpson's fame and the abdication as evidence that America was becoming the world's dominant power:

> In the single year 1936 she became the most-talked-about, written-about, headlined and interest-compelling person in the world. In these respects no woman in history has ever equaled Mrs. Simpson, for no press or radio existed to spread the world news they made.
>
> In England the news that the King, as King, wanted to marry Mrs. Simpson was the final culmination of a tide of events sweeping the United Kingdom out of its cozy past and into a more or less hectic and "American" future. (WY 14)

A British king had sided with an American divorcée over the throne! The "cozy past" had no inhabitants! While this patriotic interpretation was overreaching, freedom of choice had trumped tradition. The couple chose each other, and for their home-in-exile they chose France, maintaining residences in Paris and Cannes—a parallel to Stein's residences in Paris and Bilignin.

Stein was in England in February 1936 and in April 1937, but she hardly needed to visit England in person to hear the gossip. As the *Time* article noted, Wallis was the most "headlined" person in the world. Stein was also friends with two socialites, Daisy Fellowes and Lady Sibyl Colefax, who would have known every scandalous detail.[3] (In her autobiography, the duchess mentions seeing both Fellowes and Colefax over the Christmas 1936 holidays.) Stein's familiarity with the infamous Mrs. Simpson was thus well established when, in early spring 1937, she wrote in *Everybody's Autobiography* that recently "everybody cheered up because of course there was Mrs. Simpson. Everybody needs being excited by the story of Mrs. Simpson at least once a year, it cheered up the gloom of organization, and the difference between sovietism and fascism and new deal and sit-down striking. [. . .] Well organization has its gloom and the only thing for a long time that really cut that gloom was Mrs. Simpson and King Edward and the abdication" (*EA* 319–320).[4]

Stein must have recalled her years as a Johns Hopkins University medical student (1897–1901) and wondered whether she had encountered little Wallis, the only child of a single parent, on the Baltimore streets. (Wallis's father died of tuberculosis when she was five months old.) Until Wallis moved from Baltimore in 1917, she lived in the same neighborhood that Stein had, and during the four years of overlap they were only a couple of blocks apart.

As well, not long after Stein left, Wallis and her mother moved to 212 E. Biddle Street; Stein had lived at 215 E. Biddle. At that time she was called Bessiewallis, according to the southern custom of running a girl's first two names together; as a young woman she dropped "Bessie" because of its cow association, she said. Wallis had been her father's middle name. Growing up she was taught to appreciate her dual nature, as a Warfield (stern and industrious) of Maryland and a Montague (witty and handsome) of Virginia. Names were significant.

Wallis Warfield and her Montague mother, Alice, relied on family support. First they lived with Grandmother and Uncle Sol Warfield, then with the widow Aunt Bessie Merryman, Alice's older sister, then for a few years they lived independently, with Alice providing meals to local tenants. Wallis then acquired a stepfather. (He died in 1913, and in 1927 her mother became thrice married.) Despite all the moving around, she "passed a happy childhood" (*HHR* 11). She attended excellent schools, yet "not a single girl from [her] class at Oldfields went to college" (*HHR* 36). Her education was designed for marriage, her first coming when she was twenty: while visiting a cousin of her mother's in Florida, she met Earl Winfield ("Win") Spencer, "the Navy's twentieth pilot to earn his wings," and they married in November 1916 (*HHR* 49). Win trained fighter pilots for the war, first in Boston and then San Diego, where they lived until 1921, by which point the marriage had come apart. For a number of years they lived separately with brief reunions determined by Win's naval stationing. Through much of the 1920s Wallis was primarily in Washington, DC, or the DC area, with time also in Paris, Hong Kong, Shanghai, Peking, and Seattle. It was in Peking that she first stayed with Katherine and Herman Rogers, who would shelter her in Cannes after the abdication crisis. In *Ida* we read, "Edith and William were the married couple with whom Ida was staying."

Also stated in *Ida*, describing Ida's time in Washington: "There are so many men." In Wallis's autobiography that bland fact receives elaboration. "[I]t is remarkable how many 'men Friday' will emerge from the underbrush to help a lonely woman," she notes. There was "good company in the Washington of the early 1920s, perhaps the most charming, exciting, and cosmopolitan company to be found in the United States" (*HHR* 82). Wallis did attempt an independent career, however. First she applied to write for a New York fashion magazine, and later she went to Pittsburgh to train as a salesperson for a metal scaffolding company. *Ida*: "So Ida decided to earn a living. She did not have to, she never had to but she decided to do it. / [. . .] She thought it was best to begin with one way which would be most easy to leave. So she tried photography and then she tried just talking. [. . .] Ida never starved." While visiting New York friends, Wallis met Ernest Simpson, who was also currently married. Consulting an astrologer she learned that she would have two more marriages and "become a famous woman" through "power [. . .] related to a man" (*HHR* 119). A second marriage would help her reach the third, so Wallis and Ernest divorced their respective spouses and by summer 1928 they were Mr. and Mrs. Simpson in London, England. (Although born and raised in America, Ernest had become a British citizen.) By 1930, despite the economic depression, Ernest's shipping business was prosperous enough to support a lifestyle of country-house weekends and snappy fashions. *Ida*: "There they lived almost as if Ida had not been Ida and Gerald Seaton had married any woman."

Wallis met the Prince of Wales, David Windsor, in 1931, and a year later she visited his private residence, Fort Belvedere. Their romance began in earnest in 1934: he wooed her with jewels and a cairn terrier named Slipper. Above all David's appeal for Wallis lay in his status—she could admit the obvious: "Over and beyond the charm of his personality and the warmth of his manner, he was the open sesame to a new and glittering world that excited me as nothing in my life had ever done before. [. . .] His slightest wish seemed always to be translated instantly into the most impressive kind of reality" (*HHR* 192). *The Heart Has Its Reasons* is an interesting autobiography in part because of its famously unlikely story, but also because of this frankness of expression. Wallis Simpson was excited to be inside the castle walls, yet her feet still found solid ground. Still, by the years 1936–1940, nothing was certain in the glare of flashbulbs, the prison of exile, and the onset of war.

In the novel, Ida's primary action, especially as an adult, is to rest; that is what readers have invariably noticed. Yet the first time we see Ida at rest she says, "I like to be moving." Reading Ida in the context of Wallis clarifies this seeming contradiction. To rest was all Wallis had to do because from December 1936 on, she lived under various restrictions. Moreover, this condition was not new to her. As Win Spencer's wife she moved from naval station to naval station, and then twice she established a "residence" in order to divorce: for over two years in Warrenton, Virginia, and again in Felixstowe, England (the first because divorces were cheaper in Virginia than elsewhere, and the second to ensure divorce-court proceedings would be held outside London). Whether waiting for the next naval assignment or for divorce, Wallis knew the experience of "resting": the temporary stay. Then she had to flee England for Cannes and wait months before seeing David again.[5] This was followed by a royal ban on their visiting England; they did not return until September 1939, when Britain rallied for war (Figure

*Figure 11:* The Duke and Duchess of Windsor in September 1939, in Ashdown Forest, Sussex, England (Keystone / Hulton Archive / Getty Images).

11). Then came more waiting in Paris during the "Phony War" of 1939–1940.[6] In June 1940, after Germany had finally attacked Paris, they fled, and Wallis would say of that time, "David and I were more or less back where we were in December, 1936—certainly homeless, once more adrift in a strange country, our possessions scattered, David without a post" (*HHR* 329).[7]

Wallis excelled, however, at finding room to move within limits, and this refined ability drew David to her. He had suffered within the strict expectations of his titles, as the Prince of Wales and then King Edward VIII. Wallis did puzzle over David's attraction to her:

> I certainly was no beauty, and [. . .] no longer very young. [. . .]
>
> The only reason to which I could ascribe his interest in me, such as it was, was perhaps my American independence of spirit, my directness, what I would like to think is a sense of humor and of fun, and, well, my breezy curiosity about him and everything concerning him. [. . .] Then, too, he was lonely, and perhaps I had been one of the first to penetrate the heart of his inner loneliness, his sense of separateness. (*HHR* 191–192)

Her reading of their early romance sets the stage for an explanation of the abdication. In May 1936 he privately stated his intention to marry her: "As a Prince his loneliness could be assuaged by passing companionships. But as King he was discovering that his loneliness was now absolute [. . .]. It was my fate to be the object of his affection at the crucial moment of his decision" (*HHR* 216–217). The irony of the situation could not have been more stark. The lonely king was forced to abdicate and then separate from his beloved; at the same time, with their romance "a topic of dinner-table conversation for every newspaper reader in the United

States, Europe, and the Dominions," Wallis was losing that "sense of humor and of fun" (*HHR* 227).

"It was by now almost impossible for me to get about the streets without strangers turning to stare. [...] I began to feel like a hunted animal," she wrote (*HHR* 241–242). Smuggled into France under a false name, Wallis found the hunt was still on when she reached the gates of the Rogers villa: there were "several hundred reporters and photographers" howling to see her (*HHR* 261). As the weeks of separation and "resting" dragged on, her emotions turned blank: "I must have been a depressing companion. [...] it was the experience of a prolonged blankness of the mind and spirit. [...] [T]he storm that had howled around the person of 'Mrs. Simpson' had left me spent. For hours, I remained in my room, staring, I suspect, into space. At night sleep would not come" (*HHR* 277–278). She was experiencing a disassociation of self-image. Several thousand letters were delivered to her at Cannes, and most of them were hateful (for having brought dishonor to the crown). Scotland Yard would investigate death threats and offer protection. As her host Herman Rogers told her, "It's not just that you've become a celebrity; you've become a historical figure, and a controversial one. [...] Much of what is being said concerns a woman who does not exist and never did exist" (*HHR* 272). With "Mrs. Simpson" considered a monster she did not want to recognize, she was glad to receive her divorce on May 3 and live for a month as Wallis Warfield once again.

Her experience at Cannes was not unlike Ida's when she "went somewhere and there she just sat, she did not even have a dog, she did not have a town, she lived alone and just sat." Autobiography gives the writer an occasion to draw lessons, but Wallis Windsor remained candid even during such scripted moments: "In enduring this ordeal, I, who had always been impatient, learned something of the virtue of patience. [. . .] I survived at Cannes by mastering my own emotions. [. . .] I learned that one can live alone. / Perhaps, on second thought, I should modify that judgment. One can never live alone and be said really to live at all" (*HHR* 273). Bessie Wallis (Montague) Warfield Spencer Simpson Windsor and Edward Albert Christian George Andrew Patrick David Windsor were a good match; they were not unlike Ida and Andrew, who "got on so well together." When one's life is appropriated in a media storm, the temptation to cut all familiar ties or create an alternative identity, to regain self-control, can be difficult to resist. In the end, Wallis looked past such measures. As is stated in *Ida*, "You can't change everything even if everything is changed." And later,

> It is not easy to lead a different life, much of it never happens but when it does it is different.
>
> So Ida and Andrew never knew but it was true they were to lead a different life and yet again they were not.
>
> If one did the other did not, and if the other did then the other did not.
>
> And this is what happened.
>
> If they had any friends they had so many friends.
>
> They were always accompanied, Andrew when he came and went and wherever he was, Ida was not accompanied but she was never alone and when they were together they were always accompanied.
>
> This was natural enough because Andrew always had been and it was natural enough because Ida always had been.

> Men were with them and women were with them and men and women were with them.
>
> It was this that made Ida say let's talk.

Beyond what Stein knew about the duchess's life from friends and the press, she also seems uncanny in surmising its details. The act of walking is ubiquitous in *Ida*, for instance. Especially when Ida is younger, she enjoys walking in the company of a dog, and later it is Andrew who walks every day. Likewise, the newly married Duke and Duchess of Windsor "walked every day," a habit carried over from Wallis's life in Cannes, where her main activity had been to walk in the hills, and from the Château de Candé, where the wedding was held: "I gradually came alive again. [. . .] I walked a great deal" (*HRR* 291, 277, 285).[8] It was on a walk near the Château in April 1937 that the dog David had given her, Slipper, ran "afoul of a viper" and died, a "frightful omen" for their imminent wedding (HRR 286–287). Later in 1937, Stein wrote an episode in which Ida, distracted by her dog Iris, is bitten by a viper. (This episode is in the genealogy.) Critics have noted that Stein was herself bitten by a snake in October 1933 (see *LR* 563). But did Stein know that Wallis's dog had died from snake poison? Odds are, yes.

Stein paid close attention to "Mrs. Simpson" for personal reasons—they had both traveled from Baltimore to international fame—and professional ones. Throughout Stein's career, from *Q.E.D.*, based on her experience in a lesbian love triangle, to the story of her extended family in *The Making Of Americans*, and even to her more abstract compositions, her texts were made from the stuff of everyday life. Especially with *Ida*, there was faith in the notion that reality—in this case, the Duchess of Windsor's life—was stranger than fiction;

twentieth-century writers did not need to invent. Observation and following the news filled them with strange and complex stories. The media is a great storyteller. Indeed, as Stein would say in a 1946 interview, the power to *create* reality—the raison d'être of literary writers—had been siphoned off by the popular press. Whereas in the nineteenth century, when fictional characters were "more real to the average human being than the people they knew," readers in the twentieth century were more interested in the novel's formal aspects than its characters. So in the twentieth century,

> biographies have been more successful than novels. This is due in part to this enormous publicity business. The Duchess of Windsor was a more real person to the public than anyone could create. In the Nineteenth Century no one was played up like that, like the Lindbergh kidnapping really roused people's feelings. Then Eleanor Roosevelt is an actuality more than any character in the Twentieth Century novel ever achieved. [. . .] One falls back on the thing like I did in *Ida*, where you try to handle a more or less satirical picture within the individual. No individual that you can conceive can hold their own beside life. [. . .] People now know the details of important people's daily life unlike they did in the Nineteenth Century. Then the novel supplied imagination where now you have it in publicity, and this changed the whole cast of the novel. So the novel is not a living form. (*PGU* 21–22)[9]

This is a version of what Ezra Pound had argued in "A Retrospect" (1918): "Do not retell in mediocre verse what has already been done in good prose."[10] In other words, do not retell in a novel something from the popular press—its "characters" are more real than what an author could invent. The popular press trumps the fiction writer because at some point it stops reporting and begins creating (which was what so upset Wallis Simpson): competing for attention on a story, media outlets go further and further into the private lives of their subjects. And when someone appears more real in print than in person, when the copy supplants the original, she becomes a legend (which was the gist of Herman Rogers's counsel). As far as characters go, then, unless the individual novelist can endow a main character with celebrity status, she cannot outdo the collective authorship of the writing and reading public.

Stein used the inverse technique for *Ida*, borrowing from the life of a celebrity to create her main character. In doing this, Stein tested the novel genre for its continued relevance—which is just one reason *Ida* remains relevant to us now. Since the 1930s, the novel has faced ever increasing competition, from television to documentaries to social networking sites and blogs. Stein accepted that literature was just one among the many forms of media that tell stories. As she noted in the interview, however, literature has satire, a mode generally unavailable to the news media: with a straight face, it sells trivial updates on currently popular figures. My favorite moment is the narrator's report that "Ida ate no fruit," which comes after the announcement that "Ida began to be known." Was Ida's not eating fruit interesting? This is Stein's satirical take on celebrity gossip, but it is also interesting because it makes Ida, as publicity had made Wallis, "a more real person." Overall, if *Ida* plays on the line between fiction and gossip report, it does so without the naive intention of reining in public fascination with private lives. News junkies could be passionately interested in someone who rests a lot or does not eat fruit, so why not readers of fiction? With *Ida*, Stein was thinking about the stories we tell that explain our interest in one person and not another. Even famous people walk their dogs.

# Selected Letters

In Stein's correspondence with Thornton Wilder, Carl Van Vechten, and Bennett Cerf, we can track *Ida A Novel* from its beginning, when Stein wanted to collaborate with Wilder, to a decisive moment when Cerf approved publication, and on to Stein's happy relief upon receiving the book: "I am all xcited because it is a novel it really is." There are periods when *Ida* goes unmentioned, but overall these letters constitute a primary resource for dating the stages of composition. While Stein's friendship with Van Vechten went back to 1913, she did not meet Wilder or Cerf until she came to the United States for her lecture tour. As founder and president of Random House, Cerf wrote to Stein in 1933 to arrange a reprinting of *Three Lives* under his Modern Library imprint. Thereafter, Random House was Stein's main publisher, and Stein and Cerf met the day of her arrival in New York in October 1934. A month after that Stein met Wilder in Chicago. Still quite young, Wilder was already a highly regarded novelist and playwright.

So by the late 1930s, Van Vechten had offered unwavering support and love for a quarter century. Cerf was inherently a commercial publisher and wanted books from her that would sell well. He published *Everybody's Autobiography* (1937) but then refused *Doctor Faustus Lights The Lights* (1938, not published until 1949), and Stein responded by working with other publishers for *Picasso* (1938), *The World Is Round* (1939) and *Paris France* (1940). *Ida* thus marked Stein's return to the Random House list after more than three years away. About her friendship with Wilder she was passionate, and he would visit her biannually, in 1935, 1937 and 1939. During the last visit she recorded something he said: "What is important is that you are one of the rare writers in America who is not haunted by the spoken word. You write the written word and the written word speaks, the spoken word written never speaks" (YCAL 74.1356). In these three men, Stein had a steady friend, a relatively dedicated publisher, and an understanding interlocutor.

## 1937

### May 17, Bilignin

Gertrude Stein to Thornton Wilder: "[L]isten perhaps I will do a novel about you and call it Ida about you or about Mrs Simpson, I think it is time for me to write a novel, now Mrs Simpson is not a puzzle to me but you are, but I can see that she might be a puzzle to me, so perhaps I could write that novel, come, Thornton, come, I could do it so much better with you to make commentaries but now that [Everybody's] Autobiography is done I must do it, I have begun Ida, a novel" (*TW* 144).

**[June?], Bilignin**

Stein to Bennett Cerf: "I am working at a novel, it is called Ida a novel and it seems to begin well, and finishing the Daniel Webster play" (RHC).

**June 26, Bilignin**

Stein to Carl Van Vechten: "I have started a pleasing novel called Ida a novel, I think you will like it I hope it goes on and is a novel I always do want to write one" (*CVV* 553).

**July 18, Bilignin**

Stein to Wilder: "[W]ill you but you would never say no to me but will you really will you, ever since my earliest days [. . .] I have loved the word collaborate and I always always wanted to and now will you oh Thornton will you will you collaborate on Ida the Novel, we must do it together [. . .] a really truly novel is too much for me all alone we must do it together, how we will talk about it and talk about it oh dear it will be wonderful to collaborate at last, you would not say no Thornton and worse still you would not do no, just think how we could do Ida a novel together and what a theme" (*TW* 154).[1]

### July [18?], Paris

Wilder to Stein: He tells of receiving an invitation to visit the Duke and Duchess of Windsor in Austria (*TW* 155–156).[2]

### July 20, Paris

Wilder to Stein: On the idea of collaborating, he writes, "I certainly don't say *no* yet I tremble to say *yes*. / So I am thinking about it all the time" (*TW* 158).[3]

### August 28, Bilignin

Stein to Wilder: "[William and Mildred Rogers] have been and gone [. . .] and now once more I am left to Woodward and to Ida" (*TW* 163).[4]

### September 7, Bilignin

Stein to Wilder: "I am brimming with ideas [about Ida], nothing [practical?] yet but quite xcitable" (*TW* 168).

### September 9, Zurich

Wilder to Stein: "I received a long letter from Sibyl [Colefax] at Wasserleonburg—from which I send you a glittering letterhead [with the coat of arms of England]. She said she talked with [the Duke and Duchess of Windsor] from lunchtime until 2:15 in the morning; that they are completely happy: that he is abounding in vitality of mind; that between lunch and tea they joined the haymakers in the valley and that he took a scythe and cut the best swathe of them all.[5] [. . .] I keep thinking a lot about [Ida]. And especially at Salzburg where the world was composed of people who know in their bones what pure Ida-ness is and hopefully—hopelessly struggle along to attain it. Salzburg is a Walpurgisnacht of Celebrities. / But I just about despair of finding out what our Ida did, despair just in proportion as I close in more and more happily on what Ida was. . . . But as for 'plot' about Ida, I'm stuck, like a mule in a bog" (*TW* 170–171).

**September 22, Bilignin**

Stein to Wilder: "Dearest of collaborators, / Ida has started pretty nearly nearly started, there are going to be one or some from every state perhaps every country and they well they are not to get to Bay Shore and they are not to know about Ida but they are going to leave where they are, two from Utah have been very good, but the rest well anyway did you use to say shame shame fie for shame everybody knows your name well it is going to be the other way" (*TW* 178).

**[Late September], Zurich**

Wilder to Alice Toklas: "As Gertrude says: [']The world's full of plots. Your life's full of plots; my life's full of plots. Plots aren't interesting anymore'" (*TW* 181).

### September 29, Bilignin

Stein to Van Vechten: "I am writing an American novel called Ida, it begins well, but then it begins to get too funny and one must not be too funny" (*CVV* 570).

### October 4, Zurich

Wilder to Stein: Writing the plays *Our Town* and *The Merchant of Yonkers* has his full attention, and he writes, "It's too late. I dare not turn aside now, not even for Ida. Besides, she obstinately refuses to give up the secret of her 'action.' There she is: glorious as 'description' and like Aristotle's god: the mover—unmoved. / Perhaps her description is all her narration. / Perhaps just as poetry now gives way to prose; so narration gives way to description" (*TW* 182).

### October 5, Bilignin

Stein to Van Vechten: "[A]nd just what is the sadness of America and its [sweetness?] I am awfully interested in it, and trying to do it in Ida" (*CVV* 571).

### October 16, Bilignin

Stein to Wilder: "[A]nd Thornton have you by any chance on your person and could be parted from it a map of these United States I kind of need it to make Ida go on, she is going on some, but a map would help, and here there are none" (*TW* 187).

### October 20, Zurich

Wilder to Stein: "The best bookstore in Zürich is sending you a map of the greatest country in the world. Love it dearly. Someday we'll drive all over it together pointing out BEAUTIES to left and right. [. . .] I feel all funny and ants-in-my-. . . . . . . shirt to think that IDA is leaning on that glorious map and going on. If I see light on Ida, the light on Ida that I've been groping for two-and-a-half months I shall become very obstreperous and wish to share it with you" (*TW* 188).

### October 22, Bilignin

Stein to Wilder: "Thanks for the map, the big one was not right but on the back some little ones with the straight lines of the states and they are inspiring they are so good for Ida" (*TW* 190).

### October 26, Bilignin

Stein to Wilder: "[G]etting ready to go [back to Paris] and so getting ready to see you, yes Ida needs helping she goes on but any kind thought is more than welcome" (*TW* 191).

### November 3, Paris

Stein to Wilder: "[W]e forgot to talk about the ms for Yale, but we will on Thursday, I have an idea for rewriting Ida, lots of love" (*TW* 192).

**November 4, Paris**

Wilder to Stein: "So I read and reread IDA. / And often with bewitched delight; and sometimes in the dark—oh, yes, confident for *her*; but in the dark, for me. / But my incomprehensions are an old story. / I'm proud of being a slow-digester, a struggler-de-bonne-volonté and a ruminator. / Oh, Ida" (*TW* 193).

**November 11, Paris**

Stein to Wilder: "[A]nd there is lots xciting, Ida gently progressing but just now not so much" (*TW* 194).

**December 8, Paris**

Stein to Wilder: "I think I have a scheme for Ida which will pull it together, it came out of our last talk together the one about the difference between Making of Americans and Freud, I have an idea I have not yet had time to put it in order it is just commencing but in a couple of days I xpect to begin and then later we will send it to you" (*TW* 199).

**1938**

**[March?], Paris**

Stein to Wilder: "[A]nd you will do the novel yet yes we will, you know Thornton I find so many on the quays and I read them all and I begin to really know what a novel is, come Thornton come and I'll tell you" (*TW* 211).

### April 23, Tucson, Arizona

Wilder to Stein: "Is IDA A NOVEL still the chief work on the desk [?]" (*TW* 216).

### May 11, Paris

Stein to Wilder: "Ida has become an opera, and it is a beauty, really is, an opera about Faust, I am dying to show it to you, I have the first act done [. . .] some day she will be a novel too, she is getting ready for that, but as an opera she is a wonder" (*TW* 217–218).

### [June?], Bilignin

Stein to Cerf: "Here we are my opera is done and nothing else is yet begun but I have a scheme for a novel in my head a long one" (RHC).

### June [27?], Bilignin

Stein to Wilder: "[A]nd now once more I am going to do the novel Ida, I am beginning all over again just as if it never had been done" (*TW* 220).

### [July?], Bilignin

Stein to Cerf: "I have just begun a longish novel, simple and I hope will turn into an adventure story, I am now on the second chapter, Alice likes it very much, she says it is like early America" (RHC).

### July 26, Bilignin

Stein to Van Vechten: "I garden and I have started a novel that Mama Woojums [Toklas] says is early American" (*CVV* 601).[6]

### August 15, Bilignin

Stein to Van Vechten: "I am going on writing a long novel so I am busy [. . .] I have been working a lot, nobody in the house just lots of friends around, and that makes everything peaceful" (*CVV* 604).

### August [25?], Bilignin

Stein to Wilder: "[A]nd now about Faust, here it is and I think a wonderful play, and please get somebody to play it cinema stage but somewhere, it is our old friend Ida but I think completely created, and I think it would be very popular, I judge from the people who love it" (*TW* 222).

### November 25, Paris

Stein to Van Vechten: "I am afraid Bennett [Cerf] is getting solemn, he is just and sweet and kind but I think he is beginning to believe in the importance of being earnest, and alas, I seem to see its importance less rather than more" (*CVV* 616).

### December 23, New York

Van Vechten to Stein: "I see you are in the Oxford Dictionary of American Literature [with "How Writing Is Written"] & I *love* Ida!—one of my favorites" (*CVV* 619).[7]

**December 26, Paris**

Stein to Van Vechten: "[A]nd now I am going on with the great American novel which I have begun so often and under such different titles—now I have forgotten just which it is now but I think it is Jenny and Arthur, it was Ida but it is not Ida any longer" (*CVV* 620).

**1939**

**January 1, Paris**

Stein to Van Vechten: "I am once more in the throes of writing the great American novel, now it is called Jenny and Arthur" (*CVV* 621).

**January 16, New York**

Van Vechten to Stein: "Jenny & Arthur is a good name for a great American novel, & I am sure it will be. Is this going to be long?" (*CVV* 623).

**February 8, Paris**

Stein to Van Vechten: "I am going on with my novel, it goes better in the summer than in the winter, winters seem more occupying than they used to be" (*CVV* 624).

**[April?], Paris**

Stein to Cerf: "I am working on my novel, often typing it half a dozen times to seem to really have it started, and the Baby Basket is keeping us busy" (RHC).

**[July?], Bilignin**

Stein to Cerf: "My novel is getting on, it is a kind of a novel of The Duchess of Windsor in relation to publicity, I like it, it is about a third done" (RHC).

**September 18, Bilignin**

Stein to Wilder: "[W]e have now settled down to go on, Alice is type-writing Ida I am writing, Basket and Pepe are asleep the rain is raining and the fire is crackling" (*TW* 244).[8]

**[Early December], Bilignin**

Stein to Cerf: "I have just finished my book Paris, France, and now I am back to the novel, you do or at least I do always feel like writing a lot in war-time, I do wish you were doing something of mine, you know I do, well here I go to saw the family wood" (RHC).

**December 28, Bilignin**

Stein to Van Vechten: "I like wintering in the country, I had no idea there would be so much to do, and that I could walk so much as I do, the new Basket jumps and walks, but he does not care for the moon, he says it is too bright, and too unxpected" (*CVV* 661).

1940

**January 11, New York**

Cerf to Stein: "I hope that you are going to let us see both your book about Paris and the novel that you are working on. I agree with you that it is high time that a new book by you appears under the Random House imprint!" (YCAL 101.1950).

**[February?], Bilignin**

Stein to Cerf: "[T]he book Paris, France is just a short one that I have written for Batsford, sort of France and the village in wartime, and the novel, I tell you Bennett I do not know anything about that novel. I have worked at it and written it over and over again and now it is about half or three quarters done and I really do not know a thing about it, usually you know I know what I know and I put it down but this time I have worked at it until I am all bothered, it was based originally on the idea of a character like the Duchess of Windsor, what is publicity, and then it kind of is something else, well anyway I am sending you as much as is more or less done, but do not think if you and Donald [Klopfer] do not like it that I will mind, I do not know what it is like, and it might easily not be anything, I dropped it to finish the book for Batsford and now I want to know what you think, it troubles me, I always want to begin it again, I never felt like that before, well anyway there it is as much as is done, now do tell me just what you think" (RHC).

**February 28, New York**

Random House to Stein: Random House sends sales figures for two years of selling her Plain Edition books: *Matisse Picasso And Gertrude Stein*, seventeen copies sold; *How To Write*, eight copies sold; *Operas And Plays*, three copies sold; *Lucy Church Amiably*, one copy sold. Stein is due 50 percent of the total sale price, $72.50. She is also due royalties for *The Autobiography Of Alice B. Toklas* ($15.21); *Four Saints In Three Acts* ($10.00); *Three Lives* ($2.36); *Everybody's Autobiography* ($2.25); and *Portraits And Prayers* ($0.75) (YCAL 101.1950).

**March 19, New York**

Van Vechten to Stein: About the possibility of Hollywood making a movie version of *The Autobiography Of Alice B. Toklas*, Van Vechten writes, "Of course you both would have to appear in the picture. Even Greta Garbo and Lillian Gish couldn't be you and Alice. [. . .] Bennett [Cerf] says he has part of a novel by you. You haven't written me about this" (*CVV* 670).

**March 25, Bilignin**

Stein to Wilder: "Bennett Cerf sounds as if he would very much like to do a book of mine again" (*TW* 260).

**April 2, New York**

Cerf to Stein: "I am delighted that you have gotten so much of a novel written. It must be many years now since you have written a novel, and everybody who loves you and admires you will be impatient to read it. I enjoyed everything that I understood about the part that you have sent us and I really understood a lot of it, which, as you know, is a new record for me. In fact, I have fallen in love with Ida and can't wait to hear the end of her adventures. Please hurry up and finish the book. / I'm returning the part of the manuscript that you sent me and ask you to go over it very carefully, because there are a lot of words missing where Alice, for very understandable reasons, probably couldn't figure out your handwriting. There are also a number of typographical errors that I think you will want to correct yourself. I hope that you will write just about as much more to finish the book as you have sent us here, because that will make just about the right size from a commercial point of view. Get it finished and send it to me, and we'll publish it in just as lovely a format as we can devise for it. It's a long time since we've had a new Gertrude Stein book on our list and I'm rarin' to go!" (*FF* 350–351).[9]

**April 21, Bilignin**

Stein to Van Vechten: "Yes you know about the novel, don't you remember oh about three years ago I told you I was doing a novel about the Duchess of Windsor and it was to be called Ida, I worked at it and then I wrote it over and I have written it over almost three times completely and now Bennett likes it and so I am finishing it for him and he will do it in the fall" (*CVV* 672).

**[April?], Bilignin**

Stein to Wilder: "I sent Bennett Cerf the first half of Ida and he liked it, so I am finishing it for him" (*TW* 265).

**[April], Bilignin**

Stein to Cerf: "My dear dear Bennett, / I am as happy as happy can be that it will be one, and that it will come out at Random House, I am a faithful soul and I have always liked everything you ever did for me and you did an awful lot for me, and so I am hard at work, and getting the whole book ready for you. It was originally inspired by Mrs. Simpson Duchess of Windsor and a girl in this village and the two became one and she was called Ida, they are still one and they are going on being, and now you like it and it's fine, I have worked very hard at it going over it and over it to simplify it, and now if you understood a lot that much was worth it, it is lovely spring weather and we have been very peaceful and I am working steadily and I hope to have it all done for you in a couple of months but I work at it very slowly and carefully so Bennett will understand" (RHC).

**May 13, New York**

Cerf to Stein: "I have just received your cheerful note telling me that you are going to finish your novel as quickly as possible. I will be looking forward to getting the complete manuscript" (YCAL 101.1950).

**[May?], Bilignin**

Stein to Cerf: "Ida is getting on, just getting on, in these dark days I seem to like to write, it leads one on and on, Ida is not done but it very well might be in a week or so and then Alice will type it all and we will correct carefully carefully and send it to you and I hope you will like the way Ida goes on, she does go on even when she does not go on any more, and it will be wonderfully nice to have Random House doing a book again, nicer than I can say, I know you will be pleased that the Yale University library is going to have an xhibition of all my ms. they have and all the books they have of mine and everything including a complete bibliography that Robert Haas is doing for them, and which they are printing" (RHC).

### May 18, Bilignin

Stein to Wilder: "Bennett [Cerf] is doing Ida this fall, it has finally gotten itself done, and now I am xciting myself with a child's book called To Do" (*TW* 265).[10]

### June 3, Bilignin

Stein to Van Vechten: "[I]n about a week I will send you the copy of the Novel Ida and will you let Bennett know you have Ida when you have her in case he has not had his. Thanks so much, we are going through some pretty awful days, but we have lots of friends around and we all console each other" (*CVV* 676).

### [June?], Bilignin

Stein to Cerf: "Ida is done and is leaving to-morrow to go to you, I hope you will like her to the end. I am sending a duplicate copy to Carl so in case yours does not turn up, you can get his, I do hope you like it. I am starting another novel called Mrs. Reynolds, and if you like one well the other may get done, but it takes a long time to write a novel, Ida took about three years, we are having dark days but I guess it will all be better and better soon, anyway we love you we go on loving you, and I can not tell you how pleased I will be to be in a Random House catalogue again, you were my first true publisher, who really believed in the whole of one and do not think I ever can forget that" (RHC).

### June 25, New York

Cerf to Stein: "This morning I received your letter telling me that IDA would soon be finished. It is good to learn this and it was better still to see your familiar handwriting again. We have been thinking about you constantly and praying that you and Alice were safe and happy in Bilignin" (YCAL 101.1950).

### July 15, New York

Cerf to Stein: "Just a line to tell you that the manuscript of IDA has arrived. I will write you again just as soon as we have had a chance to read the book. / I too am happy that you are going to be back on the Random House list and hope that you will stay there for the rest of all of our lives" (YCAL 101.1950).

### July 29, New York

Van Vechten to Stein: "*Ida* is *here!* I just got Bennett [Cerf] on the phone & *Ida* is *here!*" (*CVV* 677).

### August 5, New York

Cerf to Stein: "IDA is here, primping herself in preparation for a nice little trip to the printers, so you needn't send a duplicate copy" (YCAL 101.1950).

### September 6, New York

Cerf to Stein: "Ida is on the Spring list of Random House, and is already at the printer's" (YCAL 101.1950).

### October 8, New York

Cerf to Stein: "We are expecting to have the book ready for publication right after the beginning of the New Year" (YCAL 101.1950).

### December 18, Bilignin

Stein to Wilder: "[W]e see a good many people, and I work quite a bit, I am on a new novel now, Mrs. Reynolds it is called, Ida you know is to be published in January, and now I wonder is this Mrs. Reynolds more a novel than Ida. Sometimes I dream that I have found a way to write a novel and sometimes I dream that I only dream it, but I like novels bad novels, poor novels, detective novels, sentimental novels, these days I read all the wishy washy novels of the end of the last and the beginning of this century" (*TW* 276–277).

### 1941

### January 2, New York

Cerf to Stein: "IDA is scheduled for publication on February 15th, and I will have copies to send you in a very short while [three packages with two copies each, in case any of them go astray. . . .] It is going to be a fine looking book and I am sure that you will be pleased with it" (YCAL 101.1950).

### January 24, New York

Van Vechten to Stein: "I LOVE Ida. It is gay and ironic and delightful and in a new vein for you. In the series of letters I have been collating there are many references to this book, sometimes called Jennie and Arthur, and one of these references is worth quoting [from September 29, 1937]: 'Ida begins to be funny and we mustn't be too funny!' Well, it isn't TOO funny, but of course it is funny. The dog passage is epic and will be used in anthologies till the end of time" (*CVV* 697).

**February 20, Bilignin**

Stein to Van Vechten: "I am so xcited about Ida, it has not come yet and I am so pleased you like it. I am working steadily on a new one, Mrs. Reynolds, Ida and Mrs. Reynolds both were each one suggested by somebody in the village, and when you come they will pose for you, Mrs. Reynolds is turning out to be a bit of a mystic, it goes slowly I have about 50 pages done, Ida you know was done over and over again, before it finally became what it is" (*CVV* 705).

**March 5, Bilignin**

Stein to Cerf: "My dearest Bennett, / The first two copies of Ida have come and it is the very prettiest book that was ever made, I am mad about it [Figure 12], I think the title page with its powdered color and the lettering is marvelous [Figure 13], who did it, will you thank them for me and thank them again and the printed page with the lovely dancing three letters of Ida on top [Figure 14] and the really heavenly color of the binding, I do really believe it to be the prettiest book I ever saw, it is really a museum piece, and the shape, do tell me who designed it, it is too lovely, and then I am reading it and I do think it is awfully funny, really funny, it is a nice

*Figure 12:* Book jacket for *Ida A Novel* (Random House, 1941). The inset box color is light blue.

*Figure 13:* Title page of *Ida A Novel* (Random House, 1941). The "powdered color" (as Stein says) is green. Having Ida's name in powder or sand captures her evanescent aspect.

❋ ❋ I D A ❋ ❋

## PART ONE

There was a baby born named Ida. Its mother held it with her hands to keep Ida from being born but when the time came Ida came. And as Ida came, with her came her twin, so there she was Ida-Ida.

The mother was sweet and gentle and so was the father. The whole family was sweet and gentle except the great-aunt. She was the only exception.

An old woman who was no relation and who had known the great-aunt when she was young was always telling that the great-aunt had had something happen to her oh many years ago, it was a soldier, and then the great-aunt had had little twins born to her and then she had quietly, the twins were dead then, born so, she had buried them under a pear tree and nobody knew.

Nobody believed the old woman perhaps it was true but nobody believed it, but all the family always looked at every pear tree and had a funny feeling.

The grandfather was sweet and gentle too. He liked

❋ 7 ❋

*Figure 14:* First page of *Ida A Novel* (Random House, 1941).

ushering in of spring-time, because the prim roses are in blossom over in the woods and meadows, and I feel very Wordsworthian indeed, bless you Bennett" (Bennett Cerf Collection, box 2, Rare Book and Manuscript Library, Columbia University).

**March 6, Bilignin**

Stein to Wilder: "[A]nd now there is Ida. Have you seen the book, it has just come and I am all xcited because it is a novel it really is, and it has characters just like a real novel" (*TW* 284).

**March 6, Bilignin**

Stein to Van Vechten: "Ida has just come and they have made a lovely book of it, I am so pleased and happy about it and it is funny, funnier than I remembered it" (*CVV* 706).

**March 13, New York**

Van Vechten to Stein: "Ida is getting some fine reviews" (*CVV* 710).

**March 19, New York**

Cerf to Stein: "I wonder if you have seen any of the reviews of IDA. If not, please let me know, and I will make a collection of the more important ones to send to you. There have been, of course, the usual number of smart alecks who have tried to imitate your style but, on the whole, I think that you will be really pleased with the reception that has been accorded the book. / And I am still waiting to hear how you like the looks of the volume" (YCAL 101.1950).

**March 25, New York**

Cerf to Stein: "I am so very, very happy that you liked the looks of IDA. It has been reviewed beautifully all over the country and it is selling very nicely. People seem to have been vastly amused that a publisher should admit in print that he doesn't understand one of his own books, and they laugh still harder when I tell them that you said from the very start that I was 'nice but dumb'" (YCAL 101.1950).

**April 1, Medellín, Colombia**

Wilder to Stein: "You should have seen the beauty and wit and thoroughness and dignity of the Exhibition at Yale [University Library]. / And forgive me if I say I spoke all right. The Librarian says it was the best speech he ever heard. Many said that you were in the room: wise, good, beautiful, earnest, playful and great. [. . .] From Ecuador, I hope to write to you [. . .] a letter about *Ida*" (*TW* 285–286).[11]

**[April], Bilignin**

Stein to Cerf: "Some one has just sent me the New York Times Book Review of Ida and it does please me, will you thank Marianne Hauser for me I liked her describing Ida as being equipped with beauty conversational charm and herself, and Bennett might one send a copy to the Duchess with the compliments of the author. She was [included?] in an interview I once gave the Paris Herald Tribune, in which I told about the novel I was writing and described the heroine as everything I called a publicity saint, the modern saint being somebody who achieves publicity without having done anything in particular everybody told me I could not do it, without making her do something, but by God I did and I am proud of it and I did it enough so reviewers knew it, so I am proud, bless you Bennett, I was to meet the Duchess a propos of this just before leaving Paris, and then it was put off to our return and then we did not return, so if you think it would be alright to do send her a copy with the compliments of the author" (RHC).[12]

**May 5, Bilignin**

Stein to Van Vechten: "Bennett says Ida is selling nicely" (*CVV* 720).

**May 14, New York**

Cerf to Stein: "Of course we will send a copy of IDA at once to the Duchess—and I will let you know immediately how and if she replies" (YCAL 101.1950).

**May 15, Bilignin**

Stein to Wilder: "Everybody says it [his Yale lecture] was like that, just as good as you said it was and helas it was not recorded, it just bloomed like a flower, bless it and you. [. . .] Bennett says Ida is selling quite nicely and that is a pleasure" (*TW* 288).

### June 13, New York

Cerf to Stein: "Wally Windsor was evidently very pleased to receive a copy of IDA. In her note of thanks she wrote: 'I hope to emerge from the literary labyrinth with some idea of Ida's thoughts and ways! Will you say to Miss Stein how pleased I am that she should have thought of sending me the book, and how fortunate I think she is *still* to be in her own villa. We had to leave ours and all our possessions last June'" (YCAL 101.1950).

### September 16, New York

Cerf to Stein: "IDA has sold over 1700 copies so far, and we think that is mighty good" (YCAL 101.1950).

### October 7, New York

Cerf to Stein: Random House owes Stein $406.69 (YCAL 101.1950).

# Intertexts

These texts represent some of the family relations of *Ida A Novel.* Included are two older texts that Stein incorporated, in modified form, into the novel, one that indirectly relates to the novel, and three that grew out of the *Ida* manuscripts and returned to them.

The eponymous character in "Hortense Sänger" suffers from a lack of what she calls "sufficient company." She prefers her own company—she likes reading and walking—but the overall insufficiency of that relationship leads to misbehavior in the eyes of her family. Stuck between her desire to be with others and her short temper with those who moralize, she may be, by the end, permanently adrift. One point of difference between Hortense and Ida is that the former is "dark-skinned" and the latter would appear to be white. For instance, Ida encounters a racist woman who, we can assume, would say what she says only if she believed Ida shared her prejudice:

> A woman said to Ida, I only like a white skin. If when I die I come back again and I find I have any other kind of skin then I will be sure that I was very wicked before.
>
> This made Ida think about talking.

Ida's silence implies that she regarded this woman as yet another who was not "sufficient company."

Stein's use of "Film Deux Soeurs Qui Ne Sont Pas Soeurs" puts Ida in front of an audience, as the winner of a beauty pageant. Moreover, because the original text is a movie scenario, Stein connects Ida's emerging celebrity status with that of movie stars. On her way home from the pageant, Ida walks into a movie, as it were: "[S]he saw a woman carrying a large bundle of wash. This woman stopped [. . .], Ida stopped too." "Film Deux Soeurs" also plays, as *Ida* does, with the twin figure (two washerwomen, two poodles, two ladies, two parcels), the repetition of action, and the sudden, inexplicable encounter. In "Film Deux Soeurs," even when a live poodle replaces the photographic version, "they understand nothing." By coincidence, not long after Stein incorporated "Deux Soeurs" into the "Arthur And Jenny" version of *Ida*, she was asked for "a text in French that could be set to music" (*LR* 422–427). She wrote "Les Superstitions." Stein did not write in French very often, but two primary intertexts for *Ida* were originally in that language.

"The Superstitions Of Fred Anneday, Annday, Anday A Novel Of Real Life" combines a portrait of a man who acquires fame with a meditation on the difference between fiction and real life. An American, Fred moves to Europe and eventually becomes a celebrated topic of conversation: "[E]verybody had to say or do something about Fred Annday." Unfortunately, the fame he had hoped for, once in hand, made him ill at ease (as was true for Stein). Because Fred has had an experience that affirmed the superstition of the cuckoo, that if it sings when you have money in your pocket "you will have money for all that year," he has become subject to a world of overwhelming significance. Anything might mean something. He "loved superstition," but this habit of reading everything as predictive of his future is now a burden. Fred is saved by love for a woman whose name we do not learn, which suggests that the privacy of their relationship is part of what revives his health. As the narrator unfolds her depiction of Fred, she also tells us that a novel is far more selective than real life. Whereas in everyday life one "meet[s] everyone," a novel should be "like a dream at night" where one "comes to know relatively few persons." Like the novelist for whom not everything is foreshadow, Fred learns how to be selective.

While writing *Doctor Faustus Lights The Lights*, Stein received a request from Page Cooper on May 9, 1938, to contribute to "a witty, satirical book expressing feminine viewpoints on some aspect of the dominant male or, perhaps, some other subject near the woman's heart—should I say nerves. [. . .] There are no inhibitions as to form or content except that it be light satire and from a definitely feminine angle. It may be verse, drama, essay, or fiction. Perhaps you already have something you have written just for your own delight" (YCAL 27.539). Stein immediately drafted some of "Ida" on Cooper's letter, and the finished piece was in New York by the end of May. "Ida" quite literally follows Cooper's request for women characters who offer, or at least contemplate offering, resistance to the "dominant male": "And then well then the question came should you do what they tell you or should you not." While Ida eventually becomes the very essence of popularity ("think of anything to eat, there was only Ida"), she also has the ability to "rest," which allows her to slip away from the trap of gendered or familial identity.

The references to Jenny in *Lucretia Borgia A Play* date its composition to 1938–1939, when Stein was writing the "Arthur And Jenny" version of *Ida*. The latter year has been chosen because "A Portrait Of Daisy To Daisy On Her Birthday" shares so much with *Lucretia Borgia*, and the birthday of Daisy Fellowes was April 29; as well, Stein copied some of *Lucretia Borgia* onto a 1939 typescript of "Arthur And Jenny." The textual intimacy between *Lucretia* and "Portrait" makes them an excellent example of Stein's working method in this period, her use of already existing texts as she made new ones. In "do be careful of eights" (from *Lucretia* and "do be very careful of fives" (from "Portrait"), we see more evidence of Stein's interest in superstitions and prophecies, which leads to "Les Superstitions" a couple of months later, in June 1939. Like the Duchess of Windsor, Lucretia Borgia and Daisy Fellowes enjoyed the marriage bond for its status and within its confines were able to pursue other romances. The Ida of the novel (not the story) has her own multiple marriages and affairs in common with these women, but like Fred Anneday she ultimately enjoys the mutual love in companionship.

# Hortense Sänger[I]

*(1895)*

*

## Chapter I
### In the Library[2]

It was an ideal library for literary browsers, out of the noise and bustle of the city and yet within easy reach. The books were all in one vast room with high ceilings and great windows that let in a flood of sunshine. The place was undisturbed save for some ten or twelve habitual readers, who each sought out his favorite nook on some leathern lounge or great arm-chair, out of sight between tall rows of books. Occasionally an unwary stranger would inadvertently enter and disturb the silence by his resounding footsteps, but soon he would withdraw awed by the stillness and emptiness of the vast room. Sometimes the strains of Chopin's funeral march would reach the ears of the quiet readers, as a military band, accompanying some local celebrity, on his last journey, passed down the street.

One day as the last long sad notes of the march died on the air, a young girl who had been listening intently, threw down her book with an impatient gesture, and dropped her face on the arm of the leathern couch. She was screened from all view by the heavy book-cases in front of her. There she sat in the full-glare of the noon-day sun, her book at her side, motionless. Finally with a resigned shrug she picked up her book, once more curled herself on her sofa and tried to go on reading. It was useless, a wild impatience possessed her. She was a dark-skinned girl in the full sensuous development of budding woman-hood. Her whole passionate nature had been deeply stirred by those few melancholy strains and with the sun-light heating her blood, she could not endure to rest longer. "Books, books" she muttered, "is there no end to it? Nothing but myself to feed my own eager nature. Nothing given me but musty books." She paused her eyes glowing and her fists nervously clenched. She was not an impotent child, but a strong vigorous girl, with a full nature and a fertile brain that must be occupied, or burst its bounds.

At last she rose and left the library where most of her young life had been passed. As she passed out of the quiet retreat, the east wind struck her, and increased the tumult in her soul. "I will walk it down" she said aloud. "I must escape from myself." She started up over the hills at a quick pace, but even that did not satisfy her, faster and faster she went, panting as she climbed the steep hills, but utterly oblivious of her bodily strain, anxious only to escape from self. At last she reached the top-most hill climbed it and paused for breath. Below her lay the blue ocean; the fresh breeze blew on her. She took off her hat and stood there bathed in sunshine, drinking in deep breaths of ocean air, and muttering her satisfaction to herself. At last she turned and now more slowly retraced her steps down the long hills until she reached her home.

Circumstances had forced Hortense Sänger to live much alone. For many years this had suited her completely. With her intense and imaginative temperament, books and her own visions had been sufficient company. She had been early inured to heavy responsibilities, and had handled them firmly for, though a dreamer by nature she had a strong practical sense.

She had now come to a period of her life, when she could no longer content herself with her own nature. She fairly lived in her favorite library. She was motherless and so at liberty to come and go at her own pleasure. Now the time had come when her old well-beloved companions began to pall. One could not live on books, she felt that she must have some human sympathy. Her passionate yearnings made her fear for the endurance of her own reason. Vague fears began to crowd on her. Her longings and desires had become morbid. She felt that she must have an outlet. Some change must come into her life, or she would no longer be able to struggle with the wild moods that now so often possessed her.

Just at this critical time her father died and thus the only tie that bound her to her old home was snapped. Not long after she accepted the invitation of some relatives and left her old haunts and, she hoped her old fears, to lead an entirely new life in a large family circle.[3]

*

## The Temptation

As they drew near the church the crowd in the streets increased. All Baltimore seemed to have turned out to hear the new preacher. They pressed through the throng and entered the church but as soon as they got within the door they were brought to a halt. The place was packed, every nook and corner was filled with its full allowance of uncomfortable humanity. (So closely were they crowded, that no one could see anything except the persons directly in front of them.)

After waiting a while, the crowd gradually, with that peculiar indefinable movement there is in even the densest throng, began to loosen. The pressure on the door was slightly lessened and our party by dint of pushing, waiting, squeezing, waiting again and so managing to insert themselves between the people, succeeded in forcing their way to the steps leading up to the choir-loft. Hortense who was ahead mounted two of the steps and then turned to look at the crowd below her.

Never had she seen a more motley assembly. Negroes and whites, working men and elegant youths all together. A beautiful girl with a graceful figure and dressed in those light-veil-like gowns that add so much to the charm of a Southern city was forced close up to a villainous looking Italian who was trying to push past her.

On the other side were some nuns in their long black gowns, whispering kindly to each other, frightened at finding themselves in the midst of such a thing. One delicate little woman had fainted and the crowd were forced back enough to let her husband support her out.

Other women with that rudeness peculiar to their sex, were abusing their neighbors and impatiently trying to see over their heads. An old woman barely able to totter, was trying to kneel before the central aisle, as is the custom on passing the figure of Christ. At last she succeeded but was almost crushed by a sudden movement in the throng around her.

All those strange and curiously assorted types were there, that are always to be found in a Catholic church where all ranks and conditions find a common mother. The impressive ceremonies, the wealth and imagery displayed in the building, the poetic and mystic emblems, in the church particularly in the dim evening light attract alike the ignorant and the cultured. The passivity of obedience that the church teaches is an inestimable boon in this hurried struggling life of ours.

The crowd for a moment would be still and then without any definable cause, the swaying and pushing would begin again. The heat was intense. The noises of the street came through the widely-open windows adding to the confused hum within. To avoid the heat the lights were low but the moon shone in making strange lights and shadows through the stained windows and making that strange crowd look still more weird.

Far away in the end of the church hardly distinguishable in the dim light stood the young preacher in his priestly robes waiting for the people to be still. At last he raised his hand and began his prayer. None could kneel in that densely packed throng and so all simply bowed their heads.

This attitude of prayer to an observer not participating in it has always a strange fascination. The sight of all those people bowing before a power that they dimly recognize, little children, aged grandfathers and strong men all joining in that act of prayer, is peculiarly impressive. It is a solemn and a melancholy sight to the skeptic filling him with disquieting reflections on the real worth of things. What does it all mean? Why this universal bending before, what, a God of wrath, a God of love which or neither? Are we really only the victims of blind force. "Into this universe and why not knowing,

Nor whence, like water willy-nilly flowing;
And out of it, as Wind along the wastes,
I know not whither, willy nilly blowing."[4]

Why?, why?, thus Hortense, her whole soul filled with longing thought and questioned, "A longing and for what," she muttered, "I would not be as they." What then, she did not know. She struggled with her thought, she tried to throw off the weight, the intolerable burden of solving for herself the great world-questions.

"After all" she continued to herself dreamily Omar Khayyam is right. "The me within thee blind" "While you live drink: —for, once dead, you never shall return; Dream-life is the only life worth living." And then with new fervor, she muttered looking at the preacher over that sea of bowed heads, "Go on, I'll catch your ecstacy. I'll bow my soul to the melody of your voice and yield myself to all the suggestions of the moment. Let me only be at rest and cease to wonder why, why, why. There is no answer, there shall no longer be a questioning." Her muttering ceased and with it, the prayer came to an end. The heads were raised and again a movement began among the crowd.

More people were forced in front of Hortense and she stepped back on to a landing.[5] Behind her there were also some people but not so tightly pressed together. The girl was forced back against one of the men standing in a corner, her friends were just below her. She had not noticed this man before, she did not look at him now, but he taking advantage of the position leaned toward her rather heavily. She felt his touch. At first she was only half-aware of it, but soon she became conscious of his presence. The sensuous impressions had done their work only too well. The magic charm of a human touch was on her and she could not stir. She loathed herself but still she did not move.

Now she became conscious that possibly her friends would notice her proximity to this fellow. Even that did not stir her. Her busy brain was active in weaving excuses. She remembered her well-known tendency to absent-mindedness. "I can tell them I was unconscious and grow indignant if they accuse me."

The voice of the preacher continued off in the distance but the words did not penetrate her brain. At last she became unconscious of the voice and of the crowd, she only felt the human touch and thought of the reasons she should give for her position.

At last she noticed her aunt motioning to her. "Not yet," she said to herself, "I won't see her." Then with a quick revulsion she continued fiercely, "Liar and coward, will you continue this, have you no sense of shame?" and all the while her eyes were fixed on the preacher and she looked the embodiment of intelligent interest.

She seemed to herself, to be growing apathetic. She tried to force herself to move but she could not. She upbraided herself, she grew more violent in her thoughts and yet she did not move.

At last one of her cousins forced her way to her, touched her arm and said that her mother wanted to go home. Hortense stepped down & together they made their way out of the crowded church.

*

After leaving the church they all walked on very silently for some time. A chill had crept into the air. The joy had gone out of the streets. In place of the dancing children and the careless groups of elders, there were now but the weird wavering shadows of the trees. The sky had become over-cast, all nature seemed to feel the reaction of sadness and chill after the excitement of this summer evening.

The group began to separate slightly, Hortense walking ahead with her favorite cousin. There was an uneasy silence that she tried again and again to break, but could not. A strange feeling came over her as they walked on. She began to wonder whether she had really done this thing, whether she had yielded herself consciously or whether after all the position was accidental and she not a willing subject. The excuses that she had framed to herself in the height of the excitement had taken an abiding hold on her and had become not excuses but a reality.

She wondered to see the process go on within herself. She tried to shake off her apathy but could not. She was only a spectator and within herself gradually began without any effort of her own, a growing conviction that after all it had been absent-mindedness. Again she tried to struggle against this process, tried to force herself to confess the truth to her companion. It was useless, the false conviction increasing, soon took possession of her entirely, she was mentally paralysed.

Her cousin now also attempted to break the silence. At last they began to talk in rather a strained fashion. The tension was too much for Hortense, she drew the accusation down upon herself at last by asking somewhat indignantly, what the matter was. At this her cousin began telling her how pained and ashamed they all had been at seeing her so far forget herself.

When the accusation was actually worded, all Hortense's doubts were at an end. She became filled completely with the sense of her own guiltlessness. She grew indignant and her anger passed directly into words. "What" she said frowning, "do you think as meanly of me as that? Can you believe that I could do a thing of that sort consciously? You all are ready enough to think ill of me if you can so easily accuse me of this. Don't you know well enough, how unconscious I am of the things about me when I get interested? You know how absent-minded I am and yet it does not seem to have occurred to you that I was unconscious of that fellow's presence."

Her indignation grew stronger with its expression and she now only felt that she was innocent and wronged. Her cousin only too glad to receive her justification promised to tell the rest as soon as possible. This brought from Hortense another out-burst of wrath. "Tell them or not as you please, if you all have thought me guilty you can continue to do so for aught I care." She continued the walk home silently, deeply angered, convinced now beyond question that she had been wronged. She felt that she was innocent, that her violation was only a hideous fantasy.

The next morning, according to her wont Hortense lay out on the grass basking in the sun-shine. Doubts began to assail her. Was she innocent, was she guilty? Had she been willing or had she only had a delusive sense of volition and could she really not have avoided her position. She lay there looking into the depths of the blue sky wondering and struggling.

Now the full conviction of her guilt would rush upon her and gritting her teeth muttering fiercely, she would struggle with the thought, then an apathetic feeling would succeed, and she would be certain that she had not been in the wrong.

Her old sense of isolation began to surge over her. Again she had become one apart. Again there was something that none knew beside herself, that no one else of those about her had been guilty of. The struggle continued at intervals all that day. She was outwardly as usual. In fact she herself seemed to take very little part in the war of doubts waged so hotly within her. She felt the struggle, she heard the reasons given again and again, but she herself seemed to be but an apathetic spectator.

YCAL 10.239

# Film

## *Deux Soeurs Qui Ne Sont Pas Soeurs*

## *(1929)*

Au coin d'une rue d'un boulevard extérieur de Paris une blanchisseuse d'un certain âge avec son paquet de linge qu'elle était en train de livrer, s'arrête pour prendre dans ses mains et regarder la photo de deux caniches blancs et elle la regarde avec ardeur. Une automobile de deux places stationnait le long du trottoir. Tout à coup, deux dames en descendent et se précipitent sur la blanchisseuse en demandant à voir la photo. Elle la fait voir et les deux dames sont pleines d'admiration jusqu'au moment où une jeune femme qui est coiffée comme si elle venait d'avoir un prix au concours de beauté et après s'être égarée dans la rue, passe et à ce moment voit l'auto vide, se dépêche d'entrer et se met à pleurer. A ce moment, les deux dames entrent dans l'auto et jettent la jeune femme dehors. Elle tombe contre la blanchisseuse qui commence à la questionner, et l'auto, conduite par les deux dames part, et tout à coup la blanchisseuse voit qu'elle n'a plus sa photo. Elle voit un jeune homme et elle lui raconte tout de suite l'histoire.

Quelques heures plus tard, devant un bureau de placement, rue du Dragon, il y a une autre blanchisseuse plus jeune avec son paquet de linge. La voiture des deux dames approche, s'arrête, et les deux dames descendent et font voir à la blanchisseuse la photo des deux caniches blancs. Elle regarde avec plaisir et excitation, mais c'est tout. Juste à ce moment la jeune femme du prix de beauté approche pousse un cri de joie et se précipite vers la voiture. Les deux dames entrent dans leur auto et, en entrant, laissent tomber un petit paquet, mais toujours elles sont en possession de la photo et elles partent précipitamment.

Le surlendemain la première blanchisseuse est encore dans sa rue avec son paquet de linge et elle voit la jeune femme du prix de beauté approcher avec un petit paquet à la main. Et en même temps elle voit le jeune homme. Ils sont tous les trois alors ensemble et tout à coup elle passe, l'auto, avec les deux dames et il y a avec elles un vrai caniche blanc et dans la bouche du caniche est un petit paquet. Les trois sur le trottoir le regarde passer et n'y comprennent rien.

*Revue Européene* 5–7 (May–July 1930): 600–601; *Operas And Plays* (1932; repr., Barrytown, NY: Station Hill Press, 1987), 399–400

# Film

## *Two Sisters Who Are Not Sisters*

Trans. Kathleen Douglas

Around the corner from a boulevard outside of Paris a washerwoman of a certain age with a bundle of laundry that she is busy delivering pauses to pick up a photograph of two white poodles, at which she gazes intently. A two-seater automobile is parking at the curb. All of a sudden, two ladies get out of the car and rush over to the washerwoman and ask to see the photograph. She shows them and the two ladies are full of admiration for the photo until a young woman who is made up as though she has just won a prize in a beauty pageant and then got herself lost on the street, walks by, notices the empty car, scurries into it and begins to cry. At this moment, the two ladies get back into the car and throw the young woman out. She stumbles into the washerwoman, who begins questioning her, and the car is driven off by the two ladies, and suddenly the washerwoman realizes that her photo is missing.

She spots a young man and immediately begins telling him what has happened.

A few hours later, in front of an employment agency on rue du Dragon, there is another, younger washerwoman with a bundle of laundry. The car belonging to the two ladies drives up, stops, and the two ladies get out and show the washerwoman the photo of the two white poodles. The washerwoman looks at it with pleasure and excitement, but that is all. At this very moment the beauty queen walks up, cries for joy and hurries over to the car. As the two ladies get back into their car they drop a parcel, but they still have the photo and they drive off quickly.

Two days later, the first washerwoman is back on her street with a bundle of laundry and she notices the beauty queen walking up with a parcel in her hand. And at the same time she sees the young man. Then all three of them are together and suddenly the car drives by with the two ladies, and with them is a real live white poodle, and in the poodle's mouth is a parcel. The washerwoman, the beauty queen and the young man watch the dog go by and they understand nothing.

# The Superstitions Of Fred Anneday, Annday, Anday

## *A Novel Of Real Life*

## *(1934)*

A cuckoo bird is singing in a cuckoo tree, singing to me oh singing to me.

It was many years before it happened that that song was written and sung but it did happen.

A cuckoo bird did come and sit in a tree close by and sing, sing cuckoo to me.

And this is the way it came to happen.

As I say the song was written and sung many years before, before this happening.

The song was written and sung in Italy.

There Fred Annday was living in a villa in Fiesole. He had been born and raised in America had Fred Anday and there in America he had naturally never heard a cuckoo sing although he had heard a cuckoo clock sing.

And when he first heard a cuckoo sing cuckoo, and that was in Germany he was convinced that it was a clock and not a bird and it took a great deal of argument to convince him that it really was a bird and that birds did sing cuckoo.

Then a number of years afterwards in Italy and he was thinking then of one he loved and one who loved him and he did not see a cuckoo and perhaps he did not hear a cuckoo sing but he made the song, a cuckoo bird is sitting in a cuckoo tree singing to me oh singing to me.

And then many years after in France he was thinking of how pleasant it is to be rich and he had as a matter of fact for him a fair amount of money in his pocket and all of a sudden he heard a cuckoo at a distance and he was pleased because he had money in his pocket and if you hear the first cuckoo of the season and there is money in your pocket it means that you will have money for all that year.

And then the miracle happened. The cuckoo came and did what cuckoos never do and it came and sat in a tree right close to him and he could see it and it could see him and it gave a single loud cuckoo and flew away. And this was the beginning of something for him because from that time on he was successful and he believed in superstition yes he did.[1]

Fred Anneday knew all that and he knew better than that. He knew something else about the cuckoo. The cuckoo is a bird who occupies other birds' nests. Perhaps that is the reason he brings money and success. Because he certainly does.

And Fred Anday knew that there was a monastery where there had been monks and the monks had been forced to leave and others who were not monks had taken their place and the neighborhood gathered around at night and made cuckoo noises around the place at night. Cuckoo they said and they meant that the cuckoo takes other birds' nests and that is what these people had done. And so Fred Anneday's life was based on superstition and he was right.

What had Fred Anday done all his life.

A novel is what you dream in your night sleep. A novel is not waking thoughts although it is written and thought with waking thoughts. But really a novel goes as dreams go in sleeping at night and some dreams are like anything and some dreams are like something and some dreams change and some dreams are quiet and some dreams are not. And some dreams are just what anyone would do only a little different always just a little different and that is what a novel is.

And this is what a novel is.

Fred Anneday all his life had loved not only one woman not only one thing not only managing everything, not only being troubled so that he could not sleep, not only his mother and religion, not only being the oldest and nevertheless always young enough, not only all this but all his life he had loved superstition and he was right.

He had a great deal to do with everything. This was not only because he was one and the eldest of a very large family which he was but it was because he did have a great deal to do with anything.

One of his friends was Brim Beauvais but he met him later later even than when he loved the only woman whom he ever loved and who was larger and older. And he did not meet Brim Beauvais through her although he might have. It made him think of nightingales. Everything made him think of nightingales and express these thoughts.

If any one is the youngest of seven children and likes it he does not care to hear about birth control because supposing he had not been. If one is the eldest of eight children and likes it he too does not care to hear about birth control but then any one knowing him would know what he would say if any one asked him.

If anyone is an only child and likes it well then he is an only child and likes it as men or women, or as children. And they may or may not like birth control. There you are that is the answer and even superstition is not always necessary. But really it is. Of course really it is.

Fred Anneday loved a woman and it made all the difference in his life not only that but that he continued to have a great deal to do with everything only it worried him less that is to say not at all and he slept well, that is after he had found that he loved this woman.

Oh Fred Anneday how many things have happened, more than you can say. And Brim Beauvais how many things have happened to Brim Beauvais. Not so many although he thought as many did. And this goes to show how many have told how many so. And this was because Brim Beauvais did not have to count for superstition. Which is a mistake.

Fred Annday was not tall he changed and his forehead was high. And he changed.

Brim Beauvais was fat that is to say he grew fatter which was not fair as he had been very good looking when he was thin.

Fred Anday loved one woman and she had had a strange thing happen. Not that he loved her for that but it was that which brought them together.

Listen it is very strange. But first how long has Anday lived. About thirty-eight years. And how was he feeling then. Very badly because he was very nervous and did not sleep and his mother was older and thinner and active and wore a wig but bowed as he did.

The woman that he loved was not at all like that although some men love to love a woman who might have looked like their mother if she had looked like that.

There had been a great many women in the life of Fred Anday before he loved the only woman whom he ever loved. First there was his mother.

If there where they lived there had been a mother's day she would have celebrated it eight times and Fred Anday the eldest always would have been there. He would have taken care that he was there with her to celebrate it with and for her.

What does he say and what does she say or what does she say and what does he say.

Another man was Enoch Mariner and he had a beard and violet eyes and stood and looked at one place any time a long time.

He said to her to the mother of Fred you are sixty but if everything is alright and it is it is not too late to take a lover. Did she Mrs. Anneday think he meant her. He certainly did and said so. But nobody knew because she never told and besides her sister had just died. This did not interest Enoch Mariner. Enoch Mariner was about forty-one years old at that time.

So now there are three men and there are also more than as many women and there had been as many children.

Fred Annday had no child nor did most of his sisters and his brothers. One had a child just one and only had one child just one.

Brim Beauvais never had a child. His sister had.

Enoch Mariner never had a child and he had no brothers and no sisters to have one.

So there you have a great many things that happened and remember what a novel is it is just that.

And now everyone wishes to see any one see the family Annday although a great many were very cross about them. They thought they exaggerated being what they were and that everybody had to say or do something about Fred Annday. Which once he loved the only woman he ever loved slowly nobody did. And this in a way ceased to be exciting. But the way it came about was very exciting as exciting as Dillinger and almost as many knew about it that is if you remember the size of their town and country.[2]

A Motto.

How could it be a little whatever he liked.

## Chapter II

It is impossible perfectly impossible to mention everybody with whom Anday had something to do. And why. Because there are so many of them. This is true of everyone and therefore that is not what a novel is. A novel is like a dream at night where in spite of everything happening anyone comes to know relatively few persons. And superstition. Superstition does not come in in dreaming. But in waking oh yes in waking and being waking oh yes it is nothing but superstition. And that is right. That is the way it should be. And anybody likes what they like and anybody likes superstition and so did Fred Anday and the only woman he loved but not in the same way. She was not superstitious in his way and he was not superstitious in her way. But he was right right to be superstitious. Oh yes he was.

What is superstition.

Superstition is believing that something means anything and that anything means something and that each thing means a particular thing and will mean a particular thing is coming. Oh yes it does.

Fred Annday had been superstitious as a little boy. Which of course he had not better not.

Brim Beauvais was superstitious but it moved slowly and as well as not he was not.

Enoch Mariner was superstitious and if he was nobody came to ask him to like it. He liked whatever he did or did not like. He was not very alike. And he made no reference to a wound in his stomach which he had had.

And in this town was a hotel and this at any rate is so. In this town there was a hotel and there was a hotel keeper and his wife and his four children three boys and a girl and his mother and his father and his maiden sister and a governess for the daughter and a woman who helped manage everything and she was a sister of Fred Annday. She came very near being older than Fred only she was not although she felt herself to be in spite of the fact that she had an older sister who still was not older but younger than Fred for Fred after all was the older. Any superstition will help. And it did. He was the eldest and he was older. He knew to a day how he came to be there to stay.

It is not at all confusing to live every day and to meet everyone not at all confusing but to tell anyone yes it is confusing even if only telling it to anyone how you lived anyone day and met everybody all of that day. And now what more can one do than that.

And doing more than that is this.

A Motto.

Once. It is always excited to say twice.
He came twice and she coughed.

## Chapter III

Now I need no reason to wonder if he went to say farewell. But he never did. Fred Anday never said farewell to anyone in a day no one ever does because everyone sees everyone every day which is a natural way for a day to be. Think of any village town or city or desert island or country house or anything. Of course no dream is like that because after all there has to be all day to be like that. And all day is like that. And there cannot be a novel like that because it is too confusing written down if it is like that so a novel is like a dream when it is not like that.

But what is this yes what is this. It is this.

Now having gotten a little tired of Fred Anday but not of Mariner let us begin with the hotel and the hotel keeper. Everybody can go on talking about Fred Anday at any time. When two or three or ten people are together and you ask them what are they talking about they say oh about Fred Anday and some people are like that. They just naturally are the subject of discussion although everybody has said everything about that one and yet once again everybody begins again. What is the mystery of Fred Anday. Any conversation about him is a conversation about him. That is the way it is. Does he know it. Well I do not know that he does. And if he does it does not add to his superstitions. And about that he is right it does not add to his superstitions.

How could Enoch Mariner have loved more than one woman, of course he did and could. He could even very well remember asking the first woman he asked to marry him. Not only he remembered but also everybody who saw the letter and quite a few did see it because the girl proposed to was so surprised that she had to show it to several of her friends to help her bear it.

She was going to be a school teacher and she and Enoch had met once. He sat down the next day so he said in his letter and took off his coat and he got all ready and he wrote her this letter. He said he knew she would not say yes but she would if he had said all he had to say. And he did say all he had to say and she said no. That is the way life began for Enoch and many years later anyone would have married him but he was a bachelor and he had a beard and he walked well and he always proposed to anyone to be their lover but was he, this nobody knows.

See how very well Fred Anday might have come to know him but as a matter of fact did he I am not at all sure that he did. And if one were to ask Fred Anday, he would not remember.

A Motto.

Pens by hens.

## Chapter III

Slowly he felt as he did.

So many things happen that nobody knows that it is necessary to say that he was right to have his superstitions. Of course he is. What is the use of knowing what has happened if one is not to know what is to happen. But of course one is to know what is to happen because it does. Not like it might but might it not happen as it does of course it does. And Anday Fred Anday is never in tears. Not in consequence but never in tears.

And yet Fred Anday could be treated as if he should be in tears but he was not because he had other things. He always did have other things even when it was not true that he slept.

And best of all he knew how he did. He did it very well. And because of this they knew how to say so.

Every one said Anday was not like a hill or like a ball. They said he was not well to do but he had everything to do and he did everything. Nobody could look better than best at that.

For how many reasons was Anday loved or if not loved. Just for how many reasons. Anybody can and could tell just for how many reasons.

And just for how many reasons is a chinaman loved if he comes from Indo China. Just for how many reasons.

Just for how many reasons is everybody loved or please just for how many reasons. Best of all let this be an introduction to how they feel when they do not remember anybody's first name.

One remembers only the names one has heard.

Motto.

Why should he go with him when he stays here for him.

## Chapter IV

Do not bother. Do not bother about a story oh do not bother. Inevitably one has to know how a story ends even if it does not. Fred Annday's story does not end but that is because there is no more interest in it. And in a way yes in a way that is yes that is always so. I can tell this story as I go. I like to tell a story so.

Anybody will have to learn that novels are like that.

*Nassau Lit* 94.2 (Dec. 1935): 6–8, 24–26; *HWW* 24–30

# Ida

*(1938)*

## Chapter I

Ida is her name.

She was thinking about it she was thinking about life. She knew it was just like that through and through.

She never did want to leave it.

She did not stop thinking about it thinking about life, so that is what she was thinking about. She was thinking about how she was feeling and what the people all over everywhere on the earth were doing. How could she not think about it when every day she knew what she was feeling at least she thought she did and every day she knew what everybody everywhere was doing, anyway they told her she did and she did.

You might as well just as well call her Bessie as call her Ida and if nobody likes that you might call her Emily.[1] Perhaps

Henrietta might be better because you can say Henrietta wont let her. But now let's be serious as ever is and her name is Ida, dear Ida. Somebody says that she is dead now and adored and loves everybody and somebody else likes to have it said again, dear Ida.

She always had done she always did what her husband had said she should do and then she did, well she did do what her son said she should do, but she was best of all all day either in her bed that is when she was tired or not. Please be careful not to wake her up although she mostly is awake. She does waste some time in sleep but not really. It is easy to be half awake and half asleep and to say yes I love you you do look very grand.

Now long ago Ida was like that and everybody mentioned it, dear Ida.

## Chapter II

There is no use in Ida remembering Ernest no use at all because Ernest will always come in and stand there there where Ida has a chair even when Ida is in and out. Ida complains that all that is to come and to go. Ida is named Ida, dear Ida.

Now we are serious and circumstantial and this is the way.

Ida knew, everybody knows that they like it of course they like it if they did not it just would not go on and it does go on so what else can they do. Of course sometimes he wont let her and sometimes she wont let him and that is what life is and once in a while nobody will let anybody and then well then Ida says no no, yes I will, yes I will Ida says and she says yes and then they begin again. What do they begin. They begin going on not letting anybody do anything and by that time Ida is rested of course she is. She is rested but she thinks her son might be more careful and pretty soon he is and everybody is more careful. And then pretty soon everybody is forgetting and forgot, nice Ida.

## Chapter III

Like all who are on a boat Ida is on land, now there are three things there is up in the air.

Ida lived through it all not that she ever did it, she did nothing, she neither waited nor refused, how busy she was doing neither the one or the other, how busy she was.

It could make anybody cry to think how busy she was, and she was busy very very busy.

And then well then the question came should you do what they tell you or should you not.

Who tells you what to do. Well somebody always tells somebody what to do. That is what life is. Believe it or not they do they do tell you what to do.

Policemen are like that they just hold up their hand.

Like everything Ida thinks about she thinks about that.

She thinks everybody will be a policeman by and by even you and I.

Not that she will, not that I will. Ida will not she will not be a policeman she has to rest and a policeman has a vacation but he never takes a rest.

Dear Ida, sweet Ida, Ida, Ida.

## Chapter IV

Once upon a time Ida had a father and a mother. Once upon a time she had a husband and a stepfather, once upon a time she had a brother and a cousin once upon a time she had two sets of children.

Dear Ida.

But really what was Ida.

## Chapter V

Ida used to sit and as she sat she said am I one or am I two. Little by little she was one of two, that is to say sometimes she went out as one and sometimes she went out as the other.

Everybody got confused they did not know which was which but Ida did, whichever one she was she had always to think about what life was and what was it.

Well now just what was it.

When she was one that is when she was not the other one, everybody admired her, she even had a beauty prize for being the most beautiful one, when she was the other one she had a prize too she had a prize for not remembering any one or anything.[2]

That is not the same as a beauty prize, no policeman and no beauty can have that prize, the prize for not remembering anything or any one.

And so Ida dear Ida had everything she even had two sets of children and two husbands, the first one died before the other one, he was really dead, you see Ida did have everything.

Dear Ida.

## Chapter VI

And now comes the really exciting moment in the life of Ida. She had it to tell and she did tell it and every one wanted it. Oh yes they did.

Ida was no longer two she was one and she had every one.

Everybody knew about her.

Oh yes they did.

And why

Ida was her name.

That was her fame.

Ida was her name.

Oh yes it was.

That is the way it comes about.

After that everybody knew just who Ida was where she came from and what happened

It did happen.

Everybody knew her name.

And Ida was her name.

It was an exciting time.

That was what happened to Ida.

Nobody said dear Ida any more they just said Ida and when they said Ida everybody knew it was Ida.

Alas nobody cried when they said it was Ida.

She knew, she knew that five is more than ten she knew that six is more than eight, she knew the weight, the real weight of the slate it was a large slate upon which she wrote, she did not really write but on the slate there it was, it was Ida.

Anybody can happen to be there and Ida was always there.

All who knew better than that knew better than to be fat.

Now let us make it all careful and clear.

Everybody is an Ida.

Dear Ida.

Everybody hears everybody when they are heard but that might mean that there is a third but there is not there is only Ida.

Don't all cry although you might all have a try yes you might, you might all have a try just as well as Ida.

It is just as easy to please.

Now Ida never pleased she never had to they were all pleased.

Just like that they were all pleased, oh yes why not, it was Ida, yes it was.

## Chapter VII

And so from the beginning and there was no end there was Ida.

Think of any advertisement, think of anything to eat, there was only Ida.

Dear brave Ida.

Anybody can see that it was all stored all the love of Ida.

Stored and adored.

Bored and reward

All for love of Ida.

Not that they loved Ida.

Nobody does that but they did know and Ida told them so that it was so. Of course it was so. Dear Ida.

So you see now again they say dear Ida.

Don't you see how it all happened.

Of course it does happen.

But you do see how it will happen.

It will always happen.

Nobody neglects anything.

There is always that, he says she says, there is always that.

Dear Ida.

Once more dear Ida.

I wonder if you understand about that if you did well if you did remember me to Ida. Dear Ida.

*BC*

# Lucretia Borgia

## *A Play*

## *(1939)*

For a while Lucretia Borgia was hurt because she had no cousins. She would have liked to have cousins. Then she suddenly said, he knows, and when she said he knows she meant my lord the duke. The duke was cut off by his position from listening and every little while he liked to be patient, they were often all happy together dear duke and dear Lucretia Borgia but not really very often.

Lucretia Borgia.
A play.

5 characters and a crowd, a house, a hill and a moon.

Act one.

Hands open to receive and to give. Lucretia had a house a hill and a moon, she had had to see why she was not early to bed. Gentle

Lucretia. What was the trouble. What was it she said. She said that Lucretias are often very nicely received by everybody, and why not, when all a moon does is to stare. Alright. Forget it. This is the first act of Lucretia Borgia.

Lucretia Borgia.

Be careful of eights.

Lucretia's name has eight letters in it, do be careful of eights. With Winnie and Jenny one does not have to be so particular.

But with the name Lucretia it is unpardonable not to be careful with the name Lucretia Borgia quite unpardonable.

Lucretia Borgia.

Lucretia Borgia
An opera

Act I

Lucretia's name was Gloria and her brother's name was Wake William. They kept calling to each other Gloria Wake William. And little by little the name stuck to her the name Gloria, really her name was Lucretia Borgia when it was not Jenny or Winnie. How useful names are.[1] Thank you robin, kind robin.

Lucretia Borgia.

Act I

Lucretia's name was Jenny, and her sister's name was Winnie. She did not have any sisters.

Lucretia's name was Jenny that is the best thing to do.

Jenny's twin was Winnie and that was the thing to do.

Lucretia Borgia.

Act I

Jenny was a twin. That is she made herself one.

Jenny like Jenny liked Jenny did not like Jenny.

So then Jenny said Winnie.

It is wonderful when Jenny says Winnie.

It just is.

Winnie oh Winnie. Then she said and they all looked just liked Winnie.

Part II

Jenny began to sit and write.
Lucretia Borgia—an opera.

Act I

They called her a suicide blonde because she dyed her own hair.

They called her a murderess because she killed her twin whom she first made come.

If you made her can you kill her.[2]

One one one.

YCAL 35.725

# A Portrait Of Daisy To Daisy On Her Birthday

*(1939)*

Particularly which they never need a wish
Because it always comes.
This is her life.
On her birthday and every other day.

She would have liked to have everything, which she had, then she suddenly said, she knows, by which she meant she did. She was not cut off by her position from listening and every little while she liked to be patient, she was very often happy together dear Daisy and Daisy but not really very often.

Hands open to receive and to give. Daisy had a house and a hill a river and a door, she had the sea and the moon and she had to see why she was early to bed. What was the trouble. What was it, she said. She said that Daisies were always very nicely received by

Daisies, and why not, when all a moon does is to stare. Alright. Forget it. This is an act of Daisy's.

Daisy's name has five letters in it do be very careful of fives.

With Pansy and Violet one does not have to be so particular but with the name Daisy, it is unpardonable not to be careful with the name Daisy, quite unpardonable.

Daisy.

Daisy's name was Daisy and she kept calling to herself, Daisy. And little by little the name stuck to her the name of Daisy really her name was Daisy. How useful names are. Thank you nightingale dear kind nightingale.

Daisy's name was Daisy that was the best thing to do.

Daisy's twin name was Daisy and that was the best thing to do.

Daisy was a twin. That is she made herself one. Daisy like Daisy, liked Daisy. So then Daisy said Daisy.

It is wonderful when Daisy says Daisy.

It just is.

Daisy oh Daisy. Then she said they all looked like Daisy. All Daisy.

Daisy began to sit and write.

She made Daisy.

If you made her can you kill her.

Not if she is Daisy.

And Daisy made Daisy.

One one one.

YCAL 67.1200

# Contexts II

Although these three essays were published at different times, they have the year 1935 in common. Stein gave "How Writing Is Written" as a lecture on January 12, 1935, at the Choate School, a boys' preparatory school in Wallingford, Connecticut, and it was published in the February issue of the *Choate Literary Magazine*. There is some mystery regarding the text of this lecture. Although Stein did write something in advance, she also extemporized during the event, and separating one from the other now appears impossible. The magazine text was based on a stenographer's transcript; it remains the only extant version, and all subsequent printings have used it.

Dudley Fitts, a teacher at Choate and later a well-known Greek translator, wrote to Stein on January 18 about the transcript: "The stenographer who took down your lecture had difficulties which

I have tried to iron out, but I'm not sure I've been successful" (*FF* 285). On February 5 he sent the page proofs and said, "I had to 'restore' a great deal of the lecture from memory. I hope I didn't spoil anything. Sorry to have missed entirely what you said about the noun; but the text was so corrupt that I couldn't do anything with it. If you will be so kind as to look it over, making any additions or deletions you want, we shall be most grateful" (YCAL 106.2109). We do not know what, if any, changes Stein made.

"How Writing Is Written" thus occupies a unique place in Stein's corpus as a social text that carries the marks of its particular occasion. It includes thoughts that arose as she spoke, moments of direct address to her audience (around sixty boys, as well as faculty and some former students), and the restoration handiwork of Fitts. William Rice has noted that during her 1934–1935 lectures she "often improvised at some length," but such moments were recorded in audience recollections, not in her published texts (*TW* 337). "I have been trying in every possible way to get the sense of immediacy," she said, and this lecture, even if unintentionally, embodies that aim.

A month after Wilder finished an introductory essay for Stein's *Narration* in May 1935, he set sail for Europe. During his visit with Stein in Bilignin he talked at length with her about the ideas then shaping *The Geographical History Of America*, and he read *Four In America* (1933–1934) in typescript. When Wilder returned to the United States in November, he delivered to Random House the finished typescript of *Geographical History* and told Stein that he was reading *Four In America* again (*TW* 66). He continued to read and reread Stein in the years to come, but it was in 1935 that the groundwork of his impressions was built.

Wilder wrote his second Stein introduction, for *Geographical History*, in 1936 and a third in 1947 for *Four In America*. "Gertrude Stein Makes Sense" was Wilder's slightly condensed version of that third introduction's opening ten pages. His essays complement the Stein lecture and together they describe her mind as she moved toward *Ida*. Although Wilder's essays were written to accompany particular Stein texts, they also work more generally as a formal voicing of his insider's perspective. It's clear from Stein's letters to Wilder that she trusted his insights and believed that her audience would find his essays useful.

# How Writing Is Written

*(1935)*

Gertrude Stein

What I want to talk about to you tonight is just the general subject of how writing is written. It is a large subject, but one can discuss it in a very short space of time. The beginning of it is what everybody has to know: everybody is contemporary with his period. A very bad painter once said to a very great painter, "Do what you like, you cannot get rid of the fact that we are contemporaries." That is what goes on in writing. The whole crowd of you are contemporary to each other, and the whole business of writing is the question of living in that contemporariness. Each generation has to live in that. The thing that is important is that nobody knows what the contemporariness is. In other words, they don't know where they are going, but they are on their way.

Each generation has to do with what you would call the daily life: and a writer, painter, or any sort of creative artist, is not at all ahead of his time. He is contemporary. He can't live in the past, because it is gone. He can't live in the future because no one knows what it is. He can live only in the present of his daily life. He is expressing the thing that is being expressed by everybody else in their daily lives. The thing you have to remember is that everybody lives a contemporary daily life. The writer lives it, too, and expresses it imperceptibly. The fact remains that in the act of living, everybody has to live contemporarily. But in the things concerning art and literature they don't have to live contemporarily, because it doesn't make any difference; and they live about forty years behind their time. And that is the real explanation of why the artist or painter is not recognized by his contemporaries. He is expressing the time-sense of his contemporaries, but nobody is really interested. After the new generation has come, after the grandchildren, so to speak, then the opposition dies out: because after all there is then a new contemporary expression to oppose.

That is really the fact about contemporariness. As I see the whole crowd of you, if there are any of you who are going to express yourselves contemporarily, you will do something which most people won't want to look at. Most of you will be so busy living the contemporary life that it will be like the tired businessman: in the things of the mind you will want the things you know. And too, if you don't live contemporarily, you are a nuisance. That is why we live contemporarily. If a man goes along the street with horse and carriage in New York in the snow, that man is a nuisance; and he knows it, so now he doesn't do it. He would not be living, or acting, contemporarily: he would only be in the way, a drag.

The world can accept me now because there is coming out of *your* generation somebody they don't like, and therefore they accept me because I am sufficiently past in having been contemporary so they don't have to dislike me. So thirty years from now I shall be accepted. And the same thing will happen again: that is the reason why every generation has the same thing happen. It will always be the same story, because there is always the same situation presented. The contemporary thing in art and literature is the thing which doesn't make enough difference to the people of that generation so that they can accept it or reject it.

Most of you know that in a funny kind of way you are nearer your grandparents than your parents. Since this contemporariness is always there, nobody realizes that you cannot follow it up. That is the reason people discover—those interested in the activities of other people—that they cannot understand their contemporaries. If you kids started in to write, I wouldn't be a good judge of you, because I am of the third generation. What you are going to do I don't know any more than anyone else. But I created a movement of which you are the grandchildren. The contemporary thing is the thing you can't get away from. That is the fundamental thing in all writing.

Another thing you have to remember is that each period of time not only has its contemporary quality, but it has a time-sense. Things move more quickly, slowly, or differently, from one generation to another. Take the Nineteenth Century. The Nineteenth Century was roughly the Englishman's Century. And their method, as they themselves, in their worst moments, speak of it, is that of "muddling through." They begin at one end and hope to come out at the other: their grammar, parts of speech, methods of talk, go with this fashion. The United States began a different phase when, after the Civil War, they discovered and created out of their inner need a different way of life. They created the Twentieth Century. The United States, instead of having the feeling of beginning at one end and ending at another, had the conception of assembling the whole thing out of its parts, the whole thing which made the Twentieth Century productive. The Twentieth Century conceived an automobile as a whole, so to speak, and then created it, built it up out of its parts. It was an entirely different point of view from the Nineteenth Century's. The Nineteenth Century would have seen the parts, and worked towards the automobile through them.

Now in a funny sort of way this expresses, in different terms, the difference between the literature of the Nineteenth Century and the literature of the Twentieth. Think of your reading. If you look at it from the days of Chaucer, you will see that what you might call the "internal history" of a country always affects its use of writing. It makes a difference in the expression, in the vocabulary, even in the handling of grammar. In [Robert T.] Vanderbilt's amusing story in your *Literary Magazine*, when he speaks of the fact that he is tired of using quotation marks and isn't going to use them any more, with him that is a joke; but when I began writing, the whole question of punctuation was a vital question.[1] You see, I had this new conception: I had this conception of the whole paragraph, and in *The Making Of Americans* I had this idea of a whole thing. But if you think of contemporary English writers, it doesn't work like that at all. They conceive of it as pieces put together to make a whole, and I conceived it as a whole made up of its parts. I didn't know what I was doing any more than you know, but in response to the need of my period I was doing this thing. That is why I came in contact with people who were unconsciously doing the same thing. They had the Twentieth Century conception of a whole. So the element of punctuation was very vital. The comma was just a nuisance. If you got the thing as a whole, the comma kept irritating you all along the line. If you think of a thing as a whole, and the comma keeps sticking out, it gets on your nerves; because, after all, it destroys the reality of the whole. So I got rid more and more of commas. Not because I had any prejudice against commas; but the comma was a stumbling-block. When you were conceiving a sentence, the comma stopped you. That is the illustration of the question of grammar and parts of speech, as part of the daily life as we live it.

The other thing which I accomplished was the getting rid of nouns. In the Twentieth Century you feel like movement. The Nineteenth Century didn't feel that way. The element of movement was not the predominating thing that they felt. You know that in your lives movement is the thing that occupies you most—you feel movement all the time. And the United States had the first instance of what I call Twentieth Century writing. You see it first in Walt Whitman. He was the beginning of the movement. He didn't see it very clearly, but there was a sense of movement that the European was much influenced by, because the Twentieth Century has become the American Century. That is what I mean when I say that each generation has its own literature.

There is a third element. You see, everybody in his generation has his sense of time which belongs to his crowd. But then, you always have the memory of what you were brought up with. In most people that makes a double time, which makes confusion. When one is beginning to write he is always under the shadow of the thing that is just past. And that is the reason why the creative person always has the appearance of ugliness. There is this persistent drag of the habits that belong to you. And in struggling away from this thing there is always an ugliness. That is the other reason why the contemporary writer is always refused. It is the effort of escaping from the thing which is a drag upon you that is so strong that the result is an apparent ugliness: and the world always says of the new writer, "It is so ugly!" And they are right, because it *is* ugly. If you disagree with your parents, there is an ugliness in the relation. There is a double resistance that makes the essence of this thing ugly.

You always have in your writing the resistance outside of you and inside of you, a shadow upon you, and the thing which you must express. In the beginning of your writing, this struggle is so tremendous that the result is ugly; and that is the reason why the followers are always accepted before the person who made the revolution. The person who has made the fight probably makes it seem ugly, although the struggle has the much greater beauty. But the followers die out; and the man who made the struggle and the quality of beauty remains in the intensity of the fight. Eventually it comes out all right, and so you have this very queer situation which always happens with the followers: the original person has to have in him a certain element of ugliness. You know that is what happens over and over again: the statement made that it is ugly—the statement made against me for the last twenty years. And they are quite right, because it *is* ugly. But the essence of that ugliness is the thing which will always make it beautiful. I myself think it is much more interesting when it seems ugly, because in it you see the element of the fight. The literature of one hundred years ago is perfectly easy to see, because the sediment of ugliness has settled down and you get the solemnity of its beauty. But to a person of my temperament, it is much more amusing when it has the vitality of the struggle.

In my own case, the Twentieth Century, which America created after the Civil War, and which had certain elements, had a definite influence on me. And in *The Making Of Americans*, which is a book I would like to talk about, I gradually and slowly found out that there were two things I had to think about; the fact that knowledge is acquired, so to speak, by memory; but that when you know anything, memory doesn't come in. At any moment that you are conscious of knowing anything, memory plays no part. When any of you feels anybody else, memory doesn't come into it. You have the sense of the immediate. Remember that my immediate forebears were people like [George] Meredith, Thomas Hardy, and so forth, and you will see what a struggle it was to do this thing. This was one of my first efforts to give the appearance of one time-knowledge, and not to make it a narrative story. This is what I mean by immediacy of description: you will find it in *The Making Of Americans*, on page 284: "It happens very often that a man has it in him, that a man does something, that he does it very often that he does many things, when he is a young man when he is an old man, when he is an older man." Do you see what I mean? And here is a description of a thing that is very interesting:

> One of such of these kind of them had a little boy and this one, the little son wanted to make a collection of butterflies and beetles and it was all exciting to him and it was all arranged then and then the father said to the son you are certain this is not a cruel thing that you are wanting to be doing, killing things to make collections of them, and the son was very disturbed then and they talked about it together the two of them and more and more they talked about it then and then at last the boy was convinced it was a cruel thing and he said he would not do it and the father said the little boy was a noble boy to give up pleasure when it was a cruel one. The boy went to bed then and then the father when he got up in the

early morning saw a wonderfully beautiful moth in the room and he caught him and he killed him and he pinned him and he woke up his son then and showed it to him and he said to him "see what a good father I am to have caught and killed this one," the boy was all mixed up inside him and then he said he would go on with his collection and that was all there was then of discussing and this is a little description of something that happened once and it is very interesting.[2]

I was trying to get this present immediacy without trying to drag in anything else. I had to use present participles, new constructions of grammar. The grammar-constructions are correct, but they are changed, in order to get this immediacy. In short, from that time I have been trying in every possible way to get the sense of immediacy, and practically all the work I have done has been in that direction.

In *The Making Of Americans* I had an idea that I could get a sense of immediacy if I made a description of every kind of human being that existed, the rules for resemblances and all the other things, until really I had made a description of every human being—I found this out when I was at Harvard working under William James.

Did you ever see that article that came out in *The Atlantic Monthly* a year or two ago, about my experiments with automatic writing? It was very amusing. The experiment that I did was to take a lot of people in moments of fatigue and rest and activity of various kinds, and see if they could do anything with automatic writing. I found that they could not do anything with automatic writing, but I found out a great deal about how people act. I found there a certain kind of human being who acted in a certain way, and another kind who acted in another kind of way, and their resemblances and their differences. And then I wanted to find out if you could make a history of the whole world, if you could know the whole life history of everyone in the world, their slight resemblances and lack of resemblances. I made enormous charts, and I tried to carry these charts out. You start in and you take everyone that you know, and then when you see anybody who has a certain expression or turn of the face that reminds you of some one, you find out where he agrees or disagrees with the character, until you build up the whole scheme. I got to the place where I didn't know whether I knew people or not. I made so many charts that when I used to go down the streets of Paris I wondered whether they were people I knew or ones I didn't. That is what *The Making Of Americans* was intended to be. I was to make a description of every kind of human being until I could know by these variations how everybody was to be known. Then I got very much interested in this thing, and I wrote about nine hundred pages, and I came to a logical conclusion that this thing could be done. Anybody who has patience enough could literally and entirely make of the whole world a history of human nature. When I found it could be done, I lost interest in it. As soon as I found definitely and clearly and completely that I could do it, I stopped writing the long book. It didn't interest me any longer. In doing the thing, I found out this question of resemblances, and I found making these analyses that the resemblances were not of memory. I had to remember what person looked like the other person. Then I found this contradiction: that the resemblances were a matter of memory. There were two prime elements involved, the element of memory and the other of immediacy.

The element of memory was a perfectly feasible thing, so then I gave it up. I then started a book which I called "A Long Gay Book" to see if I could work the thing up to a faster tempo. I wanted to see if I could make that a more complete vision. I wanted to see if I could hold it in the frame. Ordinarily the novels of the Nineteenth Century live by association; they are wont to call up other pictures than the one they present to you. I didn't want, when I said "water," to have you think of running water. Therefore I began by limiting my vocabulary, because I wanted to get rid of anything except the picture within the frame. While I was writing I didn't want, when I used one word, to make it carry with it too many associations. I wanted as far as possible to make it exact, as exact as mathematics; that is to say, for example, if one and one make two, I wanted to get words to have as much exactness as that. When I put them down they were to have this quality. The whole history of my work, from *The Making Of Americans*, has been a history of that. I made a great many discoveries, but the thing that I was always trying to do was this thing.

One thing which came to me is that the Twentieth Century gives of itself a feeling of movement, and has in its way no feeling for events. To the Twentieth Century events are not important. You must know that. Events are not exciting. Events have lost their interest for people. You read them more like a soothing syrup, and if you listen over the radio you don't get very excited. The thing has got to this place, that events are so wonderful that they are not exciting. Now you have to remember that the business of an artist is to be exciting. If the thing has its proper vitality, the result must be exciting. I was struck with it during the War: the average doughboy standing on a street corner doing nothing—(they say, at the end of their doing nothing, "I guess I'll go home")—was much more exciting to people than when the soldiers went over the top. The populace were passionately interested in their standing on the street corners, more so than in the St. Mihiel drive.[3] And it is a perfectly natural thing. Events had got so continuous that the fact that events were taking place no longer stimulated anybody. To see three men, strangers, standing, expressed their personality to the European man so much more than anything else they could do. That thing impressed me very much. But the novel which tells about what happens is of no interest to anybody. It is quite characteristic that in *The Making Of Americans*, Proust, *Ulysses*, nothing much happens. People are interested in existence. Newspapers excite people very little. Sometimes a personality breaks through the newspapers—[Charles] Lindbergh, [John] Dillinger—when the personality has vitality. It wasn't what Dillinger *did* that excited anybody. The feeling is perfectly simple. You can see it in my *Four Saints [In Three Acts]*. Saints shouldn't do anything. The fact that a saint is there is enough for anybody. The *Four Saints* was written about as static as I could make it. The saints conversed a little, and it all did something. It did something more than the theatre which has tried to make events has done. For our purposes, for our contemporary purposes, events have no importance. I merely say that for the last thirty years events are of no importance. They make a great many people unhappy, they may cause convulsions in history, but from the standpoint of excitement, the kind of excitement the Nineteenth Century got out of events doesn't exist.

And so what I am trying to make you understand is that every contemporary writer has to find out what is the inner time-sense of his contemporariness. The writer or painter, or what not, feels this thing more vibrantly, and he has a passionate need of putting it down; and that is what creativeness does. He spends his life in putting down this thing which he doesn't know is a contemporary thing. If he doesn't put down the contemporary thing, he isn't a great writer, for he has to live in the past. That is what I mean by "everything is contemporary." The minor poets of the period, or the precious poets of the period, are all people who are under the shadow of the past. A man who is making a revolution has to be contemporary. A minor person can live in the imagination. That tells the story pretty completely.

The question of repetition is very important. It is important because there is no such thing as repetition. Everybody tells every story in about the same way. You know perfectly well that when you and your roommates tell something, you are telling the same story in about the same way. But the point about it is this. Everybody is telling the story in the same way. But if you listen carefully, you will see that not all the story is the same. There is always a slight variation. Somebody comes in and you tell the story over again. Every time you tell the story it is told slightly differently. All my early work was a careful listening to all the people telling their story, and I conceived the idea which is, funnily enough, the same as the idea of the cinema. The cinema goes on the same principle: each picture is just infinitesimally different from the one before. If you listen carefully, you say something, the other person says something; but each time it changes just a little, until finally you come to the point where you convince him or you don't convince him. I used to listen very carefully to people talking. I had a passion for knowing just what I call their "insides." And in *The Making Of Americans* I did this thing; but of course to my mind there is no repetition. For instance, in these early *Portraits*, and in a whole lot of them in this book [*Portraits And Prayers*] you will see that every time a statement is made about someone being somewhere, that statement is different. If I had repeated, nobody would listen. Nobody could be in the room with a person who said the same thing over and over and over. He would drive everybody mad. There has to be a very slight change. Really listen to the way you talk and every time you change it a little bit. That change, to me, was a very important thing to find out. You will see that when I kept on saying something was something or somebody was somebody, I changed it just a little bit until I got a whole portrait. I conceived the idea of building this thing up. It was all based upon this thing of everybody's slightly building this thing up. What I was after was this immediacy. A single photograph doesn't give it. I was trying for this thing, and so to my mind there is no repetition. The only thing that is repetition is when somebody tells you what he has learned. No matter how you say it, you say it differently. It was this that led me in all that early work.

You see, finally, after I got this thing as completely as I could, then, of course, it being my nature, I wanted to tear it down. I attacked the problem from another way. I listened to people. I condensed it in about three words. There again, if you read those later *Portraits*, you will see that I used three or four words instead of making a cinema of it. I wanted to condense it as much as possible and change it around, until you could get the movement of a human being. If I wanted to make a picture of you as you sit there, I would wait until I got a picture of you as individuals and then I'd change them until I got a picture of you as a whole.

I did these *Portraits*, and then I got the idea of doing plays. I had the *Portraits* so much in my head that I would almost know how you differ one from the other. I got this idea of the play, and put it down in a few words. I wanted to put them down in that way, and I began writing plays and I wrote a great many of them. The Nineteenth Century wrote a great many plays, and none of them are now read, because the Nineteenth Century wanted to put their novels on the stage. The better the play the more static. The minute you try to make a play a novel, it doesn't work. That is the reason I got interested in doing these plays.

When you get to that point there is no essential difference between prose and poetry. This is essentially the problem with which your generation will have to wrestle. The thing has got to the point where poetry and prose have to concern themselves with the static thing. That is up to you.

*CLM*

# Introduction to *The Geographical History Of America*

## *(1936)*

Thornton Wilder

This book grew out of Miss Stein's meditations on literary masterpieces. Why are there so few of them? For what reasons have they survived? What qualities separate the masterpieces from the works that are almost masterpieces?[1] The answers usually given to these questions did not satisfy her. It was not enough to say that these books were distinguished by their "universality," or their "style," or their "psychology" or their "profound knowledge of the human heart." She thought a great deal about the Iliad and the Old Testament and Shakespeare, about *Robinson Crusoe* and the novels of Jane Austen—to quote the works that appeared most frequently in her conversation during the months that this book was approaching completion—and the answer she found in regard to them lay in their possession of a certain relation to the problems of identity and time.[2]

In order to approach their treatment of identity and time Miss Stein made her own distinction between Human Nature and the Human Mind. Human Nature clings to identity, its insistence on itself as personality, and to do this it must employ memory and the sense of an audience. By memory it is reassured of its existence through consciousness of itself in time-succession. By an audience it is reassured of itself through its effect on another—"'I am I,' said the little old lady, 'because my dog knows me.'"[3] From Human Nature, therefore, come all the assertions of the self and all the rhetorical attitudes that require the audience—wars, politics, propaganda, jealousy, and so on. The Human Mind, however, has no identity; every moment "it knows what it knows when it knows it." It gazes at pure existing. It is deflected by no consideration of an audience, for when it is aware of an audience it has ceased to "know." In its highest expression it is not even an audience to itself. It knows and it writes, for its principal expression is in writing and its highest achievement has been in literary masterpieces. These masterpieces, though they may be about human nature are not of it. Time and identity and memory may be in them as subject-matter—as that existing at which the Human Mind gazes—but the absence from the creative mind of those qualities has been acknowledged by the vast multitudes of the world who, striving to escape from the identity-bound and time-immersed state, recognize that such a liberation has been achieved in these works.

If then Miss Stein is writing metaphysics, why does she not state her ideas in the manner that metaphysicians generally employ?

There are three answers to this question.

In the first place, a creative metaphysician must always invent his own terms. Even though his concepts may have something in common with those of his predecessors—with such concepts as subjective, objective, soul, imagination, and consciousness—he cannot in certain places employ those terms, because they come bringing associations of (for him) varying validity and bringing with them the whole systems of which they were a part. The contemporaries of Kant complained (as the contemporaries of Professor Whitehead are now complaining) that the philosopher's terminology was arbitrary and obscure.

In the second place, Miss Stein is not only a metaphysician; she is an artist. In varying degrees artists, likewise, have always sought to invent their own terms. The highest intuitions towards a theory of time, of knowledge or of the creative act have always passed beyond the realm of "text-book" exposition. When the metaphysician is combined with the poet we get such unusual modes of expression as the myths in Plato, the prophetic books of [William] Blake, and the difficult highly-figured phrases in [John] Keats's letters. Miss Stein's style in this book might be described as a succession of "metaphysical metaphors." On the first page, for example, we read:

"If nobody had to die how would there be room for us who now live to have lived. We never could have been if all the others had not died there would have been no room.

Now the relation of human nature to the human mind is this.

Human nature does not know this. . . .

But the human mind can."

(Human Nature, hugging identity-survival cannot realize a non-self situation. The Human Mind, knowing no time and identity in itself, can realize this as an objective fact of experience.)

Similarly, further down we come upon the question:

"What is the use of being a little boy if you are growing up to be a man?"

(Since the Human Mind, existing, does not feel its past as relevant, why does succession in identity have any importance? What is the purpose of living in time? One cannot realize what one was like four seconds ago, four months ago, twenty years ago. "Only when I look in the mirror," said Picasso's mother, "do I realize that I am the mother of a grown-up man.")

This book is a series of such condensations, some of them, like the plays and the "detective stories" about pigeons, of considerable difficulty. These latter, it is only fair to add, have, with a number of other passages, so far exceeded the delighted but inadequate powers of this commentator. The book presupposes that the reader has long speculated on such matters and is willing and able to assimilate another person's "private language,"—and in this realm what can one give or receive, at best, but glimpses of an inevitably private language?

The third reason that renders this style difficult for many readers proceeds from the author's humor. Metaphysics is difficult enough; metaphysics by an artist is still more difficult; but metaphysics by an artist in a mood of gaiety is the most difficult of all. The subject-matter of this book is grave, indeed; and there is evidence throughout of the pain it cost to express and think these things. (It is not without "tears" that Human Nature is found to be uninteresting and through a gradual revelation is discovered to be sharing most of its dignities with dogs.) But Miss Stein has always placed much emphasis on the spirit of play in an artist's work. The reward of difficult thinking is an inner exhilaration. Here is delight in words and in the virtuosity of using them exactly; here is wit;

here is mockery at the predecessors who approached these matters with so cumbrous a solemnity. One of the aspects of play that most upsets some readers is what might be called "the irruption of the daily life" into the texture of the work. Miss Stein chooses her illustrations from the life about her. She introduces her friends, her dogs, her neighbors. Lolo, about whom gather the speculations as to the nature of romance, lived and died in a house that could be seen from Miss Stein's terrace in the south of France. She weaves into the book the very remarks let fall in her vicinity during the act of writing. Similarly at one period, Picasso pasted subway-tickets upon his oil-paintings; one aspect of the "real" by juxtaposition gives vitality to another aspect of the real, the created.

But why doesn't Miss Stein at least aid the reader by punctuating her sentences as we are accustomed to find them? And why does she repeat herself so often?

A great many authors have lately become impatient with the inadequacy of punctuation. Many think that new signs should be invented; signs to imitate the variation in human speech; signs for emphasis; signs for word-groupings. Miss Stein, however, feels that such indications harm rather than help the practice of reading. They impair the collaborative participation of the reader. "A comma by helping you along holding your coat for you and putting on your shoes keeps you from living your life as actively as you should live it. . . . A long complicated sentence should force itself upon you, make yourself know yourself knowing it."[4]

The answer to the charge of repetition is on many levels. On one level Miss Stein points out that repetition is in all nature. It is in human life: "if you listen to anyone, behind what anyone is saying whether it's about the weather or anything, you will hear that person repeating and repeating himself." Repeating is emphasis. Every time a thing is repeated it is slightly different. "The only time that repeating is really repeating, that is when it is dead, is when something is being taught."[5] Then it does not come from the creating mind, but from unliving forms. Sometimes Miss Stein's repeating is for emphasis in a progression of ideas; sometimes it is as a musical refrain; sometimes it is for a reassembling of the motifs of the book and their re-emergence into a later stage of the discussion; sometimes it is in the spirit of play.

But if this book is about the psychology of the creative act, why is it also called *The Geographical History Of America*?

Miss Stein, believing the intermittent emergence of the Human Mind and its record in literary masterpieces to be the most important manifestation of human culture, observed that these emergences were dependent upon the geographical situations in which the authors lived. The valley-born and the hill-bounded tended to exhibit a localization in their thinking, an insistence on identity with all the resultant traits that dwell in Human Nature; flat lands or countries surrounded by the long straight lines of the sea were conducive toward developing the power of abstraction. Flat lands are an invitation to wander, as well as a release from local assertion. Consequently, a country like the United States, bounded by two oceans and with vast portions so flat that the state boundaries must be drawn by "imaginary lines," without dependence on geographical features, promises to produce a civilization in which the Human Mind may not only appear in the occasional masterpiece, but may in many of its aspects be distributed throughout the people.

Miss Stein's theory of the audience insists upon the fact that the richest rewards for the reader have come from those works in which the authors admitted no consideration of an audience into their creating mind. There have been too many books that attempted to flatter or woo or persuade or coerce the reader. Here is a book that says what it knows: a work of philosophy, a work of art, and a work of gaiety.

From Gertrude Stein, *The Geographical History Of America Or The Relation Of Human Nature To The Human Mind* (New York: Random House, 1936), pp. 7–14

# Gertrude Stein Makes Sense

*(1947)*

Thornton Wilder

Miss Gertrude Stein, answering a question about her famous line, *A rose is a rose is a rose is a rose*,[1] once said with characteristic vehemence:

"Now listen! I'm no fool. I know that in daily life we don't say 'is a . . . is a . . . is a . . .'"

She knew that she was a difficult and an idiosyncratic author. She pursued her aims, however, with such conviction and intensity that occasionally she forgot that the results could be difficult to others. At such times the achievements she had made in writing, in "telling what she knew" (her most frequent formulization of the aim of writing), had to her the character of self-evident beauty and clarity. A friend, to whom she showed recently completed samples of her poetry, was frequently driven to reply sadly: "But you forget that I don't understand examples of your extremer styles."[2] To this she would reply with a mixture of bewilderment and exasperation:

"But what's the difficulty? Just read the words on the paper. They're in English. Just read them. Be simple and you'll understand these things."

Now let me quote the speech from which the opening remark on this page has been extracted. A student in her seminar at the University of Chicago had asked her for an "explanation" of the famous line.

She leaned forward, giving all of herself to the questioner in that unforgettable way which endeared her to thousands of students and to thousands of soldiers in two wars, trenchant, humorous, but above all urgently concerned over the enlightenment of even the most obtuse questioner:

"Now listen! Can't you see that when the language was new—as it was with Chaucer and Homer—the poet could use the name of a thing and the thing was really there? He could say 'Oh, moon,' 'O sea,' 'O love' and the moon and the sea and love were really there. And can't you see that after hundreds of years had gone by and thousands of poems had been written, he could call on those words and find that they were just worn out literary words? The excitingness of pure being had withdrawn from them; they were just rather stale, literary words. Now the poet has to work in the excitingness of pure being; he has to get back that intensity into the language. You all have seen hundreds of poems about roses and you know in your bones that the rose is not there. I don't want to put too much emphasis on that line of mine because it's just one line in a longer poem. But I notice that you all know it; you make fun of it, but you know it. Now listen! I'm no fool. I know that in daily life we don't go around saying 'is a . . . is a . . . is a . . .' Yes, I'm no fool; but I think that in that line the rose is red for the first time in English poetry for a hundred years."

There are certain of Miss Stein's idiosyncrasies which by this time should not require discussion, for example, her punctuation and recourse to repetition. The majority of readers ask of literature the kind of pleasure they have always received; they want "more of the same"; they accept idiosyncrasy in author and periods only when it has been consecrated by long accumulated prestige, as in the cases of the earliest and the latest of Shakespeare's styles, and in the poetry of [John] Donne, Gerard Manley Hopkins, or Emily Dickinson. They arrogate to themselves a superiority in condemning the novels of [Franz] Kafka or of the later [James] Joyce or the later Henry James, forgetting that they allow a no less astonishing individuality to Laurence Sterne and to [François] Rabelais.

This work is for those who not only largely accord to others "another's way," but who rejoice in the diversity of minds and the tension of difference.

It is perhaps not enough to say: "Be simple and you will understand these things"; but it is necessary to say: "Relax your predilections for the accustomed, the received, and be ready to accept an extreme example of idiosyncratic writing."

A brief recapitulation of Miss Stein's aims as a writer will help us to understand her work. She left Radcliffe College, with William James's warm endorsement, to study psychology at Johns Hopkins University. There, as a research problem, her professor gave her a study of automatic writing.[3] For this work she called upon her fellow students—the number ran into the hundreds—to serve as experimental subjects. Her interest, however, took an unexpected turn; she became more absorbed in the subjects' varying approach to the experiments than in the experiments themselves. They entered the room with alarm, with docility, with bravado, with gravity, with scorn, or with indifference. This striking variation re-awoke within her an interest which had obsessed her even in very early childhood—the conviction that a description could be made of all the types of human character and that these types could be related to two basic types (she called them independent-dependents and dependent-independents).

She left the University and, settling in Paris, applied herself to the problem. The result was a novel of one thousand pages, *The Making Of Americans*, which is at once an account of a large family from the time of the grandparents' coming to this country from Europe, and a description of "everyone who is, or has been, or will be." She then went on to tell in "A Long Gay Book" of all possible relations of two persons.

This book, however, broke down soon after it began. Miss Stein had been invaded by another compelling problem: How, in our time, do you describe anything? In the previous centuries writers had managed pretty well by assembling a number of adjectives and adjectival clauses side by side; the reader "obeyed" by furnishing images and concepts in his mind and the resultant "thing" in the reader's mind corresponded fairly well with that in the writer's. Miss Stein felt that that process did not work any more. Her painter friends were showing clearly that the corresponding method of "description" had broken down in painting, and she was sure that it had broken down in writing.

In the first place, words were no longer precise, they were full of extraneous matter. They were full of "remembering," and describing a thing in front of us, an "objective thing," is no time for remembering. Miss Stein felt that writing must accomplish a revolution whereby it could report things as they were in themselves before our minds had appropriated them and robbed them of their objectivity "in pure existing."

Those who had the opportunity of seeing Miss Stein in the daily life of her home will never forget her practice of meditating. She set aside a certain part of every day for it. In Bilignin, her summer home in the south of France, she would sit in her rocking chair facing the valley she has described so often, holding one or the other of her dogs on her lap. Following the practice of a lifetime she would rigorously pursue some subject in thought, taking it up where she had left it on the previous day. Her conversation would reveal the current preoccupation: It would be the nature of "money" or "masterpieces" or "superstition" or "the Republican Party."

She had always been an omnivorous reader. As a small girl she had sat for days at a time in a window seat in the Marine Institute Library in San Francisco, an endowed institution with few visitors, reading all Elizabethan literature, including its prose, reading all [Jonathan] Swift, [Edmund] Burke, and [Daniel] Defoe. Later in life her reading remained as wide but was strangely nonselective. She read whatever books came her way. ("I have a great deal of inertia. I need things from outside to start me off.") The Church of England at Aix-les-Bains sold its Sunday School library, the accumulation of seventy years, at a few francs for every ten volumes. They included some thirty minor English novels of the '70s, the stately lives of Colonial governors, the lives of missionaries. She read them all. Any written thing had become sheer phenomenon; for the purposes of her reflections absence of quality was as instructive as quality. Quality was sufficiently supplied by Shakespeare, whose works lay often at her hand. If there was any subject which drew her from her inertia and led her actually to seek out works, it was American history and particularly books about the Civil War.

And always with her great relish for human beings she was listening to people. She was listening with genial absorption to the matters in which they were involved. "Everybody's life is full of stories; your life is full of stories; my life is full of stories. They are very occupying, but they are not really interesting. What is interesting is the way everyone tells their stories"; and at the same time she was listening to the tellers' revelation of their "basic nature." "If you listen, really listen, you will hear people repeating themselves. You will hear their pleading nature or their attacking nature or their asserting nature. People who say that I repeat too much do not really listen; they cannot hear that every moment of life is full of repeating."

It can be easily understood that the questions she was asking concerning personality and the nature of language and concerning "how you tell a thing" would inevitably lead to the formulation of a metaphysics. In fact, I think it can be said that the fundamental occupation of Miss Stein's life was not the work of art but the shaping of a theory of knowledge, a theory of time, and a theory of the passions. These theories finally converged on the master question: What are the various ways that creativity works in everyone?

Miss Stein held a doctrine which informs her theory of creativity, which plays a large part in her demonstration of what an American is, and which helps to explain some of the great difficulty we feel in reading her work. It is the Doctrine of Audience. From consciousness of audience, she felt, come all the evils of thinking, writing, and creating.

In *The Geographical History Of America* she illustrates the idea by distinguishing between our human nature and our human mind. Our human nature is a serpents' nest, all directed to audience; from it proceed self-justification, jealousy, propaganda, individualism, moralizing, and edification. How comforting it is, and how ignobly pleased we are, when we see it expressed in literature. The human mind, however, gazes at experience, and without deflection by the insidious pressures from human nature, tells what it sees and knows. Its subject matter is indeed human nature; to cite two of Miss Stein's favorites, *Hamlet* and *Pride and Prejudice* are about human nature, but not of it. The survival of masterpieces, and there are very few of them, is due to our astonishment that certain minds can occasionally repeat life without adulterating the report with the gratifying movements of their own self-assertion, their private quarrel with what it has been to be a human being.

Miss Stein pushed to its furthest extreme the position that, at the moment of writing, one should rigorously exclude from the mind all thought of praise and blame, of persuasion or conciliation. In the early days she used to say: "I write for myself and strangers." Then she eliminated the strangers; then she had a great deal of trouble with the idea that one is an audience to oneself, which she solves in her posthumous book, *Four In America*, with the far-reaching concept: "I am not I when I see."

It has often seemed to me that Miss Stein was engaged in a series of spiritual exercises whose aim was to eliminate during the hours of writing all those whispers into the ear from the outside and inside world where audience dwells. She knew that she was the object of derision to many and to some extent the knowledge fortified her. Some of the devices that most exasperate readers are at bottom merely attempts to nip in the bud by a drastic intrusion of apparent incoherence any ambition she may have felt within herself to woo for acceptance as a "respectable" philosopher. Yet it is very moving to learn that on one occasion when a friend asked what a writer most wanted, she replied, throwing up her hands and laughing, "Oh, praise, praise, praise!"

Miss Stein's writing is the record of her thoughts, from the beginning, as she "closes in" on them. It is *being written* before our eyes; she does not, as other writers do, suppress and erase the hesitations, the recapitulations, the connectives, in order to give you the completed fine result of her meditations. She gives us the process. From time to time we hear her groping towards the next idea; we hear her cry of joy when she has found it; sometimes, it seems to me that we hear her reiterating the already achieved idea and, as it were, pumping it in order to force out the next development that lies hidden within it. We hear her talking to herself about the book that is growing and glowing (to borrow her often irritating habit of rhyming) within her.

Many readers will not like this, but at least it is evidence that she is ensuring the purity of her indifference as to whether her readers will like it or not. It is as though she were afraid that if she weeded out all gropings, shapings, re-assemblings, if she gave us only the completed thoughts, the truth would have slipped away like water through a sieve because such a final marshalling of her thoughts would have been directed towards audience. Her description of existence would be, like so many hundreds of thousands of descriptions of existence, like most literature—dead.

*'47: The Magazine of the Year* 1.8 (Oct. 1947): 10–15

# Reviews of *Ida A Novel* in 1941

In one of Stein's lectures, "Portraits And Repetition," she noted the irony of the response her work had gotten in the popular press: "[E]very time one of the hundreds of times a newspaper man makes fun of my writing and of my repetition he always has the same theme" (*LIA* 167). The reviews gathered here put that irony—one review repeating another—on display. One after the other, they describe the novel as obscure, and cut short their analysis of the novel to reference Bennett Cerf's address to the reader (Figure 15). Of course there are deviations: the Hauser, Rogers, *Time*, and Roscher reviews are sincere and insightful, while those by O. O. and Auden mimic her style, and Littell and Mann, in the face of a novel with little plot, invent their own stories in response.

The useful criticism in these reviews is partly what makes them a necessary adjunct to the novel. Their primary function is

$2.00

# Ida

**by GERTRUDE STEIN**

During the tragic upheaval in France in the Spring of 1940, many famous persons and landmarks, as well as long-cherished ideals, vanished forever in the confusion. For a time it was impossible to contact anybody in France, in the unoccupied areas as well as the occupied ones.

That Gertrude Stein should have been one of the first to emerge from the chaos, living relatively undisturbed with Alice Toklas in her beloved villa in Belignin, was no surprise whatever to American friends who know of her indomitable spirit and uncanny ability to get just exactly what she wants out of life. War and disaster surrounded her on every side, but she went calmly about her business of finishing her first novel in eleven years. (*Lucy Church Amiably* was her last one, written in 1930, and never published in America.) *Ida* was the name she chose for the new one, and here it is, presented faithfully to you by a publisher who rarely has the faintest idea of what Miss Stein is talking about, but who admires her from the bottom of his heart for her courage and for her abounding love of humanity and freedom.

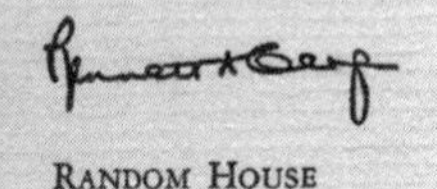

RANDOM HOUSE

*Figure 15:* Bennett Cerf's address to the reader, on the jacket flap of *Ida A Novel* (Random House, 1941).

to reconstruct the culture of expectation. Stein had read such reviews for years and knew the attitude that was ostensibly working against her; with these reviews, we can know it too. Moreover, *Ida* came from this news world. In 1937 Stein wrote to her friend William Rogers about her plans for *Ida*: "I want to write a novel about publicity a novel where a person is so publicized that there isn't any personality left. I want to write about the effect on people of the Hollywood cinema kind of publicity that takes away all identity" (*RM* 168). These *Ida* reviews illuminate a similar process of publicization—in this case of a novel. To the extent that collectively these reviews "took away" the complex personality of *Ida*, our discussions will bring it back.

## O. O., "WHAT HAS GERTRUDE STEIN DONE NOW?"

There was a writer erupting named Gertrude Stein. Critics tried to keep Gertrude from being born but when the time came, well, Gertrude came. And as Gertrude came with her also came Alice, so there she was, Stein-Stein.

She always had an Alice B. Toklas. That was Gertrude. Not Ida.

One month was not March and a book came out of Gertrude. She always had to have a book. One month was not March but it was eleven years and Gertrude Stein had not written any novel that is a story of course. This is called a book but it does easily lose itself. So much for Gertrude.

Everybody said well that is just Gertrude Stein not Ida. All of a sudden there was Gertrude Stein again.

What has Gertrude done now?

It is easier for Gertrude Stein to write a book than not a book well why should it be and not be about the Duchess of Windsor.

Little by little it is not.

We said one day.

Is there anything strange in just being Bennett Cerf and publishing Gertrude Stein anyway?

One day in Random House it is not an accident. Yes and no.

It is so easy not to be lucid.

This too happened to Gertrude Stein.

She never was a mother.

Not ever.

Miss Stein not Ida knows that is she does not exactly know some people who are always willing to read her writings.

The wackier the writing the more willing those people are just to read it.

There it is.

Thank Miss Gertrude Stein. Thank Ida. Thank Bennett.

Dear Gertrude.

Yes.

*Boston Evening Transcript* (Feb. 15, 1941): sec. 5, p. 1.

## CLIFTON FADIMAN, "GETTING GERTIE'S IDA"

A rumor circulating a couple of months ago hinted that Gertrude Stein's new novel, *Ida*, was really about the Duchess of Windsor. Now that I have tottered through *Ida*, I find I cannot categorically deny the rumor. It is certainly as much about the Duchess of Windsor as it is about anything or anyone else. If it is not about the Duchess of Windsor, what is it about? Don't look at me; I'm not your man.

*Ida* is Miss Stein's first novel in eleven years. "It is presented faithfully to you," says the amiable Mr. Bennett Cerf, "by a publisher who rarely has the faintest idea of what Miss Stein is talking about, but who admires her from the bottom of his heart for her courage and for her abounding love of humanity and freedom." This statement would seem to mark an interesting departure in editorial policy. Doubtless we shall soon be reading the works of authors who cannot tell a lie, are kind to their younger brothers, or have contributed heavily to the Salvation Army.

Out of her abounding love for humanity, Miss Stein gives us an elusive creature named Ida. The story of Ida is divided, like a football game, into two halves, called, for purposes of ready reference, First Half and Second Half. The printer and binder have ingeniously arranged to make Second Half follow First Half, so quite an effect of sequence and coherence is produced. It's never made quite clear whether Ida (who dominates both halves) is on her own or whether she is twins. On page 43 we have this: "Ida decided that she was just going to talk to herself. Anybody could stand around and listen but as for her she was just going to talk to herself. She no longer even needed a twin." This seems a forthright statement, but at other points the twin situation is not as lucid as one would wish. On page 52, however, Ida is definitely not a twin. Fifty-two is my favorite page.

Ida (or her twin) has certain quirks: she is very careful about Tuesday, she always hesitates before eating, and she rests a good deal during and between marriages. I should inform you that Ida is the marrying type. Among her various husbands is a man named Frank Arthur, and why not? We do not learn much about her marital habits, but we are told that "she was always good friends with all her husbands."

This goodness of Ida's also extends to other matters. "She was kind to politics while she was in Washington very kind. She told politics that it was very nice of them to have her be kind to them." No record exists of politics' reply.

Furthermore, there is a man in the book named Philip. "Philip was the kind that said everything out loud." This sentence about Philip appears on page 40, and he is never mentioned again. Philip is my favorite character.

I have a theory about Miss Stein's novel which—give me just a second—I should like to outline for you. My notion is that Miss Stein has set herself to solve, and has succeeded in solving, the most difficult problem in prose composition—to write something that will not arrest the attention in any way, manner, shape, or form. If you think this easy, try it. I know of no one except Miss Stein who can roll out this completely non-resistant prose, prose that puts you at once in a condition resembling the early stages of grippe—the eyes and legs heavy, the top of the skull wandering around in an uncertain and independent manner, the heart ponderously, tiredly beating. Take a sentence at random: "Ida instead of going on the way she was going went back the way she had come." Repeat it slowly once or twice and you will find that your head has fallen to one side and your eyelids are a little sandy. Try this: "Ida woke up. After a while she got up. Then she stood up. Then she ate something. After that she sat down. That was Ida."

See what I mean? Sleep tight.

*New Yorker* (Feb. 15, 1941): 78.

## LEWIS GANNETT

Bennett Cerf, who, under the corporate pseudonym of Random House, publishes the works of Gertrude Stein, says of her new "novel," *Ida* (Random House, $2), that he rarely has the faintest idea what Miss Stein is talking about but that he admires her from the bottom of his heart.

So do I. Mr. Cerf adds, however, that he admires Miss Stein "for her courage and for her abounding love of humanity and freedom." That's well enough, but it is hardly the impression I get from reading *Ida*. I admire Miss Stein, and enjoy reading her "novel," much as I used to enjoy reading the works of the eleven-year-olds at a certain progressive school on West Twelfth Street, particularly a story written by my daughter Ruth, which concerned the somewhat incomprehensible quarrels of Mrs. Babbitt and Mrs. Dutch Cleanser.

You will hardly read *Ida* for its plot, though careful study might reveal quite a lot of plot. Ida was a twin, and then she wasn't, which seldom happens in novels published by Doubleday or Macmillan. Her life never began again because it was always there, which is so different from life in the works of the life-reborn school. Ida liked sitting. She did not hear what they said. She just sat and everything was hers without her asking for it, and when she was ready she went away in an automobile by airplane. She was very fond of dogs, and quite a lot of marrying happened to her.

First there was Arthur, who had slept too often under a bridge to care about fishing; they were married and they went to live in Ohio, but Ida did not love anybody in Ohio. She loved apples. Then in Washington Frederick came to see Ida; they were there together; everything just happened in those days; Ida did not remember how many years she was with Frederick and in Ohio and in Texas because in those days she did not count. The third time it was Andrew and he came from Boston, and it is very usual of them, Gertrude Stein says, when they come from Boston to be selfish, very usual indeed. It was not exciting, it was what they did. They did get married.

. . . It is rather like modern poetry, this novel of Gertrude Stein's, except that it has somewhat more rhythm and a great deal more charm. Miss Stein conveys, as do the progressive school children, a sense that she really enjoys writing, and doesn't care a bit whether you, or her publisher, know what she is talking about or not.

Books and Things, *New York Herald Tribune* (Feb. 15, 1941)

## HARRY HANSEN

When I first began reviewing books a veteran editor, who had been reviewing Gertrude Stein's works for a generation or two, explained the traditional way of reviewing her books. "You take a slice out of them for a sample," said he. "Nobody can understand any of it, anyhow."

But I find that parts of *Ida*, Miss Stein's "first novel in 11 years," do seem to make sense, although I can't get interested in Ida herself. The passages that seem to be written in English run like these, about Ida and the dogs:

"So one changed to two and two changed to five and the next dog was also not a big one, his name was Lillieman and he was black and a French bull and not welcome. He was that kind of a dog he just was not welcome.

"When he came he was not welcome and he came very often. He was good-looking, he was not old, he did finally die and was buried under a white lilac tree in a garden but he just was not welcome.

"He had his little ways, he always wanted to see something that was just too high or too low for him to reach and so everything was sure to get broken. He did not break it but it did just get broken. Nobody could blame him but of course he was not welcome."

The French bull may not have been welcome, but the French poodle named Dick was. "Dick was the first poodle I ever knew and he was always welcome, round roly-poly and old and gray and lively and pleasant, he was always welcome," writes Miss Stein.

"He had only one fault. He stole eggs, he could indeed steal a whole basket of them and then break them and eat them, the cook would hit him with a broom when she caught him but nothing could stop him, when he saw a basket of eggs he had to steal them and break them and eat them. He only liked eggs raw, he never stole cooked eggs, whether he liked breaking them, or the looks of them or just, well anyway it was the only fault he had. Perhaps because he was a black dog and eggs are white and then yellow, well anyway he could steal a whole basket of them and break them and eat them, not the shells of course just the egg."

Dick came to a cruel end—at the age of 14 he ran off to see a distant lady dog and on the way was run over and, "alas poor Dick he was never buried anywhere."

Miss Stein concludes: "Dogs are dogs, you sometimes think that they are not but they are. And they always are here there and everywhere."

Bennett Cerf, president of Random House, signs a statement on the jacket saying he "rarely has the faintest idea of what Miss Stein is talking about, but admires her from the bottom of his heart for her courage and for her abounding love of humanity and freedom." We can inform Bennett that in the above extract Miss Stein is talking about two dogs, of which one was not welcome and the other liked raw eggs. As for her abounding love of humanity and freedom, we take that for granted. We always knew Miss Stein must have some redeeming qualities; surely people didn't continue to publish her just because she made words stand on end.

The rest of *Ida* will cost you $2, but this much is free.

The First Reader, *New York World-Telegram* (Feb. 15, 1941)

## MARIANNE HAUSER, "MISS STEIN'S *IDA*"

On the flap of this novel Bennett Cerf states somewhat evasively that though he admires Miss Stein "from the bottom of his heart," he rarely has the faintest idea of what she is talking about. This statement, we feel, does not do full justice to Gertrude Stein. Whenever she talks about something, and she oftentimes does, her thoughts are neither very complex nor enigmatic. More often, however, she does not talk about anything in particular, but just talks, putting words together rhythmically and for their own sake. To look for an underlying idea in those instances seems as futile as to look for apples in an orange tree.

*Ida*, Miss Stein's first new novel in eleven years, is not her most eccentric work, though it surely is a queer enough book. One might call it a short novel, a long poem, or a modern fairy tale; or a painting in words, reminding of a Dali rather than of a Picasso.

The plot itself, simple and essentially satirical, leaves little to guess. Ida was born in America, of "sweet and gentle" parents. She grew up, fond of resting, also fond of changing places, doing nothing at all. She was nobody, but she was everybody because she was Ida. She traveled all over the country, doing nothing. She won in a beauty contest, and she owned a blind dog, called Love, and dozens of other dogs, one after the other. She said "well," and "how do you do," and "how nice of you. Come again." There was no one for her but Ida, except for her twin Ida, a double whom she had created to have some one to talk to. Thus equipped with beauty, conversational charm, and herself, she was to advance far in life.

She married many times. She had all sorts of husbands, and all sorts of clothes and hats. One day she left America, and with one of her husbands she went to a foreign country. There she lived in a comfortable house as mistress of the most prominent, the most talked-about man in the country: Andrew the first. Andrew was good looking. He never read anything, and he took a walk every day. The affair of Andrew the first and Ida was known and discussed by every one, and every one wondered if they would or would not marry. There were distinguished guests at Ida's house day in day out, and Ida was well dressed, and she said, "how do you do," and "yes, do," and finally she said, "yes."

So much about the plot. Miss Stein tells it all in her own, highly conscious manner, sarcastically, poetically, absurdly, saying everything precisely as no one else would say it.

It is a curious little book, too thin, too deliberate to be called crazy, and too well done to be laughed off. There is little sense in approaching it from a normal literary point of view. To get hold of its substance seems as impossible as to catch a moonbeam or define the shape of an amoeba. One cannot search for the concrete in the abstract and complain if there isn't anything to be found.

Nor would it make sense to say critically that Ida is unreal as a person; for unreal is precisely what she is meant to be. Things happen to her and within her as in a dream, and are told as they might be told in a dream. One passes through the story somnambulistically, feeling one's self once in a while slapped soberly on the back by Miss Stein's sense of humor. Those moments are the happiest, and the most refreshing, in the book.

When there is nothing else, there is always Miss Stein's personal style, following its own eccentric rules. To quote some of the weirdest passages would be amusing, yet unjust; almost as unjust as to pick for the sheer fun of it some phrases from *Finnegans Wake*. Miss Stein's book, however futuristic or surrealistic, is a rounded piece of writing, cleverly balanced in its own way and not to be torn apart. Whether one likes or dislikes *Ida* is a matter of taste as well as patience. This, we admit readily, is quite a commonplace criticism. Yet we also feel it is the only final thing we can say about both the book and the heroine.

*New York Times Book Review* (Feb. 16, 1941): sec. 6, p. 7

## "ABSTRACT PROSE"

Most readers require of prose that it make concrete sense as they think sense should be made. So Gertrude Stein, who uses prose to build a series of abstractions, either infuriates most readers or elicits defensive jeers. But readers who are willing to read words as they are willing to listen to notes in music—as things without an explicit message—can get from her work a rare pleasure. The three stories in her earliest (1909) book, *Three Lives*, being anchored to sense, are good ones to start on. Her latest book, *Ida*, much more abstract, is a good one to go on with.

The heroine of *Ida* is purportedly modeled on the Duchess of Windsor. That fact need trouble no one, short of a tenth reading or so. Ida is a woman who likes to rest, to talk to herself, to move around. In the course of her lifetime she has several dogs, marries several men (mostly Army officers), lives in several of the 48 States. She seems at times to be some sort of dim, potent symbol or half-goddess, sometimes a plain case of schizophrenia, sometimes a stooge for Miss Stein. In the long run, after several icily beautiful pages of suspense, she appears to settle down with a man named Andrew.

How much or how little sense Ida makes as a story is not important. The words in which it is told are stripped of normal logic, and totally cleansed of emotion. The result is something as intricately clean as a fugue or a quadratic equation.

For those who wish to make the effort, the following suggestions:

- Read it with care, but require no sense of it that it does not yield.
- Read it aloud.
- Read it as poetry must be read or music listened to: several times.
- Read it for pleasure only. If it displeases you, quit.

Gertrude Stein says of Ida: "Ida decided that she was just going to talk to herself. Anybody could stand around and listen but as for her she was just going to talk to herself."

*Time* 37.7 (Feb. 17, 1941): 99–100

## W. H. AUDEN, "ALL ABOUT IDA"

IDA is not about IDA, but about Dear Ida. Who is Dear Ida? Why, everybody knows Dear Ida, but not everybody knows whom they know. Most people call the Dear Ida they know IDA, but most people do not know IDA. Then who is Dear Ida whom everybody knows? Miss Stein knows who Dear Ida is. Dear Ida lives from day to day, but a day is not really all day to Dear Ida because she does not need all day. She does not need all day because, of course, she is mostly sitting and resting and being there. Resting is what she likes best and sitting is what she does best. That is being natural, and, of course, being natural does not take all day. That is why she can only use the part of the day and night that she chooses to sit in. She stays there as long as she can, then she goes walking.

Dear Ida walks in the afternoon when she is not resting. Everything happens to Dear Ida, funny things happen, husbands happen, going away happens, and Dear Ida does not know whether they are happening slowly or not. It might be slowly, it might be not. Dear Ida does not know because she does not begin, no, never, because, as Miss Stein says, if you begin, nothing happens to you. You happen. Dear Ida does not happen, Dear Ida is not funny. The only funny thing about Dear Ida is her dislike of doors. Otherwise Dear Ida is very well, very well indeed. Does Dear Ida know IDA? No, she does not know IDA, she only knows that IDA is beside her. She cannot know IDA because she thinks IDA is like what she thinks Dear Ida is like. Dear Ida does not even know Dear Ida. Only once in her life does she know Dear Ida. That is the only time Dear Ida cries. Knowing IDA beside her, and not knowing Dear Ida, like the Dear Ida she is, she thinks that IDA is Dear Ida, my twin, my twin Winnie who is winning everything and will never make me cry. When she tries to think of IDA, she can only think of her twin Winnie. When she tries to think of Dear Ida, she can only think a dog is a dog because it is always there. If Dear Ida does not know Dear Ida, who does? IDA knows. IDA is funny and is always beginning. Nothing happens to IDA. IDA does not call Dear Ida dear Ida. But Poor Ida, Lazy Ida, Bad Ida, why do you let such funny things happen to you, why don't you begin, why don't you cry? Dear Ida, you are wrong. The first of everything is not a sign of anything. Anything can be the first of everything. Perhaps ten can be a sign of something. Yes, perhaps everything after ten is a sign. I am not your twin Winnie, Dear Ida, I am IDA. If you knew this, you would not be resting. Perhaps you would be crying, but you would know IDA, and that would be as well. Most novels are Dear Ida writing about her twin Winnie, but they do not say so. O dear no, they say this is IDA writing about IDA. But it is only Dear Ida writing, and what does Dear Ida know about Ida as she sits, Dear Ida, and lets funny things happen and does not cry. When she writes IDA she only says, My twin Winnie who is always winning, always counting, never sitting but always crying. There is too much winning, too much counting, too much crying, too much of not resting altogether. Ida is not Dear Ida writing about her twin Winnie. Ida is IDA writing about Dear Ida. There is not too much of anything, only one hundred and fifty pages, and Dear Ida only cries once. IDA does not pretend that Dear Ida is not resting and not thinking about her twin Winnie. Dear Ida writes very often but I do not like what she writes because it is neither about IDA nor Dear Ida, only about her twin Winnie, and that is too much. I like IDA best when she writes about IDA but she does not write about her very often. Next to IDA writing about IDA, I like IDA writing about Dear Ida.

This is what Ida is. I like Ida.

*Saturday Review of Literature* 23 (Feb. 22, 1941): 8

## AUBREY L. THOMAS

Gertrude Stein's first novel in the last 11 years, *Ida* (Random House, $2), makes its appearance today, the first of her work to be published first in the United States. That sounds somewhat like the repetitious Miss Stein herself, doesn't it?

Nevertheless, these are facts and susceptible to demonstration and proof. But frankly, that was about all we could understand about Miss Stein's creation. The rest of it, except that it is about a gal named Ida—or was she Ida-Ida?—is completely beyond our comprehension.

We even made use of a key which the publisher of a children's book by Miss Stein two years dared to say would unlock the door to an understanding of her prose. This key went something like this:

"Don't bother about the commas which aren't there, read the words. Don't worry about the sense that is there, read the words faster. If you have any trouble, read faster and faster until you don't."

But it didn't work and the door is still locked. Nevertheless, we felt somewhat better when we read the blurb on the jacket of *Ida*. Here Bennett A. Cerf, president of the firm publishing the novel, says:

"That Gertrude Stein should have been one of the first to emerge from the chaos, living relatively undisturbed with Alice Toklas in her beloved villa in Belignin, was no surprise whatever to American friends who knew of her indomitable spirit and uncanny ability to get just exactly what she wants out of life. War and disaster surrounded her on every side, but she went calmly about her business of finishing her first novel in eleven years. (*Lucy Church Amiably* was her last one, written in 1930, and never published in America.) *Ida* was the name she chose for the new one, and here it is, presented faithfully to you by a publisher who rarely has the faintest idea of what Miss Stein is talking about, but who admires her from the bottom of his heart for her courage and for her abounding love of humanity and freedom."

True, we haven't said anything about the plot of the novel but then, we don't know what it is. Maybe you will have better luck.

Book of the Day, [Feb. 1941?] (YCAL 28.553)

## J. E. MOLLOY, "IDA, DEAR IDA, AND THE FUNNY THINGS SHE DID: AN INSIGHT INTO STEIN-WAYS WILL HELP THE LAUGHS"

This is the story of Ida, dear Ida. "There was nothing funny about Ida, but funny things did happen to Ida," and this is the story of the funny things that kept happening to Ida. And that, dear reader, is putting it mildly.

Ida really was a little funny herself. The funny thing she did best was resting. "Whenever anybody needed Ida, Ida was resting," very busy resting. She was especially good at sitting. And the funny thing Ida did easiest was changing places. She always "liked to change places, otherwise she had nothing to do all day." If she wasn't living with her great-aunt (who wasn't sweet and gentle), she was staying with her sweet and gentle grandfather, or with a woman named Eleanor Angle in California, or with a cousin of her uncle, or with a cousin of the doctor's wife.

But all that was before she began to get married. For the funny things Ida had most of were husbands. There was Frank Arthur, and Benjamin Williams, and Frederick, and Andrew Hamilton, and at long last Andrew, who was Andrew the first, and even after he wasn't Andrew the first, Andrew was still his name. And of course "Ida was good friends with all her husbands, she was always good friends with all her husbands." Ida was that kind of girl.

Then there was Tuesday. "She was very careful about Tuesday. She always just had to have Tuesday. Tuesday was Tuesday to her." And the dogs. "She always had a dog, at every address she had a dog and the dog always had a name. . . ." There were thirteen dogs in all, one, a Chinese dog, named William.

Now, whether or not Ida is really one Wallis Warfield Spencer Simpson, Duchess of Windsor (as has been rumored, but nowhere claimed in this book), *Ida* is the funniest thing that has happened to Gertrude Stein since that last funny thing she wrote and called a novel in 1930.

[Feb. 1941?] (YCAL 28.553)

## ROBERT LITTELL

I began reading Gertrude Stein's *Ida* in the back seat of an automobile on a long, cold, foggy ride. The first few pages slid over the surface of my consciousness without making a scratch. The fog settled down more thickly on the landscape; another kind of fog, curiously ordered and patterned, rose from the pages of the book. Nothing meant anything, but all of it was meant to mean something quite definite. A purpose was hidden there, like those shapeless shapes I saw through the car's window which might have been trees, or might just as well have been only thicker places in the fog. I was aware of no deliberate attempt to mystify the reader; it all sounded far too serious for a joke at my expense. I reread again from the beginning, and was overcome by the helpless despair of those who are going under ether. The more I reread, the less it meant, and the more certain I was that there was something there eager to be unlocked if only I had the key. These gropings were rudely interrupted by an accident. The left front wheel of the car came off, state troopers came to the rescue; finally, we were towed through the fog with the nose of the car ignominiously hoisted into the air. I regard this as an omen of some kind, and have abandoned my search for the key to what may very well be the door beyond which lies the future of American literature.

Outstanding Novels, *Yale Review* 30.3 (Mar. 1941): xiv

## E. C. S., "GERTRUDE STEIN AS NOVELIST"

If you wish to find out whether you can approach a novel without prejudice, try *Ida*. You will learn how much store you set on a command of grammar and rhetoric as a basis for writing. Gertrude Stein writes without regard for any of the supposed rudiments of literary expression, so if Macaulay and Lindley Murray are your mentors you may not have much fun trying to read *Ida*. You have to keep your attention on Miss Stein's words or you will get nowhere. She doesn't approach the reader with any of the ordinary aids of commas, question marks, or quotation marks. There are sometimes two or three commas on a page but they seem so lonesome and so overburdened with the work of the 20 or 30 commas that one might expect to find there that they count hardly at all.

*Ida* provides reading enjoyment for those who are willing to work at it. The grand thing about Miss Stein is that she is original, not merely in punctuation and parts of speech, but in expression. She puts together words that were never before associated in just such arrangements and yet they make sense in a personal way, by means of Gertrude's all-her-own style. There are times when you think you have the clue to her aims, then again you wonder.

Just to indicate the positive side of Gertrude's accomplishment, now that so many reviews of her novel are arousing smiles by the negative process of quoting her oddities, consider the following bits of original expression:

> She was very careful about Tuesday. She always just had to have Tuesday . . . when she said to herself no there is nobody at home she decided not to go in . . . I am tired of being just one and when I am a twin one of us can go out and one of us can stay in . . . they were nobody's aunts but they felt like aunts and Ida went to church with them . . . But then Ida liked living anywhere . . . Ida was out, she was always out or in, both being exciting . . . Ida went out first locking the door she went out and as she went out she knew she was a beauty and that they would all vote for her.

Ida might have gone out of the window after locking the door. And with Ida one thing leads to two or three things, all in one sentence sometimes. Ida gets married two or three times, depending upon what part of the story you are reading. It might be two times in the back of the book and three times in the front of the book. The story tells how Ida found her twin, or did she? Really, the curious should find out for themselves, relishing the Steinisms as they read, and perhaps share some of Ida's thoughts, such as "She liked to look at black shoes when she was not going to buy any shoes at all."

*Christian Science Monitor* (Mar. 22, 1941): WM12

## DOROTHY CHAMBERLAIN, "GERTRUDE STEIN, AMIABLY"

*Ida* is classified as Gertrude Stein's "first novel in eleven years." (*Lucy Church Amiably*, printed in Paris in 1930, is as hard to read as the telephone book and not much more interesting.) The new novel is about Ida, who is born in the first paragraph, grows up, likes dogs and army officers, is geographically restless but otherwise lazy and has even she couldn't figure how many husbands. I think the ending is happy.

Entire pages are understandable; but most of it goes:

> And so Winnie was coming to be known to be Winnie.
>
> Winnie Winnie is what they said when they saw her and they were beginning to see her.
>
> They said it in different ways. They said Winnie. And then they said Winnie.
>
> She knew.
>
> It is easy to make everybody say Winnie, yes Winnie. Sure I know Winnie. Everybody knows who Winnie is. It is not so easy, but there it is, everybody did begin to notice that Winnie is Winnie.

Which is not clarified by the fact that there was no Winnie; she existed only in Ida's imagination. This lack of clarification is one clue to the customary reaction to Miss Stein's work—it is either ridiculed, or reverenced as the creation of genius. Rarely is an effort made to understand or criticize on the basis of how well she succeeded in what she tried to do. That she herself is an extraordinary woman—for years a monolith in the expatriate art and literary world of Paris—no one denies. No first-line critic dares ignore her; yet in general her work is taken as a joke.

By experimenting with automatic writing, fabricated language—soon abandoned—and style, Gertrude Stein attempted to free words from their emotional associations, so that, purified, they might be used intellectually, almost mathematically, to build exact descriptions of people and things, unsullied by the words' accumulated meanings. To depict inner and outer reality, divorced from emotion and events, and to "express the rhythm of the visible world" became her goal.

To the consequent writing—as overintellectualized as surrealism and futurism—only the initiate has a key; it is unintelligible to the reading public. The most popular and successful work in this manner, *Four Saints In Three Acts*, was an opera, not fiction, and it depended for its effectiveness largely on music, color, motion, costumes and stage setting. So the original by-product of the theory—its influence on young writers, its reawakening of interest in language and style—has become of greater importance than the specific results of the experimentation.

*Ida* retains many of Gertrude Stein's earlier tricks: association of words and ideas through sound, rhyming, repetition, singsong rhythm, naïveté of thought, language, structure. (There are those who believe her works should be sung. It's a free country.) But the gibberishlike *Lucy* style has given way to a more conventional manner and form.

Here Miss Stein tells the story of a woman's life in America; but she has succeeded in giving that life an eerie, disembodied quality that resembles nothing you know. The incongruous sequence of inexplicable episodes and characters is like a jumbled dream, or a motion picture of the hallucinations of an insane mind—rising, focusing, dissolving. You feel rather crazy yourself, lured on into this curious world by simple words, short sentences, conversational ease, narrative force, alertness, rapidity and imminence of events, and the unforeseen, unpredictable turns of the author's mind. *Ida* is entertaining, stimulating, often funny. Also it is an anodyne, which bewilders and befogs. You don't know what it's all about.

And you don't believe in it. Not only is this word experimentation fundamentally perverse, for fumigation cannot rid language of its human associations; but it leads nowhere. A book need not be comprehensible to all the world; neither should it require elucidation. Miss Stein can be readable when she wishes to be. There's *The Autobiography Of Alice B. Toklas*, which you should read sometime. It's good.

*New Republic* 104.14 (Apr. 7, 1941): 477

## DONALD G. ROSCHER, "EINSTEIN IS FINE, BUT ZWEI IS TOO MANY"

This is the story of a woman who, as a child, lusts for life and lives and lives and lives. And then Ida (poor Ida) just exists. So this book takes you from her birth to her death, because to "just exist" is to be dead.

The life story of Ida is buried beneath Miss Stein's exquisite prose, consisting of pure word forms which are used to develop a series of magnificently abstract abstractions. Gertrude Stein plays with words, and her play on words deliberately overshadows her usually delightfully-dubious, sometimes dubiously-delightful story. Stein's prose is often poetry in the guise of prose; read it for the sheer joy of reading the words that make up our language; read it aloud for the sheer joy of hearing the sounds of the words that make up our language; read it for the sheer joy of realizing that words are music. Read Stein with abandon; look for no concrete sense that is not obviously there as far as you are concerned.

Of Ida's family: "It was a nice family but they did easily lose each other." "There was nothing funny about Ida but funny things did happen to her."

Funny here means queer, and Ida wasn't queer, but queer things did happen to her when she was really living, and not just resting and existing, because life is queer; everything about life is queer; everthing in life is queer; life is indeed queer.

(Queer: Odd; singular. Everything which is something is singular, and therefore odd. There was only one Bach. There was only one Cezanne. There is only one Stein.)

The secret of life is living, and living is not existing, and existing is not living; existing is just existing; living is a multitude of things.

As a child Ida lives by her imagination . . . And when you imagine, you know, and when you know, it is because you believe, and to believe is to live. One must believe.

"A great many make fun of those who believe this thing. But those who believe they know, female dwarf bad luck male dwarf good luck, all that is eternal."

Sheer knowing is too coldly logical, but knowing you are by imagining you are is glorious . . . And real living is knowing you are, but knowing via a voice in the clouds.

"She was very young and as she had nothing to do she walked as if she was tall as tall as anyone."

Her imagination (her beautifully active imagination) bore her a twin. "She began to sing about her twin——."

She was as fond as fond could be of dogs; Ida loved dogs. She had many dogs over a period of time.

Ida lived and lived and lived; moved and moved and moved; lived and moved. She moved to lots of places, and she lived in lots of places (before she died the death that is "just existing").

The metamorphosis of enthusiastic-Ida into blasé-Ida was slow, but sure, but deadly.

The rattle of Death: "She always remembered that the first real hat she ever had was a turban made of pansies. The second real hat she ever had was a turban made of poppies.

"For which she was interested in pansies and gradually she was not. She had liked pansies and heliotrope, then she liked wild flowers, then she liked tube-roses, then she liked orchids and then she was not interested in flowers.

"Of course she was not interested. Flowers should stay where they grow, there was no door for flowers to come through, they should stay where they grew. She was more interested in birds than in flowers but she was not really interested in birds."

Ida was dead. She died.

(* *The editor of this page is not responsible for the opinions of this reviewer. Personally we think Gertrude peddles plain and fancy literary hokum, Thornton Wilder notwithstanding.—S. N.*)

*Chicago Daily News* (Apr. 16, 1941)

## W. G. ROGERS

Ida, born but not born a twin, fond of dogs, married several times, living with a serenity and detachment we may take for happiness, is the subject and title of the latest novel by Gertrude Stein.

The publisher offers it as Miss Stein's first novel in 11 years. This lapse of time has not, however, found the noted American writer idle. If she has not produced fiction, she has turned out a long series of books on a great diversity of subjects, most of them printed in the United States and some in England, France and Italy as well.

America knew about Miss Stein long before it had, to any extent, read her books. She was the glamorous figure whose Rue de Fleurus salon in Paris attracted the leaders in literary, artistic and music circles in Europe and this country. Before she came back to the United States for her lecture tour in 1934 and 1935, she had done only one book which enjoyed a wide audience: *The Autobiography Of Alice B. Toklas*. That was nowhere near enough to explain the extraordinary welcoming fanfares which sounded as she landed, when most New York papers used two and three and four column pictures of her on their front pages and accompanied them with exhaustive, colorful stories of the lively shipboard interviews. It was not the author but the person whom the press paid its highest tribute: It regarded her as news.

Thousands of Americans have seen Miss Stein since that exciting day, and more thousands have read the books on which she wants her fame to rest. They have allowed themselves to be puzzled by expecting both more and less than she cares to give, in much the way in which they have been puzzled by the works of the late James Joyce, or the paintings of Picasso, Braque, Gris, Picabia and other personal friends of Miss Stein's.

This present book, which in some respects is the most fascinating from her hand—from her and on to you via Alice B. Toklas's typewriter and the publisher's and binder's workrooms—is her first novel since *Lucy Church Amiably*, appearing in France in 1930. But it is not Miss Stein's only "Ida." Another one was started about the middle of the last decade, and the manuscript of it was on display in the recent Yale University Library exhibition of Steiniana.

Possibly it was the existence of the bibliographical predecessor that led the author to make her heroine long for a twin, a twin which in fact she did have in fiction. Miss Stein picks out of her own past and out of her incredibly wide experience with human nature the stuff she uses in fiction. But what she does with that material is another matter.

She believes in giving her readers only fractional glimpses, in starting but not finishing, in implying but not revealing. *Ida* is a book of half-told tales. Facts are never encountered face to face but subtly skirted. And to make it more intriguing, there are occasional insertions of a startling, bold realism which heighten markedly our interest in the other, usual incompletions.

To complain of her work that it does not make sense is like complaining of Dickens that he did. He wanted to. Miss Stein is "not interested" in that, as Saint Theresa of the opera [*Four Saints In Three Acts*] produced in Hartford [in 1934] was "not interested." She doesn't care about the kind of sense which makes two plus two equal four and adds up to a neat love story. Words for her are tools; they are more than the barren labels listed in Webster.

*Ida*, I find, is full of excitement and drama. It has its own meanings too, even though they are not the kind you can put your finger on. If you approach the book willing to let Miss Stein talk to you, instead of insisting that she present you the kind of writing you are accustomed to, you will find her new novel a stirring pleasure.

[*Springfield Union*?], [Apr. 1941?] (YCAL 28.553)

## EARLE BIRNEY

When something happens nothing begins. When anything begins then nothing happens and you could always say with Ida that nothing began.

Nothing ever did begin.

Partly that and nothing more.

The above is a fair sample of the style and material in Miss Stein's latest little bundle of words. It is also a fair description of what happens. Not, of course, that Miss Stein intends anything to happen. She warned us, in the pseudo *Autobiography Of Alice B Toklas*, that "events should never be the material of poetry or prose. They should consist of an exact reproduction of either an outer or inner reality." Unless my eyes have deceived me all these years, *Ida* does not even inexactly reproduce any outer reality known to man. As for the inner verities, no doubt the book is chock-full of them, but the dilettantish babble of babytalk which serves Miss Stein for a language got in the way of this reviewer whenever he tried to get his trembling hands on any of them.

This is not written to discourage any *Forum* readers who feel they have steadier fingers for grasping Ida's soul. Take it simply as the baffled cry of one who would like to get his claws around Ida's neck. I am all for defending Miss Stein's right to experiment in literature, and for commending the publisher who, by his own confession on the jacket, doesn't know what she's talking about but nevertheless prints her. And it would no doubt be more pleasing to the publisher if I imitated W. H. Auden and other reviewers who have dodged the issue by writing parody-reviews of *Ida* in the hope that their readers would think that they understood it.

Moreover, Mr. Auden says he likes *Ida* and Ida's ideas alike (this is catching) whereas whenever this reviewer felt that he understood Ida he didn't like her. She is a chicken-minded self-satisfied enervated self-conscious little bore and so is her imaginary Twin-Ida and her great-aunts and her numerous and shadowy husbands and dogs. And so is Miss Stein.

Miss Stein was a bore when, in 1909, she wrote her one intelligible book, *Three Lives*. But then she was not much more boring than Frank Norris and the other second-rate Americans whom she was imitating. Now, after thirty years practise, she is without doubt the greatest bore among modern writers.

Fiction and Diction, *Canadian Forum* 21 (Apr. 1941): 28

## KLAUS MANN, "TWO GENERATIONS"

Neither Gertrude Stein nor Carson McCullers needs an introduction to the readers of this magazine. For Miss Stein is certainly not yet forgotten—not at all!—and Miss McCullers has made a rather sensational entry into American Literature with her remarkable first novel, *The Heart Is a Lonely Hunter.*

It's not really that they resemble each other—Miss Stein and Miss McCullers—quite the contrary. But since their two slender volumes, *Ida* and *Reflections in a Golden Eye*, happen to lie side by side on my reading table, it allows me to visualize these two extraordinary women walking through the amazing scenery of their capricious imaginations. They don't look like two sisters, to be sure: the difference of age and attitude is enough to banish such an idea. Nor do they give the impression of being mother and daughter or a couple of intimate friends. Rather, they might be taken for two individuals distantly akin to each other—a well-preserved aunt, perhaps, accompanying her niece on a walk in the darkling plain.

Says Aunt Gertrude, with a toneless laugh: "It's too funny for words. All those funny things that happened to Ida. There was nothing funny about Ida but funny things happened to her. Dear Ida. So she was born and a very little while after her parents went off on a trip and never came back. That was the first funny thing that happened to Ida. Then, of course, many other funny things happened. And then, of course, all her marriages. Arthur. And

Andrew. Andrew never read. Of course not. Ida was careless but not that way. She did read."

"I read quite a bit, too," observes niece Carson in a hollow, mournful voice.

"Oh, yes," Aunt Gertrude says, shrugging her shoulders, impatiently.

"I'm afraid," says the girl, and she suddenly stands still, as if petrified. "I am dreadfully scared. There is a chill in the air. . . ."

She remains motionless, her obstinate, wan little face bent backwards, staring into space, in the attitude of one who listens for a call from a long distance.

"Don't get excited, child," Aunt Gertrude suggests, with the mild and cruel superiority of a sage. "No matter what the day is it always ends the same way, no matter what happens in the year the year always ends one day."

"The air is full of sordid mysteries," whispers the younger one, withdrawing into her ominous trance as into a cave. "Private Williams. . . . The mute expression in his eyes—He had never seen a naked woman till he watched Eleonora Penderton. . . . The Captain's wife, you must know, feared neither man, beast, nor devil; hence all the lively gossip among the ladies of the post. . . ."

"Oh, yes. Thank you." Aunt Gertrude seems slightly irritated. "What you just said about 'neither beast nor devil' sounds rather feeble. Oh yes. Kind of Ibsen-like. So that is the way it sounds. Reminds me of Hedda Gabler. *Femme fatale*. What a bore. Not at all the kind of thing a young person should write in the twentieth century. For the twentieth century is not the nineteenth century. Not at all. Of course not."

Young Carson, absorbed in her own vision, continues, stubborn and ecstatic: "The air is charged with age-old vices—atavistic trends. . . . Jealousy, hatred, desire, parricidal obsessions—you can feel them, smell them, taste them—even in the stable. Mrs. Penderton, an indomitable Amazon, is dynamic enough to master Firebird, that terrific horse. But look!—she has bitten her lower lip quite through; there is blood on her sweater and shirt. Blood—everywhere . . . murder, madness, decay. . . . What a delightful place is a military post in peacetime!"

"Yes. Of course. Not at all." Aunt Gertrude is increasingly annoyed by the macabre vivacity of her young companion. "I prefer Ida. Of course I do. Definitely. Why should everybody talk about Ida. Why not. Dear Ida."

"Oh, those lugubrious dinner parties at the Pendertons!" the delicate niece exclaims dreamily. "The Langdons and the Pendertons, all four of them squatting around the table; all four of them doomed; on the verge of actual lunacy. Private Williams watches the whole set-up from outside. Major Langdon is so shockingly in love with Mrs. Penderton that Mrs. Langdon finally becomes nervous, leaves the room and cuts off the tender nipples of her breasts with garden shears. . . ."

"How utterly ludicrous!" cries the white-haired lady, half-irked and half-amused. "With garden shears! What a joke! Her tender nipples! Think of it! Oh yes! Thank you!"

"I will kill you," the girl says in a strangled voice, looking very pugnacious, very frail, very young. "I will do it!"

"Oh no you won't," the white-haired one assures her, full of merriment and confidence. "Of course not. How utterly amusing. Why should you? You have so much talent. So why should you do such a foolish thing?"

"Do you really think I have talent?" the young visionary asks eagerly.

"Oh course you have," shrieks the gay old girl. "Obviously so. A terrific lot of it. Undoubtedly. Silly child."

"I wonder if I ought to believe you," says the infant prodigy, wide-eyed, with a faint, musing smile. Then she gives her companion a swift, searching glance. "Of course, you are an experienced woman," she admits respectfully, though not without hesitation. "A real *femme de lettres*. Much more capable as a critic, I should say, than as a creative writer. Your little book on Picasso was full of delightful things. But *Ida* falls short of your essays. Why do you want to seem so primitive? A highly articulate person who tries to talk like a baby! Frankly, your fairy-tale trick is a trifle embarrassing."

"And how about you?" grins Aunt Gertrude. "Are you so sure that you are not embarrassing, and even more than just a trifle, with your childlike gravity and complicated inventions? An inspired youth that tries to talk like a hard-boiled psychologist! Why do you want to seem so sophisticated? You are always at your best in describing the sky, or landscape, or animals, or the emotions of very primitive beings, such as Private Williams. The Private is unforgettable but the Captain's wife is a joke. What do you know about Mrs. Penderton, or about her lover, or about her husband? But for some queer reason you *do* know something about Private Williams; just as you knew something about the deaf-mutes, in your first novel. Those lovely deaf-mutes. Oh yes. There, you had an uncanny insight. Something very enchanting. Very frightening. Yes. So you should write about those enchanting and frightening things. Not about the Captain's wife. So you should write about savage things. New things. Sad things. So you should write about American things. Not this nineteenth century stuff. With the garden shears! Many funny things happened to Ida. Dear Ida. But nothing that ridiculous. Naturally not."

"But you have your own little mannerisms yourself," Carson quietly observes.

Aunt Gertrude has a good laugh. "Plenty of them," she admits cheerfully. "But that's a different matter. Entirely. My job is done. I have done my job. And you just begin it. So it is very different. Of course it is. All I have to do—having done my job—is to stick to my little habits as a peasant sticks to his superstitions. To stick to my familiar eccentricities. People need regularity. A certain regularity. Something they can depend on. So do I. Something trustworthy. While everything crumbles. Something cosy. In the midst of general turmoil, I am a rock of Gibraltar. I am a very conservative person. So that is the way I am. Very conservative. Oh yes."

The fragile *enfant terrible* touches the hand of the older woman with a sort of timid tenderness. "Yes, there is something infinitely cosy about you. One always knows what you are going to say next; that makes your line so wonderful. Now you will say . . ."

"*Thank you*," Aunt Gertrude says, smirking majestically. "But I wonder what *you* are going to say next, strange little creature you are! Kind of incalculable, I suppose. . . . Your next book will be a masterpiece, something overwhelming—or something completely absurd. As for *Reflections in a Golden Eye*, it is an attractive mixture of both."

"Never mind," Carson giggles, suddenly casting off her dignity and capering about like a nervous imp. "*Ida* isn't so hot either, sweet old cosy Aunt! But I like you. You are lots of fun."

"I know I am." Aunt Gertrude looks more stolid than ever, half like a motherly matron, half like a wandering sorcerer; at once grim and serene, with her fine, weather-worn, generous face. "Naturally I am. Because I am having fun—always. So that is why I am funny. Because funny things happen to me. The funny things of the twentieth century. Yes."

She keeps taking vigorous, majestic strides, finding her way without difficulty in the midst of the spooky darkness. Carson, however, has transformed herself into a tiny will-o'-the-wisp, hovering, fluttering, giggling among the bushes and trees. What a wan and attractive light!—wavering and intense, oversensitive, savage, charming and corruptible. The experienced aunt watches her with apprehensive admiration. "Stop this monkey business, child!" she shouts. "You might fall! You'll break your neck! You'd better be careful, or you will go astray. This is tricky ground, kind of swampy, too, and the abyss is not far! Don't take a chance, crazy kid! We still need you! Who do you think you are?" thunders the gallant veteran of so many intellectual adventures, the tireless discoverer of authentic talents and amusing fakes. "An elf? A whirlwind? A psychological problem? Not at all, darling. Of course not. You are something much more vulnerable and more important. You are a poet, Carson McCullers. So if you destroy yourself, you destroy a poet. You deprive the twentieth century of a bit of poetry—if you destroy yourself."

"So then you have the unfathomable heart of a poet. Yes. The intricate splendor. Of course. The madness. The golden eye.

"So then you have the golden eye of the poet.

"(But the title of your book sounds affected.)

"A poet.

"Yes.

"Thank you."

"Thank God."

*Decision* 1 (May 1941): 71–74

# *Bibliography of Criticism on* Ida A Novel

Berry, Ellen. "Postmodern Melodrama and Simulational Aesthetics in *Ida*." *Curved Thought and Textual Wandering: Gertrude Stein's Postmodernism*. Ann Arbor: University of Michigan Press, 1992. 153–177.

Bessière, Jean. "L'incommencement du commencement: Carlos Fuentes, Gertrude Stein, Nathalie Sarraute." In *Commencements du roman*, ed. Jean Bessière. Paris: Champion, 2001. 187–211.

bpNichol. "When the Time Came." In *Gertrude Stein and the Making of Literature*, ed. Shirley Neuman and Ira B. Nadel. Boston: Northeastern University Press, 1988. 194–209.

Bridgman, Richard. *Gertrude Stein in Pieces*. New York: Oxford University Press, 1970. 306–310.

Brinnin, John Malcolm. *The Third Rose: Gertrude Stein and Her World*. Boston: Little, Brown, 1959. 359–360.

Chessman, Harriet. "*Ida* and Twins." *The Public Is Invited to Dance: Representation, the Body, and Dialogue in Gertrude Stein*. Stanford, CA: Stanford University Press, 1989. 167–198.

Copeland, Carolyn Faunce. *Language and Time and Gertrude Stein*. Iowa City: University of Iowa Press, 1975. 147–155.

Danhi, Jamie Allison. "*Ida* (Naive Historiography)." In "First Persons Singular: A Study of Narrative Incoherence in the

Novels of Samuel Beckett and Gertrude Stein." Diss., University of California, Berkeley, 1983. 236–263.

Dubnick, Randa. "Clarity Returns: 'Ida' and 'The Geographical History of America.'" *The Structure of Obscurity: Gertrude Stein, Language, and Cubism*. Urbana: University of Illinois Press, 1984. 65–85.

Franken, Claudia. "Ida and Andrew: Dissoluble Allegories." *Gertrude Stein: Writer and Thinker*. Piscataway, NJ: Transaction, 2000. 337–373.

Gygax, Franziska. "Ida and Id-Entity." *Gender and Genre in Gertrude Stein*. Westport, CT: Greenwood Press, 1998. 27–37.

Hoffman, Michael J. *Gertrude Stein*. Boston: Twayne, 1976. 98–100.

Kellner, Bruce. *A Gertrude Stein Companion: Content with the Example*. New York: Greenwood Press, 1988. 39–40.

Knapp, Bettina L. *Gertrude Stein*. New York: Continuum, 1990. 166–169.

McFarlin, Patricia Ann. "Stein's *Ida, a Novel*: Disembodying Ida, Changing Places and Resting." In "Embodying and Disembodying Feminine Selves: Zora Neale Hurston's *Their Eyes Were Watching God*, Djuna Barnes's *Nightwood*, and Gertrude Stein's *Ida, a Novel*." Diss., University of Houston, 1994. 178–255.

Miller, Rosalind S. *Gertrude Stein: Form and Intelligibility*. New York: Exposition Press, 1949. 43–46.

Morbiducci, Marina. "'Ida *Did* Go *In-directly Everywhere*': The Escaping Pervasion of Space." *How2* 2.2 (2004). http://www.asu.edu/pipercwcenter/how2journal/archive/online_archive/v2_2_2004/current/stein/morbiducci.htm.

Murphy, Sean P. "'Ida Did Not Go Directly Anywhere': Symbolic Peregrinations, Desire, and Linearity in Gertrude Stein's *Ida*." *Literature and Psychology* 47.1–2 (2001): 1–11.

Neuman, Shirley. "'Would a Viper Have Stung Her if She Had Only Had One Name?': *Doctor Faustus Lights the Lights*." In *Gertrude Stein and the Making of Literature*, ed. Shirley Neuman and Ira B. Nadel. Boston: Northeastern University Press, 1988. 168–193.

Nguyen, Tram. "*Ida*: 'Who Is Careful?'" In "Gertrude Stein and the Destruction of the Subject." Diss., University of Alberta, 2008. 117–152.

Schmitz, Neil. *Of Huck and Alice: Humorous Writing in American Literature*. Minneapolis: University of Minnesota Press, 1983. 226–239.

Secor, Cynthia. "*Ida*, a Great American Novel." *Twentieth Century Literature* 24.1 (Spring 1978): 96–107.

Sontag, Susan. "Performance Art." *PEN America* 3 (2004): 92–96.

Sutherland, Donald. *Gertrude Stein: A Biography of Her Work*. New Haven: Yale University Press, 1951. 153–159.

Tomiche, Anne. "Repetition: Memory and Oblivion: Freud, Duras, and Stein." *Revue de Litterature Comparee* 65.3 (July–Sept. 1991): 261–276.

Watson, Dana Cairns. "Talking Boundaries into Thresholds in *Ida*." *Gertrude Stein and the Essence of What Happens*. Nashville, TN: Vanderbilt University Press, 2005. 119–148.

# *Notes*

## *Introduction*

1. Following Ulla Dydo's example in *Gertrude Stein: The Language That Rises, 1923–1934* (2003), I capitalize every word in a Stein title and do not use punctuation. This suits the democratic poetics of Stein—her rejection of hierarchy among words, so that an article was as important as a noun—and also what one finds in the manuscripts: Stein capitalized the "A" in the title and did not use punctuation between "Ida" and "A Novel." While she dropped the latter part down a line on the page, a visual and not a political (title/subtitle) distinction was created. Toklas used all caps when she typed a Stein title, which again indicates a desire for parity. One exception here to the rule is *To Do: A Book Of Alphabets And Birthdays*. Stein meant for a colon (or period) to be there—were it not, the title would be unnecessarily ambiguous.

2. This edition of *Ida* uses for its copy text the novel as it was first published in 1941. However, more than forty minor changes have been made based on a comparison of the 1941 text with the manuscripts. Words have been added (e.g., *did, Soon, where, a zebra, to*) and deleted (*and, not, ready*), and some have been altered: for example, a "them" is now "then," a "said" is now "saw," a "died" is now "dried," and an "Anyhow" is now "Andrew." Five new paragraphs have been created. Some punctuation has been modified—including question marks changed to periods—and uppercase and lowercase have been inverted three times. Some apparent errors ("I do not win [want?] him to come"; "She found out [the?] next day"; "He let go [of?] her") have been left because the manuscripts do not authorize a change. Ideally, we could have compared the published novel with both the manuscripts and the final typescript that Stein sent to her publisher Bennett Cerf in June 1940, but the latter is not extant.

3. Because Stein had a lifelong regard for Shakespeare's plays, readers may want to consider *The Comedy of Errors*, which contains two pairs of twins, each with identical names—twin brothers (Antipholus) and their twin servants (Dromio)—and *Twelfth Night*, which casts the fraternal twins Viola and Sebastian. *The Comedy of Errors* also contains a line, "But if that I am I" (3.2.41), that may be behind Stein's often used expression in the mid-1930s, "I am I because my little dog knows me."

4. After "Ida married Frank Arthur," there follow at least four more husbands: Frederick ("He married her and she married him"), Andrew Hamilton ("Ida married again. He was Andrew Hamilton"), Gerald Seaton ("Ida was Mrs. Gerald Seaton"); and Andrew ("The day had been set for their marriage"). Between Frank Arthur and Frederick there may have been one other: the comment "This time she was married" does not point definitively to either man.

5. In a passage that addresses her twinship and emerging renown, we read, "Ida was her name and she had won. / Nobody knew anything about her except that she was Ida but that was enough because she was Ida." In a 1937 letter to Thornton Wilder, Stein recalled the expression "shame shame fie for shame everybody knows your name" and noted that in *Ida*, "it is going to be the other way" (see "Selected Letters").

6. One echo of the period's dark times is in the scene where Ida meets a man who says, "I feel that it is easy to expect that we all wish to do good but do we. I know that I will follow any one who asks me to do anything. I myself am strong and I will help myself to anything I need."

7. Rae Armantrout, *Up to Speed* (Middletown, CT: Wesleyan University Press, 2004), 68–69.

8. Don DeLillo, *White Noise* (New York: Penguin, 1985), 12.

9. The Ida character was based on the Duchess of Windsor. See "Mrs. Simpson" for information on that connection. YCAL refers to the Gertrude Stein and Alice B. Toklas Papers at the Beinecke Rare Book and Manuscript Library, and the numbers indicate box and folder.

10. Ida finally speaks for herself: "Ida returned more and more to be Ida. She even said she was Ida. [. . .] I say yes because I am Ida." Before this, answering questions (or not) had been her only option in conversation. Now she begins to ask questions of her visitors, and those unwilling to talk in a back-and-forth manner are unwelcome: "When any one came well they did Ida could even say how do you do and where did you come from. / Dear Ida. / And if they did not come from anywhere they did not come."

11. Over the course of the narrative, the times when Ida overtly takes the lead are few. Ida does not function as a typical title character; indeed, she is more like a minor character who does not direct or shape the narrative's events.

12. For more on the quality of stillness (or silence) in narrative, see Stein's lecture "Portraits And Repetition" (1935). She wonders whether, "if it were possible that a movement were lively enough, it would exist so completely that it would not be necessary to see it moving against anything to know that it is moving" (*LIA* 170). She also notes, "I wonder now if it is necessary to stand still to live if it is not necessary to stand still to live, and if it is if that is not perhaps a new way to write a novel. I wonder if you know what I mean. I do not quite know whether I do myself. I will not know until I have written that novel" (*LIA* 172). It is possible to read *Ida* as "that novel."

13. "My Life With Dogs" and "Superstitions" were listed as separate pieces in *A Catalogue of the Published and Unpublished Writings of Gertrude Stein* (New Haven: Yale University Library, 1941), by Robert Bartlett Haas and Donald Clifford Gallup.

14. Apparently Sontag did not know that Stein adapted her 1929 movie scenario, "Film Deux Soeurs Qui Ne Sont Pas Soeurs" (included here), for *Ida*, a move that supports Sontag's silent-film argument. Besides silence, Sontag identifies the comic performer by a use of repetition; a use of deadpan; an apparent defect of feeling; an apparent defect of cognition, which makes the audience feel superior; inappropriate behavior, either relentless niceness or outrageousness; and childlike behavior.

15. Some sentences from "What Does She See When She Shuts Her Eyes A Novel" (1936) characterize Stein's more disjunctive style: "Gabrielle said to any one, I like to say sleep well to each one, and he does like to say it. / He likes to do one thing at a time a long time. / More sky in why why do they not like to have clouds be that color. / Remember anything being atrocious. / And then once in a while it rains. If it rains at the wrong time there is no fruit if it rains at the right time there are no roses. But if it rains at the wrong time then the wild roses last a long time and are dark in color darker than white" (*GSW* 492). Stein knew that a wrong time for one thing (fruit or grammar) is a right time for something else (wild roses or poetic language).

16. See as well Stein's "Three Sisters Who Are Not Sisters," written in 1944 (*GSW* 707–711). Beyond the similar titles and play with the twin relation, these texts go in different directions. In "Three Sisters" five young women and men

pretend to kill each other because they anticipate being actually killed—a thinly veiled Holocaust narrative.

17. Stein argues in "How Writing Is Written" that as a philosophical principle "there is no such thing as repetition": "There is always a slight variation. [. . .] Every time you tell the story it is told slightly differently." This principle can apply to the repetition of a phrase within a text or to the repetition of one text within another, as is the case with *Ida*.

18. By the time of the 1941 exhibition, as Norman Holmes Pearson said then, the Stein archive was "unrivaled in scope for any living author." Pearson, "The Gertrude Stein Collection," *Yale University Library Gazette* 16.3 (Jan. 1942): 45.

19. Two bibliographies were also produced then: *A Catalogue of the Published and Unpublished Writings of Gertrude Stein*, by Haas and Gallup; and *Gertrude Stein: A Bibliography* (New York: Arrow Editions, 1941), by Julian Sawyer. These bibliographies offered one more way, along with the exhibition and the archive, for readers to see the place of *Ida* in Stein's career as a whole.

20. Three of those "daily themes" are printed here under the title "Hortense Sänger." Stein's use of the Hortense story in 1938–1939 is described at the close of the essay. Did Stein make a copy of this story before she gave the original to Wilder for deposit at Yale? Probably, although a copy is not extant.

21. The previous four paragraphs borrow from an essay of mine, "Gertrude Stein's Twin" (*Textual Practice*, 25.6 [Dec. 2011]), which examines more at length Stein's archive in relation to *Ida*.

22. *The Geographical History Of America Or The Relation Of Human Nature To The Human Mind* (Baltimore: Johns Hopkins University Press, 1993), 108. See Wilder's "Introduction to *The Geographical History Of America*" (included here) for more on these terms.

23. "Finally he became an officer in the army and he married Ida but before that he lived around," and "He decided to enter the army and he became an officer and some few years after he met Ida."

## *Ida A Novel*

1. Aspects of Stein's *The World Is Round* (1938) came from the *Ida* drafts, including the relationship between Rose and Willie, which resembles the one between Ida and Andrew. Like Ida, Rose also has a dog named Love.

2. This reference to a "suicide blonde" has its source in Stein's *Lucretia Borgia A Play* (1939).

3. This paragraph and the next three have their source in the "Hortense Sänger" stories that Stein wrote in 1895.

4. This scene alludes to Stein's experience witnessing a walking marathon in Chicago in November 1934, which she describes in more detail in *Everybody's Autobiography* (*EA* 215–216).

5. Stein added this paragraph to *Ida* in the third stage of the novel's composition. For Richard Bridgman (307), this scene alludes to the broken arm of Melanctha in Stein's *Three Lives* (New York: Vintage, 1936; see 102). Although Melanctha broke her left arm in a fall, not her right, Ida may have considered the girl with a broken arm "a sign" because like Melanctha, Ida was entering the identity and sexual consciousness of a young adult.

6. This paragraph and the next four have their source in Stein's "Film Deux Soeurs Qui Ne Sont Pas Soeurs" (1929).

7. Stein drafted this episode in 1938, and in 1939 she told another version of it in *Paris France* (New York: Liveright, 1970; see 34).

8. In the "Arthur And Jenny" version of the novel, Arthur is also known as Philip Arthur. See the end of the Introduction for the passage that gives this information.

9. Stein had earlier used the story of Madame Pernollet, who fell to her death in 1933, in her detective novel *Blood On The Dining Room Floor* (1933). Stein had known Madame Pernollet for many years, having stayed (in Belley) at the Hotel Pernollet in the mid- to late 1920s (see *LR* 563–565).

10. The name Lady Helen Button alludes to Hélène Bouton, a seventeen-year-old who began working for Stein and Toklas in September 1939. Stein liked Hélène's stories and used them for "Helen Button A War-Time Story," which she then incorporated into *Paris France* (80–92).

11. Here begins "My Life With Dogs," which Stein wrote shortly before beginning the novel's Second Half in April 1940.

12. The dog Never Sleeps also appears in *To Do: A Book Of Alphabets And Birthdays* (see *AB* 5–6, 11, 21–22, 79, 82–85), which Stein wrote while finishing *Ida* in spring 1940.

13. Here ends "My Life With Dogs."

14. Stein is probably being self-reflexive, the "she" being the novel itself. After hearing from her publisher Bennett Cerf that he liked the novel's First Half, Stein began work on finishing *Ida* with fresh enthusiasm.

15. The Lurline Baths were built in 1894, two years after Stein moved from San Francisco to Baltimore, but she spent summers in San Francisco in the late 1890s and probably visited the baths then.

16. From this point to the end of Part Five, minus the final sentence and with some additions indicating Andrew's presence as a listener, the text is Stein's translation of her "Les Superstitions," which she wrote in June 1939 (see *LR* 426n). For more on Stein's use of the cuckoo bird as a sign, see "The Superstitions Of Fred Anneday, Annday, Anday A Novel of Real Life" (1934).

## *Genealogy of* Ida A Novel

1. Two years earlier, in *Narration*, she had stated her preference for the sentence over the paragraph. While a paragraph contains "succession" and encourages a beginning-middle-end structure, a sentence embodies not succession but existing: it can have a "complete inner balance of something that state[s] something as being existing," and "anything really contained within itself has no beginning or middle or ending" (*NA* 20).

2. For the final version of *Ida*, Stein makes the sentence more concrete: "Ida went out walking later on and the rain came down but by that time Ida was at home reading, she was not walking any more."

3. Stein also carries the viper episode over to "Arthur And Jenny," but that is where it ends in the *Ida* drafts. See Shirley Neuman's "'Would a Viper Have Stung Her if She Had Only Had One Name?': *Doctor Faustus Lights the Lights*" for a thorough description of the textual relationship of *Ida* and *Faustus*.

4. For example, compare "Nobody can listen to Ida sing but she does like to sing and Ida likes it to be singing. / Everybody did know everything she was doing and nobody could know she was singing" (YCAL 27.552) with the next incarnation: "Nobody can listen to Ida sing but she does like to sing. It might be singing and Ida likes it to be singing. Ida would like to listen to Ida singing but this cannot happen because if she did sing then she would be singing and everybody could know that she did sing, but everybody did know everything she was doing and nobody could know she was singing so though she would have liked to be singing and she almost sang she never did sing singing. Thornton Woodward had a plan" (YCAL 27.545).

5. Another two are Henry and Hawthorne, who "left Utah" and later returned: "[I]t was all to do over again and they did it they did it over again. / This is what

I mean, the earth is round" (YCAL 27.547). Earlier in her career Stein was known for the phrase "begin again." In this later period the key phrase is "the world is round," which has a similar emphasis on cyclic time though with an ambiguous inflection. A "round world" has the quality of the infinite and the inescapable, and Stein used it in the name of both possibility and uncertainty.

6. See Nichol's essay "When the Time Came" for more on Stein's wordplay and doubling: he discusses both "[t]he I's continual strategy of creating a not-I" and how in *Ida* "the *one* has the potential to become more than one" (203). "There is the notion," he says, "that in the twinning, the recognition of the other, the not-I, is what brings the I into its true existence" (204).

7. In this and the next two paragraphs, Stein used a lowercase "l" for the dog, but when Toklas typed this draft she made it uppercase. I have followed Toklas.

8. For instance, compare these Arthur passages with this one in *Ida*: "Once upon a time Ida stood all alone in the twilight. She was down in a field and leaning against a wall, her arms were folded and she looked very tall. Later she was walking up the road and she walked slowly."

9. For another example of how in revision Ida took from Arthur, compare (in manuscript) "He did not talk to them he talked to himself. / He said if I was married I'd have children and if I had children then I'd be a father and if I was a father I'd tell them what to do and so I'm not going to be married" (YCAL 27.537) with (in *Ida*) "She did not talk to them. / Of course she did think about marrying. She had not married yet but she was going to marry. She said if I was married I'd have children and if I had children then I'd be a mother and if I was a mother I'd tell them what to do. / She decided that she was not going to marry."

10. Typescript A is in YCAL 27.537, B in 27.540, C1 in 27.541, and C2 in 27.542.

11. The first notebook, 166 sheets (both sides), takes the narrative a little more than halfway through Part Four: "No use saying that he only remembered Ida because he didn't." The next notebook, 118 sheets (both sides), goes from there, and nine-tenths of it is used to finish the First Half.

12. The shock comes from seeing the contrast between all the draft material of the first two stages and the clean-copy notebooks of this third stage, and from the recognition that Stein transformed the text so much. The third stage is relatively straightforward to describe but it must have been the most complicated for Stein. See the end of the Introduction for an example of this extraordinary rewriting process. I picture Stein at a large table with the first- and second-stage drafts in front of her, reading and copying and modifying.

13. See note 2, for example.

14. See *The World Is Round*, which has a similar chapter structure to the first and second stages of *Ida*.

15. In *A Catalogue of the Published and Unpublished Writings of Gertrude Stein* (New Haven: Yale University Library, 1941), by Robert Bartlett Haas and Donald Clifford Gallup, the first two stages were listed as separate texts, "Ida" in 1937, and "Arthur And Jenny" in 1938.

16. The first of the last two notebooks (YCAL 27.550) goes from "Andrew had a mother" to "nothing ever made Andrew careless," and the second finishes the text.

17. For more on Stein's war years, see her memoir *Wars I Have Seen* (1945), as well as Janet Malcolm's *Two Lives: Gertrude and Alice* (New Haven: Yale University Press, 2007) and Ulla Dydo and Edward Burns's "Gertrude Stein: September 1942 to September 1944" (*TW* 401–421).

18. Of that 1939–1940 winter, Stein would say in her autobiographical essay "The Winner Loses, A Picture Of Occupied France" that "every day Basket II, our new poodle, and I took long walks. We took them by day and we took them in the evening [. . .] in the dark" (*HWW* 114).

19. The first notebook (YCAL 27.548) contains three separate sections of *Ida*: from "The road is awfully wide" to "her life with dogs and this was it"; from "took a train, she did not like trains" to "I, I am a cuckoo, I am not a clock"; and from "looked at Ida and that was that" to "she had been settled very well." The "Dogs" narrative uses all of the second notebook (YCAL 27.549) and carries over to the third (YCAL 27.549). In the third notebook, coming between the end of "Dogs" ("Basket rather liked best pussy wants a corner") and the resumption of the Ida-and-Andrew narrative ("Ida never knew who knew what she said") are some pages (*AB* 11–12) from *To Do: A Book Of Alphabets And Birthdays* (see Figure 10). The third notebook ends, "Once upon a time Ida." The "Superstitions" section begins and ends in the first notebook (see Figure 9), but for her typescript Toklas copied almost all of it from a separate thirty-sheet sequence, Stein's translation of her French version ("Les Superstitions") from the year before (YCAL 74.1355).

### *Mrs. Simpson*

1. The more recent biographies of the duchess include Stephen Birmingham's *Duchess: The Story of Wallis Warfield Windsor* (Boston: Little, Brown, 1981) and

Charles Higham's *The Duchess of Windsor: The Secret Life* (New York: McGraw-Hill, 1988). They are, however, only slightly less sensational than the books published in the late 1930s. *Wallis and Edward: Letters 1931–1937: The Intimate Correspondence of the Duke and Duchess of Windsor* (London: Weidenfeld & Nicolson, 1986), edited by Michael Bloch, prints some original documents, and *A King's Story: The Memoirs of the Duke of Windsor* (New York: Putnam, 1951), which inspired Wallis to write her own story, is a useful point of comparison.

2. This title was devised for him then, but not until his brother's coronation on May 12, 1937, did he officially become the Duke of Windsor.

3. Consider the implied promise of gossip to come in Fellowes's letter to Stein on November 21, 1936, from London, which noted that she would be back in Paris the following week: in the meantime, "London is thrilling. I am a student of the new reign, and take a keen interest in all developments" (YCAL 106.2103). In the summer of 1935, Fellowes had lent the Prince of Wales and Wallis "her yacht, *Sister Anne*, for a cruise" (*HHR* 208).

4. A few months later, in the first draft of *Ida*, Stein echoes this comment about Mrs. Simpson cheering up the gloom, writing that Ida "relieved everybody of their gloom" (YCAL 27.535).

5. "My personal folk tale had gone disastrously awry. [. . .] In my darkest moments at the Fort, I had never visualized anything like this—David by his own choice a virtual outcast from the nation over which he had ruled, and each of us condemned to wait in idleness and frustration on our separate islands of exile until my divorce became absolute in early May" (*HHR* 278).

6. Compare what Wallis says about her months in Cannes before the wedding—"it was no life at all, just a dull marking of time"—with her comment on "the unreality of the lull" during the months of Phony War (*HHR* 286, 320).

7. They would soon find a post in the Bahamas, with David as governor, until 1945, when they returned to France. Given Stein's love of Shakespeare, she must have compared the banishment of David and Wallis from England with exile plots in the bard's plays. Jane Kingsley-Smith has noted in *Shakespeare's Drama of Exile* (New York: Palgrave Macmillan, 2003) that more than a third of his thirty-eight plays highlight the theme of banishment and its effect on personal identity. The characters in these plays, she says, travel "from loss of language to loss of nation, from loss of the beloved to loss of self" (2).

8. The fun of reading Ida and Wallis as twins can go much further. For instance, like Wallis, "Ida was always careful about ordering, food clothes cars, clothes food cars everything was well chosen."

9. See as well Stein's "What Are Master-pieces" (1935): "[There is a] difficulty [to] writing novels or poetry these days. The tradition has always been that you may more or less describe the things that happen you imagine them of course but you more or less describe the things that happen but nowadays everybody all day long knows what is happening and so what is happening is not really interesting, one knows it by radios cinemas newspapers biographies autobiographies until what is happening does not really thrill any one, it excites them a little but it does not really thrill them. The painter can no longer say that what he does is as the world looks to him because he cannot look at the world any more, it has been photographed too much and he has to say that he does something else. In former times a painter said he painted what he saw of course he didn't but anyway he could say it, now he does not want to say it because seeing it is not interesting. This has something to do with master-pieces and why there are so few of them but not everything" (*GSW* 357).

10. Ezra Pound, *Early Writings*, edited by Ira B. Nadel (New York: Penguin, 2005), 254.

*Selected Letters*

1. Stein had earlier invited Sherwood Anderson, Louis Bromfield, and Lloyd Lewis to collaborate with her on different projects, but as is the case here those invitations did not see fruition (see *LR* 563n).

2. Wilder did not accept the invitation, and he never did meet them.

3. Shortly after this, Wilder arrived in Bilignin, staying from July 31 to August 16. He visited Stein and Toklas again in November, in Paris, early in the month and then from the 18th to the 23rd.

4. William G. Rogers would review *Ida* (see "Reviews"), and later he wrote two books on Stein: *When This You See Remember Me: Gertrude Stein in Person* (New York: Rinehart, 1948) and *Gertrude Stein Is Gertrude Stein Is Gertrude Stein: Her Life and Work* (New York: Thomas J. Crowell, 1973).

5. The Duke and Duchess of Windsor were on their honeymoon. Lady Sibyl Colefax was also a friend of Stein's and would have been a valuable source for Windsor gossip.

6. Van Vechten was Papa Woojums and Stein was Baby Woojums.

7. Van Vechten is referring to the "Ida" story published in *The Boudoir Companion*, edited by Page Cooper (see *BC*).

8. Two months earlier, Wilder had visited them for five days.

9. Stein drafted some *Ida* sentences on the back of this letter, including "She said it was better to rest and let them come in" and "Ida does go on / She goes on even when she does not go on any more," this second one being self-reflexive for Stein about this long-in-process novel and also descriptive of the celebrity figure, whose life goes on even when the press has dropped its coverage of her.

10. Stein includes in *To Do: A Book Of Alphabets And Birthdays* a character much like the Duchess of Windsor, named Ivy. "Ivy fell in love with a pretty king" who then lost that status, as well as a fundamental component of identity, his birthday: "[H]e had had one when he was a king but now he was not a king he did not have one" (*AB* 19–20).

11. Wilder enclosed a précis of his speech written by somebody (unnamed) in attendance: "It was in the Yale Library a month ago. The big room was filled—people stood three deep around the sides of the room. [Wilder] began with some of the earliest things and came all the way up to 'Ida' [. . .]. The audience loved it all and afterward clapped and clapped—hoping he would go on for another hour. / In the next room was a collection of photographs—mostly Carl van Vechten's, I think—manuscripts and first editions" (*TW* 286–287n). If Wilder did write to Stein about *Ida*, the letter is not extant. However, he was thinking of *Ida* when he wrote to Alice Toklas in November 1947 about his new novel: "It is called The Ides of March and is the last months of Julius Caesar's life recounted by exchanges of letters between a large number of people. I like to think that you will see how largely it is influenced by Gertrude's ideas, both in form and content. Caesar is one of those 'publicity saints' [like Wallis Simpson] who arrest the attention of the world not by what they do, but by the mystery of their disinterestedness. I have tried also to get away from telling it by 'what happened next' and have tried [as Stein had tried in *Ida*] to get the quality of a landscape" (YCAL 138.3239).

12. Stein is remembering a November 1938 press release that described her play *Doctor Faustus Lights The Lights*, her forthcoming children's book *The World Is Round*, and *Ida*: "She has always wanted to write a novel and right now she is about one-quarter finished with one, which is a novel about publicity saints" (YCAL 16.337). The introduction also cites this press release, at more length.

### *Hortense Sänger*

1. "Hortense Sänger" is an umbrella title for three stories that Stein wrote as an undergraduate student in spring 1895. The last two have been known collec-

tively as "The Temptation," but I use "Hortense Sänger" simply because all three stories feature this young woman. Stein turned the stories in on March 22, May 8, and May 22.

2. Stein's note on her cover page reads, "First chap. of a connected work." Stein's teacher was William Vaughn Moody, the poet and playwright, and based on his review comments she later made a few changes. They have silently been accepted here.

3. Stein said to Moody, who had asked her to "[r]evise or rewrite" and resubmit: "I would like to have rewritten to whole theme but the German opera [which she had attended] threw me back in my work." In the next two pieces, Stein was apparently thinking of his suggestion that the "story should perhaps have been taken up at a later point and the present portion developed by way of reminiscence."

4. With incidental changes, this is quatrain 29 in Edward FitzGerald's *The Rubáiyát of Omar Khayyám*, first published in 1859; Stein is probably using the fourth edition (London: Bernard Quaritch, 1879). FitzGerald's quatrain reads, "Into this Universe, and *Why* not knowing / Nor *Whence*, like Water willy-nilly flowing; / And out of it, as Wind along the Waste, / I know not *Whither*, willy-nilly blowing." In the next paragraph Stein cites from quatrains 34 and 35: "Then of the THEE IN ME who works behind / The Veil, I lifted up my hands to find / A Lamp amid the Darkness; and I heard, / As from Without—'THE ME WITHIN THEE BLIND!' // Then to the Lip of this poor earthen Urn / I lean'd, the Secret of my Life to learn: / And Lip to Lip it murmur'd—'While you live, / Drink!—for, once dead, you never shall return.'" The line "Dream-life is the only life worth living" is Hortense's own, her gloss on the theme of impermanence.

5. It appears that Stein returned to this story some years later. In pencil—the original text is in pen—she made changes to this sentence and two more in the paragraph, and one more in another paragraph, and she squeezed this fragment between two paragraphs: "Once such a kind of one when a very young woman went with some women of." Was she gleaning text for later work, for *Ida*? Because the purpose of these changes is not clear, they have not been incorporated here.

### *The Superstitions Of Fred Anneday, Annday, Anday*

1. See Ulla Dydo's compilation of Stein's references to the cuckoo (*LR* 562). The texts include "A Circular Play" (1920), "A Sonatina Followed By Another"

(1921), and the "Grant" section of *Four In America* (1933–1934). In an August 1933 letter from Stein to Lindley Hubbell, she tells of a cuckoo that had sung to her in the spring of 1932, a few months before she wrote the book that brought her money and fame, *The Autobiography Of Alice B. Toklas*. Because the cuckoo had augured well, Stein's faith in superstitions was enhanced. Dydo has suggested that we read "Fred Anneday" in company with, besides *Four In America*, four other texts that respond to life in the Bilignin area: the detective novel *Blood On The Dining Room Floor* (1933) as well as "A Waterfall And A Piano," "Is Dead," and "The Horticulturalists" (all from 1936; *LR* 587n).

2. When Stein wrote this, John Dillinger was still a criminal on the run. He was killed by FBI agents in July 1934.

## *Ida*

1. The reference to "Bessie" is a wink in the direction of the Duchess of Windsor, who was born Bessie Wallis Warfield.

2. This play on doubles and beauty prizes may have led Stein back to "Film Deux Soeurs Qui Ne Sont Pas Soeurs" and its inclusion in *Ida*.

## *Lucretia Borgia*

1. Lucretia becoming Gloria may be a reference to Gloria Morgan Vanderbilt, who changed her name from Mercedes to Gloria when she was a teenager. Her identical twin sister, Thelma Morgan Furness, was the Prince of Wales's mistress before his attention shifted to Wallis Simpson in 1934. It was Thelma who introduced Wallis to David. Stein probably knew that David went from Thelma to Wallis, and she certainly knew about the Vanderbilts—for one thing, she arrived in America during the infamous Vanderbilt custody trial, in October and November 1934, a trial that determined that Gloria was not fit to care for her daughter, also named Gloria. Thelma Furness and Gloria Vanderbilt would later write a memoir titled *Double Exposure* (1958).

2. Stein uses modified versions of this sentence and the previous two in *Ida*. As well, compare this ending with that of "A Portrait Of Daisy To Daisy On Her Birthday."

## *How Writing Is Written*

1. Robert T. Vanderbilt was a student at the Choate School and editor-in-chief of the *Choate Literary Magazine.*

2. Stein is reading from the abridged version of *The Making Of Americans* that she first prepared, with the help of Bernard Faÿ, for a French translation of the novel in 1933. An English version of the abridgement was published in February 1934 by Harcourt, Brace. As Stein notes, the first passage she reads is from page 284, and the second is from pages 284–285.

3. The Battle of Saint-Mihiel (in September 1918) was a major offensive against German forces that featured American troops and developed in the French populace a gratitude for American involvement. A month after this lecture, in late February 1935, Stein began writing the *Narration* lectures which she gave at the University of Chicago, and in the second lecture she again used this story of the soldiers in France (see *NA* 19–20).

## *Introduction to* The Geographical History Of America

1. See as well "What Are Master-pieces And Why Are There So Few of Them" (*GSW* 355–363), a lecture Stein gave at Oxford and Cambridge universities in February 1936.

2. Stein had made Wilder her interlocutor for *The Geographical History Of America*, especially during his Bilignin visit from July 23 to August 2, 1935.

3. After publishing *The Autobiography Of Alice B. Toklas* in 1933, Stein incorporated the sentence "I am I because my [little] dog knows me" into various texts as she thought about identity existing not in herself but interpersonally—how relationships, such as with a dog, gave her a stable, recognizable identity. When a dog knows its owner, that is identity. See also the "Henry James" section (written early in 1934) in *Four In America*, where she says, "I am I not any longer when I see. / This sentence is at the bottom of all creative activity. It is just the exact opposite of I am I because my little dog knows me" (*GSW* 149); "And Now" (1934); and "Identity A Poem" (1935).

4. This quotation is from Stein's lecture "Poetry And Grammar," in *Lectures In America* (Boston: Beacon Press, 1957), 220, 221. Wilder modified the concluding verb in the first sentence. In Stein's lecture it reads, "[A]s actively as you should lead it."

5. I have not located the source of these two quotations. They may be from conversations between Wilder and Stein or his paraphrase of "Portraits And Repetition" in *Lectures In America*.

*Gertrude Stein Makes Sense*

1. This motto first appeared in Stein's "Sacred Emily" (1913) and continued to appear, on Stein's custom letterhead, for instance, and in the 1939 book *The World Is Round* (see chapter 26, "Rose Does Something").

2. This "friend" was probably Wilder himself.

3. Wilder miswrites here: Stein's research on automatic writing was done at Radcliffe, and she studied medicine at Johns Hopkins. For more on Stein's education, see *The Autobiography Of Alice B. Toklas* (New York: Vintage, 1990, 77–83); Richard Bridgman's *Gertrude Stein in Pieces* (20–39, 357–359); and Steven Meyer's *Irresistible Dictation: Gertrude Stein and the Correlation of Writing and Science* (Stanford, CA: Stanford University Press, 2001).

# *Acknowledgments*

It was while doing research on Stein's construction of her Yale archive that, in talking with the always percipient Nancy Kuhl and Richard Deming, the idea emerged for this edition of *Ida*. However, without the groundbreaking Stein scholarship of Ulla Dydo and Edward Burns, this book would never have been an idea ready for conversation in the first place.

I also offer my thanks to Alison MacKeen, my editor, for her expert resourcefulness; to her assistants, Christina Tucker and Niamh Cunningham, for the magic of turning questions into answers; to the staff at the Beinecke Rare Book and Manuscript Library, for making a scholar's work seem like play; and to Jessie Hunnicutt, my copyeditor, for her graciousness and for reading everything so carefully, the novel in particular—her questions about it were very useful as I proofed the text.

I have four students to thank: Kathleen Douglas translated Stein's "Film Deux Soeurs" from French to English, Tiffany Monroe produced transcriptions of many of the texts, Kathleen Alcott proofed the Mann review, and Jenifer Wiseman helped with the selection of Wilder letters. Working collaboratively with students makes me the student I hope always to be. I also want to acknowledge Chapman University for its help in funding research trips and permissions.

Having relied so much on family, friends, and colleagues for their dedication, interest, and willingness to read, I am thrilled to offer this book in return, as small thanks. And not long after I began work on this, my wife, Lara Odell, gave birth to our daughter, Ida—just Ida, no twins. So as she grew I was coincidentally tracing the development of *Ida*. Lara's devotion to us both during this project has been remarkable and I feel very fortunate. Now I dream ahead to the day when Ida reads *Ida*.

# *Credits*

I offer my gratitude for permission to reprint or use the following sources:

"Hortense Sänger," "Film Deux Soeurs Qui Ne Sont Pas Soeurs," "The Superstitions Of Fred Anneday, Annday, Anday A Novel Of Real Life," "Ida," "Lucretia Borgia A Play," "A Portrait Of Daisy To Daisy On Her Birthday," "How Writing Is Written," and the unpublished drafts of *Ida* that appear in the "Genealogy," by permission of the Estate of Gertrude Stein, through its Literary Executor, Mr. Stanford Gann Jr. of Levin & Gann, P.A.

The text of *Ida A Novel*, and along with images of the jacket cover, flap, title page, and first page, copyright © 1941, 1968 by Random House, Inc., from *Ida* by Gertrude Stein, copyright © 1941 and renewed 1968 by Daniel C. Joseph, Administrator of the Estate of Gertrude Stein. Used by permission of Random House, Inc.

Excerpts from letters by Bennett Cerf, copyright © by Random House, Inc. Used by permission of Random House, Inc.

Excerpts from Thornton Wilder's correspondence as it appears in *The Letters of Gertrude Stein and Thornton Wilder* (Yale University Press, 1996) or in the Thornton Wilder Collection, YCAL, Beinecke Rare Book and Manuscript Library, published with permission of Tappan Wilder.

Thornton Wilder's introduction to *The Geographical History Of America Or The Relation Of Human Nature To The Human Mind* (Random House, 1936), published with permission of Tappan Wilder.

Thornton Wilder's article "Gertrude Stein Makes Sense," from *'47: The Magazine of the Year* (Oct. 1947), published with permission of Tappan Wilder.

Excerpts from letters by Carl Van Vechten, published by permission of Bruce Kellner, Successor Trustee, Estate of Carl Van Vechten, and by permission of Edward Burns, editor of *The Letters of Gertrude Stein and Carl Van Vechten, 1913–1946* (New York: Columbia University Press, 1986).

Earle Birney, Fiction and Diction, *Canadian Forum* 21 (Apr. 1941): 28, by permission of Wailan Low.

Clifton Fadiman, "Getting Gertie's Ida," *New Yorker* (Feb. 15, 1941): 78. Copyright © Condé Nast. All rights reserved. Reprinted by permission.

"Abstract Prose," *Time* 37.7 (Feb. 17, 1941): 99–100, by permission of Time Inc.

E. C. S., "Gertrude Stein as Novelist," reprinted from the March 22, 1941, issue of the *Christian Science Monitor*. Courtesy of the *Christian Science Monitor* (www.CSMonitor.com).

W. H. Auden, "All about Ida," currently collected in *The Complete Works of W. H. Auden: Prose: Vol. 2, 1939–1948* (Princeton University Press, 2002), copyright © 1941 by W. H. Auden, used with permission of the Wylie Agency LLC.